'Adios, s

With a curt b [   ] the
exit to the co [   ] ck.

'Should you ~~discover~~ that you require further assistance after all, my room is opposite yours.'

Désirée's blue eyes widened. He was staying here at the inn!

She stared after his departing figure, feeling oddly disturbed. Rafael de Velasco might be a man of breeding, but all her instincts told her he was dangerous and she didn't want anything more to do with him!

Gail Mallin, has a passion for travel. She studied at the University of Wales, where she gained an Honours degree and met her husband, then an officer in the Merchant Navy. They spent the next three years sailing the world before settling in Cheshire. Writing soon became another means of exploring, opening up new worlds. A career move took Gail and her husband south, and they now live with their young family in St. Albans.

Recent titles by the same author:

MARRY IN HASTE
CONQUEROR'S LADY
DEBT OF HONOUR
THE DEVIL'S BARGAIN
A MOST UNSUITABLE DUCHESS

A REBELLIOUS
LADY

Gail Mallin

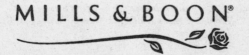
MILLS & BOON®

*First published in Great Britain 1998
Harlequin Mills & Boon Limited,
Eton House, 18-24 Paradise Road, Richmond, Surrey TW9 1SR*

© Gail Mallin 1998

ISBN 0 263 80773 8

*Set in Times 10 on 10½ pt. by
Rowland Phototypesetting Limited
Bury St Edmunds, Suffolk*

04-9804-82335

*Printed and bound in Great Britain
by Caledonian International Book Manufacturing Ltd, Glasgow*

Chapter One

1809

Midnight. A new year was born.

Rafael de Velasco left his desk and moved to the window of his study. He opened it and a draught of cold air blew in, bringing with it the sound of Riofrío's church bell.

Rafael listened, his expression grim. What would 1809 bring for his troubled country?

Just as the last chime was fading away, a discreet knock at the door roused him from his reverie.

His steward entered, a nervous expression on his lined face. 'You have a visitor, Don Rafael.'

Almost before Luis had finished speaking he was swept aside by a stout, middle-aged man wearing the black soutane of a priest.

'Come in, cousin. *Mi casa es su casa.*' Rafael's deep voice was fringed with sarcasm.

A frown marred Sancho Ortego y Castuero's well-bred face for an instant at this mocking invitation to treat the house as his own and then his expression smoothed. 'Let us not quarrel, Rafael. I did not come for that.'

Rafael motioned him to be seated by the fire. 'Then what did you come for?'

'Still the same, *amigo mio*. You are always blunt.' Sancho laughed but his mirth had a forced ring to it.

5

Rafael shrugged.

'Aren't you at least going to offer me a glass of wine in honour of the season?'

A short laugh escaped between Rafael's well-cut lips.

'Dare I trust you?' he asked with deceptive serenity. 'The last time you were here you refused to drink with me.'

Sancho turned bright red. 'I was angry,' he muttered. 'You know I didn't mean to call you a traitor.'

Rafael's black eyebrows lifted.

'All right! My behaviour was abominable. I've regretted it ever since.' Sancho dropped his gaze to the diligently polished floorboards. 'I apologise.'

Rafael was silent, remembering their furious meeting. He had known that Sancho had wanted to throw the glass of wine in his face, but at the last instant family feeling had restrained him.

Those same shared bonds going back to their childhood—when Sancho had often visited his young cousins, Rafael and his little sister, Elena—had also prevented Rafael from issuing the challenge that had risen instinctively to his own lips.

Unnerved by his silence, Sancho shifted his bulk uneasily in his chair. 'We both want the best for Spain. Don't let's quarrel over the method of achieving it.'

Rafael nodded abruptly.

'You are right,' he said, some of the tension seeping from his broad shoulders. 'Half of our country's troubles stem from the fact no one can agree on a policy.'

'Then—'

'I too have regretted our quarrel,' Rafael interrupted him. He smiled slowly. 'Welcome back, cousin.'

His broad face flushing with delight, Sancho leapt up and enthusiastically pumped the hand Rafael extended to him.

He sat down again as Rafael moved to a small simple oak table which nestled against the whitewashed wall. The wood was age-blackened but so well polished it had a silken patina that gleamed in the candlelight. On its surface stood a silver tray bearing an open bottle of wine and two fine crystal glasses.

'You were expecting company?' Sancho eyed the unused wine glasses, his brown eyes speculative.

'I hoped Elena would join me in toasting the New Year, but she was tired and went to bed early.'

Rafael poured out the wine and handed a glass to Sancho, who admired its deep ruby colour.

'This is from Casa del Aguila's own vines or I am no judge,' he exclaimed, taking an appreciative sniff of the wine's aromatic bouquet.

'I see you haven't lost your interest in the good things of life, cousin.' Rafael hid a smile. 'I thought priests were supposed to abjure all pleasures of the flesh.'

'I fasted throughout Advent!' Sancho started to protest and then, realising he was being teased, laughed instead and patted his round stomach. 'Not that you would know it!'

Ignoring his usual chair behind the carved walnut desk, Rafael sat down opposite his cousin and, settling his tall frame, took a swallow of wine before setting it aside.

'So, what else brings you here, Sancho?'

'I came to ask you to change your mind.' Sancho knew better than to try and pretend. Rafael was too shrewd!

Rafael stretched out his long legs. 'I already have,' he said quietly, his gaze fixed on his high leather boots.

'You are no longer one of the *afrancesados*?' Delight filled Sancho's voice.

Rafael lifted his dark elegant head and nodded, but Sancho's excitement faltered at his expression.

'I welcomed the French as liberators who would rid us of Godoy and his corrupt regime.' Rafael's night-black eyes were bleak. 'I was wrong.'

Knowing his cousin as he did, Sancho could guess how much that simple admission must have cost his fierce pride.

Under Godoy, lover of the queen and virtual dictator of Spain, the country had stagnated. Crippling taxes withered farmer and merchant alike. The navy had never

recovered from its losses at Trafalgar and the army was
in urgent need of reform, but King Carlos had done
nothing to stop the rot.

Then Napoleon Bonaparte, Spain's ally, sought to
secure a passage from his troops through Spain into
Portugal so that his blockade against England could be
enforced. Godoy, knowing that actions against Portugal
were always popular, had agreed. But Napoleon could
not resist the temptation to add Spain to his conquests.

The king and his heir, Prince Ferdinard, were lured
across the border to Bayonne and forced to resign their
right to the throne. French popularity had instantly faded
and a mob took to the streets of Madrid.

News of the massacre of the French garrison and Marshal Murat's bloody reprisals spread swiftly all over the
country.

Torn by conflicting emotions, Rafael had tried desperately to reconcile this betrayal with all the things he had
long admired about Napoleon.

Then, one hot summer afternoon, Sancho had arrived
at Casa del Aguila to tell Rafael that he was going to
become a military chaplain.

'You are the best swordsman I know, Rafael. Join me.
We shall push the hated invader back over the Pyrenees!'

'Fine words, but eloquence will not win battles.' Still
suffering from the shock of disillusionment, Rafael had
been curt. 'We haven't a single general worthy of
the name.'

Sancho gasped. 'We have men of true courage!'

'Where are their arms? Their supplies? A ragged mob
of peasants masquerading as a regiment will not stop the
finest military genius since Julius Caesar!'

Their quarrel rapidly escalated and it had ended with
Sancho storming out, vowing never to set foot on the
finca again. A vow he had kept until tonight.

'Does your change of heart mean that you will now
join me?' Sancho asked eagerly.

To his disappointment Rafael shook his head. 'I do
not think I have the right temperament to be a regular

soldier,' he said, a crooked grin twisting his elegant features.

Sancho gave a reluctant chuckle of understanding. 'Too independent and stubborn you mean, *amigo*!'

'Nor, in spite of what happened at Baylen, do I believe we can win this war by trying to fight Napoleon on his own terms,' Rafael continued, his expression sobering.

About to argue, Sancho paused. They had won a great victory at Baylen and the French had been forced to evacuate Madrid, but their very success had drawn Napoleon himself into the fray. As the turbulent year had drawn towards its close, the Emperor had smashed his way through Spain with his usual dramatic speed and flair, reversing his army's defeats and forcing the British, Spain's new ally, to withdraw.

'We have to find another method. One that allows us to use the advantages we do have.' Rafael's dark eyes began to gleam.

'You have a plan?' Sancho caught his excitement.

'A small band of men who know the terrain can move with speed and stealth. They can inflict demoralising losses and withdraw before the enemy has time to strike back.'

'*Guerrilleros*!' Sancho breathed the name. 'You will use the little war of the ambush and the knife against the French?'

Rafael nodded, his finely moulded lips curving into a smile that sent an involuntary chill down Sancho's spine. 'I shall make them afraid of their own shadows.'

'A toast.' Recovering his nerve, Sancho jubilantly raised his glass. 'Let us drink to a successful new year for your venture and for Spain!'

For an instant Rafael stared silently into the blood-red heart of his wineglass before raising it to his lips. 'Death to the French!'

Then in one swift movement he hurled the empty glass into the stone fireplace. It shattered noisily and the dregs of wine hissed into oblivion in the hot flames.

*   *   *

'*Ma foi, mam'selle*! What a disaster!'

Désirée Fontaine, ruefully surveying the broken axle of the chaise she had hired at such expense only three days ago in Bayonne, gave a short laugh.

'I agree, Monsieur Beauchet,' she said crisply to the plump little man who had undertaken the task of acting as her escort and guide on this journey across Spain. 'None the less, I am determined to continue.'

'But how, *mam'selle*?' Pierre, the coachman who made up the final number of their small party since Desirée's maid had succumbed to homesickness and refused to cross the border, spoke up. 'That axle is a mess.'

'If it cannot be easily repaired, we shall have to find another carriage.' Ignoring her courier's muttered grumbling, Désirée calmly proceeded to dust off her skirts.

A flicker of annoyance passed over her heart-shaped face as she noticed a tear in the hem of her fine cambric gown. She must have snagged it on the one of the splintered panels when she climbed out of the drunkenly tilted chaise.

'Monsieur Lamont isn't going to like this!' The young coachman was pale with anxiety beneath his outdoor tan.

'Don't worry,' Désirée said kindly. 'I shall write a letter of explanation for your master.'

Désirée felt sorry for him, but, as Pierre continued to lament, irritation finally overwhelmed her sympathy. Didn't he realise he was only making matters worse, standing there wringing his hands like a ninny!

'Please see to the horses, Pierre. They must be unhitched in case they take fright and injure themselves.'

'*Oui, mam'selle.*' Blushing at his own folly, Pierre hurried to obey.

Désirée took a deep calming breath.

Her hope of gaining a short respite in which to collect her thoughts was crushed when Beauchet, who had been sitting slumped at the roadside refreshing himself from the silver hip-flask full of cognac which was always at his side, roused himself from his gloomy reverie.

'We must return to France,' he announced loudly.

'What?' Desiree was shocked. 'But that is ridiculous!'

'I insist on it, *chérie*.' He struggled clumsily to his feet.

Worried that he might have been injured, she stifled her dislike of his familiar manner and moved swiftly to help him.

'Are you hurt, *monsieur*?'

'I ache all over.'

He had made the same complaint every few hours since they had left the château behind them, so Désirée felt quite justified in releasing her steadying hand.

'A hot bath will help soothe any bruises,' she said cheerfully.

He shot her a look of active dislike.

Désirée ignored it and continued in the same optimistic tone. 'The inn in Vitoria which was recommended to me is said to keep a good table.'

'I very much doubt it!' he snapped back. 'In fact, I have yet to eat a decent meal in this wretched country! Or obtain a proper night's sleep! The bedbugs are intolerable!'

Désirée resisted the impulse to scream and silently counted to ten.

Oh, why on earth had she listened when Madame de Tolly had recommended him as just the man to see her safely to Burgos!

Her good neighbour had been persuasive.

'I can understand your reasons for wishing to visit Etienne, *ma petite*. You are bored living here with only Hortense for company. It is a great pity there are no suitable young people in the district for you to mix with. A girl of your age ought to be out enjoying parties.'

'It is rather lonely at times,' Désirée had admitted. 'Particularly since *Maman* died.'

'And you have always wanted to travel.' *Madame* had nodded sagely. 'But you cannot venture so far afield with only your maid for company. It is not *comme il faut*!'

Désirée had willingly agreed with this pronouncement, but when she suggested that Hortense, the elderly cousin who lived with her, could accompany her to Spain, Madame de Tolly had laughed merrily.

'I know Hortense was your mother's devoted companion and she has willingly acted as a kind of surrogate guardian to you since her death, but she is much too old to undertake such a trip!' *Madame* chuckled. 'I suspect the very idea would horrify her!'

Désirée had been forced to concur.

'No, Hortense will not do, *ma petite*. It is male protection that you require.'

A frown creased *Madame*'s brow. Désirée was an orphan. Etienne and Hortense were her only family, apart from the unspeakable English relatives from whom she was estranged.

Her discreetly painted face cleared as inspiration struck her. '*Voilà*, I believe I know the right person!'

It was settled that *Madame* would write to Monsieur Beauchet, but when he had arrived a few weeks later at the small château near Orléans which was Désirée's home, Désirée had been surprised.

Sixteen years had passed since Claude Beauchet had helped Madame de Tolly to escape from the Reign of Terror then afflicting Paris, and the intervening years had not treated him kindly. Almost sixty, his tongue remained plausible, but a fondness for cognac had weakened his once-sharp wits and added considerably to his girth.

Anxious to be on her way and thinking that he was at least honest and would not cheat her, Désirée had hired his services. Prior to the start of the trip, she found him helpful enough, but once the journey was actually underway she had discovered he was lazy and inclined to fuss and fret, making a mountain out of every minor molehill.

Time, it seemed, had blunted his appetite for adventure!

'I'm sorry you are not enjoying this journey, *monsieur*,' Désirée said, abandoning her futile attempt to raise his spirits. 'However, since none of us was injured, I see no reason to cancel my plans.'

'You are being wilfully blind, *mam'selle*!'

Realising that he was about to resume his protests, Désirée shook her head at him quickly and turned away.

She could hear him muttering indignantly as she walked towards the coach, but she was tired of trying to remain courteous in the face of his constant whining.

Forcing herself to dismiss the courier from her thoughts, she examined the chaise and quickly came to the conclusion that they would indeed have to abandon it.

'The horses are none the worse for what happened, *mam'selle*.' Pierre came up to give her his report.

'Good. Could you fashion some kind of reins?'

He shrugged doubtfully. 'They ain't riding animals. You'd not stay on, *mam'selle*.'

It was on the tip of Désirée's tongue to refute his statement. Her strict English grandfather had seen to it that she was a very competent horsewoman, but then she realised Pierre's expression was utterly miserable.

'I promise I won't let Monsieur Lamont blame you,' she reassured him.

'It ain't just the accident what's bothering me, Mam'selle Fontaine. It's them rumours. About them guerrillas, I mean.'

Désirée's big blue eyes widened. 'Surely you don't believe that nonsense, do you?'

'It ain't nonsense, *mam'selle*. Don't forget, I come from Bayonne. We're much closer to Spain than you northerners. If I had a *sou* for every story I've heard about them devils, I'd be a rich man. Everyone knows they torture any poor Frenchman they get their evil hands on.'

Désirée didn't believe a word of it.

'My brother is close to King Joseph and in a position to know the truth,' she said firmly. 'He would never have mentioned the idea of my joining him in Madrid if he thought it was unsafe.'

Pierre nodded acknowledgment, but the nervous way in which he twisted his hands together warned Désirée he persisted in believing the ridiculous notion that their journey was dangerous.

Controlling her impatience, Désirée gave him her most charming smile. 'The Emperor himself has said that the problems we experienced here last year are finished. The Spanish armies have been routed.'

'Aye, but do the Spanish people know they are beaten, *mam'selle*?' Pierre's face wore a gloomy frown. 'The Emperor might have made his brother king, but what's the good of that if most Spaniards hate us? There's bound to be trouble.'

Désirée fell silent for a moment. Pierre was young and nervous, but he wasn't stupid. Was it possible that her own keen desire to join Etienne was preventing her from recognising the truth?

Until they had reached the border area, she had never heard a word about these partisans. Everyone at home had assumed the Spanish were beaten. Certainly, Napoleon, who ought to know more than a mere coachman, had proclaimed that the French were the masters of Spain. Indeed, he frequently claimed that a large proportion of the Spanish population actively supported his rule.

It was a complicated situation, she knew. Old King Carlos had been deeply unpopular with most of his subjects. He was little better than an imbecile and his queen, Maria-Luisa, was a shameless trollop! Unfortunately, Napoleon's swift installation of his elder brother, Joseph Bonaparte, on the Spanish throne had outraged national pride.

But the French *were* in control. They had chased the British to Corunna, forcing them to withdraw from Spain. Before long they would secure Portugal—Marshal Soult was already in Oporto—and then the whole peninsula would be in French hands.

No, logic dictated that Pierre's rumours must be wrong and, having come so far already, it would be silly to turn back without much stronger evidence of any danger.

Dismissing her doubts, Désirée shrugged lightly.

'I think these tales of guerrilla atrocities have been greatly exaggerated,' she said with a return of the airy confidence which had borne her through all the difficulties so far.

Beauchet, who had been listening to their conversation, suddenly chimed in. 'That is all very well, *chérie*, but just how do you propose we get to Vitoria?'

Stung by the sarcasm in his high-pitched voice, Désirée glared at him.

'Another vehicle is bound to come along soon. After all, this *is* the Royal Road to Madrid. I'm sure we shall obtain a ride.'

'Bah! We might wait for hours!'

'Then we must walk!'

Her announcement seemed to strike both her listeners dumb.

'We are only a league or two from Vitoria,' she continued in a more moderate tone. 'We could reach the inn in a couple of hours or less if we walk briskly.'

'Walk!' Beauchet whipped out a large spotted silk handkerchief and mopped his brow. He was already sweating profusely, although the sunshine on this new May morning was no more than pleasantly warm.

'You have another suggestion?' Désirée enquired sweetly.

'Yes! Abandon this crazy enterprise!'

Désirée's intensely blue eyes flashed with scorn. 'You were quick enough to accept the task only a few weeks ago, *Monsieur*.'

He shrugged, his expression as sulky as a thwarted baby's. 'The situation appeared different in Orléans,' he muttered. 'But now I have had the opportunity to gather new information and assess the true facts. Without a proper armed escort, I do not feel that I can continue with this journey, *mam'selle*.'

'*You* were paid to escort me to Burgos where my brother is to meet me,' Désirée said tightly, striving to hang on to her temper.

What was the fellow up to? Surely he had more sense than to believe in unlikely rumours?

Désirée eyed him suspiciously. The man was bone idle

and had made it plain he had no taste for the journey.
He wanted to go home, but he needn't think he could
scare her into giving up her plans.

'What you ask is impossible, *monsieur*. Do you expect
me to conjure up an armed guard out of thin air? Let us
forget this nonsense and continue at once if you please.'

'We must turn back,' Beauchet repeated stubbornly,
ignoring her acid comments. 'You can always write to
your brother and ask him to meet you at the border.'

Désirée bit back a very unladylike English oath. 'Do
not be a fool! He is a busy man.' Taking a calming
breath, she continued in a quieter tone. 'I haven't come
all this way merely for the sake of enjoying a holiday.
It is my hope that my brother will let me stay.'

'*Ma foi*! You will be murdered in your bed!'

'Do not be ridiculous, *monsieur*!'

Beauchet drew himself up haughtily. 'If you will not
listen, then I am afraid I must resign my services and
take leave of you.'

'You refuse to fulfil your obligations?' Désirée was
shocked. Beauchet might be lazy and half-addled by
drink, but she had assumed he was a gentleman.

'You paid only half my fee in advance,' he reminded
her. 'We have already travelled several hundred miles
from Orléans. I consider I have amply fulfilled my duty.'

'You are a despicable rogue!'

Beauchet's fat jowls quivered with indignation. 'You
are insulting, *mam'selle*, but, honour aside, I think I
should prefer to be a rogue than a dead fool!'

Désirée would have found his pose of affronted dignity
quite laughable in other circumstances. Unfortunately, to
be stranded alone in a strange land was not an amusing
prospect!

Overcoming the pang of dismay which had momentarily sent an icy shiver down her spine, Désirée
gracefully inclined her fair head.

'As you wish, *monsieur*. I have no doubt I shall do
better without an idle drunkard for company.'

Ignoring the gobbles of outrage which greeted her

remark, Désirée pointedly turned her back on him and asked Pierre to extract her baggage from the chaise.

The light blue carriage-dress she was wearing had fashionably narrow skirts. She ought to change into something more practical.

In spite of Pierre's objections, Désirée still thought it might be possible to ride the carriage horses. She had a riding-habit with her and it was worth a try.

Pondering the difficulties, Désirée suddenly realised that Beauchet was conferring with the coachman in agitated whispers.

'What is going on?' Alarm flashed through Désirée's slender frame.

'I told you, I'm leaving.' Beauchet snatched up his own valise and thrust it at Pierre. 'Here, find some way to secure this,' he ordered.

'Leave those animals alone!'

Désirée ran forward, but the courier thrust out an arm to prevent her.

'You have no right to take them.' Désirée's high-boned cheeks were scarlet with fury.

He sniggered. 'I'll admit it was your money that paid for their hire, *chérie*, but since they can't take us to Vitoria, I reckon that contract is void.'

Désirée threw him a look of disgust. 'You are little better than a thief!' she exclaimed.

An indignant expression crossed his plump face. 'I don't intend to keep them. I shall return them to their own stables on our way home,' he asserted loftily. 'I'll even call in on Lamont when we get to Bayonne. It'll save you the trouble of writing to the fellow.'

'Oh, I suppose that makes everything all right! Or do expect me to *thank* you?'

'There is no need to take that tone,' he retorted huffily. 'I have every right to terminate my services since you have not paid me in full.'

Sickened by his deviousness, Désirée clamped her lips shut before temper led her into saying more. It was obvious he had lost all sense of honour, she would not humiliate herself by entering into further discussion with him.

Returning to her valises, she stooped to feel their combined weight and knew that they were too heavy for her to carry any distance.

'Do you think you could take one of these for me, Pierre?' she asked, still contemplating her bags. 'I won't be able to manage both of them.'

'He can't do that.' There was a note of triumphant spite in Beauchet's high voice.

'You are turning back?' Désirée's gaze jerked up and she stared at Pierre with dismay.

Hanging his head, the coachman avoided her eyes and nodded silently.

Désirée moistened her suddenly dry lips with the tip of her tongue. 'See me safely to Burgos and you shall receive generous reward,' she said, swallowing her pride.

'I'm sorry, *mam'selle*, truly I am.' Pierre shuffled his feet in sheepish embarrassment. 'I'd like to help you, but Monsieur Lamont is going to have my hide over this accident as it is. I might lose my job if I don't report to him as soon as possible.'

'I'll explain to him—'

Hastily, Pierre shook his head. 'My wife is expecting our first child. She's bound to hear what's happened and if I don't go back, she'll worry herself sick. You see, she didn't want me to cross over the border in the first place.'

'Come on, we're wasting time.' Beauchet cut across the servant's red-faced apologies and ordered Pierre to give him a leg up to mount the horse he had selected. Without saddle or stirrups it was a tricky business, but the roan was a placid beast and stood still while the courier settled himself on its broad back.

Désirée hoped he was as uncomfortable as he looked!

Pierre moved to the second mount and then hesitated. 'Come with us, *mam'selle*.'

Désirée shook her head, outrage stiffening her spine.

'I want the money you were holding for me, Beauchet,' she said, her anger at the courier's underhand behaviour hardening into a stubborn resolve to manage on her own.

A look of shifty disappointment flashed over the courier's face at her blunt demand, deepening Désirée's suspicion that he had been planning to cheat her.

'And all my official papers, if you please,' she added grimly.

'Aye, hand everything over,' Pierre echoed, his expression stern.

Eyeing the young groom's big fists, Beauchet sighed and reluctantly complied.

'Thank you.' Désirée stood back with a look of scorn.

Hortense had insisted she sew pockets into each chemise. She would take care to bestow her valuables safely as soon as the two men departed.

'Sure you won't change your mind, *chérie*?' A faint note of shame underlay Beauchet's farewell.

Hearing it, Désirée smiled coldly. Had he just realised what an awkward time he was going to have of it, trying to excuse the despicable way he had abandoned her?

'Go and be damned to you,' she said sweetly and, turning her back on him, began to calmly repack her belongings to fit the most important items into the smaller valise.

The slim golden spires of Vitoria seemed to waver before Désirée's eyes and with a little groan she set down her bag and, removing her gloves, flexed her cramped fingers. The sun, which earlier had seemed so pleasant, was now blazing at its zenith and she felt as if she might melt.

Wiping the back of her sleeve across her damp forehead, Désirée surveyed the small plain of Vitoria, which lay aslant like a diamond among the surrounding hills. The town itself stood on an eminence, with the Royal Road sweeping in from Madrid in the south-west and out to Bayonne in the north-east. It was just her luck that no vehicle had appeared!

Not that she looked very respectable to ask for a ride. She cast a rueful glance over her dust-streaked skirts.

And her hair had tumbled down under her bonnet, which she had reluctantly kept on for fear of sunburn.

Maman had always insisted that neatness was one of the true marks of a lady. Désirée grinned to herself. She had never shown proper attention to her mother's scolds, preferring to scramble after Etienne no matter how she ripped her clothes.

With a sigh, she thrust her gloves into her valise and picked it up. It wasn't far now and feeling sorry for herself wasn't going to do any good!

Her mouth twisted wryly. How often her grandfather had used that phrase to her! Whenever she had fallen off her pony or failed in any of the other tasks he had set for her, Sir William had insisted she try again until she achieved success. No matter how bruised or humiliated she might have been, she had always been forced to obey.

'You may be the daughter of a penniless *émigré*, but you also have Cavendish blood in your veins. Oblige me by showing some courage, Anne!'

Her grandparents had always refused to call her Désirée. They insisted on using her second name, Anne, ignoring Corinne Fontaine's protests. As a little girl, Désirée had accepted their dictates without thinking; the ways of grown-ups were often mystifying. It was only when she was older that she had realised it was one of the many methods by which they had sought to destroy her mother's influence.

Entering the town, Désirée firmly dismissed the past and its disturbing memories. She needed to keep her wits sharp. The inn she wanted, the White Virgin, lay just off the main square. It was apparently named after the famous white jasper statue which stood enshrined in a niche over the door of the old church of San Miguel.

'Look for *la Virgen Blanca* at the top of the square,' her informant had said. 'Behind the church turn right and you will find the inn.'

Concentrating hard, Désirée was scarcely aware of the curious glances she received.

To her surprise, many of the houses were made of

grey stone and some had bay windows. Allied to the green, hilly scenery, it wasn't at all how she had pictured a Spanish town. In fact, if it hadn't been for the heat, Désirée could have almost imagined herself back in England.

There! That little street was the one she was looking for.

Désirée hastened forward just as two men came out of one of the buildings. They stopped with their backs to her and stood talking, blocking the entrance to the narrow *calle*.

Désirée came to a halt. She had no intention of being forced to squeeze past them.

'Excuse me, gentlemen.' The Castilian phrase had slipped her memory—she knew only a little of the language which was used in this part of Spain—but made subconsciously wary by Pierre's mutterings, she instinctively spoke in English, not French.

The taller man turned round and Désirée found herself looking into a hard austere face, deeply tanned by the sun. From beneath thin black brows, equally dark eyes surveyed her. The glance lasted only a second or two, but Désirée could have sworn that he had taken in every detail of her appearance, from her tangled blonde ringlets to her dusty leather shoes.

Then, with a curt nod, he stood back, allowing her to pass.

Désirée could feel his eyes boring into her back all the way up the street!

To her relief, she found the inn easily. A pair of big wooden doors stood open, revealing a shady courtyard and Désirée quickly stepped inside, glad for some reason she could not name to escape the tall, dark-haired man's gaze.

A stout woman dressed in black appeared. She looked amazed to see Désirée standing alone in her courtyard.

Acutely conscious of her lack of suitable escort, Désirée attempted to explain that she required a room.

A flood of rapid Castilian answered her.

'I'm sorry. *No le entiendo*. I don't understand.' Longing to sit down and desperate for something to cool her dry throat, Désirée cudgelled her brains for some way to convince the frowning landlady that she was respectable.

'May I be of assistance?'

The voice was ice wrapped in sable velvet.

Désirée swung round. The tall Spaniard she had encountered earlier had materialised at her side, although she had heard no sound to indicate his arrival.

'Forgive me, but you *do* want a room?'

Désirée nodded, tongue-tied by surprise. His English, although marked by a strong accent, was excellent!

A quickfire exchange followed. The woman was clearly reluctant, but Désirée's unexpected champion was obviously a man accustomed to obedience.

'I have made arrangements for you to have a room at the rear. It will be quieter.'

'Thank you.' Désirée had recovered her composure. 'You are very kind. . .' Her voice trailed off slowly.

'Permit me to introduce myself.' His expression did not change as he responded to her hint, but Désirée was sure she saw a brief flicker of amusement in his dark eyes. 'Rafael de Velasco.' He executed an elegant bow. 'And you, *señorita*?'

So he had noticed she wore no wedding ring.

'My name is Anne Cavendish.' Désirée smiled at him innocently, the same instinctive sense of caution which had operated earlier prompting her to conceal the whole truth.

At the moment Spain and England were allies. It might be safer to claim her father's nationality, although on his last leave home Etienne had complained that Spaniards were notoriously insular in their outlook and generally hostile to all foreigners.

Rafael de Velasco appeared to be an exception to this rule but, helpful though he had been, he was still an unknown quantity.

He was also undeniably attractive. Under that rather shabby coat his shoulders were broad, but there wasn't an ounce of fat on his long lean body. In fact, he looked to be in peak physical condition, an impression heightened by the lithe grace with which he moved.

Désirée wasn't sure how old he was. Thirty, perhaps? His thick, somewhat unruly hair was free of any hint of grey and his olive skin was smooth, but there was a cynically weary twist to his mouth. It was a beautifully cut mouth with a sensually full lower lip in contrast to the hard angles of his determined chin, thin high-bridged nose and elegant cheekbones.

Patrician features, but the plainest of clothes. He looked like a pirate with that mop of black curling hair and those dark mysterious eyes, but he had a gentleman's manners.

Désirée wasn't sure what to make of him, but she would have wagered her best earrings that he would make an excellent dancer. . .or duellist!

The stout woman reappeared, interrupting Désirée's thoughts. She was carrying a tall jug and two earthenware beakers. Beads of moisture clung to the jug and Désirée licked her lips thirstily as she watched the woman set it down on a small table in a corner of the courtyard before departing again.

'I told Consuelo to bring you some food. It will be ready soon. In the meantime. . .' Rafael de Velasco indicated a pair of rickety-looking chairs pulled up to the table '. . .shall we sit down?'

Désirée hesitated.

Why did he make her feel so unsure of herself? She was self-reliant by nature and, at twenty-one, had grown accustomed to acting independently, for Hortense had left all the decisions to her after *Maman* had died. That was almost two years ago and she had learnt to run the household and act as hostess to Etienne's brother-officers and friends.

Désirée, who was bored by the unchanging, dull routine of her everyday existence, had loved it when Etienne came home on leave. In fact, Hortense had accused her of flirting at the parties he gave. She had objected, defending herself by saying she preferred to discuss horses with the men rather than the latest fashions with the women, but all the same she knew her elderly chaperon had a point.

Among Etienne's friends she came alive, just as the château itself did when they arrived. She didn't deliberately set out to flirt, but she never felt self-conscious or awkward with them. Perhaps her lack of shyness was a legacy of her strange upbringing. Her grandfather had treated her like a boy, even to teaching her how to shoot and fish.

Whatever the reason, she enjoyed male company, but, attractive though she found him, Désirée knew she ought not to encourage Rafael de Velasco's attentions.

It wasn't just because he was a stranger. *Dieu*, it wasn't even because he was a Spaniard and therefore a potential enemy of her country! No, her unease went deeper. It was an instinctive response to the incredibly strong magnetism of the man. He radiated an aura of intense virility. Allied to his natural air of command and stunning good looks, it was having a devastating effect on her senses!

She might not be able to stop wondering what it would feel like to be kissed by that intriguingly sensual mouth, but at least she ought not to sit drinking with him!

On the other hand, however, that table was shaded by a horse-chestnut tree and she was dying of thirst and her feet were sore from all that walking!

'You don't wish to rest, *señorita*?' A tiny lift of enquiry quirked his thin black brows. 'Or is it that you don't you trust me?'

'Is there any reason why I shouldn't, sir?' Désirée's chin came up.

Amusement gleamed in the jet-black eyes. 'Do you think I would *admit* it, if there was?'

She couldn't help laughing at his impudence, but as she allowed him to pull out a chair for her and sat down, she found herself resenting both his charm and his high-handed tactics. He seemed altogether too sure of himself!

Watching him pour out the contents of the jug with a deft grace, it also occurred to her that he must have had plenty of success with women. Unexpectedly, Désirée found herself wishing that she didn't look so dishevelled.

Imbecile! What did it matter what he thought of her! In a few minutes he would be gone and she would never see him again.

Somehow, it was a rather depressing thought.

Trying to hide her oddly mixed feelings, Désirée took the beaker he handed her and sipped the cool milky-looking beverage. It was sweet but refreshing, with a hint of cinnamon and lemon underlying a taste she did not recognise.

'This is delicious. What is it called?' she asked appreciatively.

'*Horchata*. It is made from almonds. One of the specialities of the house.'

Glad to slake her thirst, Désirée finished her drink. Here in the quiet shade, the temperature was pleasant and she could feel herself beginning to relax. She hadn't realised until now how the events of the morning had drained her.

'May I ask why you are here in Vitoria, Miss Cavendish?'

His abrupt question made Désirée jump. Hastily, she gathered her wits and sought for an answer. She was pleased that he had made the assumption she had hoped for and concluded she was English, but she didn't want to encourage further curiosity.

'I don't think my reasons can be of any interest to you, sir.' A distinct hauteur infused her tone.

His swift frown told her that he did not care to be spoken to in such a manner, but his voice remained perfectly courteous when he answered her.

'Your business is your own, of course, but surely you realise it is unwise to travel alone? Leaving aside the fact that you do not speak the language well, a beautiful woman without a protector is always at risk.'

Did he think she was beautiful? To her annoyance, Désirée blushed.

'Someone is to meet me,' she said curtly.

'Today?'

His persistence alarmed her. What business was it of his?

'Tomorrow,' she lied, adding firmly, 'Thank you for your help, but I believe I can manage now.' She rose abruptly to her feet. 'Do not let me detain you any longer, *señor*.'

He stood up, his face darkening at her dismissive tone.
'*Adios, Señorita.*'

With a curt bow he turned on his heel but at the exit to the courtyard he paused and glanced back.

'Should you discover that you require further assistance after all, my room is opposite yours.'

Désirées blue eyes widened. He was staying here at the inn!

She stared after his departing figure, feeling oddly disturbed.

Rafael de Velasco might be a man of breeding, but all her instincts told her he was dangerous and she didn't want anything more to do with him!

Chapter Two

Shortly before seven the following morning Rafael ordered breakfast and sat down at the long dining-table which took pride of place in the Virgen Blanca's main parlour.

Last night he had finished the business which had brought him to Vitoria. The Basque smuggler he had contacted earlier in the year had obtained the rifles he needed. Rafael had handed over the rest of the gold and the English-made guns were his.

They now lay concealed in the vast travelling berlin which had once belonged to his father. He even had a perfect decoy prepared in case he encountered a French patrol.

It had taken a good deal of money to arrange, but a smile of satisfaction lit his features as he contemplated the success of his venture so far.

The sound of light footsteps alerted him to the fact that someone approached and he looked up to see the lovely blonde girl he had befriended yesterday entering the room.

'Good morning, *señorita*.' He rose politely to his feet. 'I did not expect to see you again before I left.'

'Nor I you, Señor Velasco.' Désirée kept her tone cool, but she couldn't prevent a little flare of excitement quickening her heartbeat.

'I have just ordered breakfast. Will you join me?'

'I suppose I may as well,' she said, adopting an offhand

manner in order to conceal the pleasure she felt at his invitation.

Dressed casually in cord breeches and a short leather coat, he was even more attractive than she remembered. The earth-coloured jacket was unbuttoned and his white shirt lay open at the neck. Désirée stared at the strong column of his throat. In contrast to the linen, his skin was very brown.

What would it feel like to touch that olive flesh? Was it as warm and smooth as it looked?

'*Por favor.*' Rafael indicated a chair opposite him.

Coming to her senses, Désirée realised that he was waiting for her to sit down and she hurried to take her place.

He called to someone in the back room and a moment later they were served with a platter of fresh crusty bread-rolls and two large bowls of steaming black coffee.

A small pot of some sticky-looking conserve accompanied the bread and Désirée spread a little on her roll. It tasted of cherries, sweet and ripe.

'It is to your liking?'

She murmured agreement, suddenly feeling a little ashamed of her ungracious behaviour. Whatever his motives, he was being nice to her.

'Did I understand you to say that you were leaving today?' she asked in a much warmer tone than she had previously employed.

He nodded, but did not elaborate.

'Have you hired horses here in Vitoria?' Désirée continued to probe. When he affirmed it, she asked which livery stables he had used.

'Why do you want to know, Miss Cavendish?'

Irritation sent the answer bubbling to Désirée's tongue. 'Because I can't make Consuelo understand me and I need to get to Burgos as quickly as possible.'

'I thought you said someone was meeting you in Vitoria?'

Désirée coloured. 'Did I? How silly of me! I meant in Burgos.'

She was a poor liar, Rafael decided. Her vivid little face was too expressive of her inner thoughts. He had known yesterday that she was concealing something.

Could it be that she was running away to meet a lover?

Dios! What demon had put that idea into his head?

Rafael stared at her flushed face. She had beautiful skin, clear and smooth-textured, and he had never seen such intensely blue eyes!

Admit it, *amigo*, she is lovely enough to tempt any man!

The thought annoyed him. Was he a foolish boy to be distracted by an enticing figure and glorious hair!

Désirée dropped her eyes to her plate, but she could still feel his speculative gaze on her.

Oh why had she blurted out the truth? She had meant to keep her destination secret.

To cover her confusion, she took a sip of her coffee. It was hot and strong, reviving her to meet his gaze again.

'Tell me, are you running away from your family?'

Rafael's abrupt demand broke the silence.

'No!' Désirée's gasp revealed her astonishment. Recovering, she informed him that she was an orphan.

He looked sceptical and Désirée decided that, providing she was careful to omit certain details, there was nothing to be lost by explaining the reason for her journey.

'Does he know what you intend?' Rafael asked, wondering what an Englishman was doing living in the Burgos area and concluding he was probably involved somehow in the wine trade. 'He gave his consent for you to travel alone?'

Désirée winced at his shrewdness. No one else had thought to ask her if Etienne had actually agreed to her plan. They had all assumed she had his permission.

'Not exactly, no,' she confessed. 'We talked about it the last time he came home and he didn't say no.' Her eyes twinkled naughtily. 'So I just wrote and told him I was on my way.'

'I think you are foolhardy, Miss Cavendish.' Rafael's

deep voice held a note of censure, but his disapproval
was mixed with admiration for her spirit. Few women
would have dared undertake such a bold venture.

'You are probably right. But I was bored and thought
I might enjoy more excitement if I came to Spain.'

She laughed. 'Unfortunately, so far I have only found
the wrong kind!'

He quirked his eyebrows in enquiry and, without
meaning to, Désirée found herself obeying his unspoken
command.

Rafael felt anger flare in him. '*Por Dios*, you have
been ill served! Those fools deserved to be whipped!
Tell me the names of these lazy rogues and I shall see
to it for you.'

'It doesn't matter,' Désirée replied hastily. 'No harm
came to me. They aren't worth worrying about.'

He frowned but then nodded. 'As you wish.'

Désirée suppressed a sigh of relief.

Or was she being over-cautious? Perhaps there had
been no need to edit the truth of Beauchet's desertion
and pretend her escort had been Spanish.

Swallowing hard, Désirée wished she knew. But even
if he didn't give a fig she was French, he might well be
annoyed that she had deliberately misled him.

If only she had never claimed to be English, this tangle
could have been avoided! It had seemed a good idea at
the time, but as *Maman*, who surely had cause to know,
used to say, deception always came home to roost!

Désirée knew she would only feel at peace with herself
again if she made a clean breast of it and confessed her
deliberate prevarication, but she didn't want to take the
risk of alienating him. Somehow, without her quite knowing why it should be so, Rafael de Velasco's good opinion
was important to her.

In fact, it was unnerving to realise that she hadn't
stopped thinking about him since they met. He had been
able to dominate her thoughts just as easily as he had
taken control of events yesterday.

He wasn't like any other man she had met. She'd had

several beaux, but none of them had been able to cope
with her desire for independence and Désirée had inevi-
tably ended by despising them.

But she couldn't imagine Rafael de Velasco playing
second fiddle to a woman. He possessed an inherent air
of command and a vibrant masculinity which tugged
insistently at her senses.

Her pulse began to hammer. She barely knew him, but
she felt more alive in his company than she had ever
done before. In his presence, every fibre of her being
seemed to tingle with a strange new awareness.

Mon Dieu, what was the matter with her? She was
behaving like a green sixteen-year-old! Admittedly, he
was handsome and he intrigued her, but she ought to
know better than let her head be turned.

'I won't let what happened yesterday affect my plans.'
Resentment at her own foolishness clipped Désirée's
voice. 'I am still determined to join my brother. I asked
him to meet me in Burgos and I know he will be waiting
for me.'

She glared at him as if daring him to challenge her
and Rafael shrugged.

'I may think you foolish, *señorita*, but it is not my
place to dissuade you,' he responded drily.

'Then you will help me find transport?' Désirée could
not keep the eagerness from her voice.

'I am headed south. Burgos lies on my route. If you
wish, we could travel there together. I have a comfortable
carriage.'

Désirée's heart slammed against her ribs in sharp short
strokes.

'It is kind of you to make such a generous offer, but
I barely know you, *señor*,' she said stiffly. 'I do not think
it would be—'

'You think it would be an offence against propriety.'
With an impatient wave of one long-fingered brown
hand, Rafael interrupted her. 'Forgive me, I should have
explained that several outriders and a distant female
cousin of mine accompany me. I am escorting her home.

She speaks no English, but I think you will find her an adequate chaperon.'

Désirée bit her lip. Now she had offended him!

Meeting his dark eyes, she realised she was mistaken.

There was warm approval in his gaze and feeling suddenly dizzy, Désirée realised something else, something which anxiety and a certain innate modesty had prevented her from seeing before.

There was no mystery about Rafael de Velasco's motive in befriending her. He wasn't being helpful merely out of kindness or good manners. He found her as attractive as she found him!

'In that case, I should be delighted to accept your offer,' she said, trying to quell her excitement.

'We must leave in a few minutes.' Rafael rose to his feet. 'Can you be ready?'

Désirée nodded. 'My bag is already packed.' She drained her bowl and stood up, determined to ignore the strange quivering in her thighs.

'I will meet you in the courtyard.'

Désirée started to turn away, but on impulse she swung back to face him.

'I don't think I have properly thanked you for your kindness, but, believe me, I am grateful.'

'*De nada, señorita*. Do not concern yourself. It is a pleasure to help.' Rafael accepted her thanks with a charming smile and graceful gesture of disclaim.

But even as he spoke Rafael suspected he was going to regret his quixotic gallantry. Beautiful and intriguing, this foreign girl was much too desirable for his peace of mind!

When Rafael handed Désirée up into the berlin, she immediately understood why he had thought she would find his cousin a suitable chaperon——the lady already seated in the carriage was dressed in the white flowing robes of a Cistercian nun.

'She lives at the convent of Las Heulgas, near Burgos,' Rafael said softly, catching Désirée's startled eye.

A gurgle of amusement sought for escape, but Désirée quickly smothered it while her rescuer exchanged a few words with Sor Isabella in their native tongue.

'My cousin asks me to bid you welcome. She apologises for her lack of English and hopes that you will forgive her silence.'

'Did you explain why I am travelling with you?' Désirée asked awkwardly, hoping that the old lady didn't think her a trollop.

'Not in any detail.' Guessing at her concern, Rafael sought to reassure her with a smile.

She didn't look in the least like an adventuress. Before joining him in the courtyard she had rearranged her pale gold hair, securing it in a single thick plait which was tied back with a piece of blue ribbon. She had also exchanged her high-waisted morning gown with its short puff sleeves for a dark blue riding-habit. The well-tailored jacket was buttoned high at the neck, but it was closely fitted to the body.

Rafael wondered if she knew how it accentuated the perfection of pert breasts and small waist. A full skirt, shorter than that of an ordinary gown, flared out over her slim hips and stout leather boots completed the outfit.

She looked prepared for any mishap, not surprising perhaps in view of yesterday. She also looked very young and heart-stoppingly fragile.

Disturbed by his susceptibility, Rafael quickly closed the door of the carriage after her.

'You are not travelling inside?' Désirée strove to keep the disappointment from her voice.

He shook his head. 'I prefer horseback,' he answered and with an elegant bow of farewell stepped away from the window.

Settling herself more comfortably against the velvet squabs, Désirée wished she could have joined him. It was a fine morning and she would have enjoyed a gallop.

Suppressing this thought, she smiled politely at the small elderly woman seated opposite her and Sor Isabella nodded back. Then, indicating the fine rosary of carved

ivory which lay in her lap, the nun picked it up and
began to tell the beads, her lips moving silently.

Left her own devices, Désirée gazed out of the
window. It was possible to catch the occasional glimpse
of her benefactor. He looked thoroughly at ease on his
handsome grey stallion and Désirée admired his handling
of the big horse.

Once they were free of the town, Rafael waved a hand
in salute and rode on ahead. Désirée endeavoured to
concentrate on the passing scenery. Unfortunately, the
landscape became harsher and more arid as they travelled
further south.

After a while it failed to hold her attention and she
fell to pondering how her brother would receive her.
Knowing Etienne, he would greet her warmly, but once
they were in private she was in for a fierce scold.

Désirée's lips curved in a reminiscent smile. Eight
years older than herself, Etienne had often found her
slavish devotion a sore trial. To his credit, when they
were younger, he had allowed her to dog his footsteps
without complaint, but his patience had exploded on
occasion, particularly when she had tried to copy his
more daring exploits. Luckily, his anger hadn't usually
lasted and he always forgave her in the end.

Or nearly always. In spite of his easygoing nature,
Etienne possessed the same stubborn streak they had both
inherited from *Maman*. Once he had come to a final
decision, nothing could change his mind.

Désirée shivered. On more than one occasion her
grandfather had thrashed Etienne for refusing to obey his
commands. The leather strap he'd used had sometimes
raised such severe welts that Etienne could barely stand,
but he had never given in.

The beatings had become more frequent as Etienne
grew older and in the end even *Maman* had agreed it
was best if Etienne left the Manor. He had fled in secret
one night a few months before his seventeenth birthday,
leaving them to face Sir William's cold wrath. Désirée's
punishment for refusing to say where Etienne had gone

was a week of nothing but water and gruel, but it had been worth it to know she had given him the chance of making it safely back to France.

Twelve years had passed since his escape and her brother had not only achieved his a ambition to become a soldier, but had caught the eye of Napoleon himself. His promotion had been rapid, achieving deserved renown and enough riches along the way to buy back the château which had been lost to the family during the Revolution.

Désirée envied him. It was the lot of girls to stay at home and be obedient, but she had always wanted to experience adventure and see new places. She *needed* to be active and doing something.

Cousin Hortense blamed it on her irregular upbringing!

Not that Désirée had expected the actual process of travelling to be so boring. The journey from Orléans had been bad enough, but today she lacked any means of occupation. However, since the road was very bumpy she doubted she could have read or used the portable chess-set she had been forced to leave behind in her wrecked chaise. How Sor Isabella, having at last concluded her lengthy prayers, could have nodded off to sleep was beyond her understanding!

The day wore on, growing hotter by the minute and Désirée's boredom grew with the heat. It was a relief when Rafael finally called a halt outside a small *posada*, but when she descended from the coach he announced that they would stay only for a short time while the horses were watered and rested.

'They will bring some food out. Or do you wish to go inside?'

Désirée shook her head firmly. 'It looks flea-infested,' she said bluntly.

Rafael grinned. Her outspoken honesty was refreshing after the timidity of most Spanish girls!

Sor Isabella also declined to leave the carriage. Having spoken to her, Rafael turned back to his other guest.

'Unless you intend to return to the berlin, I suggest you seek some shade, *Señorita*.' He indicated a cork-oak tree growing to one side of the inn.

She nodded obedience.

'Good. Now, if you will excuse me, I must check that the horses are being properly treated.'

Désirée watched him stride away. He moved with the lithe grace of some big powerful jungle cat!

She had no appetite for the plate of bread and sliced spicy sausage brought out to her by a slatternly looking maid, but sat down with her back against the trunk of the tree Rafael had recommended, toying with the cup of rough red wine that had accompanied the food.

'You have hardly touched your meal.'

Désirée jumped, sending her wine flying.

'Must you always creep up on people!' she exclaimed crossly, scrubbing at the stain which blossomed on the skirts of her riding-habit with an irritated hand.

Rafael laughed, dropping down to sit besides her with loose-limbed ease. 'I was making enough noise for a regiment! You must have been daydreaming, *Señorita*.'

Désirée's frown faded in response to his laughter.

He had discarded his jacket and his hair was a tangled riot of windblown curls. She was aware of a crazy longing to smooth back a stray lock which had fallen across his forehead.

'Here. Try this.' He held out a large clean hand-kerchief.

'It might stain,' she warned.

He shrugged. '*De nada*. It doesn't matter.'

Désirée reached out to take the handkerchief and their fingers touched.

His hand was so warm, so vital! A strange sensation seemed to radiate from the point where their fingers met, a twisting hot spiral that snaked swiftly along her veins to explode with burning heat in the pit of her stomach.

Hastily, Rafael pulled his hand away. From the dazed expression on her face, he knew she had felt it too, that hot stab of desire. The shock of it had sliced through his defences like a knife!

Striving for normality, he moved to pick up the empty cup. 'Can I get you a replacement?'

Coming to her senses, Désirée shook her head. 'No, thank you,' she murmured, apparently busy wiping her skirt.

Rafael glanced at her untouched plate. 'What about something else to eat?'

The wine stain attended to, Désirée summoned the courage to look up and meet his gaze with a semblance of calm. 'I'm not very hungry,' she admitted, hoping he would think she had been affected by the heat.

Rafael crushed the urge to take her in his arms. He very much wanted to kiss her, but it would be wrong to take advantage of her friendless state. At present, she was under his protection and honour demanded he treat her as he would Sor Isabella.

Once they reached Burgos, it would be a different matter!

'Actually, I'm rather tired. I didn't sleep well last night.' Desperately aware of his nearness, Désirée said the first thing that came into her head to fill the tense silence.

In the dappled light under their leafy canopy it was hard to be sure, but Rafael thought he detected faint shadows beneath her lovely eyes.

'Are you afraid of what your brother will say?'

Taken aback by his abrupt demand, Désirée reflected ruefully that she ought to be growing used to his shrewdness.

'He will be angry. I just hope he won't send me back home.'

Rafael, grappling with the disturbing realisation that he didn't want to let her go, could volunteer no safe reply.

Disappointment washed over Désirée. Angrily, she tried to curb it. There was no reason to think he would care whether or not she stayed in Spain!

Another silence stretched out between them until Désirée could stand it no longer.

'Is it much further to Burgos?' she asked, getting to her feet.

'We should be there before sunset.' Rafael copied her action. 'Providing we don't break a wheel or meet a French patrol.'

Désirée stiffened. There was an odd note in his deep smooth voice.

'You don't like the French, *señor*?' she enquired hesitantly.

His sensual mouth twisted. 'Do you?' he retorted. 'I thought all the English hated Napoleon.'

Désirée swallowed hard, a strange hollow feeling sweeping over her, but couldn't think of any answer.

Impatiently, Rafael dismissed the subject. 'Come, it is time we left.'

They walked back towards the coach and an involuntary sigh escaped Désirée. 'I wish I didn't have to get back in!'

'You would prefer travelling on horseback?' Amazement coloured Rafael's tone.

'Yes, of course. Don't Spanish ladies like riding?' Désirée chuckled at his expression.

'Most of them prefer to stay in their carriages. . .and out of the sun.'

'I have a shady hat.'

He relented at the hopeful note in her voice.

'Then I shall see what I can arrange, *señorita*.'

He disappeared into the stables at the rear of the inn; a few minutes later, to Désirée delight, he emerged leading a pretty little black mare.

'Oh she is lovely!' Désirée exclaimed, glad that she had not known of the animal's presence earlier. Awareness would have made that hot, stuffy coach journey even more intolerable!

'A present I am taking home for my sister,' Rafael explained.

'She won't mind my riding her?' Désirée asked anxiously.

Rafael shook his head. 'Elena is not the jealous type.'

'I promise I'll be very careful.' Désirée moved forward joyfully.

'Haven't you forgotten something?' Rafael was amused.

She cocked her blonde head at him in enquiry.

'It would be a pity to spoil so fair and lovely a complexion.'

'Oh, yes! My hat!' Blushing a little at the unexpected compliment, Désirée swung back to the berlin.

She was rather surprised to see that her small valise had been stored beneath the coach-driver's seat. Surely there would have been enough room in the luggage compartment at the rear?'

'Let me help you.' Rafael materialised at her side. He swung agilely up to retrieve her bag and Désirée dismissed her trivial speculation.

While she donned the pretty but decidedly frivolous chip-straw hat and tied its blue satin ribbons beneath her chin, the coachman appeared and Rafael handed her valise up to him before going off to issue instructions to the outriders.

Désirée looked around her for a mounting block, but before she could find one Rafael returned.

'Allow me.'

Very conscious of what had happened last time, Désirée steeled herself for the shock of contact as his hands gripped her waist and he tossed her lightly up into the smart saddle, which was presumably another gift as it was obviously new.

Rafael gave the order to move out and, aware that she was under scrutiny, Désirée kept silent and concentrated on getting to know her mount. The little mare was beautifully behaved and after a while she relaxed.

'You like her?'

Désirée nodded enthusiastically. 'Your sister is very lucky.'

A shadow passed over his lean face. 'Unfortunately, she does not enjoy good health.'

'I am sorry to hear it, *señor*.'

There was sincerity in her voice, which prompted Rafael to remark, 'I think you also have known the sorrow of watching someone you love suffer.'

Désirée nodded. 'My mother was an invalid for the last few years of her life.'

They rode in silence for a while after that exchange, but it was a comfortable silence, allowing Désirée to savour her new freedom. In spite of the dust and the heat, she was enjoying herself.

Sure now of her competence, Rafael engaged her in conversation again and found to his surprise as the leagues flew past that she was knowledgeable on a wide variety of topics, including subjects not normally of interest to the female sex.

'I never thought to meet a woman who knew a better way than I did to tickle trout,' he chuckled, conceding defeat after a spirited exchange of ideas concerning fishing.

Désirée gave a demure smile. 'I hope you don't hold to the opinion that women should do nothing but tend their embroidery.'

Rafael shook his dark head. 'I am not quite so old-fashioned in my notions as you might think, Miss Cavendish. My late father was a noted scholar and when I was twelve he took me with him on a tour of Europe to visit the many friends with whom he corresponded, including several ladies of great intelligence. My provincial eyes were opened and I soon realised femininity was no bar to intellect.'

'Is that when you learnt to speak English so well?' Désirée asked interestedly.

Rafael acknowledged it. 'I discovered I had a talent for languages. When we returned home, my father arranged an extra tutor for me and I studied both English and French.'

'Didn't you go away to school?' Désirée enquired,

remembering what a fuss there had been when *Maman* had refused to send Etienne to the strict boarding-school that Grandfather had decreed suitable.

'My father felt he could teach me better himself, but later on I attended the university at Salamanca.'

It was here at this ancient centre of learning that he had first become interested in the ideas of liberty and equality. Liberalism had never appealed to his father, who was a traditionalist at heart for all his learning, but Rafael had eagerly soaked up the history of how the American colonists had freed themselves from the British yoke.

The more recent events happening in France also stirred his fervour but, like many others, he watched in dismay as those ideals of freedom were stained with blood. The eventual fall of the monsters who had promoted the Reign of Terror and the emergence of Napoleon had encouraged hope that the Republic might survive, but the Corsican had proved no champion of liberty.

The idealistic hopes Rafael had cherished finally died with Bonaparte's betrayal of Spain. Perhaps true freedom was an impossible dream. All he was certain of was that his people could not and would not exist under the rule of a foreign tyrant. They would fight to the death to prevent it!

Désirée wondered at his suddenly fierce expression.

'Was your time in Salamanca so awful, *señor*?'

Realising he was frowning, Rafael smoothed his features and made a light answer before excusing himself to ride on ahead and speak to his men before proposing a halt to rest the horses.

Glad to stop and take a drink from the leather water-bottle offered to her, Désirée made the most of the opportunity to stretch her legs before the order to remount came. To her delight, Rafael again elected to ride by her side.

Their conversation was so natural and easy that

Désirée found herself thinking that she might have known him for years.

He was, of course, well born. His careless mode of dressing had confused her at first, but she suspected he was actually quite wealthy. Certainly, he travelled in style!

Désirée didn't really care. She was interested in the man, not his position, and she found him wonderful company. They seemed to have any tastes in common, not least of which was a similar sense of humour.

The journey, enlivened by laughter, drew towards its close.

Rafael couldn't remember when he last felt so relaxed, which was ironic in the circumstances. But surely God would not be so unkind as to send them a French patrol on this day of all days?

'Don Rafael!'

Burgos was in sight when one of the outriders galloped up, shouting to attract his attention.

Rafael stiffened. The Deity, it seemed, was in a mood to mock!

'What is it?' Désirée asked, raising an arm to shield her eyes from the glare of the westering sun. She didn't know what that cloud of dust portended, but she could sense the sudden tension that vibrated in the air all around her. 'Trouble?'

Rafael nodded, silently cursing. 'Of a surety, Miss Cavendish.'

The swirling dust cloud grew nearer and Desiree was able to make out blue uniforms.

She bit her lip with savage anxiety. French *chasseurs*!

'Don't be afraid.' Instinctively, Rafael reached across to grip her hand and give it a comforting squeeze. 'You need not reveal your name. You are under my protection and I will not let them harm you.'

Désirée wanted to thank him, but her throat seemed filled with a huge ball of sand.

They watched the riders approach.

Frozen into immobility, Désirée stared at the leading

officer. There was something familiar about his blond
moustaches!

With tight feeling in her chest, she let out a small
strangled gasp.

'What is wrong, *mi ninfa*?'

Désirée heard him but was unable to reply. The colour
drained from her cheeks as a wave of dizziness
assailed her.

Of course she recognised the officer riding towards
them like a vengeful Fury! It was Etienne!

'Pretty, ain't it? Makes a fine front door, whatever it's
called.' Captain Duclos laughed heartily at his own joke
as he waved his hand at the glistening white gateway,
decorated with pinnacles and statues, which they were
approaching.

'It is known as the Arco de Santa Maria.' Rafael spoke
courteously in French, but his voice was very cold. 'Once
part of the medieval walls of Burgos.'

The Frenchman flicked him a hesitant look. Not given
to introspection, he was aware, none the less, of a firm
conviction that he wouldn't care to meet this particular
Spaniard without a troop at his back. Everything about
Rafael de Velasco and his small party appeared to be in
order, but behind that mask of icy civility he sensed
murderous antagonism.

'Ah, *oui*, it's an old place. Not that I care for ancient
towns myself. Give me something modern with good
straight roads a man can rid down in comfort!' Duclos
laughed again as they clattered through the gateway, local
inhabitants scattering nervously out of their path. 'How
about you, *señorita*?'

'Burgos appears to be a fine town,' Désirée said carefully, keeping her gaze firmly fixed upon the twin gothic
spires of the Cathedral looming ahead. She dare not
refuse to answer Duclos, but she had no intention of
agreeing with the man.

How could she had thought this buffoon was Etienne?
At a distance, Duclos possessed the same build and blond

colouring, down to an identical dashing moustache, but as soon as he had drawn closer she had realised her mistake.

Relief had mingled with apprehension. *She* might have cause to be feel reprieved, but it was obvious that Rafael felt only anger and distaste at the interruption. Even a thick-skinned idiot like Duclos must have sensed he was unwelcome!

The Captain had willingly accepted Rafael's curt explanation that she was a family friend travelling under his protection, but he had insisted on peering into the carriage. A barrage of furious Spanish had greeted him as he had opened the door. Désirée had hidden an amused smile as he beat a hasty retreat from Sor Isabella's indignant protests.

Not that the situation was in the least bit funny. Désirée could almost taste the hatred hanging in the air. Rafael's outriders were looking daggers at the French troopers and it wouldn't have surprised her if violence had erupted.

Thankfully, Rafael had his men well in hand; with a few sharp words from him, the threat was removed. Désirée sensed his choice might have been different if he had not known perfectly well that violence would serve him nothing. Outnumbered and with two women to consider, resistance was futile, but the angry glitter in his dark eyes warned her that she had been right to think he might hold the French in aversion.

A cold lump of misery settled in Désirée's stomach. No matter that he had politely agreed that they all ride into Burgos together, she *knew* he loathed Duclos and all he stood for!

'Well, I must leave you now.' Duclos reined in his showy bay as they reached the Cathedral. 'No doubt you can find your own way.'

Rafael acknowledged the remark with a stiff inclination of his head.

Turning to Désirée, the captain bowed forward in the saddle. 'Enchanted to have made your acquaintance, *señorita*. Remember me if you should ever want to practise your French. A message will find me at the Castle most days.'

Seeing a muscle flicker angrily at the corner of Rafael's mouth, Désirée hastily thanked him, employing her prettiest smile.

The troop of soldiers clattered off and Désirée let out a deep sigh, releasing the tension which had cramped her muscles since they had first come into view.

'Where are you to meet your brother?' Rafael's question brought her attention sharply into focus and she named the inn which had been recommended to her several lifetimes ago in Orléans.

'Then we must go east along the river.' Rafael prepared to turn his mount's head in the right direction.

'But don't you want to escort your cousin to the convent first?'

'Las Heulgas lies to the west.' Rafael thought for a instant and then, with a quick gesture, excused himself while he spoke first to his cousin and then to his senior outrider.

'Come. It is arranged. Pepe can escort Sor Isabella and I shall take you to the inn.'

'Are you sure? I don't want to put you to any further inconvenience,' Désirée murmured, secretly pleased that they would spend a little longer in each other's company.

'I want to satisfy myself that you are safe.' Rafael knew it was not his sole reason. He wanted a few moments alone with her without a dozen eyes watching their every move! 'I can easily catch the others up later.'

'Very well, *señor*.' Désirée urged the little mare up to the coach and said a polite farewell to Sor Isabella.

The elderly nun smiled at her. '*Vaya con Dios, niña.*'

The old lady's words rang in Désirée's ears as they rode off. Go with God. It was a conventional blessing, but Désirée was aware of a deep sense of guilt stealing over her.

She had misled Sor Isabella and she had lied to Rafael. They had been kind to her and she had repaid them with dishonesty. It didn't matter that she had acted from expediency. It was wrong!

Lifting up her chin, Désirée came to a decision, but before she could act upon it Rafael signalled a halt.

'What is it? Are we lost?'

'I know the way.' He shook his dark head. 'We must leave the river bank here. The inn lies behind that plaza.'

'Then why have we stopped?'

'Because I wish to speak to you in private.' Rafael gave a little smile. 'This seemed a good place for it.'

Désirée glanced around and saw what he meant. This stretch of the river bank was empty. Above them, the sky was flaming to its rest, painting the waters of the Arlanzon red and gold, and the only sound was the soft snickering of their horses mingling with the melancholy croaking of frogs in the river.

'I suppose everyone has gone home to supper,' she said a little breathlessly.

'And so must you in a moment.' Rafael's voice was gentle. 'I know you must be weary.'

Désirée didn't bother to deny it. She was fit and accustomed to frequent riding, but the long hot hours she had spent in the saddle today had been bone-achingly hard.

Rafael had expected her to complain about the heat or the dust, if nothing else. It pleased him that she had not, enduring every discomfort with a cheerful smile.

'I admired your fortitude today, but that isn't what I wish to talk of.' Rafael wished she would stop staring at the gap between her horse's ears and look up at him. 'Can't you guess what I want to say, *ninfa*?'

'You called me that earlier,' Désirée replied, almost in a whisper. 'What does it mean?'

'Nymph describes you perfectly.' Rafael's voice was a soft caress. 'Beautiful and mysterious, a slender creature of gold and sapphire and pearl, who can enchant this mere mortal man.'

Blushing, Désirée forced herself to lift her head and meet his eyes.

'You must not pay me compliments, *señor*,' she said, her tone bleak. 'I do not deserve them.'

Désirée could feel her courage dribbling away. She didn't want that lovely warmth in his gaze to vanish and be replaced with contempt!

He stared at her. 'I don't understand.' A frown tugged his eyebrows together. 'Have I made a mistake? I do not wish to sound a. . .a. . .how do you say? Yes, a coxcomb, but I thought you liked me.' He hesitated. 'I want to get to know you better, but if we part now without making any plans to meet again we may not get another chance.'

His austere features softened. 'And I would regret that, *ninfa*.'

'Please don't say anything more, Señor Velasco,' Désirée begged hastily. 'I do not believe it is possible for us to be friends.'

Her agitation conveyed itself to the little mare who began to cavort nervously. It took a moment for Désirée to regain control, but when she did she saw that Rafael's expression had hardened.

'What are you trying to tell me? Are you married, is that it?'

'No!' Désirée suppressed an urge to burst into tears. 'But I have lied to you! I let you think I was English, but I'm not. Oh, my real father was English and I lived in England for several years, but I have no right to claim the Cavendish name!'

'Explain yourself, *por favor*.' Rafael had his expression under control, but his mount bridled, betraying the tension in his body vibrating down the leather reins.

Désirée gritted her teeth and, switching to her native tongue, said baldly. 'Very well, *monsieur*. I was born in France. My mother was French. *I* am French. And, unless I am very much mistaken, that makes us enemies!'

Chapter Three

Watching him closely, Désirée saw Rafael de Velasco recoil. Her heart sank at the stunned expression which flashed across his handsome face. It disappeared so quickly she might have been tempted to ignore it, but there was no mistaking the coldness in his deep voice when at last he spoke.

'Your parents were not married, I assume?'

Désirée jerked her chin a fraction in assent. She was not going to apologise! Her mother and father had adored each other, but *Maman* was already married when they had met.

'I wish you had thought to be honest with me earlier, *mademoiselle*.' His French was as elegant as her own. 'It would have saved us both embarrassment.'

Désirée winced. 'My intention was not to deliberately deceive you, but to protect myself.'

His black brows flew together in a frown. What a poor opinion of him she must have formed!

'Did you really think I would attack a defenceless woman?' he demanded scornfully. 'I may despise your Emperor, *mam'selle*, but I have not sunk so low!'

Fuelled by humiliation, an answering anger stirred in Désirée. 'How was I to know I could trust you? You were a stranger to me! For all I could knew, you could have been one of those guerrillas I have heard so much about lately, liable to cut my throat just for speaking to you in French!'

She saw him pale beneath his tan. Realising she was
spouting nonsense, she reined in her runaway temper.

'I mean you no insult, *señor*,' she continued in a
quieter voice. 'All I am trying to do is to explain why I
thought prudence was in order.'

A part of him conceded that her argument was sound,
but Rafael's pride was stung by the fact it had taken her
so long to decide he was trustworthy.

'You have a strange idea of what is prudent!' he
said, seizing on the fatal weakness in her defence. 'A
sensible woman would have gone straight home. Why
didn't you?'

'I've told you already!' Désirée snapped.

'You told me many things, *mam'selle*,' Rafael replied
sarcastically. 'Even assuming this brother exists, what is
he doing here in Spain? I don't suppose he is English—'

Abruptly, Rafael stopped speaking. *Dios*, what a
fool he was!

'He is a soldier, this brother of yours, isn't he?
One of Napoleon's vultures come to pick over my
country's bones!'

'How dare you describe Etienne in that horrible way!'
Rage brightened Désirée's eyes, intensifying their colour
almost to violet. 'Yes, he is an officer in the French
army, but he is a fine, honourable man! Unlike you,
monsieur, he did not inherit wealth and privilege. When
we were just children, our château was stormed by a
rioting mob. We lost everything!'

Désirée shivered at the memory. She had been five
years old, but the screams of brutal hatred and the sound
of the windows smashing under a hail of stones still rang
with dreadful clarity in her ears.

The man she had always believed to be her father, the
elderly Chevalier, had had a heart seizure and collapsed
while they were escaping. He died before their eyes,
leaving Etienne to take care of her and their distraught
maman on that nightmare journey to the coast where they
finally managed to bribe a fisherman to carry them across
to England.

Shaking off remembered horror, Désirée glared furiously at Rafael de Velasco.

'You have no right to criticise my brother, *monsieur*. You do not know him. But everything I own today was achieved through his hard work and talent and I will not allow you to slight him.'

Startled by the fierceness of her attack, Rafael emitted a reluctant laugh. 'I wonder if your brother knows what a champion he has in you, *mam'selle*.'

Désirée bit her lip. 'It pleases you to mock me.'

He shook his dark head, wishing he could tell her that he admired her loyalty, but he could not permit such a weakness in himself. Already he had learnt to admire too much about her!

'You were right to think your real nationality would change things,' he said, finally breaking the painful silence which had fallen. 'I detest what the French have done to my country.'

'It is hardly fair to blame me for the Emperor's ambitions!'

'Logic doesn't enter into it,' Rafael retorted savagely. 'Even if I accept your innocence, your brother *is* a soldier and therefore one of those responsible. If you stand by him, you condone Napoleon's behaviour.'

Désirée could not deny it.

'Anne Cavendish could have been my friend, but between us. . .' He shrugged heavily.

There can be nothing but enmity. The words hung unspoken in the air.

Désirée understood. Pierre had been right. The Spanish were not beaten. The war had not ended and there could be no future for two people on opposing sides. Yet knowing it was inevitable did not lessen the crushing disappointment she felt at his rejection.

She liked Rafael de Velasco better than any man she had ever met and longed to discover if their mutual attraction might flower into something deeper, but she wasn't about to beg him to change his mind.

'Since you are determined to see me as your enemy,

then let us say goodbye here and now, *monsieur*.' Pride
ensured that her farewell was nothing more than coolly
polite. 'I thank you for your assistance and hope I may
be given an opportunity to repay you one day.'

He inclined his head in acknowledgment, but to
Désirée's surprise refused to let her go on to the inn alone.

'I promised to see you there safely and I never break
my word,' he said flatly when she protested.

'But I don't—'

'It will not take long if you stop wasting my time.
Come.' He urged his horse forward, leaving Désirée to
follow.

After a moment she obeyed, simmering with indignation at his high-handed arrogance.

They halted outside a tall stone building and Rafael
swung himself out of the saddle.

Envying his lithe ability, Désirée dismounted more
slowly as a boy came running to take their horses. She
would be stiff tomorrow.

She followed Rafael inside, glancing around the
gloomy hallway with nervous interest. At least the place
was clean, if somewhat spartan.

A middle-aged man appeared and Rafael greeted him.

'Can you ask him if my brother has arrived?'

He nodded curtly. 'His name?'

'Colonel Fontaine.'

At least he now knew her real surname. Banishing a
foolish desire to know the rest, Rafael sternly told himself
to be glad that he was about to be rid of her.

Blank looks of incomprehension greeted his questions
and Désirée's heart sank.

'No one of that name has been here.'

'I don't understand. There must be some mistake,'
she said.

'I assure you that he would not forget if a French
officer had stayed here.' Rafael's tone was dry.

Glancing at the closed, shuttered face of the landlord,
Désirée repressed a shiver. She could feel his resentment

towards her. Fleetingly, she wondered how she would have coped without Rafael's presence.

Trying another tack, she asked him to check if any message had been left for her, but this enquiry drew another blank.

'I suggest you try asking at the Castle.' Stupid as it was, Rafael could not rid himself of a feeling of responsibility towards her. 'The French are garrisoned there. Someone might know his whereabouts.'

Désirée nodded. It was a good idea.

'Thank you.' She hesitated. 'If you would be so kind, please ask him to let me have supper and a room for the night and I will go to the Castle as soon as I have eaten.'

'Are you mad?' Incredulous anger sharpened Rafael's tone. 'You cannot visit a garrison full of soldiers alone. Particularly not at night.'

'They will not harm me. They are my fellow countrymen,' Désirée replied stiffly, hoping her cheeks hadn't gone as red as they felt.

'They are men, *mademoiselle*, and liable to be drunk after supper. You are a beautiful woman. They might not stop to ask your nationality. Send your message in the morning.'

Flinching at the brutal cynicism in his velvet voice, Désirée shook her head. 'I will write a note if you think it best, but it must go tonight. I will not be able to sleep otherwise.'

She glanced at her host. Would he oblige her and provide someone to take her letter or would he be too afraid to have dealings with the Castle?

Guessing at her thoughts, Rafael said abruptly, 'There is no need to write a note. I will go myself.'

'It is very good of you to offer, but I have no claim on your time, Señor Velasco. You are engaged to visit your cousin and I do not wish to delay you any further.'

The words felt awkward and stiff on Désirée's tongue, but she might as well have spared herself the effort for all the notice he took of her refusal.

'I shall not be long. You will have time to change before joining me for supper.'

'I don't remember inviting you to sup with me, *monsieur*,' Désirée snapped.

'You didn't.' A brief smile flickered over his lean dark face. 'However, it is getting late and I am hungry. By the time I return from the garrison we may as well discuss the matter over supper like civilised beings.'

To her surprise, he reached out one long brown hand and touched her lightly on the shoulder.

'Just for tonight, let us declare a truce,' he suggested. 'I shall endeavour to think of you as Anne Cavendish and you can pretend I am anything but a Spaniard, if that is your wish.'

Realising he was attempting to reassure her and allay her worries about Etienne, Désirée nodded. 'Anne is actually my second name,' she murmured shyly.

'May I make so bold as to enquire your first?' Rafael assumed a casual tone to cover his intense interest.

Entering into the spirit of their truce, she swept him a graceful curtsy and informed him.

Caught off guard, Rafael almost betrayed himself but his quick reflexes enabled him to make his exit without revealing his inner perturbation.

Désirée. Her name hammered in his head as he waited for his horse to be brought to him. Désirée. The desired one. *Por Dios*, how cruelly, how unattainably appropriate!

The room into which Désirée was shown was large, but that was the only thing in its favour. She stared at the high wooden bed draped in dismal dark brown curtains and, all at once, wished she had never set out on this mad journey, but was safe at home in her own pretty pink and white bedroom.

The loud thump of her valise as the maid who had accompanied her dumped it down on the bare wooden floorboards recalled Désirée's wandering attention.

'*Gracias*,' Désirée thanked her and asked her to bring up some hot water.

A sullen look greeted her request. Désirée repeated it more firmly.

'*Si, señorita*.' The maid nodded and backed hastily out of the room as if she feared Désirée might ask her to unpack.

Désirée had finished this task by the time the girl returned. Taking the jug, she dismissed the maid and, locking the door, removed her clothes to enjoy a thorough wash. Refreshed, she donned the least creased of the three gowns she had brought with her.

There was a small mirror hanging on one wall, enabling her to rearrange her hair. Taking up the silver hairbrush Etienne had given her two birthdays ago, she swept the pale mass up into a simple knot at the back of her head, securing it deftly with a handful of ivory-headed pins.

It was now growing dark in the room and Désirée found it difficult to judge how she looked, but she comforted herself with the knowledge that at least her white muslin dress was pretty, with its delicately embroidered bodice and deeply flounced hem, although it could have done with pressing.

She would have to hire another maid when she got to Madrid. But would she able to find one as good as Louise? Wishing her maid had not succumbed to home-sickness, Désirée slipped on a pair of white satin pumps and sat down on the bed to wait.

A loud knocking at the door roused her and she scrambled up to answer it, dazedly aware she must have dozed off.

'Why are you in the dark?' Rafael de Velasco stood there, a branch of candles held high in one hand.

Désirée blinked at him. 'I. . .I think I fell asleep. What time is it?'

A slight involuntary smile curving his mouth, Rafael told her.

'Come.' He held out his free arm. 'A meal awaits us.'

Désirée placed her fingers on his dark sleeve. Somehow he had found the time to change. He was now wearing a coat of smooth black cloth and he'd shaved too. Struggling to make her sleepy brain work, she wondered how he had accomplished it.

'After visiting the Castle, I went to pay a call at Las Heulgas to ensure that my cousin had arrived safely. I brought my men back with me. We will stay here overnight. It is too late to continue our journey now.'

Rafael had intended to camp out near the convent, but he did not tell her so. *She* was the reason for changing his mind. He had tried to pretend to himself that since he had to return to the inn he might as well pass the night in comfort in a proper bed, but he knew he was lying. He had even gone to the trouble of smartening himself up, a habit he ought to cultivate more often according to his sister!

He had guessed her thoughts again, but Désirée was too wound up to wonder at his uncanny perception.

'Did you find out any news about my brother?' she asked urgently, all her senses snapping fully awake.

'They had not heard he was in Burgos,' Rafael replied quietly.

Her face fell. 'I see. Thank you for trying anyway.'

They descended the stairs in silence, but instead of leading her into the main dining-room, Rafael turned aside.

'I thought you might prefer to sup in private,' he said, ushering her towards the small *sala* he had commandeered.

Désirée halted and, removing her hand from his arm, met his gaze with a challenging frown. 'Is it the custom of unmarried Spanish ladies to eat alone with men who are no relation to them?'

Did he think she was easy game now that he knew she was a love-child?

'No, it is not. Nor do they travel without a chaperon.' He shook his dark head, a mocking gleam in his eyes. 'Do you intend to start standing on ceremony, *mam'selle*?'

'I suppose not.' Désirée gave a reluctant laugh, aware of the dangers in letting over-sensitivity lead her into assuming the worst.

She had no reason to think he despised her for being born on the wrong side of the blanket. His manner had not altered towards her. She had obviously been reared a lady; perhaps he thought good blood counted for more than a wedding ring.

Not that his opinion mattered anyway!

Besides, it was too late to worry about propriety, she reflected as he waited politely to one side, allowing her to enter the room before him. She had acted as the odd circumstances demanded and she would just have to hope that Etienne would understand.

A fire had been lit to ward off the evening chill and in the candlelight the small room looked cosy and inviting. A table stood in front of the fireplace already laid with a white cloth.

The meal was not the usual dainty fare Désirée was used to at home, but it was plentiful and well-cooked. Their attentive young waiter brought in a tureen of bean soup, which was followed by an omelette, described to her by Rafael as a *tortilla*, a dish of salted cod, assorted offerings of hot and cold vegetables and a platter of roast lamb.

'Can I give you some of this wine?' Rafael held up the bottle he had ordered earlier from the cellar.

Désirée nodded and allowed him to fill her glass.

Knowing she must be hungry after her day in the saddle, Rafael kept the conversation to light trivialities, encouraging her to forget her anxiety and satisfy her appetite before dismissing the waiter with the announcement that they would help themselves to the dessert of sugar-coated almonds, honey cakes and fruit.

'What do you intend to do now, Mademoiselle Fontaine?' Rafael asked, returning to the vexed subject of her brother's absence. 'Will you remain here in Burgos or go home to France?'

Désirée swallowed the last piece of juicy orange she

had been eating and shook her head. 'Neither. I intend to go on to Madrid.'

For an instant Rafael was taken aback by her crisp answer. 'Impossible!'

'Why? I have enough money. For all that the French are hated, I am sure it will hire the necessary service.'

'Money talks, I agree, but have you considered all the difficulties?'

'I am not such a fool as to think it is going to be easy. But I cannot sit here doing nothing!'

'Are you sure he knows you are coming? Letters go astray.'

Désirée nodded her head so violently that a few tendrils of pale gold hair floated free. 'I sent several. One of them must have reached him.'

From her worried expression, Rafael saw that she had grasped that something might have occurred to prevent the colonel from keeping the rendezvous.

'It might be less distressing to send an envoy in your place,' he suggested. 'An uncle, perhaps?'

'We have no one but each other, *señor*.' Désirée clasped her hands together, unseen beneath the table, to stop them trembling as she tried to put her feelings into words.

'I haven't seen much of Etienne these last few years. He is older than I am and our paths have diverged. I suppose you might even say that, strictly speaking, he is only my half-brother. But none of that matters.' She sighed. 'If he is ill or has suffered an accident, I don't want to waste time floundering around in ignorance.'

Rafael regarded her closely. Her lovely heart-shaped face wore a look of determination, but her eyes told him she was afraid.

'He may have been merely delayed. The duty officer I spoke to said that they were expecting dispatches from Madrid any day now. There might be a letter for you.'

'I hope so!'

The prospect of a long wait for news filled Désirée with dismay. Patience was not one of her virtues!

Reaching for her wineglass, she sipped the rich red liquid thoughtfully. Dare she ask Rafael de Velasco to help her yet again?

Stealing a glance at his handsome face from beneath her downcast lashes, she decided to gamble on his undoubted chivalry.

'You said you were going south. Will you take me with you?' she asked boldly. 'I swear I won't get in your way or hold you up.'

For a brief instant Rafael allowed himself to be tempted, but sanity prevailed.

'I'm afraid that will not be possible, *mam'selle*.'

Désirée gave a bitter laugh. 'I see. You dislike me so much you cannot bear to remain in my company.'

Rafael wished he *could* dislike her. It would make things simpler. Reminding himself that she was French didn't seem to be the solution. Every time he looked at the graceful line of her white shoulders rising out of that soft embroidered gauze his loins ached.

He wanted to pull her up out of that chair and into his arms. To entangle his hands in the pale glory of her hair. To taste her soft lips. And bury himself to the hilt within the hot secret depths of her delectable body!

Madness!

'My decision has nothing to do with personal feelings. My home lies near Covarrubias. I am not going on as far as Madrid.'

'Please.' Désirée dropped her voice to a sweet husky murmur. 'I would not ask if the circumstances were not desperate.'

'Believe me, I am not indifferent to your plight, but I have other commitments.' He could not tell her about the guns. 'Duty requires me to leave Burgos tomorrow. I cannot delay here any longer.'

Désirée leant forward towards him, allowing her lips to part a little as she fluttered her eyelashes. 'You could change your mind,' she said softly. 'I would willingly pay you for your time and trouble—'

'I am not a lackey for hire, Mademoiselle Fontaine.'

Rafael's voice turned cold. 'My services cannot be bought. I have helped you so far because you are a woman of gentle birth in obvious need. Honour demanded I render you aid, but do not presume to play upon my sympathy, I beg of you.'

Désirée flushed. Anger that her ploy had failed mingled with embarrassment. He wasn't interested. She had made a fool of herself and to no purpose!

Thrusting back her chair, she stood up.

'I shall waste no more of your valuable time, *señor*. No doubt one of the officers at the Castle will be able to suggest a friendly guide if the need arises.'

She stalked towards the door, but before she could reach it Rafael came up out of his chair in one swift fluid movement and strode across the *sala* to stand with his back to the oak panels to prevent her exit.

Désirée stopped short. He was so close she could feel the heat emanating from him and his impressive height meant that in order to glare at him she had to tilt her head back on the slender stem of her neck.

'Let me pass. You are blocking my path.' Frustration raged in Désirée's voice.

'Why are you so angry with me, *ninfa*?'

'Don't call me that!' Désirée began to wish she hadn't tried to flirt with him. There was a wicked gleam of mischief in his smile.

He laughed recklessly, enjoying the way her eyes glittered. 'I thought you liked it,' he murmured and, succumbing to temptation, ran one finger down the flawless curve of her cheek. Her skin felt like the softest silk!

The breath caught in Désirée's throat. His nearness was making her feel dizzy. He was much too big, much too male!

'Well, I don't!' Her voice came out in a choked whisper. 'And please don't touch me.'

'Why not?' An inner voice warned Rafael that he was dicing with danger, but he chose to ignore it. 'Don't you want me to, *mi perla*?'

'No!' Désirée's heart began to slam against her ribs. My pearl, indeed!

'I don't think I believe you.' Throwing sense to the winds, Rafael decided to extract a revenge of the sweetest kind to repay her attempt to manipulate him.

'Shall we try an experiment to see if I am right?' He gathered her firmly into his embrace.

Too late, Désirée remembered that if you play with fire you risk getting burnt.

'Have you run mad, *señor*?' She struggled futilely in his hold.

'Hush, *ninfa*.' Wicked lights danced in Rafael's eyes as he bent towards her.

Held motionless by his strength, Désirée decided to accept her fate with dignity and stood stiff in his arms, allowing him to take possession of her mouth without further protest.

Softly, his lips caressed hers. Expecting a fierce assault, she was shaken by his gentle tenderness. Pleasure suffused her as he slowly deepened the kiss. Her senses reeling, she yielded, her lips parting eagerly beneath his.

Waves of heat swept through her as he explored her mouth with thorough expertise. All thoughts of resistance faded. She clung to him, kissing him back with a fervour that made him groan deep in his throat.

In the dim recesses of his brain, Rafael was vaguely aware that he ought to put a stop to this lunacy, but when she pressed herself against him even closer his hand slid up of its own volition to cup her breast. The warm soft weight of it fitted perfectly into his palm and he could not resist the need to brush his thumb backwards and forwards across her nipple. It hardened to his touch and she shivered in his arms, but did not pull away.

Revelling in the exciting new sensations he was arousing in her, Désirée forgot everything but the wonderful feel of his body against hers. The heady male scent of him filled her nostrils and she sighed voluptuously against his mouth. Their wine-sweetened breath mingled and the kiss went on and on until she thought she might faint.

Lifting his head at last, Rafael gazed down into her face. Her eyes were still closed, she was breathing very fast and her expression was drugged with unashamed pleasure.

Involuntarily, his arms tightened. He found her unexpected abandon intensely arousing! Every sense clamoured to continue but, summoning up the last remaining vestige of self-control he forced himself to release her.

Désirée swayed and he put out a hand to support her, but withdrew it when her eyes opened.

There was a look of shy confusion in their violet depths that tore at his determination, but Rafael knew he could not let her see how deeply their embrace had affected him. He could not afford such weakness!

'Point proven, I think, *mam'selle*!' he remarked in a cool drawl. He stepped away from the door. 'Our little experiment undoubtedly confirmed that you liked my touch.'

Désirée gasped and went white.

'You bastard!'

Before he had time to stop her, she raised one hand and slapped him hard across the face. Then, wrenching open the door, she picked up her skirts and fled.

Rubbing his stinging cheek, Rafael gave a twisted smile.

'You asked for that, *amigo*!' he murmured ruefully, and strolled back to the table to pour himself another glass of wine.

After a restless night Désirée woke up feeling headachy and tired. She rang for hot water and dressed in her one remaining clean gown, a blossom-pink sprigged muslin, glad her limbs were not as stiff as she'd feared they would be after all that riding. Quickly arranging her hair in a neat practical chignon, she headed for the door.

Her hand on the knob, she paused.

Did she or didn't she want to go downstairs?

Coward! You cannot hide up here for ever!

Désirée caught a glimpse of her reflection in the look-ing-glass on the wall. Her face was pale and set, but her eyes were glittering with nervous excitement.

'Perhaps he has already left,' she whispered to her reflection.

You ought to hope he is long gone, answered a little warning voice in her mind, but, in spite of the anger and embarrassment that had ruined her attempts to sleep last night, she could not prevent her pulse from racing at the thought of seeing Rafael de Velasco again.

Admit it, you wanted him to kiss you! You still want him to even now!

Désirée sighed. Oh, why was she such a fool? That lovely kiss, which had thrilled her to her very soul, had meant nothing at all to him! His mocking comments had made it quite clear that he'd merely been amusing himself.

She couldn't even pretend that it was his fault. She had deliberately tried to flirt with him in the hope that he would agree to her demands. His response had been to pay her back in her own coin and the result had been devastating.

His teasing had turned to passion, sweeping away her inhibitions. She had been kissed before, but never like that! The sensations he had aroused were so pleasurable that she had wanted it to go on for ever!

Désirée groaned aloud. What must he think of her? She had behaved shamelessly. If he had demanded more, she would have willingly surrendered!

How on earth was she going to face him? The very thought of having to meet his night-black gaze was making her go hot and cold all over!

Désirée gave herself a mental shake. She had to stop thinking about last night and start behaving in a rational manner. She needed to write to the commander of the garrison.

'Breakfast first,' she told herself. It might help set her disordered thinking straight.

There was no one else in the dining-room and she was

able to consume her meal in peace. When she had finished, she sought out the landlord to ask him if he could supply her with pen and paper.

Her request, when he finally understood what it was she wanted, provoked a frown. Désirée wasn't sure whether he was being deliberately unhelpful or not, but it took much head-scratching and a great deal of time before the items she required were finally brought to her.

'*Gracias, señor.*' Désirée endeavoured to keep the sarcasm from her voice as she thanked him for the small scrap of paper, ink and a pen that badly needed trimming.

A trip to the kitchen produced a knife to mend it and, armed for the task, she was at last ready to write her note. About to return to her room, a glance out of the window reminded her it was another fine sunny morning and suddenly a longing to get outside, away from these dark and gloomy surroundings, overcame her.

At the back of the inn she found a walled garden. A fountain stood in the centre of a brick patio. It was silent and dry, but she could hear birds singing and there was a faint sweet smell of herbs coming from somewhere.

Her lips curved in a smile as she spotted a wooden bench against the far wall.

Spreading out her sheet of paper beside her, Désirée chewed on the end of the pen and tried to compose a suitable letter. It took a long time.

Lost in thought, she didn't hear footsteps approaching.

'*Buenos días*, Mademoiselle Fontaine.'

Désirée jumped, her hand jerking in surprise. A blob of ink splattered from her pen on to her carefully composed note.

'Damn and blast it!' she exclaimed in English, unthinkingly using one of her grandfather's favourite expressions.

'I apologise. I did not mean to startle you.' Rafael de Velasco said quietly.

There was a tiny silence.

'I must also apologise for last night.' Rafael extended

his olive branch cautiously. 'I had no right to kiss you. I can only plead your beauty as my excuse.'

Désirée sought frantically for a formal reply, but then her sense of humour overcame her and she began to giggle helplessly. 'You sound like a poet in search of a verse!'

He grinned. 'A bad poet,' he corrected.

The ice broken, Désirée found that her embarrassment had fled with their laughter.

'I should apologise too,' she admitted, remembering how hard she had slapped him.

Rafael struggled with his pride for a moment and then spread his hands wide in a gesture of wry contrition. 'I deserved it.'

Glad that he bore no grudge, Désirée coloured rosily when he added wickedly, 'Besides, it was worth it!'

'I think we ought to draw a veil over last night, Señor Velasco,' she announced with mock severity, 'and pretend that embrace never happened.'

Rafael wasn't sure if he could. His dreams had been haunted by a slim blonde nymph, whose eyes were the colour of a summer sky.

Assuming that his silence meant consent, Désirée smiled up at him invitingly. 'Won't you sit down?' she asked, moving her letter out of the way.

Rafael caught his breath. That warm open smile of hers was truly enchanting!

A wave of regret washed over him. If she had not been French. . .if she had not been of gentle birth. . .if she had not been such a trusting innocent. . .

He wanted her, but the price of gratifying his desire was too high. She was neither a whore nor a married woman in search of sport and he would not stain his honour by ruining her reputation. Despoiling innocents had never been in his line and too much stood between them for anything other than a brief dalliance.

Duty, honour and common sense demanded he bid her farewell. But he ached to hold her in his arms again and discover whether she really was as passionate as her abandoned response last night seemed to promise.

Something of his thoughts showed on his dark lean face and Désirée's heartbeat quickened in response.

She took a deep calming breath and sought refuge in rearranging her skirts, needlessly smoothing out their graceful folds. When she raised her gaze again, the look of desire had vanished from his face and she rewarded her good sense by allowing her eyes to feast on his elegant appearance.

Today he was wearing cream pantaloons and a coat she hadn't seen before, a dark blue broadcloth, which fitted across his wide shoulders with scarcely a crease. A handsome brocade waistcoat and smartly tied neckcloth added to his splendour. Someone had even polished his boots!

'You are looking very fine, sir.' An impish smile flitted across Désirée's face as she wondered how long it had taken him to tame his unruly hair.

'But not feeling comfortable, I assure you.' Self-mockery twisted Rafael's answering grin as he moved to sit down beside her.

'Are you sure you want to risk sullying such perfection?' she teased, knowing full well that the bench was clean since she had dusted it off with her own handkerchief.

His grin broadened. 'I'm glad you approve of my efforts.'

Désirée blinked. Surely he hadn't gone to such trouble just for her?

'I thought I had better smarten myself up.' Rafael sat down, careful to keep at a discreet distance. 'I needed to pay a call on one of my aunts. She owns a property not far out of town and likes visitors.'

Désirée chuckled. 'I hope she appreciated your splendour.'

'I think she did.' Rafael's expression grew sombre. 'You see, I had a favour to ask and she agreed to grant it.'

Désirée wondered what he was leading up to. 'Why

are you telling me all this?' she enquired curiously.

'I asked her if she would accept you as her guest.'
Rafael was watching her closely, trying to gauge her
reaction. 'You would be far more comfortable in her
house than staying here on your own.'

'I. . .I don't know what to say,' Désirée stammered,
shaken by this new evidence of his thoughtfulness. She
hesitated and then blurted out, 'Why are you going to
such trouble to help me? You obviously hate the French.'

He shrugged. 'I cannot explain it,' he admitted with
rueful honesty. 'My head tells me that you are my enemy
but. . .somehow my heart cannot believe it.'

A faint smile softened his austere features.

'All I know is that I want us to part as friends, even
if there is no hope of us ever seeing one another again.'

'You are leaving?'

'I must. I came to say goodbye.'

Désirée bit her lower lip to still its trembling.

'I have some further business to conduct, but if you
wish to avail yourself of my aunt's offer I shall escort you
there myself later this afternoon after the *siesta* is over.'

A dozen considerations swirled in Désirée's brain, all
jostling for attention, but she all she could think of was
that soon she would see him no more.

Struggling to shake off the desolation that threatened
to overwhelm her, Désirée managed a polite smile. 'I
am grateful for your kind concern, but I think I should
remain here.'

'In a busy public inn? Without any protector?' Rafael
couldn't conceal his disapproval.

'I agree that your aunt's house would be more far
more respectable, but I'm sure she cannot wish to have
a Frenchwoman as her guest.'

His silence confirmed her suspicion. He had forced
his aunt into agreeing to take her in.

'It does not suit my pride to accept help which is not
freely given,' she said quietly. 'Besides, Etienne will
look for me here.'

'What if your brother does not come?'

Désirée upturned her palms in a fatalistic gesture.

'It makes no odds, *señor*. If Etienne fails to arrive within the next day or so, I shall seek him in Madrid. Even if I wished to go home, I could never do so without knowing what has gone wrong.' Her glance travelled sideways towards her letter. 'I have already written to the commanding officer of the garrison to ask for his help in finding a suitable escort.'

Rafael stood up. 'Then there is no more for me to say, but to wish you luck.'

'Thank you.' Désirée could feel a tearful lump rising in her throat and prayed she would not disgrace herself.

'If you have finished your note, I will see to it that it is delivered.'

Sternly quelling her stupid desire to burst into tears, Désirée folded the sheet of paper up and handed it to him.

'I suggest we find the landlord and ask him for some sealing wax.'

Désirée gathered her pen and ink and stood up.

Rafael extended his arm to her and, with the faintest of hesitations, Désirée laid her hand upon his sleeve.

She could feel the steel of his muscles beneath the smooth cloth and a tremor of longing feathered through her veins. Confined by the narrowness of the path, they had to walk so close together that her skirts were brushing against his thigh. The heat from his body seemed to scorch her and she could smell the fresh lemon tang of his cologne. It mingled with the balm of his shaving-soap and the clean, masculine scent of his skin, making her head spin.

If he had given the slightest hint of wanting her, Désirée knew she would have been unable to resist falling into his arms. She longed to feel his lips on hers. She knew it was utter insanity, but she wanted him so much it hurt!

Disconcerted by her wanton thoughts, Désirée was glad when they stepped indoors and their unsettling intimacy was lost in the flurry of summoning the landlord.

While they waited in the main *sala* for him to return

with the sealing wax, loud booted footsteps sounded in
the entrance hallway. Going to the door, Rafael saw the
Frenchman they had encountered the day before.

'It is Captain Duclos,' Désirée exclaimed, coming to
join him and recognising the new visitor.

The sound of her voice attracted the Frenchman's
attention and he marched over towards them, his dress-
sword clanking at his side.

'Mademoiselle Fontaine.' He bowed low in her
direction.

'Captain.' Désirée dipped a neat curtsy, wondering
how he knew her name.

'Forgive me for not paying you more attention yesterday. I didn't realise you were French.'

Désirée stifled a giggle at the ineptness of this speech.
'You know Señor Velasco, of course,' she murmured
mischievously.

Duclos jerked his chin curtly in Rafael's direction,
acknowledging his presence for the first time.

Rafael returned this salute with an mockingly
elegant bow.

'I heard you came up to the Castle last night. You were
in search of news about Colonel Fontaine, I believe?'

Désirée stiffened and Rafael placed a hand under her
elbow in a silent gesture of support.

'I was acting on Mademoiselle Fontaine's behalf.'

'It's very odd that you didn't mention she was a
Frenchwoman yesterday.' The blond moustache bristled
with suspicion.

'We are such old family friends, it quite escaped my
memory.'

There was a challenging insolence in the way Rafael
spoke; seeing the glittering dislike in his eyes as he
looked down on the shorter man, Désirée's amusement
fled and she quickly intervened with a polite enquiry
after the Captain's health.

The last thing she wanted was for them to quarrel, she
told herself, but she knew she didn't care about Duclos.
Her instinct was to protect Rafael de Velasco.

'Why did you come here, Captain?' Rafael cut into the conversation.

The Frenchman coughed, suddenly looking uncomfortable as if he had just remembered something unpleasant.

'As a matter of fact, Velasco, I've brought the information you wanted,' he said gruffly. 'Er. . .can we speak in private, do you think?'

Sensing that the hussar had bad news to convey, Rafael nodded but, as he turned to lead the Frenchman away, Désirée stepped forward to bar their path.

'No! If your information concerns my brother, then I have the right to hear it.'

Duclos nodded and, awkwardly fingering the hilt of his sword, said, 'We heard from Madrid this morning, but I'm afraid it is not good news, *mademoiselle*. Perhaps you would like to sit down? Shall we summon your maid?'

Désirée impatiently waved these well-meant suggestions aside. 'Your information please, *monsieur*!'

'Forgive me. I don't know quite how to tell you. . .' Duclos's ruddy face reflected his discomfort.

'There is no easy way to deliver bad news, *hombre*! Break it to her quickly!'

Automatically obeying the authority in Rafael's snapped order, Duclos jerked the words out in a rapid, devastating stream.

'Three weeks ago your brother was ambushed by *guerrillas* while out on patrol with his men. He was badly injured during the action. The wound festered and he died a few days later at his house in Madrid.'

'No! You are lying!' Désirée stared at him wildly, her voice rising in a scream of denial. 'It isn't possible! Etienne cannot be dead!'

Chapter Four

'**D**rink this.'

As the benumbing fog cleared from her head, Désirée felt Rafael de Velasco hold a glass to her lips. It seemed easier to obey his command than argue and she swallowed.

A fiery liquid burned down her throat and she coughed in protest, but the brandy helped to restore her senses.

She was seated in a chair by one of the windows in in the main *sala*.

'How did I get here?' she whispered.

'I carried you. You were half-swooning from shock.' Rafael stepped back and placed the empty glass upon a convenient side-table.

'Where. . .where did Duclos go?'

'He had to get back to the castle.' Contempt curled Rafael's lip. After dropping his bombshell, the Frenchman couldn't wait to escape the consequences!

She had seemed very light and fragile in his arms, but for once no desire had stirred in him. All he had felt was pity, a pity which overwhelmed his satisfaction at hearing that Napoleon had lost one of his finest young officers.

'Did he give you any more details of what happened?'

The stricken look in her eyes tore at Rafael's self-control and his voice hardened in an involuntary effort to protect himself.

'There wasn't much else he knew. Apparently the patrol was attacked by a band of *guerrillas*. Several of his men were killed outright, but the others managed to help your brother get clear.'

Désirée shuddered, struggling to control her grief.

Lacking the right words to comfort her, Rafael put a silent hand on her shoulder.

Just then one of the maids knocked at the open door and entered at Rafael's signal.

'She will take you to your room.'

The maid's expression was suitably sympathetic, but Desiree saw gloating triumph in her eyes and knew the girl rejoiced at the death of one of the hated French soldiers.

Like a child, Désirée immediately clutched Rafael's arm. At the moment he seemed the only strong, the only secure thing in the universe!

'You won't leave, will you?' she asked, hating to hear herself beg, but unable to stop herself. 'Not yet, please!'

'I shall wait until you are feeling more composed.' Rafael spoke gently and, bending forwards, lightly brushed a stray lock of pale hair from her brow. 'Go now and rest and we will speak later, I promise.'

Désirée nodded, glad to obey. Once safely alone in the privacy of her room, the tears began to flow and she wept for hours until fatigue dragged her into oblivion.

When she awoke the room was darkening with shadows. She stretched her cramped limbs and slowly sat up. It was time to take stock of the situation.

She would not stay here. Nor was there any reason now to journey to the capital. She would go home again to the château near Orléans.

Where every room held memories. . .

A tiny sob escaped her, but Désirée quickly stifled it. Her grandfather always used to say tears were only for weaklings and she had to be strong. Somehow, she would have to find the courage to resume her old life.

Désirée could hardly believe this nightmare was real. She had trusted in Napoleon's assertion that Spain was conquered, but those *guerrillas* had been confident

enough to attack a well-led patrol. They were extremely
dangerous.

And how she hated them!

A surge of fury brought her to her feet and she hurried
to the window. Flinging it open, she gulped in the cool
evening air, feeling as if she might choke.

The numbing effect of shock was beginning to wear
off and she was so angry she didn't know how to deal
with it. She wanted to scream, to punch and kick and
claw and inflict the same kind of pain which was tearing
at her guts on those who were responsible for
Etienne's death!

Shuddering with the effort, Désirée struggled to bring
the raw agony under control. Blind emotion would not
serve her—she needed to think!

A knock sounded at the door, interrupting her deliber-
ations, and she turned away from the window to unlock
it before remembering there was no need. Earlier, she
had been too devastated to think of locking her door.

'Come in.'

It opened to admit the dour innkeeper's wife carrying
a tray which bore a small coffee-pot and a cup. With a
nod to Désirée, she set it down on the table near the
window.

'Don Rafael gave orders to bring you this,' she said
very slowly, as if addressing a stupid child. 'He asks you
to join him in the small *sala* as soon as you have drunk it.'

Understanding the gist of her meaning, Désirée
thanked the woman, who lit candles and poured the
coffee for her before leaving the room.

A large moth flew in, attracted by the light, and Désirée
shut the window. Catching a glimpse of her reflection in
the mirror, she grimaced. She ought to have asked for
some hot water but it was too late now. Instead, she
quickly splashed her pale cheeks with the remaining inch
left over in the ewer from that morning.

Feeling slightly better, she drank the bitter black coffee
before it went cold and then combed out the tangles in
her hair. There wasn't time to change her crumpled gown.

She had kept Rafael de Velasco waiting too long already.

He was standing with his back to door, staring at the age-blackened painting in oils which hung above the mantelpiece. The furniture they had used last night had been replaced against the walls and the grate lacked a cheery fire. Gloomy and unwelcoming in the gathering dusk, Désirée scarcely recognised it as the same room.

Rafael swung round. He had been so absorbed in thought as he stared unseeingly at the painted angels and saints he hadn't consciously registered any sound, but his well-honed instincts sprang into action, warning him someone was behind him.

'*Buenos tardes, mam'selle.*'

She looked very pale and her eyelids were swollen and red, betraying the intensity of her grief. He took a step towards her and then checked.

'Good evening, *señor.*' Désirée noticed that he had changed out of his smart clothes and was wearing the battered leather coat he had worn the day before when travelling.

Rafael bowed to her formally. 'I hope you are feeling a little better.'

Désirée nodded, glad of his restraint. She did not think she could have coped with a display of sympathy.

'Please excuse the length of my absence,' she said quietly. 'I did not mean to delay you this long.'

He waved her apology aside, knowing he could not have left Burgos without checking she was all right. 'Have you thought about how you are going to get home? I can arrange an escort for you, providing you are willing to wait here for a few days until I can return. In the meantime, my aunt's offer is still open.'

Désirée shook her head. 'I am not going home,' she said slowly, suddenly realising what it was that she must do.

He gazed at her in astonishment.

'I am going to Madrid.'

'*Dios!* Are you out of your mind?'

The anger in his voice brought a flush of annoyance to Desirée's pale cheeks.

'I do not understand your objection, *señor*,' she said hotly.

'There is no reason for you to go there!'

'You are wrong. I intend to learn more about what happened and to find out what, if anything, has been done to bring my brother's murderers to justice.'

Rafael swore beneath his breath.

Finally, seeing she would not be moved, he asked if she had any acquaintance in the city. 'Do you have a place to stay?'

'Etienne has. . .had taken a house in the Calle del Clavel. I doubt if anyone will object to my staying there.' A look of determination flickered across her white face. 'If they do, I shall appeal to King Joseph. I'm sure he will support me.'

Her mention of the Emperor's brother brought a frown to Rafael's face. How could he have so easily forgotten her connections! Last night he had learnt at the garrison that Colonel Fontaine had been favoured by Napoleon himself. His sister would not lack protectors. She might even be able to persuade the commander of the garrison to furnish her with a military escort to Madrid.

'Even if he does, I do not think it is wise for you to remain in Spain.'

Désirée nodded, understanding his meaning all too well. But she no longer had any choice.

'It is my duty to see that Etienne's murderers are punished.' Her voice shook with emotion.

'Your staying here will accomplish nothing.' Rafael spoke with a brutal frankness, hoping to shock her into seeing sense. 'The *guerrilleros* hide in the hills. They know the terrain as your soldiers do not and can evade capture.'

Her expression was disbelieving and Rafael wanted to shake her.

'Take my advice and go home.' Anxiety for her roughened his tone.

Too upset to register his underlying concern, Désirée heard only his anger. 'No!'

'You are very stubborn!' Rafael drew in a ragged breath.

'So I have been told.'

They glared at one another for a moment in silence and then Désirée shrugged.

'*Adieu*, señor Velasco,' she said, sinking into a graceful curtsy. 'I thank you for your many kindnesses and shall strive to remember you in my prayers.'

'*Vaya con Dios*.' Rafael curbed a fierce desire to pull her to him and held out his hand to her instead.

Désirée backed away, a tormented expression appearing in her eyes.

'You will not take my hand in farewell?' Rafael's face twisted in surprise.

'The man who killed my brother was a Spaniard.'

'You hate me for being Spanish?' Rafael discovered a painful irony in having their positions reversed.

She nodded. 'I find that I, too, have my prejudices.'

Her voice was cold and hard, striking Rafael like a mallet. The protest which had risen to his lips stilled and he let her go without another word.

The house in the Calle del Clavel was small, but quite modern. It was smartly painted in white and a gleaming copper door-knocker adorned the front door, which opened to reveal a charming little hallway paved with marble.

'Shall I come in with you, Mademoiselle Fontaine?'

Désirée shook her head at the dapper little man whose task it had been to escort her here. One of King Joseph's secretaries, he had been dispatched to Charmartin, a small village one league north of the city, to collect her.

The commanding officer at Burgos had arranged for her to travel to the capital under the protection of a detachment of his soldiers who were bound for the garrison there. He hadn't been too pleased by her request, but Désirée had persisted in her demands, swearing she would not delay his men. She had kept her word, handling her borrowed mount with a skill that had provoked respect, but when they reached Charmartin she had agreed to the chaplain's suggestion that it would be more fitting for her to wait while the news of her arrival was conveyed to the king and her new home was made ready to receive her.

'Thank you, Monsieur Dubec, but I should prefer to be alone.'

'Very well, *mam'selle*. The servants I hired for you are already in residence. I hope you will find them satisfactory.'

'I'm sure I shall, *monsieur*.' Désirée kept her tone polite, but she was anxious for him to go.

After further advice and a promise that he would return to escort her to the Palace in due course, Dubec kissed her hand and took his leave.

Désirée stared at her new abode. It reminded her of her aunt's little house in Portsmouth, the first place they had stayed on landing in England. Aunt Caroline, her father's elder sister, had greeted the trio of bedraggled exiles kindly. She hadn't even minded when Etienne had trampled in mud all over her drawing-room carpet.

A shiver ran down Désirée's spine and she abruptly dismissed the memory. But it was no use. Even two weeks after hearing the news of his death, she still couldn't get the idea out of her head that Etienne would be here to greet her.

Biting her lip, she controlled her grief and went inside. Having heard her arrive, the three servants Dubec had hired were standing waiting for her in the hall. Désirée asked their names and, after asking them to attend to her luggage and fetch a cool drink to the drawing-room, dismissed them.

Free to explore, she wandered slowly from room to room. After the luxurious country villa at Charmartin, where Napoleon himself had stayed the previous year, it seemed a doll's house, but everything was spotlessly clean.

The furnishings were fashionably expensive, but too elaborate for Désirée's taste. Staring at the large gilt bronze lamp in the drawing-room decorated with chiselled flowers, she decided that the owners must be wealthy people.

She doubted that Etienne had cared for all the lavish gilding and fancy carving. He had probably chosen the house for its convenient position, halfway between the Royal Palace and the garrison in the Retiro Park.

She climbed the staircase and, glancing into the largest bedroom, which was situated at the front of the house, found evidence of his occupation. Dashing away the tears which had sprung to her eyes, Désirée hastily closed the door again. She was not ready to sort out his clothes and books yet.

'Where shall I put your things, *señorita*? Do you wish to sleep in here?' The dark-eyed personal maid found for her by Dubec appeared at her elbow.

'No.' Désirée shook her head. 'Not in this room.'

Rosita stood respectfully waiting for her decision.

Désirée opened another door and found a smaller bedroom which overlooked a courtyard garden at the rear of the house. 'I'll take this one.'

Rosita nodded approval. 'Shall I prepare a bath for you, *señorita*, when I have unpacked everything?'

'Thank you. I should like that,' Désirée responded to the maid's cheerful smile.

Returning to the drawing-room, she saw a tray of refreshments had been set out for her and she sat down with the intention of trying to sort out her first impressions of her new home.

Aware of the sullen looks thrown their way by the Madrileños they had passed on their way through the streets, Rosita's friendly manner struck Désirée as a good omen for the future. She seemed competent too, as did the other servants. The house was well kept and to judge by the *mojicónes*, which she had just enjoyed, the cook had a light hand with sponge cake.

Her initial anxieties allayed, Désirée's concentration

faltered. A dark austere face instantly filled the void, taking ruthless possession of her thoughts.

'*Dieu!*' Realising what she was doing, Désirée's fingers tightened upon the glass of cold fresh lemonade she held as she struggled to banish the image.

It wasn't as easy as she would have wished. When she had said goodbye to Rafael de Velasco she had been determined to dismiss him from her thoughts, but somehow he kept coming back, invading her privacy, destroying her peace.

Hating her own weakness, a wave of angry resentment swept over her. She would not let her foolish heart cherish warm memories of a Spaniard

Rising swiftly to her feet, she left the room and headed for the stairs. Once she had bathed and put on some clean clothes, she would feel more composed and be ready to make a fresh start.

And begin the search to find Etienne's murderers.

'Do you know a good dressmaker, Rosita?'

'*Si.*' The maid nodded, handing Désirée her morning cup of hot chocolate as her mistress sat up in bed. 'In the Calle de Carretas.'

'Is that close to here? Shall we need to arrange a carriage?'

'We can walk there easily, *señorita.*'

'Then we must visit her today.' Désirée sipped her chocolate. 'My wardrobe needs replenishing.'

Etienne had not cared to see her in black. He had scorned the habit of wearing mourning for a year or more merely for the sake of convention, but she would need to order one or two black gowns to wear on formal occasions. She was due to visit the Palace for a private interview with the king and she had written to Etienne's superior officers requesting a meeting.

A faint grimace twisted Désirée's face. She had been in Madrid for almost a week now. For the most part, she had stayed indoors, attending to the sad task of sorting out Etienne's belongings. However, the strain of her journey and her initial shock at hearing of his death had faded.

'We shall go directly after breakfast,' she said decisively, realising she would be glad to get out of the house.

It was a warm bright morning and Désirée relished the feel of the crisp clear air on her face as they set out to walk to the dressmakers. The streets, a warren of old stone buildings and narrow alleyways interspersed with tiny squares where fountains played and people congregated to chat, were busy.

Désirée commented on the number of well-dressed women and Rosita informed her that these ladies were probably on their way home from hearing mass.

Désirée had already discovered that Madrileños were extremely devout. They had barely reached the end of their own *calle* before they heard the ringing of a handbell which signified the approach of the Holy Sacrament. With a muttered explanation that the priest was probably on his way to visit someone sick, Rosita grabbed her arm and they both flattened themselves against the wall, yielding their place to the small procession as local custom demanded.

Careless of her skirts, Rosita had dropped to her knees as the Host went by. Désirée contented herself with a respectful bow of her head.

Aware of the maid's reproachful gaze as they carried on their way, Désirée decided that she would have to take more care not to offend. Her grandfather, although a firm believer in the Almighty, had abhorred excessive ritual and forbidden her to follow her mother's faith. She had reverted to Catholicism on her return to France, but by then she had absorbed the view that God was best served plainly.

Vaya con Dios. Those were virtually the last words Rafael de Velasco had said to her. Had he really meant it? Was his concern for her welfare genuine or merely polite mouthings which meant nothing at all?

She'd had plenty of time for quiet reflection since her arrival in Madrid. Her anger still burned against Etienne's murderers, but she had begun to wonder if she had been fair-minded with regard to the tall Spaniard.

Guilty that she had blamed him for the actions of his countrymen, Désirée had tried to condone her childish reaction by telling herself his interest in her had been prompted by mere lust.

However, innate honesty had finally forced her to admit that even if that was true, it didn't necessarily mean he was insincere in everything else he had said and done. He had continued to help her even after he had discovered her nationality, but she had allowed grief to blind her to that important fact.

Rafael de Velasco had managed to put aside his prejudice. Perhaps it was time for her to start practising the charity their mutual faith advocated and do the same.

'Watch your footing, *señorita*!'

Lost in her convoluted thoughts, Désirée had almost stepped into a little pile of goat droppings.

'Try to stay away from the gutter,' the maid advised, steering Désirée round the obstacle with a muttered comment that many goats were driven in each morning to supply the city with milk.

Shaking off her disquieting reflections, Désirée paid attention to this warning and found other, more fragrant obstacles in her path as they walked along. Local fruit vendors appeared to have the habit of piling up their wares on the pavement. The heaps of lemons and oranges added a bright touch of colour and a pleasant smell to the streets, although they could not drown out the pervasive odour of cooking oil that wafted out from many of the buildings.

The Calle de Carretas was one of the principle commercial streets and Désirée noted that every variety of luxury good seemed to be catered for. She was entranced by the sight of a wonderful little shop devoted to the sale of fans.

It stood squashed between a perfumer's and a shop which sold nothing but combs. When Désirée expressed surprise at this, Rosita assured her that every lady in

Madrid needed a selection to wear with her collection of *mantillas*. Having noticed this fashion for herself, Désirée came to the conclusion that she would like to try one of these decorative head-coverings, which hung down like a shawl at the back. It would help her blend in amongst the crowd and also provide useful protection from the sun.

They spent a pleasant quarter of an hour choosing what to buy in the comb shop before moving on to the dressmaker's, which lay at the end of the street.

Doña Mercedes owned premises above a silk merchant's and she greeted Désirée with a speculative smile and deferential curtsy when Rosita performed the introductions.

The size of her new customer's order produced another curtsy and, with an eager gleam in her little currant eyes, the plump dressmaker ordered one of her assistants to take Désirée's measurements. A book of fashion-plates was produced for her perusal and the morning flew past as bolts of various materials were brought out for inspection.

Désirée strongly suspected that Doña Mercedes received a commission from the silk merchant below on what she managed to persuade her customers into buying, but since the fabrics were good quality she didn't mind. It was worth paying extra for the convenience of not having to shop around when time was short.

'And I'll take a length of that lilac silk-gauze to make another evening gown,' she said, concluding her selection.

'Offer to pay her half what she asks,' Rosita whispered as the dressmaker made a note of the designs Désirée had chosen.

Deciding this was good advice, Désirée took it and a brisk haggling session ensued.

There was a gleam of respect in the older woman's eye when she bade Désirée farewell and Désirée hid her amusement. She might look like a green girl, but she hadn't run the estate in Etienne's absence for nothing!

As soon as they were out of earshot, Désirée turned to her maid.

'How did you know she was going to overcharge me?' she asked interestedly.

Rosita gave an awkward shrug. 'She knows you are French and she probably thinks you are rich.'

A thoughtful expression passed over Désirée's face. 'So I was fair game for plucking?'

Rosita looked embarrassed as she nodded. 'But she *is* a good dressmaker, *señorita*. You will be pleased with the results.'

'I hope so,' Désirée replied drily, realising that she had spent more than she had intended.

Etienne's will left everything in her favour. It was to be hoped that the lawyers would not drag their feet in releasing her inheritance, for her own supply of money would soon run out at this rate.

'Are you angry with me, *señorita*?' Rosita asked nervously, noticing her employer's frown.

'Not in the least.' Désirée smiled to reassure her. 'I am grateful you prevented me from being cheated.'

She liked Rosita. The girl was extremely willing and, although not nearly as skilled as Louise, her former maid, she was eager to learn. Her cheerful good nature acted like a tonic on her own flattened spirits and, if Rosita resented her as a foreigner, she did not show it in any way. In fact, at times she fussed over her comfort like a mother hen with one chick!

'Shall we go on to the shoemaker's?' Désirée glanced up at the flawless blue sky. The sun was at its noon position. They had been in the dressmaker's for hours!

'It is almost time for *siesta*,' Rosita reminded her. 'Soon all the shops will shut.'

Désirée hesitated. She had enjoyed the colour and lively atmosphere of these streets. In the the quiet solitude of Etienne's house, it was all too easy to sink into depression and brood over the past.

'You must not overtire yourself, *señorita*. Tomorrow you have an important meeting to attend.'

Désirée nodded agreement. She was to meet Marshal Jourdan, King Joseph's Chief of Staff, and she would need her wits about her. With any luck, he might have the information she sought—information which would bring her brother's killers to justice.

Once Etienne's murder had been punished, she might allow herself to admit how much she liked this country. A land of striking contrasts, it had already captured her imagination. The mountains and arid plains of Castile had a proud, almost cruel beauty, which haunted her soul.

Just like Rafael de Velasco. One day she might even have to admit to herself that she owed him an apology!

'*Mi hermano*, is there something troubling you?'

Rafael de Velasco looked up quickly from his desk and saw his sister standing in the doorway of the study.

'Why do you ask?' he said, injecting a note of light amusement into his voice.

Elena moved into the room. A slight, rather shy girl, she shared her elder brother's finely chiselled features, but lacked his vivid colouring.

'Because you have been staring at the same page for the last five minutes,' she said quietly in her gentle voice.

'I don't care to be spied upon.' A frown darkened Rafael's lean face.

'I'm worried about you. You have been in a strange mood ever since you came back from Vitoria.' Elena sat down opposite him. 'You have been working very hard, but I sense it gives you no peace to organise these raids.'

Rafael shrugged. 'I take no pleasure in killing, *hermana*.' He closed the report he had been reading with a decisive snap. 'But it must be done. We have to rid Spain of the French.'

'Even Mademoiselle Fontaine?'

Elena was watching him closely and saw a telltale muscle flicker at the corner of his mouth.

'Where did you hear that name?' Rafael's deep voice was creditably calm, but his pulse had quickened.

'Pepe told me what happened. Why did you help her when you regard the French as our enemies?'

'I don't make war on women.'

'Did you like her?' Elena's hazel-brown eyes were filled with curiosity. She had never seen her self-possessed brother look so ill at ease.

'I don't care to discuss my personal feelings,' Rafael growled, thrusting back his chair as if he meant to leave the room.

'There are many things you do not care to discuss, *mi hermano*.' An unaccustomed note of bitterness entered Elena's gentle voice. 'My future, for one!'

'It is too soon, *niña*, to talk of burying yourself away in a convent.' Rafael's angry expression softened. 'You are only twenty-six. There is plenty of time for you to find yourself another husband and build a new life.'

'I do not want another husband!' Elena drew in a sharp breath. 'Can't you understand that, Rafael?'

'You are still grieving for Alonso. You will feel differently—'

'My grief will never fade enough for me to want another man,' Elena interrupted him quietly.

Rafael was silent. Three years ago his sister's young husband had contracted lung fever and died. He had assumed she would eventually resume her old life, but she had never recovered from the blow. Her health had suffered and her personality had undergone a dramatic change. Always a quiet girl, she had become moody and ill-tempered.

At first, Rafael had been glad when she turned to religion for comfort. Her devotions had helped restore her interest in life, but then a few months ago she had begun to talk of retiring to a convent. He had brusquely dismissed the idea, refusing to listen.

'You mean well I know, but you have never been in love, Rafael,' Elena said, breaking the silence. 'For months after Alonso's death I wanted to die, too, so I could join him. I still miss him every minute of every single day.'

Rafael shifted uncomfortably in his seat. How could he answer her? He hadn't realised until now how deep her unhappiness went.

Was it really possible to love another human being so much? Elena was right. He couldn't judge her. All his experiences had been shallow, mere adventures in lust. He had never cared enough to lose his heart.

He had always known, of course, that one day he would have to take a bride. He was thirty-two and a man could not remain a bachelor for ever. Soon, he would need an heir. Logic told him love was not necessary to make a successful marriage, but he had seen how happy Elena and Alonso were and wondered. Was there a special woman waiting for him somewhere, a woman Fate had destined to be the mother of his children, to be his wife. . .?

Unbidden, the memory of a laughing pair of blue eyes flashed into his mind. For an instant he could almost smell the perfume of her blonde hair. . .

Por Dios! He was bewitched!

'My faith is the only thing that brings me any joy.'

Elena's gentle voice brought Rafael back to his senses.

'I *know* I shall find the peace I seek within the walls of the convent at Frias.' She smiled at him a little sadly. 'But you are my brother, the head of my family, and I do not wish to cross your will. Please, withdraw your objections and let me find happiness in my own way.'

Rafael stared at her. 'Are you really sure, *hermana*?'

She nodded serenely.

Rafael thought hard for a moment and then said crisply, 'Very well, I shall give you my permission and provide you with a suitable dowry to offer the holy sisters—'

'Oh, Rafael!' Unable to contain her relief, Elena interrupted him. 'I don't know how to thank you.'

'Wait, I haven't finished.' Rafael gestured her to silence and she listened with eager anticipation. 'I want to be completely sure that this is the right course for you.

The easiest way to find out is to put your certainty to the test. Does that sound fair to you?'

'*Sí*. What did you have in mind?'

'Since you were widowed you have spent all your time here at Casa del Aguila. A quiet life was appropriate while you were in mourning, but it is years since you have had the chance to enjoy any gaiety.'

'I did not wish for parties.'

'Perhaps not, but before you leave the world behind I want you to be very sure you won't have any regrets about what you are giving up.'

He picked up a letter from the polished surface of the desk. 'This is from Inez Arteche y Moro. It contains an invitation to a reception to be held by *El Rey Intruso*. I think we should go.'

Astonishment filled Elena's thin face. She hadn't even realised that her brother was still in contact with the glamorous Marquesa de Aranda. Once upon a time they had been close. She even suspected that they had been lovers, but Inez had put ambition first and married the elderly marquis.

'I. . .I don't understand. Why would Joseph Bonaparte invite us to the palace?'

'Here, read it for yourself.' Rafael handed the letter to her. 'It is quite simple. Joseph wishes to ingratiate himself with his subjects, particularly those of noble blood. We belong to one of the oldest families in Castile. Even more importantly, Inez thinks my loyalty is given to the *afrancesados*.'

Elena skimmed the untidy writing and then shook her dark brown head. 'I'm not sure I want to go,' she murmured.

Rafael reached out to enfold her hand in his own. 'In Madrid you will have the chance to sample all the things that you have missed. You can go to the theatre, attend parties, dance all night if you wish.' He gave her hand a comforting little squeeze. 'Don't you see, *niña*? It will be a true test to discover if your faith is really as strong as you think.'

Slowly the look of hesitation vanished from her face. 'Very well, but what of you, Rafael? I know you have important plans. Can you spare the time?'

He nodded, releasing her hand and sitting back in his chair again. 'Everything is under control here. Carlos knows what to do in my absence. Besides, I intend to use the opportunity to gather information which will be useful to our cause.'

Elena rose to her feet and shook out her black skirts. 'I shall go and start making preparations,' she said, her manner becoming brisk. 'There is a lot to do if we are to leave in time.'

Rafael watched her go, a slight smile appearing on his face. Already she looked more animated than he had seen her appear in weeks.

He glanced down, meaning to study the report detailing French troop movements once more, and caught sight of the elegant white card of invitation which his sister had placed back on the desk.

He had meant every word he had said to Elena. But he hadn't told her the whole truth.

He wasn't even sure he wanted to admit to himself that the chance of encountering a certain blue-eyed Frenchwoman had influenced his decision to accept Joseph's invitation.

To Désirée's intense disappointment, her meeting with the Chief of Staff was cancelled.

She had gone out to buy a much needed pair of new shoes to complement the mourning gown Doña Mercedes had just delivered. She returned to the Calle del Clavel to discover that a message had arrived saying that the Marshal was too busy to see her.

'The officer said he could not wait for you to return, *señorita*,' Asuncion, the middle-aged housemaid, who had answered the door, informed her. 'He asked me to tell you that the Marshal will be in touch as soon as possible.'

Désirée thanked her and went upstairs to remove her bonnet, a heavy frown marring her face.

She had recovered her usual good humour by the time Monsieur Dubec's carriage pulled up outside her door a few days later.

The dapper little secretary had come to escort her to the palace for the private audience which the king had granted her. Désirée, who had met Joseph Bonaparte on a previous occasion in Paris, found herself unaccountably nervous.

She tried to comfort herself with the knowledge that she was in good looks. After weeks of not caring a jot, she had begun to take an interest in her appearance again. It might sound heartless if voiced aloud, but she knew mourning suited her, heightening the impact of her white skin and pale gold hair.

The simple gown of black crape she had chosen for the interview lent her an air of charming fragility. Naturally, she wore no jewellery, save for a single discreet strand of pearls around her slim throat, but, after much practice, Rosita had finally managed to dress her hair in a sophisticated knot of upswept curls, threaded with black velvet ribbon. The admiration in the secretary's eyes as he handed her into the coach told Désirée that she had succeeded in recapturing all her old elegance and style.

Their progress through the narrow streets was slow, particularly at the Puerto del Sol, one of the major crossroads of the city, which was thronged with people. Madrileños seemed to enjoy being out of doors, Désirée had noticed but, anxious they might be late, she was glad when they finally reached the Royal Palace.

'I thought it would be a much older building!' she exclaimed in surprise.

'There was an Alcázar, a fortress, here, I believe, but it burnt down some seventy years ago. This replaced it. A magnificent structure, and so wonderfully French in style, *oui*?'

Désirée nodded. 'It reminds me of Versailles.'

She gazed out of the window with interest as their
carriage made its way to the principle entrance, a gateway
which led into an interior court. Pure classical architec-
ture, statues, rich polished marble and a vast multitude
of gleaming windows met her eyes.

Monsieur Dubec assisted her down from the coach.

'We go this way.' He pointed towards a grand staircase
on their right-hand side.

Désirée shook out her skirts and took his proffered
arm with a slight feeling of trepidation, which she strove
valiantly to ignore.

Armed guards lined their route, but her companion was
obviously well known and they were waved on without
stopping. They made their way through what seemed an
endless number of rooms and antechambers, each one
filled with ever more magnificent tapestries, glittering
chandeliers, inlaid furniture and wonderful paintings until
Désirée became too overwhelmed to make sense of what
she was seeing.

To her relief, Dubec told her that the audience would
take place in one of the small informal rooms which lay
off the king's enormous private library. She would have
liked a chance to examine the bookcases, but Joseph was
already waiting for them.

'No, please do not apologise for being late. It is I who
am early,' said Don José Primero genially.

Rising from her deep curtsy, Désirée reflected that he
looked very like his famous younger brother, but his
cast of expression was more amiable. From what she
remembered, he lacked Napoleon's vivid charisma, but
was a much kinder man.

Dismissing his secretary, Joseph waved her to take
one of the small gilt chairs and they both sat down.

'I was very sorry to hear of your brother's death. As
you know, we were well acquainted. He was an excellent
soldier and I shall miss him.'

Désirée blinked back the tears which threatened and
thanked him for his condolences in a choked voice.

Tactfully, he changed the subject and asked her if

she was comfortable in the little house on the Calle del Clavel.

'For my part, it is a pleasure to welcome such a lovely lady to Court,' he said with a twinkle in his eye which reminded Désirée that he had a reputation for being susceptible to pretty faces. 'But I would recommend you not to think of staying here too long.'

He let out a sigh. 'I fear my Spanish subjects are like lions who can perhaps be tamed by rational kindness, but their temper remains uncrushed by even the strongest force.'

Désirée wondered how to answer him. Her acquaintance with Rafael de Velasco had led her to suspect that Spain would never accept a foreigner as king.

Instead, she politely asked after the health of his wife and his daughters.

Joseph was very fond of his family, who had remained behind in France at his estate near Chantilly, and he was happy to talk of them for several minutes.

Listening to him, Désirée came to the conclusion he was a lonely and unhappy man. Her own grief seemed to have sharpened her senses and she guessed he bitterly regretted giving up his former Kingdon of Naples to come to Spain. Here, the real power belonged to his brother's generals and the people were not willing to accord him the admiration he craved.

No wonder he was rumoured to be consoling himself with several pretty mistresses!

A gold clock sitting on one of the ornate side-tables chimed the hour.

'I have greatly enjoyed talking to you, *mam'selle*, but I'm afraid you will have to excuse me.' Joseph prepared to rise. 'I have another appointment.'

Realising she was being dismissed, Désirée spoke up quickly. 'Sire, I have a favour to request of you.'

'What is it?' Joseph sat back in his chair again. 'I should like to help.'

'Marshal Jourdan cancelled my meeting with him. I want to discover what had been done to capture and punish the *guerrillas* who murdered Etienne. Could you arrange another meeting with him for me?'

'I'm sorry. That will not be possible. You see, we have just had bad news from our forces in Portugal. Marshal Soult was driven from Oporto by the English. He barely escaped capture.'

Désirée grasped the point of this shocking news at once.

'You expect the English to advance into Spain?' she gasped.

'Those are Sir Arthur Wellesley's orders, I under-stand.' A faint smile twisted Joseph's mouth. 'I fear I am going to have to fight to keep my throne!'

Désirée bit her lip. 'I appreciate Etienne's death must take second place to more urgent priorities, but surely it is bad for morale to let his murder go unavenged?'

Joseph nodded thoughtfully. 'I shall see what I can do. There is a major on my staff who is a capable fellow. I think he could help.'

Désirée thanked him and he rose to his feet.

'Take care of yourself, *chérie*. Those bright eyes were not meant to shed tears.' Joseph paused, as an idea of how he might cheer her up struck him. 'I shall send you an invitation to the reception I am holding at the end of next week.'

Seeing her look of hesitation, he assured her that the entertainment would be decorous enough to suit a lady in mourning. 'Do say you will come. It will give you a chance to meet some interesting people.'

'Thank you, Sire.' Désirée flashed him a brilliant smile. 'I shall look forward to it.'

Chapter Five

The large saloon, decorated with several striking equestrian paintings by Velázquez and Titian, was a sea of colour. Jewel-bedecked ladies in pastel gowns mingled with officers in a multitude of bright uniforms. Hundreds of wax candles burned, illuminating the swirling, everchanging kaleidoscope as darkness gathered beyond the tall, silk-draped windows.

Rafael de Velasco surveyed the scene. His lean face was impassive but his dark eyes betrayed his restless impatience. Most of the guests were assembled. Soon the man who called himself Don José Primero would appear.

Several of the women present wore black, a fashionable colour in Madrid. Some were obviously stout duennas, hovering protectively near to their charges. None possessed the slender figure of a nymph or hair the colour of moonlight and gold.

Was she here?

'Rafael *mio*. How lovely to see you again.'

A voluptuous woman, expensively dressed in pale green silk advanced towards him, hands outstretched. Huge emeralds glittered at her throat and in her ears and her hair had the blue-black sheen of a raven's wing beneath a *mantilla* of priceless antique lace.

'Marquesa.' He bowed gracefully over her hand.

Inez Lucia Arteche y Moro laughed, throwing back her head to show off her long white neck. 'Why so formal, *amigo*? If you won't kiss me, then at least say how delighted you are to see me. You *are* pleased, aren't you?'

'But of course and, even if I were not, I would not dream of contradicting so beautiful a lady.' Rafael smiled but the warmth did not quite reach his eyes.

Inez *was* beautiful and she knew it. Unfortunately, she also possessed morals which would have shamed an alley-cat. He had been attracted to her when they were both in their late teens. . .and shocked to discover that he was by no means her first lover!

The old Marques de Aranda did not let the whiff of scandal already attached to her name deter him from acquiring her as his third wife. Surprisingly, the marriage was a success. The Marques doted upon the four children she produced for him in rapid succession and Inez astonished everyone by turning out to be a very good mother. Satisfied, her husband now allowed her to take handsome young men as her *cortejos* and Inez had repaid his tolerance by learning to be more discreet.

It was several years since they last met, although they had kept up a sporadic correspondence, and Rafael saw that time and her inordinate fondness for sweetmeats had coarsened her once-clear features and blackened her teeth, but she remained a very attractive woman. She had kept her figure, a little riper now but still alluring, and her dark dramatic eyes were truly lovely.

'Is your husband here tonight?' Rafael asked courteously.

She shook her head, setting her elaborate earrings dancing. 'Fernando does not care for the French.' She shrugged. 'He says he is too old to learn new tricks.'

Rafael's mouth tightened. 'He should not have to!'

Inez was surprised. 'Have you lost your love for our new rulers so soon, *tesoro*?'

Although he smiled at her use of the old nickname— no one else had ever called him their treasure!—Rafael realised he needed to exercise caution.

'Joseph is an amiable man and means well,' he

answered lightly. 'However, there is a world of difference
I find between theories of liberty and reality.'

Understanding he would not be drawn further, Inez
abandoned curiosity with a careless shrug of her shapely
shoulders. 'I dare say it doesn't matter whether you are
a genuine *afrancesado*. Half of the people here only
support the French from expediency.'

'Like yourself, *querida*?' Rafael gave her a
wicked grin.

She chuckled throatily and changed the subject. 'Did
you manage to persuade Elena to come with you to
Madrid?'

'*Sí*. She is over there, talking to the *condesa*.'

'Good.' A faintly malicious smile curved Inez's
painted lips. 'We shall be safe from interruption for at
least another ten minutes.'

Rafael lifted his brows. 'You hope for privacy in a
gathering like this? Dare I hope you mean to flirt with
me, *querida*?'

Inez responded to the teasing note in his deep voice
with another throaty chuckle and a rapid fluttering of her
fan in encouragement.

'What would your latest *cortejo* say?' There was mock
reproof in Rafael's expression. 'Would I risk a knife in
the dark for my presumption?'

'You could always duel for my favours,' Inez retorted,
not bothering to deny she had a current lover.

Rafael gallantly gave her the answer she expected. 'It
would be my pleasure.'

They both knew he didn't mean it, but a remembered
thrill of excitement shot through Inez. He had been a
very good lover!

She smiled up at him, wondering if there was any
chance of rekindling the flame in him, but before she
could think of her next move she sensed him suddenly
lose interest in the game.

Turning her head, she followed the direction of
his gaze.

A gap had opened up momentarily in the crowd and

she saw that a young girl had just entered the saloon. Her slender figure was simply gowned and she wore little jewellery, but her hair blazed like living gold beneath the chandeliers.

'She is beautiful,' Inez said, watching in amused exasperation as her tall companion totally forgot she was alive. So much for her hopes!

'Do you know her?'

Rafael nodded wordlessly. Although he had hoped to see her here tonight, his instinctive reaction to Désirée Fontaine's appearance shocked him. The mixture of delight and desire she aroused in him was so strong it literally robbed him of breath.

Recovering, he excused himself with a hasty murmur and made his way though the throng.

'*Buenas noches, mam'selle*'.

A voice of ice wrapped in sable velvet.

Désirée swung round in astonishment. 'I did not expect to see *you* here!'

Rafael took her hand and touched her fingers to his lips. 'I hope it does not spoil your evening,' he replied, releasing her and stepping back.

Désirée managed an abrupt shake of her head. Her hand was tingling almost as if his lips had burnt her skin, making it difficult to think.

'Did you come alone?'

Struggling to regain her composure, Désirée said, 'I didn't feel I needed a chaperon.' Her polite smile faded and she met his dark gaze with a challenging look. 'Here, I am among friends.'

'You feel an interloper in my country,' he said flatly.

She shrugged. 'Is that a statement or a question? No, don't bother to answer. I have heard myself called *La Française* and it wasn't meant as a compliment.'

'Perhaps you wish to think of yourself as an outsider. It is an easy excuse, which allows you to alienate yourself from a country you are finding too attractive.'

Désirée bit her lower lip. She had forgotten his shrewdness.

She hadn't forgotten anything else about him. He was just as tall, just as overwhelmingly virile as memory had insisted. In his formal evening clothes, he looked remarkably distinguished and heart-renderingly handsome.

In the silence which followed his impulsive remark, Rafael allowed himself the pleasure of absorbing every detail of her appearance. Her face was a little thinner, but just as lovely. The black satin gown she was wearing was plain and unadorned, but its very simplicity merely enhanced the underlying curves of her body and he felt his loins tightening in response.

Looking into her eyes, he saw the unhappy confusion lurking in their violet depths and desire was immediately quenched.

Por Dios, he was a fool! After what happened to her brother, he should have realised she was afraid of falling under the spell of his beautiful but savage country.

'Come,' he said gruffly. 'Permit me to find you a glass of wine.'

Hearing the contrition he was too proud to voice, Désirée knew he had not meant to upset her.

With an effort, she forced herself to forget the manner of Etienne's death. She would not allow bitterness to poison her evening.

'Very well.' With a nod of assent, she placed her hand on the arm he held out to her.

The feel of his hard muscles beneath her fingers was tantalisingly familiar, bringing back all her previous feelings of attraction in a heady rush.

They made their way towards the refreshment room, stopping every now and then while Rafael introduced her to various members of his acquaintance. To Désirée's surprise, these high-ranking Spanish noblemen and their wives all spoke French and seemed eager to make her feel welcome.

It struck her as rather odd that Rafael should have such friends. Come to that, what was he doing here at all? She could have sworn that he would despise any party held by a man most Spaniards sneeringly dubbed *El Rey Intruso*, the intrusive king.

'You look a little pensive. Are you not enjoying yourself?' Rafael wondered what she was thinking, wishing he could be certain that she had forgiven him.

'I am having an excellent time.' Désirée denied his suggestion with a tiny gurgle of laughter. 'It seems years since I enjoyed an evening like this.'

She hadn't attended any parties since she had begun her preparations to leave France and she wasn't going to risk spoiling this one by asking him awkward questions.

'It pleases me that you are content, *mi ninfa*.'

Désirée coloured at the warmth in his velvet voice. She knew she ought to tell him to stop using endearments to her, but her heart gave a leap of happiness to realise that, in spite of their difficult parting, he had been worried about her.

Rafael obtained wine for them both and led her over to the long windows, where it was quieter, perhaps due to the fact that one casement had been opened a little to admit air into the very warm room.

Welcoming the cool breeze on her face, Désirée gazed out at the starlit sky. 'It is so clear you could almost touch those stars!'

'Many people think night air injurious to health,' Rafael remarked idly, watching her face, more interested in her delicate profile than the sky.

'Personally, I have never found it so,' Désirée replied with a thoughtful gravity he found enchanting. 'I enjoy being out in the garden at home on summer nights.' Désirée took a sip of her drink. 'I like warm weather.'

Rafael would have liked to hear more about her home. He would have liked to know more about her. She had told him once that she was a love-child, but not how she came to have an English father.

When and why had she returned to France? Instinct told him that she was not happy living there, but his curiosity would have to stay curbed, he decided. Any attempt to engage in such a discussion was too risky at

present. She might be offended, but, even if she was
willing to talk, he had no desire to accidentally bring
back that look of sadness which had clouded her lovely
face a few moments moment ago.

'June is often a pleasant month in Madrid. The heat,
however, will soon become very fierce. You must
remember to protect yourself.'

'I have already bought a *mantilla*,' Désirée answered
his innocuous remark with a demure twinkle in her eyes.

Abandoning bland neutrality, Rafael gave her a slow,
lazy smile. 'I should like to see you wear it.'

Désirée's pulse began to hammer. When he smiled at
her like that her heart seemed to turn somersaults!

'Am I to understand that you are staying in Madrid
for some time, *señor*?' she said a little breathlessly.

'A week or two. I have some business to conduct.'

'Then perhaps I shall see you again.'

'Will you let me call on you in the Calle del Clavel?'

Désirée hesitated. She wanted his friendship, but was
it wise to go on seeing him when she feared she liked
him too much already?

'I thought time might have healed your resentment.'

Hearing the bleak note in his voice, Désirée stared
down into her wine glass, seeking the courage she
needed.

'I owe you an apology,' she said at last, bravely raising
her gaze to meet his. 'I was unfair to you in Burgos. It was
wrong of me to lump you together with the *guerrillas*.'

'You were heart-stricken with grief, *ninfa*.'

'Thank you. It is generous of you to excuse my conduct, particularly when you have every right to be
annoyed with me. After all your kindness, I should have
been grateful, not angry with you.'

He shrugged, his expression making Désirée think her
apology made him uncomfortable.

'I wanted us to be friends,' he said abruptly. 'I still do.'

'I am not sure if that is possible,' she answered slowly.
'We both know that sooner or later Spain is going to
erupt and we each owe loyalty to our own country.'

'We need not betray that loyalty.'

Désirée had the horrible feeling that in practice it would not be so simple to put patriotism first!

'Look, I promised myself that I wouldn't pry into your motives for being here,' she blurted nervously, fiddling with the stem of her glass. 'But I find it hard to believe that you are an *afrancesad*. You hate the French!'

'Hatred is an emotion I cannot afford at present. I have business here in Madrid; if I have to be polite to your compatriots to ease matters, then I will.' He gave her a wry half-smile. 'My opinions haven't altered, but I give you my word that I will offer no violence to any Frenchman while I am in this city.'

Wondering what his business could be, but understanding it was impossible to ask, Désirée nodded tacit acceptance. She might find his pragmatism surprising, given his passionate character, but she was in no position to condemn it. Not after she had been willing to bend the truth to suit her own interests in Vitoria!

Relieved to have got over a difficult hurdle, Rafael quickly tried another approach. 'Is it the thought of gossip that is worrying you?' he asked, knowing tongues would wag if they were seen together.

Désirée shook her head. 'People will talk whatever I do! It is the penalty I must pay for failing to obeying the conventions.'

Her position was particularly vulnerable. Not only had she dared to travel alone but, to make matters worse, yesterday she refused an invitation from the wife of a senior officer to become a guest in their home.

'For myself I don't care if everyone thinks I am a reckless hoyden, but I ought to be careful. After all, I do have Etienne's reputation to consider.' She sighed. 'It is a question of honour, I suppose.'

'There is precious little honour to be had in war.'

The bitterness in his voice startled Désirée. He wore a strange expression she could not decipher.

'You think the *guerrilleros* are savages,' he continued unexpectedly. 'I know it is too much to ask you to forgive them, but you might find it easier to accept what happened to your brother if you understand that they regard themselves as patriots. They cannot hope to win conventional battles against Napoleon's troops. They fight the best way they can.'

His beautifully cut mouth hardened. 'War is usually a dirty, dangerous business and not the glorious adventure men often pretend.'

Désirée nodded thoughtfully. 'Etienne once said something very similar to me. I think he was trying to tell me that war could be both those things. That there was courage and bravery as well as terror and pain.' She gave a tiny shrug. 'Perhaps there cannot be one aspect without the other.'

Rafael stared at her in silence for a moment and then said quietly, 'Until we met I don't think I believed it was possible to discuss serious matters with a woman, no matter how clever she was. You are a revelation to me, Désirée.'

Two things immediately occurred to Désirée. The first was that he had just paid her one of the nicest compliments she had ever received and, secondly, he had rejected formality and used her given name.

'I feel I can talk to you about anything,' she admitted in a faintly tremulous murmur. She finished her wine to fortify herself. 'It seems silly, doesn't it, to deny ourselves the pleasure of becoming better friends?'

'So I may call on you?'

She nodded silently and as their gaze locked felt her heart give a queer little flutter.

'Rafael. I have been looking for you everywhere!'

Abruptly the spell was broken. Désirée dragged her eyes away from his and, as the room swung back into focus, saw that the newcomer was a small, slight-figured girl who wore a severe black gown and a black *mantilla* over her dark hair.

'Elena. I did not realise you were looking for me.' Rafael gave his sister an apologetic smile before gracefully introducing her to Désirée.

So this was Rafael's sister. Désirée eyed her curiously. She was older than Désirée had expected or at least her thin face was rather lined, but her expression held a gentle charm.

While Rafael went to fetch more wine, Elena offered Désirée her condolences with such delicate sympathy that Désirée felt herself warming to her. She might lack her brother's dramatic charisma, but she was an easy person to talk to with none of the proud stiff reserve Désirée had noticed in many Spanish women.

When Rafael returned, he was delighted to find Elena laughing at some remark Désirée had made. It was rare to see his sister look so animated and he flashed Désirée a smile of approval.

Elena caught the glance. So, her brother had more liking for this pretty blonde girl than he had admitted!

Somewhat to her own surprise, Elena realised she didn't mind. From what Pepe had told her about that journey from Vitoria, she had assumed the Frenchwoman would be a loud, bold creature, but Désirée was nothing of the sort. Lively, yes, and too careless of propriety perhaps, but a lady of good breeding none the less.

'Will you come and visit me, Mademoiselle Fontaine?' Directing an enquiring glance at her brother, Elena guessed he would not object, but for form's sake added, 'You don't mind do you, *hermano*?'

'Not in the least,' Rafael replied. His eyes glinted with repressed laughter. 'In fact, I should be delighted to receive Mademoiselle Fontaine as our guest.'

Wondering if Elena had already sensed the strong attraction flowing between them, Désirée accepted the invitation.

'We are staying at our town house in the Calle Nueva,' Elena told her. 'It is not far from you.'

'I don't think anywhere is far from anywhere else in Madrid,' Désirée commented with a slight smile. 'I didn't realise what a small city it was at first. My first impression was one of grand magnificence!'

She had been feeling apprehensive and miserable when

suddenly, almost without warning, a vision of numerous
spires and cupolas had sprung into being. The beauty of
the delicate skyline had shaken her from her introspection. Gazing at it, she was reminded vividly of a
description she had once read in one of her grandfather's
antiquarian books of some fabulous ancient city that
arose out of nothing in the midst of a desert.

'You entered the city by way of the Puerta de Alcalá?'
Rafael enquired.

Désirée confirmed it, remarking that she didn't think
she had ever seen a long, wide avenue flanked by such
fine old buildings. 'But the streets near my house are a
like a rabbit warren. I would get lost regularly if it were
not for my maid,' she chuckled.

'Madrid is a city of contrasts,' Elena agreed.

'What amazes me is that there are no foreign quarters.
No little enclaves of Jews or Huguenots or other national-
ities, as there are in Paris and London.' Désirée blurted
out this observation without thinking.

'True. The population is large but wholly Spanish.
Unless you count the French.'

Rafael's dry comment brought a tinge of colour to
Désirée's cheeks as she struggled and failed to find a
suitable retort.

'*Hermano!*' Elena's fan quivered in agitation. 'You
are embarrassing an innocent guest.'

Rafael looked at Désirée. 'Am I, *mi perla*?' he asked
wickedly.

Elena's mouth fell open and Désirée said hastily, 'Don
Rafael and I have agreed to disagree on certain matters.'

'You don't mind my brother's. . .er. . .er. . .blunt-
ness?' Elena, who had never known Rafael to behave to
a woman without due regard for *cortesia*, sounded as
confused as she looked.

Désirée was tempted to retort she was used to his
piratical lack of courtesy but, deciding that this remark
would further puzzle Elena, settled for simply
reassuring her.

'I don't think my sister will believe I am forgiven,

unless you prove it.' There was a challenge gleaming in Rafael's dark eyes.

Désirée's chin came up. 'And how do you suggest I do that, *señor*?'

'Come for a stroll with me tomorrow evening,' Rafael replied promptly. 'We can join the rest of the fashionable world on the Prado.'

'I should be delighted accompany you both of course, if you wish for the outing, Mademoiselle Fontaine,' Elena added swiftly, giving her brother a scandalised look.

What had got into him? She had never seen him act like this before, behaving as if he had known a stranger for years. It was almost as if their minds were in tune and he felt free to treat Désirée with the kind of casual ease he normally reserved for his male friends. And yet only a blind fool could fail to notice that he was very much aware of her as a desirable woman!

Désirée stifled the hasty protest which hovered on her tongue. She did not wish to offend Elena, but she knew Rafael wanted to be alone with her and, God help her, she wanted to be alone with him, not hampered by the presence of a chaperon!

'Naturally, I would expect you to bring your maid or accept my sister's offer to act as a duenna.' Rafael's carefully controlled tone hid his growing impatience, but inwardly he silently condemned all chaperons to perdition. 'However, I hope you will feel comfortable enough to dispense with your maid's attendance when you come to the *tertulia* we intend to give next week,' he continued with relentless determination.

From the way Elena stared at him, fresh astonishment written all over her face, Désirée gathered that this was the first she had heard of any intention to hold a party.

'You honour me, *señor*. *Two* such delightful invitations. I scarcely know how to answer you,' Désirée murmured, deliberately drawing out her consent in return for his provocative behaviour. What must his poor sister be thinking!

Dios! He supposed he deserved to feel her retaliatory

claws, but it was hard to remember the conventions when every fibre of his being burned!

'Well, will you come or not?' he growled, ignoring his sister's gasp of horror at his further breach of *cortesía*.

Impatient longing glittered in his eyes and Désirée coloured, knowing as if he had spoken aloud what he really wanted from her.

He was *muy hombre*, a real man, proud and passionate. Beneath that exterior of cold Castilian hauteur, a fiery temper burned. Any moment now his control might snap. If it did, she knew he would seize her in his arms and cover her in wild kisses.

With a little thrill of horror, she realised that, regardless of the scandal, she wouldn't lift a finger to prevent him!

Désirée decided it was time to stop teasing.

'Of course I will come with you,' she said simply and had her reward when he smiled.

The Paseo del Prado, Désirée discovered, was a long broad open space with rows of trees enclosing the walk. Several fountains were playing, their waters refreshing the dry Madrid atmosphere and providing harmonious background music to the conversations and laughter of the numerous, well-dressed strollers.

An area in the middle of the *paseo* had been reserved for carriages, but Désirée was more than happy to stroll along on Rafael's arm. His company gave a final gloss to the pleasure of enjoying the evening cool in such pleasant surroundings.

'Why did Elena not join us?' she asked.

'Her confessor called just as we were about to leave. She was torn between duty and pleasure.'

'Well, I suppose she felt she had to choose duty.'

Rafael glanced at her with a smile. 'Actually, *mi perla*, you are mistaken. Elena has plans to become a nun. For her, time spent on her knees with her confessor is to be preferred to secular enjoyment such as this.' He waved an arm to encompass their surroundings. 'Particularly when I reassured her that I would not forget to bring your maid along.'

Désirée had wondered at his insistence that Rosita accompany them. However, if he had made a promise to his sister she knew he would not break it, no matter his own preference.

She cast a quick glance at Rosita, who was following several paces behind them. A smile curved Désirée's lips. Whatever it was that Rafael had said to the girl when he had drawn her aside after they stepped out of his carriage, Rosita was keeping as far distant as convention allowed. Not that she would have been able to make out what they were saying in any event, for their conversation was being conducted in English.

It seemed the safest choice. In this crowd, the use of French might draw unwanted attention and Désirée's command of Castilian, although improving daily, was not yet good enough to venture into the realms of subtlety.

'Does Elena speak English?' Désirée asked, her thoughts running on.

If he was surprised by the question, Rafael did not show it. 'A little. She shared my lessons for a while.' He smiled. 'She was not a keen student and I think she would have preferred it if *Padre* had been like most fathers and frowned on education for women.'

'He sounds an unusual man,' Désirée murmured and then realising that this might sound critical, added hastily, 'I think he was right. Why shouldn't girls be allowed to study if they wish!'

'Were you allowed to do so, *ninfa*?' Rafael was curious.

Désirée shrugged. 'Not as much as I would have liked.' A little grimace twisted her mouth. 'My grandfather was in charge of my education, but he was old-fashioned in his outlook. He considered the classics and a little mathematics suitable, but he drew the line at scientific studies.'

Rafael absorbed this interesting information and remarked, 'Most people would think he already permitted too much.' He gave her a provocative smile. 'Perhaps he felt any more serious work would over-tax your brain.'

Refusing to take the bait, Désirée shook her head demurely: 'But you see, *señor*, he did not think of me as a girl. To him, I was a substitute grandson and he always treated me as a boy.'

To her amusement, he let slip what sounded suspiciously like a disbelieving oath.

A boy! The man must have been an idiot!

'Would you care to sit down?' The wind taken out of his sails, Rafael blankly indicated an area to one side where a number of cane chairs had been set out.

Désirée refused. 'I am enjoying the exercise,' she murmured, but she knew that she didn't want to relinquish his arm.

Recovering from his stupefaction, Rafael wished there was more time to indulge his curiosity. But the hour was growing late and there was something else he had to say first.

'I did not get the chance to enquire last night, but have you had any success in learning more about what befell your brother?'

As he had expected, Désirée's lovely face clouded but her voice remained creditably calm.

'Not very much, I'm afraid. The military are. . .are somewhat busy at present.' She hesitated, wondering if she dare mention the English success in Portugal.

'There is no treason in discussing a commonly known fact.'

With his usual perspicacity, he had guessed the reason for her hesitation.

'If you have heard of the capture of Oporto, then you will know why Marshal Jourdan was too busy to speak to me,' she said tartly. 'However, the king has promised me the services of one of his aides-de-camp. A Major Evrard. He wrote to me a few days ago. A very pretty letter. He has already begun to investigate. With any luck, he will soon discover who was responsible for the attack.'

A strange frown flickered over Rafael's dark face but before she could begin to interpret it, it vanished and he was asking if she would like some *agua fresca* to take away the dust from her throat before they returned to the carriage.

She nodded and he summoned one of the *aguadores* who were plying the crowd.

The water was cold and sweet, but Désirée couldn't help wondering what had disturbed him.

He concealed it well, but where Rafael de Velasco was concerned her senses had grown very sharp and she *knew* something was wrong. Something connected to her brother's death.

But what?

Two days later Rosita came flying into the *sala* where Désirée, having just finished breakfast, was engaged in writing a letter to Hortense.

'You have a visitor, *señorita*,' she gasped.

Désirée, who was expecting Rafael, looked up with a smile.

'Go and admit him,' she instructed. 'Quickly, *por favor*.'

Rosita looked doubtful, but with a shrug obeyed.

To Désirée's surprise, a stranger walked into the room.

Ignoring his hostess's startled gasp, the man crossed to the small writing-table where she was sitting and with considerable aplomb possessed himself of her nerveless hand.

'*Enchanté*, Mademoiselle Fontaine. I am Armand Evrard. Delighted to make your acquaintance at last.'

Joseph's aide-de-camp.

'Welcome, Major.' Désirée reclaimed her hand and indicated the most comfortable chair. 'Do sit down. May I offer you refreshment? Some freshly made lemonade, perhaps?'

'Thank you.' He seated himself. 'I don't care for cold drinks so early in the day, but I will take some coffee, if that is convenient?'

'Of course.' Setting aside her pen, Désirée rose gracefully to her feet and went to give the bell-pull a tug.

She was aware of being watched and for some reason his gaze made her feel uncomfortable. Some men had the repulsive habit of stripping a girl bare with their eyes. It wasn't that. His pale grey gaze lacked sexual voracity, but there was something cold, almost calculating, in his stare.

It was an odd thing how the mind could make instant judgements, she thought. Her instinct was to dislike this man, but why?

In fact, he was quite a pretty fellow, although personally, she did not much care for red hair on men. A scant few inches taller than herself, his figure was slender, but well-proportioned. She guessed him to be in his late twenties, but it was hard to tell since his skin, which was almost as fair as her own, was smooth and unlined.

The major broke the silence. 'I hope I have not called at an awkward time? I know it is rather early. Unfortunately, when I wrote to you the other day I wasn't precisely sure when I would be free.'

His light-toned voice was pleasant, his manner blending courtesy and a respectful deference as he waited for her answer. Telling herself that she must be imagining things, Désirée sat down on the sofa opposite him.

'Your visit is quite convenient, *monsieur*.'

'Good. I am sure you must be even more eager than I am to discover the truth.'

'Did you know Etienne?'

He nodded. 'We had not been acquainted long, but I think I can safely say we were friends.' The pale grey eyes softened. 'I miss him. In this Godforsaken hole of a country, a man needs every friend he can get and I was more than sorry to learn of his death.'

There was sincerity in his tone and it caused Désirée to revise her initial impression.

The Major then offered her his formal condolences before continuing carefully, 'You know why I am here, of course, but does it upset you to speak of the Colonel?'

'No. I find it helps,' she replied simply and the last of her uneasiness melted as she listened to him relate several anecdotes regarding Etienne.

By the time Asuncion brought in the coffee, they were chatting together like old friends and the look of loathing in the maid's eyes as she stared at the hated French uniform cam as a shock.

'You may go. We will serve ourselves,' Désirée said hastily, dismissing the woman.

Her servants obviously regarded her visitor as the enemy. They saw only the soldier and were not willing to try and judge the man behind the uniform.

Idly, Désirée wondered if he had grown those aggressive side-whiskers and bristling moustache to follow fashion or compensate for his slight appearance and girlish features.

She poured the coffee and handed him a cup.

'Thank you, *mademoiselle*.' Evrard took a sip and rolled his eyes in exaggerated approval. '*Much* better than we get in the garrison!'

Désirée smiled. Guessing that he was trying to create a cheerful atmosphere, she appreciated his thoughtfulness.

'May we turn to the matter which brought me here?'

At Désirée's gesture of assent, the Major set down his cup. 'I have begun my investigation by speaking to the men who were with your brother that morning,' he announced, his manner becoming brisk. 'Did you know that three others were also killed and several wounded in the attack?'

Désirée nodded.

'None of the men I have questioned so far were able to add anything to what we already know, but I haven't finished interviewing everyone yet. A couple of the wounded are still very hazy in their recollections. I doubt if one man will survive, but the other is getting better and, from what I have been told by his sergeant, he speaks a little Spanish.'

'You think he may have overheard something useful?'

Armand Evrard inclined his red head. 'It may be so.

We can but hope. However, I would suggest you do not let yourself become too optimistic, Mademoiselle Fontaine. Even if this fellow, Moreau, has the information we need, it will not be easy trying to capture the *guerrillas*.'

'I understand, *monsieur*. Thank you for the warning.'

He smiled at her. 'I had feared to find you prostrate with grief, but I should have known the Colonel's sister would show more fortitude.'

He rose to his feet. 'Now I must take my leave of you, *mademoiselle*. My thanks for the coffee.'

Désirée stood up, smoothing down her lilac cambric skirts. 'My pleasure, Major.'

She escorted him to the front door.

'I will get in touch with you as soon as I have any further news.' Armand Evrard bowed with military precision.

'Goodbye, Major.'

On the step he paused. 'I think we shall deal together very well, *mademoiselle*.'

'I hope so, *monsieur*. I will certainly do everything I can to help you for it is my dearest wish to avenge Etienne's death.'

'You may rest assured that I will do all in my power to see your wish is fulfilled.'

There was a note of steely determination in his light tones and, watching him walk away, it occurred to Désirée that in spite of his somewhat effeminate appearance, Armand Evrard was tougher than he at first seemed.

Half an hour later Rafael arrived. He was dressed casually in dark-coloured breeches and his old leather travelling jacket.

'I thought you might like to go riding this morning,' he said, seeing her look of imperfectly concealed surprise.

'With Elena's escort? Or Rosita's?'

'No escort. Just me, if that is acceptable?'

'Give me a few minutes to change.' Désirée's eyes began to shine.

She ran upstairs, her heart singing like a caged bird at the moment of release.

Within a short time she had rejoined Rafael, who glanced at her familiar dark blue riding habit with a nod of recognition.

'Do you approve of my new hat?' Désirée indicated the wide-brimmed black straw with a wave of one hand.

He grinned. 'Practical and very fetching, *mi perla*.'

Désirée laughed. 'At least it is more suitable than the one I wore the last time we rode together!'

He had brought a handsome chestnut gelding along for her use and, as they threaded their through the busy streets, Désirée was conscious of curious glances following them.

Although she had pinned up her bright hair beneath her hat she knew she did not look like a Spanish woman, but even in his casual attire no one would mistake Rafael de Velasco for anyone other than a *hidalgo*, a nobleman of the blood.

It was that autocratic bearing of his that did it, she reflected. The proud way in which he held his dark head, the decisive air of command that cloaked him, the haughty frown when something displeased him, all spoke of the high lineage bred into his very bone.

And she, what was she? A love-child. A bastard whose father would not, could not, publicly acknowledge her until he lay on his death-bed!

A sigh sought release, but Désirée repressed it savagely. What was the matter with her? So, she could not match Rafael in birth. Given their present circumstances, it hardly mattered! Anyway, only a man displaying *serious* interest would find her irregular parentage a handicap!

There was no point in wasting a lovely morning in dwelling on what could not be changed. She was not going to think about the war between their countries or her own problems when she had Rafael's company all to herself.

Désirée let her eyes rest upon him, admiring the way

in which he handled his lively mount. He and the animal moved as if they were one creature. Only a superb rider could make it seem so easy.

'Where are we going?' she asked, quickly shaking off a sudden memory of those skilful hands sliding round her waist to hold her close against his tall, firm body.

'To El Pardo. Long ago the kings of Castile built a palace on the hill there. They wanted to take advantage of the good hunting in the surrounding forest.' Rafael flashed her a quick smile. 'I thought you might enjoy a little peace and quiet.'

'It sounds lovely.' How had he known she wanted to get away from the hustle and bustle of the city? But he hadn't said how far away this place was.

'Will it take us long?' A faint note of hesitation crept into Désirée's voice.

'Don't worry. We shall be back before anyone notices you are gone and starts to talk.' A grin flickered over his elegantly austere features, making him seem suddenly boyish. 'And I promise to be on my best behaviour, even without a duenna to glare at me!'

Trusting him completely, Désirée was able to laugh back at him.

They took the road north, talking as they rode. The miles flew past and it didn't seem long to Désirée before the scenery began to change.

'How green it is,' she murmured as the trees thickened into forest, shading them from the fierce sun. 'And so quiet. Nothing but bird-song.'

Rafael chuckled. 'This forest is also inhabited by deer, eagles and wild boar.'

Désirée gave a nervous gulp. 'Really? You wouldn't imagine it so close to Madrid,' she remarked airily.

'There might even be a bear or two.'

'Rafael!' She turned wide eyes on him. 'You *are* joking, aren't you?'

He smiled at her wickedly, delighted that she had at last ventured to use his given name. 'Am I?'

For an instant she wasn't sure and then, as he began to laugh, she knew.

'Oh, you are gammoning me!' Indignation coloured her cheeks a pretty pink.

'*Lo siento*—I am sorry.' He grinned at her with a cheerful lack of repentance. 'I couldn't resist it.'

Désirée summoned up her severest frown, but her eyes were dancing with merriment. 'What a way to treat a delicate young lady, *señor*! Have you no consideration for my nerves?'

He pulled a humble face, clasping his hands together in mock contrition. 'I beg your forgiveness, *muy doña*.'

'You are a dreadful hypocrite, Rafael de Velasco!' Désirée's stern expression dissolved into laughter. 'It would have served you right if I had succumbed to hysterics!'

He shook his dark head. 'Never.' He reached out to touch her shoulder in an impulsive gesture of approval. 'You are made of sterner stuff, *mi perla*.'

Seeing genuine admiration replace his funning, Désirée blushed and hastily dropped her gaze to her reins.

When he looked at her with such warmth in his eyes, she could actually feel her heart beat quicken!

'Is something wrong?' His long fingers tightened on her shoulder.

She shook her head quickly, but did not trust herself to look at him.

'Désirée?'

Slowly, she obeyed his unspoken command and lifted her eyes to meet his.

Their gaze locked and the still, green air seemed to vibrate as passion silently answered passion.

Chapter Six

Rafael drew in his breath sharply and dropped his hand from her shoulder as if he had been burnt.

'Shall we go on and see the palace? Or would you prefer to dismount and rest for a while?' Finding his voice at last, Rafael fought to keep it steady. 'It is quite safe. The game will not trouble us.'

He gave her a faint smile. 'The last bears to roam here died hundreds of years ago.'

'Oh, well, in that case!' Désirée managed a light chuckle and slid quickly from the saddle before he could make a move to help her.

Rafael dismounted and they began to walk towards a small clearing which they could see ahead.

'It feels good to stretch my legs. I haven't ridden in weeks.'

'We can make a regular habit of riding together, if you wish.' Rafael matched her light, conversational tone.

'That would be wonderful.' Désirée's smile quickly faded. 'However, perhaps it might be better if we didn't go so far afield next time. I don't want to set the cat amongst the pigeons.'

Rafael gestured agreement. 'A wise precaution, *ninfa*.'

The last thing he wanted was to occasion talk. Gossip would hurt her and might hinder his own plans.

They came to the clearing and Rafael suggested they stop and sit down.

'I brought a few provisions,' he said, opening his saddle bag. 'Are you hungry?'

Désirée nodded; the exercise had given her an appetite.

Rafael unstrapped his rolled-up cloak and handed it to Désirée, who shook it out and spread it in a shady spot while he unpacked the food and a flask of red Val de Peñas wine.

They took their places on the makeshift rug and began to eat, sharing the loaf of bread and some cold roasted chicken.

'Thank you. That was delicious.' Désirée finished the last bite with a sigh of satisfaction.

'Would you like any of these?' Rafael, who had enjoyed watching her enthusiastically consume her simple meal, indicated the handful of dates and nuts he had brought along.

'I would rather have a drink, if I may,' she replied, wiping her hands on her handkerchief.

'It will be a little warm,' he warned as he picked up the wine-skin.

Désirée laughed. 'I don't mind.'

He showed her how to lift the skin on high and pour the wine in a steady stream straight into the mouth.

'You try.' He handed it to her.

With a shrug, Désirée lifted the wine-skin and tilted it in the way he had shown her.

'*Mon Dieu!*' As she had expected, aiming it wasn't as easy as he made it look!

Some of the wine went into her mouth, but the rest went splashing everywhere as she giggled helplessly.

Rafael rescued the wine and set it aside.

'Here. Take mine.' Seeing her fumble for her handkerchief, he quickly produced his own and held it out to her.

In the same instant the memory struck them both.

'*Two* ruined handkerchiefs! Your laundry-woman will be cursing me.' Désirée was giggling too much to take it from him.

'It is your riding-habit which will be ruined! Come, let me do it.'

He leant towards her and began to wipe the wine away. A trickle was running down her neck. Without thinking, Rafael quickly laid his fingers against the bare skin of her throat to stop it staining her gown.

Désirée's laughter suddenly stilled. Rafael could feel her pulse leap beneath his touch as desire, like a smouldering ember, flared into fresh life, stunning them both into silence.

This time Rafael did not draw back, but stared at her like a man hypnotised, unable to drag his gaze from her trembling mouth.

The damp handkerchief fell unheeded from his grasp and fluttered to the ground.

Désirée gazed up at him and the scant few inches of air separating their bodies seemed to crackle and fizzle. Heat enveloped her, scorching every inch of her skin until she felt as if the forest all around them must catch fire too.

'We...we must pack up and go.' Rafael forced the words out but found no will to move.

She couldn't answer him. She couldn't think, couldn't breathe!

'*Por Dios!*' Rafael knew he was shaking. 'We *must* leave, *querida.*'

Désirée managed to nod assent, but when she tried to stand her legs would not support her and she swayed dizzily towards him. Rafael's arms came out automatically to steady her and, even as he realised his mistake, it was already too late.

Driven by a need he could no longer deny, he let out a low growl of satisfaction and drew her to him.

With a wild little laugh, Désirée abandoned sanity. Flinging her arms around his neck, she lifted her face for his kiss.

Eagerly, their lips met and the flame became white-hot.

Waves of pulsating heat flowed through Désirée's veins, turning her giddy. Obeying a primitive longing to yield, she opened her mouth to give his tongue admittance and a new, exciting duel of touch and taste began.

Rafael's arms tightened their grip. In response, her fingers buried themselves in the dense tangle of hair at his nape. He could feel her heart pounding beneath his and a wild elation flooded over him. She wanted him as much as he wanted her!

Together, still entwined, they sank back into the folds of his cloak. Cushioned by grass, the earth felt as soft as a bed.

'You have made your jacket wet,' Rafael whispered the words against her mouth, before letting his lips trail across the delicate line of her jaw towards her ear.

Fiery, exquisite sensation detonated in the wake of each tiny kiss and Désirée's tenuous self-control exploded into oblivion.

'Then I shall have to take it off, won't I?' she murmured in a low provocative purr which she scarcely recognised as her own voice.

Before he could react, her fingers flew to undo the buttons. The edges of the garment fell aside, revealing the lace-trimmed chemise she wore beneath it.

Above the low neck of the chemise the white, rounded swell of her breasts was clearly visible. A laced front fastening, tied in a neat bow, held the chemise together.

Désirée lay very still. A part of her was utterly aghast at her shameless behaviour, but she ignored the warning voice, which was trying in vain to make itself heard. She didn't want to be sensible! She wanted to feel him stroking and caressing her!

She smiled at him invitingly and, his breathing turning ragged, Rafael reached out and untied the bow.

Watching her face closely to gauge her reaction in case she changed her mind, he slowly pulled the two edges apart.

'*Madre de Dios*, but you are beautiful!'

Her breasts were as full and lovely as he had imagined, with pale pink nipples that hardened instantly at his first, gentle touch.

The light caress became more sure, more demanding. His palms slid under each breast, feeling their soft warm fullness, circling slowly, stroking, finding the tight pink crests and rolling them hard between thumb and fore-finger.

'Hmm, that's nice!' Désirée whispered, arching her back like a cat.

Her arms encircled his neck and drew him even closer until the whole length of his tall body was taut against her own. . .and she made an interesting discovery.

A hot blush suffused her cheeks, but she didn't pull away from his male hardness.

'Kiss me again, Rafael,' she demanded, rubbing her-self against him in a slow, sensuous rhythm.

In a dim part of her brain she registered the insane folly of such reckless invitation, but it no longer seemed to matter when he dipped his head to obey.

The kiss was savage and exciting. When it ended she felt like crying, but her frustration turned to gasps of delight as his head dipped swiftly again, lower this time. His mouth enveloped first one nipple and then the other in a hot, moist suckling. Nerve-endings screaming with pleasure, Désirée writhed beneath him, clutching at his broad shoulders with frantic hands.

'Oh, yes! Oh, don't stop! It feels wonderful!'

Her throaty little whispers of pleasure encouraged Rafael to continue, each caress becoming bolder than the last.

'I want you so much, *mi perla*.' Passion thickened Rafael's voice.

'I want you too.' A wonderful sensation of blissful relief filled Désirée as she admitted the truth.

Freed at last from trying to deny her feelings, she gave a little laugh of pure joy and in that moment it struck her with all the force of summer lightning that she was in love with him.

It wasn't just a thing of the body. She wanted *all* of him! From the moment they had met he had dominated every thought, every aspect of her life. Heart, mind and soul, she longed to be his.

'Do you?' Doubt roughened Rafael's tone. Did she really understand what she was saying?

In answer, Désirée drew his head down for another passionate kiss.

Infected by her crazy recklessness, Rafael's doubts melted. Raising himself up, he threw off his jacket and stripped off his shirt, eager to feel her skin against his own.

Desirée watched him with wide eyes.

His chest was very brown, the muscles superbly delineated beneath a covering of dark, curling hair. Fascinated, she stretched out a hand towards him and then hesitated.

'Touch me, *querida*.' Rafael spoke the endearment softly as he caught her fingers in his own and guided them to his chest.

A tiny sigh of pleasure escaped him as she ran experimental fingers over his flesh. Revelling in her new-found power, Désirée switched her attention to his dark copper nipples and made the discovery that they were hard and tight, like her own.

Rafael lay down again, covering her with his body so that their naked flesh made exciting contact. Désirée shivered with anticipation as his body hair rasped across her sensitive nipples.

'You feel so warm,' she whispered.

'My blood is hot for you.' Rafael stared down into her flushed face. He could feel his pulse hammering in a savage rhythm, pounding in his brain and splintering his self-control.

Désirée pressed herself even closer and with a low exclamation, half-curse, half-prayer, Rafael gripped her skirts and flung them up to expose her long slim thighs.

'Your skin is like silk,' he murmured against her mouth as his long, skilful fingers began to explore.

Désirée kissed him, her senses reeling, and the world shrank to hold only his caressing hands and lips.

'Oh, Rafael!' She sighed his name, each and every nerve in her body afire.

Just as the tension was growing intolerable, his hand

slipped between the cleft of her thighs and Désirée gasped with exquisite relief as his questing fingers found the tender, delicate core of sensation within. Gently, he began to caress the swollen nub of flesh, sending fresh waves of delight coursing throughout her entire being.

Behind Désirée's closed lids a molten rainbow coruscated and spun, throbbing to the beat of her blood. She was blind, deaf, to everything but the wonderful sensations rippling through her body.

'Désirée.' Rafael lifted his mouth an inch away from hers. 'Désirée, tell me if this is what you truly want?'

His harsh panting voice seemed to come from many leagues away.

'Désirée, listen to me!' Rafael struggled to clear the fog of desire from his mind. Every fibre of his being longed for completion, but a tiny remnant of sanity prevailed.

'Oh, don't stop!' Désirée's eyes fluttered reluctantly open.

'*Querida*, are you a virgin?'

His hoarse demand penetrated the pleasure-drugged haze of delight that held her in thrall.

'What? I don't under—*of course* I am a virgin!'

Hearing the startled indignation in her tone, Rafael knew it was true.

Abruptly he released her and sat up.

'Rafael?' Désirée laid her hand on his thigh. 'It doesn't matter. I *want* this!'

He shook his head. '*Now*, at this moment, you do. Tomorrow you would regret it.'

'I very much doubt if I would.' She sat up and leant against him, her hair brushing his shoulder.

She could feel him stiffen in resistance and her mouth went dry as she realised the complete impossibility of confessing her true feelings.

He had asked for friendship, not love. The last few minutes had opened her eyes to the truth, but she had no proof that his feelings had changed.

Don't fool yourself! You mustn't pretend that he held

back just now out because he cares for you. He stopped because he values honour and no gentleman takes advantage of an innocent, well-bred young lady.

But, breathing in the potent male scent of him, Désirée didn't want to be a lady!

Absorbing the shocking realisation that she still wanted him, even if all he felt for her was lust, Désirée shuddered. She must be mad!

But somehow she didn't care!

'Rafael, listen to me,' she said quickly. 'In spite of what you might be thinking, I do realise that we can have no future together.'

Rafael glanced at her, his mouth curving into an involuntary smile at her solemn tone, so at odds with her disordered dress.

Her pulse racing, Désirée suddenly realised that at long last she understood why *Maman* had risked everything to consummate her love for John Cavendish.

And she was more of her mother's daughter than she had hitherto realised!

'I know that one day very soon we shall have to say goodbye, but there is no need to let Fate cheat us,' she said recklessly. 'Not when we can take a little happiness for ourselves without hurting anyone.'

She trailed her fingers slowly up his arm and over on to his warm bronzed chest, giving him a mischievous smile.

'I want today to be a lovely memory which I can take out when I am an old lady,' she murmured in a sweetly seductive whisper. 'I want to remember. . .and warm myself on cold winters' nights.'

For a brief instant his face filled with answering amusement, but then he shook his head. 'I'm not in the habit of seducing virgins, *querida*.'

Her fingers stopped and then began again, twisting themselves into his curling chest hair.

'Rafael, I know my own mind. I'm not some silly child bowled over by the first presentable man she's met! I know you don't want to marry me, but we can have a few days of happiness together.' Throwing her bonnet over the windmill, she put it as plainly as she could. 'We can be lovers.'

'Such happiness would have to be bought at a high cost.' Rafael's dark eyes bore searchingly into hers.

'I am willing to pay whatever price the future demands.' Désirée met his gaze directly and taking his hand guided it to her breast. '*You* are everything I have ever wanted in a man. I want *you* to be the first man to make love to me.'

He was silent and for an instant she thought she had won as she could feel his fingers tremble against her flesh.

Gently, Rafael loosened her grip and withdrew his hand.

'I thank you for the compliment,' he said softly. 'But I fear I cannot oblige.'

She gasped and stared at him in disbelief.

'You don't want me?' There was an incredulous note in her accusation.

He gave a harsh laugh, hoping his despair did not show on his face.

How little she really knew! What would she say if he told her the real truth of who and what he was? Would she still want him then?

He doubted it!

At the back of his mind the thought of confession had previously occurred to him, but he had swiftly dismissed it. Just as he had to reject it now. He could not afford to take the chance that she would understand. It wasn't just his neck he risked.

Beautiful, sweet and desirable though she was, Désirée Fontaine was still a Frenchwoman. He owed loyalty to Spain and the men who depended on him. He had no right to forget or ignore those simple facts.

'I want you more than I have ever wanted any other woman!' he said in a hoarse, flat voice Désirée scarcely recognised as his. 'You tempt me almost beyond bearing—I never imagined that desire could be so strong.

Between us it is like an elemental force, but I can offer you nothing.'

'I don't ask anything of you!'

A leaden weight seemed to descend on Désirée's heart. He did not want any part of her love.

'Even so, it would be wrong of me to take the gift you offer.'

Rafael raked his hand wearily through his unruly hair. He wanted her so much, but the chains of honour were even stronger than those of desire.

Without the whole, fatal truth out in the open, he could not, would not, make love to Désirée Fontaine!

'Believe me, I wish things could be different, but honour demands I return you home untouched.' Rafael forced his features into a mask of cool reason. 'There must be no stain on your reputation or damage to your future marriage prospects.'

'Honour! Is that all you can think of?' Bitter frustration exploded in Désirée and she flung herself back down on the cloak.

'*Dios!* Be grateful that I remain capable of remembering it,' he grated, and turning his back on her, made an angry grab at his shirt.

'Rafael, I. . . I. . . Oh, damn and blast it!'

A painful flush of humiliation burning in her cheeks, Désirée jumped to her feet and began to right her disordered clothes, but her hands were shaking so much she could barely manage it.

'Let me help you.' Rafael, who had finished dressing, crossed swiftly to her side.

Désirée stood very still as he did up her buttons. The longing to wind her arms about his neck was still strong in spite of her angry humiliation, but even if she had been willing to drag her pride even deeper in the dust she knew it would do no good. He was too stubborn to change his mind and she had no stomach for another rejection.

'Thank you.'

'*De nada*.' Rafael made her a small ironic bow and turned away.

Désirée glared furiously at his back. His hands had been steady, his touch impersonal. How could he!

And yet there was an unaccustomed colour in his lean cheeks. Perhaps he was not as calm as he was pretending.

In silence they packed up the remains of their impromptu picnic and stowed everything away.

Suddenly the quiet was shattered by the sound of a gun going off.

'What the devil. . .?' Désirée hastily reassured her startled horse.

'Hunters,' Rafael said tersely.

'It sounded quite close.'

'Then it is a good time to leave. We have lingered too long in any case. The Palace will have to wait for another day.'

Without waiting for her answer, Rafael boosted her up into her saddle.

As they rode away another, thought struck Désirée and, forgetting her resolve to coolly ignore him, she turned to Rafael.

'That gunfire—do you think it could have been *guerrillas*?'

'Not here. We are too close to the city. They do not operate in this area.'

'Oh, good. I'm so glad I'm not in *any* sort of danger,' she retorted with heavy sarcasm.

Rafael scowled at her two-edged implication.

'If you want me to apologise for what happened just now, I will,' he snapped. 'Otherwise, I suggest you let the subject drop!'

Too angry to think of a suitably cutting reply, Désirée fell silent once more.

It wasn't until much later, when she was relaxing in the bath Rosita had filled for her that evening, that her furious humiliation finally faded, leaving her mind clear.

Thoughtfully, she laved water over her arms. She had

been too pleased by Rafael's unexpected invitation this morning to stop and think that they might be riding into danger. However, since she had been in Madrid, she had heard many rumours to indicate that the whole country appeared to be sliding into a state of unrest and she was willing to believe it.

Fawned upon by many members of the Spanish nobility, Joseph might hold court in his lovely palace, but Etienne's murder had shattered her belief in the notion that the Spanish people were beaten. No matter what the Emperor declared, the fight wasn't over yet.

Guerrilla activity was all too real and growing daily. Désirée suspected that Rafael knew this very well, so why had he been careless of their safety? He had even brushed off her concern in a dismissive manner.

Désirée reached for the towel. His attitude was puzzling and she didn't like puzzles.

The following day was the one which had been chosen for paying a *visita de cortesía*, a courtesy call on Elena de los Dolores de León. Asking Rosita to press her new morning gown in dark-striped muslin, Désirée was aware of a certain reluctance to keep the appointment.

Coward, she scolded herself.

The house in the Calle Nueva was old, guarded by thick walls and a massive outer door. Set in the centre of the age-blackened wood was a small shuttered grille, grated with iron.

Rosita rang the heavy bell and the shutter slid open an inch.

'*Quiés es*?' said the unseen porter.

Rosita made the traditional reply, '*Gente de paz*,' informing him that they were people of peace.

The shutter opened a little more and, at Désirée's nod, Rosita proffered their names and purpose.

From the hostile looks the porter gave them as he admitted them into the courtyard, Désirée felt sure he didn't think she was worthy of the honour, but Elena's

beaming smile of welcome as she was shown into the
sala banished this wry reflection.

'Désirée. I am so pleased that you have come. Do sit
down here next to me.'

To Désirée's relief, Elena was alone.

She was seated on a large silken divan set before one
of the most elaborately carved fireplaces Désirée had
ever seen. Crossing towards her, Désirée noticed that the
tiled floor was partly covered in plaited rattan mats, but
it was hard to distinguish much else for lowered blinds
obscured the windows to keep out the sunlight.

Blinking in the gloom, Désirée sat down.

'I see you are wearing a *mantilla*. May I say that I
think it suits you?'

'Thank you.' Désirée, who had been a little uncertain
of the fashion on herself, was pleased by her new friend's
approval. 'It is more comfortable to wear than a hat in
this warm weather.'

'Allow me to offer you a cool drink.' Elena rang a
hand-bell by her side.

The summons must have been expected and one of the
servants quickly arrived, bearing a tray of refreshments.

Désirée accepted a glass of orange juice. 'I find I am
always thirsty these days,' she remarked.

An image of Rafael showing her how to pour wine
into her mouth direct from the skin flashed into her mind,
but she firmly banished it.

'You can blame Madrid's dreadful combination of
excessive heat and dry air,' Elena answered with a smile.

Désirée sipped her drink. Searching for a topic to open
the conversation, she asked her hostess how the little
black mare Rafael had bought for her did.

'Very well, thank you. She is a delight to ride.'

Désirée smiled. 'A lovely creature,' she agreed.

'Did you enjoy your ride yesterday with my brother?'
Elena posed the question shyly. 'I would have accompanied you, but I had one of my stupid migraines.'

'It was a pleasant change to get away from the bustle
of the city,' Désirée replied and quickly changed the

subject by asking how the arrangements for the *tertulia* were coming along.

Elena pulled a wry face. 'I could have done with more notice, but still, everything is almost ready now.'

'Are you inviting many guests?'

A swift nod of assent answered Désirée's question. 'Usually, my brother does not entertain when he comes to the city, but this time he has asked everyone he knows.'

A shadow passed over Désirée's face and Elena gave her a reassuring smile. 'There will be many *afrancesados* present and several French officers too. You needn't fear you will be the only foreigner.'

Désirée wanted to ask why Rafael was pretending to be an *afrancesdo* but she couldn't think of a way to do it.

'Would you like to try one of these?' Elena indicated the assorted pastries which had been brought in to accompany their drinks, tactfully ignoring the hiatus.

Désirée wasn't hungry and was about to refuse when Elena added that she was thinking of serving the *cabello de angel* at the party.

'Unfortunately, it is impossible to obtain good quality butter here in Madrid so they aren't to the recipe I would use at home. Rafael said they might not please.'

Désirée heard the doubt in her tone and obligingly sampled one of the angel's hair pastries. 'It's delicious,' she announced firmly, taking a childish delight in contradicting Rafael de Velasco's opinion. 'I'm sure your guests will enjoy them.'

'Speaking of my brother, I'm sorry he isn't here,' Elena murmured apologetically. 'I did remind him earlier that you were expected, but he insisted he had to go out.'

Désirée forced a polite smile. 'Please don't worry. It doesn't matter.'

Hearing the strained note in her voice, Elena had to curb an exclamation of surprise. The other night at the Royal Palace she had been convinced her brother and Désirée were in the throes of developing a *tendre*.

A quick frown creased her brow. Now she came to

think on it, Rafael had been in a distinctly difficult mood when he returned home yesterday.

What's more, Désirée's whole manner today lacked the enchanting sparkle Elena remembered.

She flicked her fan to and fro, wishing there was something she could do to help if they had quarrelled. Rafael would not thank her for interfering, but she had never seen him so happy as he had been this last week.

'Do you think I should keep to mourning or not?'

Belatedly realising Désirée was asking her advice on the dress appropriate for the *tertulia*, Elena forced herself to concentrate as they debated the thorny problem of what to wear.

'I want everything to be perfect for it will be my last social engagement,' Elena concluded the discussion with a faint smile.

'Rafael said you were thinking of becoming a nun.' Désirée found it impossible to restrain her curiosity.

Elena nodded firmly. '*Sí.* I intend to enter the convent in Frias.'

'Frias? You aren't staying in Madrid?'

'There are many excellent convents here, but Frias is a special place. It is one of the oldest towns in Castile.'

Désirée's expressive face revealed her puzzlement.

'It lies at the heart of the lands of Los Velasco, up in the mountains,' Elena explained.

When she casually added that the Duque de Frias was one of their cousins, Désirée felt an inexplicable *frisson* of depression feather down her spine.

She had always known that Rafael de Velasco was above her touch. What did it matter if he was cousin to a duke?

Sadly, logic was no comfort!

Last night, when she had lain sleepless for hours, she had come to the painful conclusion that love could not dismissed to order. It just wasn't possible to stop loving Rafael. The only course open to her was to bury her feelings beneath an impenetrable shield of pride. For the sake of her sanity, she *must* pretend nothing of lasting importance had happened in that forest glade!

She knew the deception would be easier if she did not have to spend time in Rafael's company. However, to cut him socially would only give rise to gossip since she was supposed to be a family friend. She would have to employ more subtle methods to withdraw from an affair that should never have begun.

It had been her intention to tell Elena this morning that she had changed her mind and would not attend the *tertulia*. Elena's obvious pleasure at seeing her and the knowledge that her new friend had been working hard for the party made Désirée's resolve waver.

Before she could make up her mind, a new visitor, Elena's confessor, was shown in.

Realising that all hope of private conversation had vanished, Désirée politely announced her departure as soon as an opportunity presented itself.

'I hope we may meet again before the *tertulia*,' Elena said shyly, ringing for a servant to inform Rosita to wait for her mistress in the courtyard.

'I am holding an at home morning tomorrow. Do come if you can find the time. I should be very pleased to see you.' Adjusting the folds of her *mantilla* around her shoulders, Désirée gave her hostess an encouraging smile, inwardly hoping she would be able to find the firmness she needed to say no when she was on her own ground.

They said their farewells and Désirée was escorted down the stairs by a footman, who showed her out.

Emerging into bright sunlight, she was dazzled after the gloom within the house and it took her a few seconds to realise that the figure standing by the elaborate statue in the centre of the courtyard was not Rosita.

By the time she had realised her mistake, Rafael had crossed to her side and was bowing over her hand with his usual deft grace.

Conscious that there might be watching eyes at any

of the many windows, she resisted the impulse to snatch
her hand away.

'I hoped to be back before you left,' Rafael said, continuing to hold on to her hand.

Désirée shrugged, trying to ignore the way her heart
was slamming against her ribs.

He released her. 'You are still angry with me.'

Disconcerted by his directness, Désirée bit her
lower lip.

'I did not mean to upset you. I want you to be happy.'

Gazing into his dark eyes, she read sincerity in his
expression.

'Will you come back inside? There is something I
wish to discuss with you.'

Shaking her head, Désirée took a step back away
from him.

'The best way for me to find happiness, Rafael de
Velasco,' she said breathlessly, 'is to do what I should
have done in the first place and stay away from you!'

Désirée soon realised that her ambition to forget her
hopeless love was going to be difficult to achieve. Everyone who came to her at home morning seemed to want
to talk about Rafael. A group of officers' wives, anxious
to offer their friendship to one reputed to have the ear of
the King, chattered speculatively about the tall handsome
afrancesado. They questioned Désirée relentlessly, determined to discover how well she knew him.

Désirée had barely recovered from their onslaught
when some of the Spanish ladies she had met at the
royal reception were shown in together with their escorts.
Within a few minutes it was clear to her that these Madrileños were intrigued by the idea of Rafael offering an
entertainment. In view of his previous distaste for society,
they seemed to think it promised to be an especially
interesting evening.

Even Armand Evrard, who arrived as the other visitors
were leaving, brought the subject up.

'*You* have been invited, *monsieur*? I did not know that you were acquainted with Don Rafael.'

'I'm not,' the Major replied cheerfully. 'However, he has issued a general invitation to all the senior officers who are free of duties that evening. They say he intends to serve only the best champagne! But then I've heard the family is very rich and he is an *afrancesado*.'

Désirée was unwilling to voice her doubts on this score. She owed Rafael too much, but she was heartily sick of having to discuss the man she wanted to forget.

'I dare say it will be a very pleasant evening, but I'm sure you did not come here just to talk of Rafael de Velasco, Major.'

He gave her a startled glance, surprised by the unusual sharpness of her tone.

Désirée reined in her irritation. 'I'm sorry. I'm afraid entertaining so many visitors has given me a headache,' she murmured apologetically.

It was actually true. After another sleepless night her brain felt woolly. She wished Elena had visited her. Then she might have come to a decision about the *tertulia*.

'You do look a little pale.' A sympathetic expression appeared on Armand's face. 'Shall I come back another time? I merely came to pay my respects. There hasn't been enough further progress to justify another report.'

'Oh, no! Please don't go.' Feeling distinctly ungracious, Désirée pressed him to take another glass of sherry.

'Thank you.' He sipped the pale dry *fino* appreciatively. 'Actually, I did have another reason for visiting you.' He gave her a smooth smile. 'I was hoping to persuade you to come with me to the theatre tomorrow night. You said you enjoyed theatrical performances and I should very much like to have your company.'

Dismay filled Désirée. There was no mistaking the caressing warmth in his light voice and persuasive manner.

'They are performing a French version of Cadalso's *La Óptica del Cortejo*. It is supposed to be an amusing

romantic satire.' He saw her expression brighten with
interest and his smile grew wider. 'We could have a
bite of supper afterwards. I'm told the Casa Botin is a
restaurant worth patronising.'

'It is kind of you to ask me, *monsieur*—'

'Oh, please, won't you call me Armand?' he interrupted quickly. 'In the circumstances, I think we may be
excused from formality.'

Désirée hesitated. He was helping her and she didn't
wish to offend him, but neither did she want to encourage
his attentions. He simply wasn't the type of man she
found attractive, even if she had not been in love with
Rafael.

'Very well,' she agreed. 'And you may call me
Désirée. However, I don't think I ought to attend a public
performance at a theatre. I am still in mourning.'

'But you mean to favour the Velasco *tertulia*,' he protested, his voice rising in a distinctly petulant manner.

'That is a private party.'

'*Oui*. Attended by half of Madrid.' His smile had faded
to a sour grimace.

Somehow his very opposition to the *tertulia* strengthened Désirée's wish to attend it!

She set her wine glass down, her spine stiffening with
annoyance beneath her black crape dress. 'It is being
given by my friends,' she said with implacable firmness.
'I don't think the two can be compared, *monsieur*.'

The Major was no fool and he knew when to make a
tactical retreat. 'Forgive me. I don't mean to press you
into behaviour you feel inappropriate,' he murmured.

Désirée, feeling that perhaps she had been a little hard
on him, gave him a friendly smile. 'There is nothing to
forgive. It is merely that I have no wish to become the
subject of gossip. Living alone as I do, people are inclined
to be critical.'

'I appreciate the difficulties of your position, but won't
you at least have supper with me? Surely, there can be
no harm in that? It must be lonely for you here on your
own. I know you have made many new acquaintances

in the last few weeks, but we are both French, both strangers in a foreign land. We could be company for one another.'

Désirée hesitated. She *was* lonely.

'All I ask is to serve you, but I should feel honoured if you could consider me a friend.' He laughed, a little too loudly. 'Who knows, in time you might come to regard me with the same admiration I have for you!'

His attempt to sound as if he was merely paying her a fashionably extravagant compliment was contradicted by the eagerness burning in his pale eyes.

Désirée experienced a sinking feeling in her stomach. It seemed that unkind Fate was playing tricks on her! Why couldn't it be the man she loved who wanted her company?

'I should be happy to have your friendship, Armand,' she replied with assumed lightness. 'But you must remember that I shall be leaving Spain soon and it is always sad when *friends* have to say *adieu*.'

He nodded, the flicker of disappointment which blighted his expression revealing that he had understood the limitations she was setting.

'I shall treasure each hour we spend together as if it was the last,' he answered extravagantly, deliberately matching her light-hearted tone.

A few moments later he set his empty wine-glass aside and rose to leave.

'Shall we celebrate our new friendship over supper tomorrow?' he asked, bowing over her hand in farewell.

Désirée decided to give in gracefully and agreed.

When he had gone a bitter smile rose to her lips. How ironic to try and warn Armand not to fall in love with someone who could not return his feelings when she had tumbled into the very same trap herself!

Chapter Seven

Unfortunately for his plans, the King required Armand to remain on duty the following evening. He sent a hasty note round to Désirée, apologising for the delay and explaining that he would be free at ten and would call for her then if that was acceptable.

Having scanned the scribbled letter Asuncion brought in to her, Désirée went out into the hall where his messenger awaited an answer.

'Please tell the Major that the new arrangement is satisfactory.'

The soldier clicked his heels in salute and briskly departed, leaving Désirée free to return to her *sala*.

She sat down, a slight frown creasing her brow. What was she to do with herself for the next two hours? Having expected Armand at any moment, she was already dressed in the black satin evening-gown Doña Mercedes had created for her.

She picked up a book but was too restless to read and went instead to her bedroom, where Rosita was engaged in tidying up discarded items of clothing.

'Oh, *señorita*, you startled me!' the maid exclaimed. 'Did you decide you preferred your ivory fan after all?'

Désirée quickly explained what had happened. 'I've decided to go out for an hour while I am waiting. It is much too pleasant an evening to waste.'

'*Sí*.' Obediently, Rosita abandoned her task, knowing she was required to accompany her mistress.

'I want to take a look at the Puente de Segovia,' Désirée announced, changing her heel-less silk sandals for a stouter pair of shoes.

She had heard that the bridge was impressive, but she hadn't had a chance so far to view it for herself.

'The river bank gets dusty in hot weather, *señorita*. You should also change your gown.'

Désirée shook her head. 'I can always change on my return if necessary,' she replied carelessly. 'Hopefully, it won't be too bad.'

Rosita gave a disbelieving sigh.

Désirée laughed. 'You know you enjoy an outing in the cool of the evening. Off you go and see if Señor Gonzalez has a carriage available for us.'

From the disapproving expression on her maid's face, she guessed that Rosita was hoping that the proprietor of their nearest livery stables, with whom Désirée had an arrangement, would not be able to oblige.

Unluckily for Rosita, the livery stable was not busy and Señor Gonzalez was able to send one of his best carriages. Settling herself comfortably, Désirée sat back to enjoy the ride.

The level of the Manzanares was shrinking fast, but a pleasant breeze wafted over its banks, cooling Désirée's warm skin.

'Shall we get out and walk?'

Rosita looked horrified by the suggestion.

Désirée grinned. She knew the Spanish girl found her passion for exercise inexplicable. In Rosita's experience, ladies confined themselves to a gentle stroll along one of fashionable promenades to show off their latest outfits.

'Very well. You can stay in the carriage.'

Rosita accepted Désirée's offer thankfully but, aware of her duty, cautioned her mistress not to go too far. 'If you stray out of sight, I shall have to come after you!'

'I won't. I just want to get a closer look at the bridge.'

Désirée admired the strong lines of this handsome structure. Other strollers were out enjoying the views and the pleasant breeze. She decided it was worth coming down to the river again, although it was indeed dusty.

She smiled to herself. She knew she lacked the indifference to comfort which was necessary if one wished to be truly fashionable. Apparently, in the height of summer, a walk-way called La Florida was actually laid along the dry river-bed. Rosita had informed her that this Paseo de Rio was a most desirable promenade, but Désirée thought it must be appallingly hot and dusty.

She began to stroll back towards the carriage, taking care to keep her long skirts clear of obstacles. In her desire to obtain a better viewpoint, she had ignored her chaperon's warning and strayed into rougher ground. While she might not be a slave to fashion, Désirée had no wish to snag her dress on the bushes or, even worse, trip and go headlong.

Away from the usual path it was remarkably quiet and, busy watching her footing, it wasn't until Désirée had almost stumbled upon them that she became aware of two men directly ahead of her.

At her gasp of surprise, the taller man whipped round and Désirée found herself looking into Rafael de Velasco's angry eyes.

'You are not eating, *ma chérie*. Is the meat not to your liking?'

Désirée forced her wandering attention to return to the man seated opposite her across the best table that the Casa Botin could boast.

'It is excellent, Armand.' Désirée took another piece of *cochinillo*. The suckling pig had been roasted to succulent perfection, but her mind was not on food.

Why had Rafael reacted with annoyance on seeing her? He had returned her greeting curtly and made no attempt to introduce his companion, a soberly clad gentleman who had surveyed her with silent hostility.

Désirée had felt decidedly *de trop*. It was a relief when Rosita had come hurrying up, providing a face-saving opportunity to bring the painfully stilted, brief conversation to an end.

On the way home, Désirée had fumed with indignation and although her temper had now cooled, she was still feeling upset.

'Would you like some strawberries? They bring them in from Aranjuez. I'm told they can grow almost anything there because it is so green, but the strawberries are said to be particularly good.'

Désirée became aware that Armand was speaking and shook her head, refusing dessert. 'If you don't mind, I would prefer to go home.'

He let out a small sigh. 'I suspected you weren't enjoying yourself.'

'Oh, I am.' Désirée felt guilty. She had tried to shake off her distraction, not wishing to spoil the evening, but she couldn't get Rafael out of her head. 'It's just that I am tired.'

'The hour *is* late. . .' He let his voice trail away and she knew he'd guessed she wasn't telling him the real truth.

'I'm sorry.' Désirée meant it. 'You deserve a more lively companion.'

Armand waved her apology aside and, calling for the waiter, organised their departure. While the carriage he had hired for the evening was brought round, he carefully confined his conversation to inconsequential trivialities.

Désirée appreciated his tact.

However, when they were safely ensconced in the chaise, he asked her if there was something wrong. About to deny it, Désirée hesitated. There was sympathy in his light voice, tempting her to respond.

'Don't answer. I should not have asked.'

'No, you are right. I am feeling low in spirits,' she confessed. 'It. . .it has been a difficult day.'

She had obviously intruded on a private moment and Rafael had every right not to wish to speak to her, but his cool rejection had hurt!

'You are missing your brother.'

Désirée agreed, glad of an honest reason she could admit to.

'Actually, I wish Etienne was here now,' she said with

a wistful sigh. 'There is so much I want to tell him.'

She could have talked to Etienne about her feelings for Rafael. He might not have approved, but he would have tried to understand.

There was an awkward silence and Désirée suddenly wondered if she had embarrassed her companion. 'Please excuse me. I am being maudlin.'

'Not in the least,' Armand protested politely. 'After all, it's barely six weeks since you learnt of the Colonel's death.' He coughed. 'I would be happy to listen, you know.'

It was too dark inside the chaise to see his expression, but Désirée heard the eagerness in his voice.

'It's not the same, of course, but I was Etienne's friend,' he continued in the same rapid tone. 'Discussing your problems with me might help you solve them.'

'You are very kind, Armand.' Désirée's voice wobbled and she bit down hard on her lower lip to stop herself bursting into tears.

She had always prided herself on rarely succumbing to tears, a habit her grandfather had taught her to despise, but her stupid love for Rafael de Velasco was turning her into a watering-pot! Just because he had looked at her in that uninterested fashion, behaving as if he barely knew her!

Unfortunately, telling herself it didn't matter if he thought she was a nuisance was absolutely no use!

'Kindness doesn't come into it, *ma chérie*. I am delighted you are here in Madrid.'

Suddenly, to her surprise, Armand seized Désirée's hand and kissed it fervently.

Involuntarily, she recoiled, her muscles stiffening in silent protest, and he let her go at once.

'However, I must confess I was amazed to hear of your arrival,' he continued quickly, his tone deliberately nonchalant.

Désirée relaxed again, realising he wasn't going to plague her with unwanted romantic advances. 'Why were you surprised?'

'Etienne told me that he had written to you, telling you not to come to Spain. . .' Armand hesitated '. . .he knew, you see, that trouble was brewing.'

'I never got his letter.'

Désirée shivered.

If she had received it, she would have known that the situation in Spain had changed for the worse. She would have never set out on her unconventional journey. Never met Rafael de Velasco.

And never had her heart broken!

The house on the Calle Neuva was transformed from Désirée's last visit. The outer door stood open and a guard of powdered footmen had replaced the surly porter. Lights blazed everywhere and music greeted her as she crossed the courtyard.

Carefully rearranging the silver-spangled scarf draped over her arms into more graceful folds, Désirée took a deep breath and entered the *sala*.

It was very crowded, the hum of conversation and laughter loud on the warm air.

'Désirée.'

She caught sight of her hostess, who was holding court before the huge fireplace.

'Come and meet everyone.'

Elena's smile was warmly welcoming and Désirée's unusual shyness evaporated.

She started out across the tiled floor and came to a sudden halt as Rafael, abandoning his conversation with another group of guests, stepped out in front of her.

'*Buenas noches*.' He bowed with elegant grace and held out his arm towards her.

A wild impulse to slap his dark face assailed Désirée. Mastering it with difficulty, she silently laid her fingers on the sleeve of his superbly cut coat and allowed him to escort her across the room.

'I must pay attention to our guests for now,' he said quietly as they approached the fireplace. 'But will you grant me the favour of a moment's conversation later?'

'What is the point?' Désirée asked bitterly.

'Meet with me and you shall find out.'

They had almost reached the group gathered around Elena. Désirée started to remove her hand from his arm, but Rafael's reaction was swift. His free hand shot out and covered her fingers, imprisoning them beneath his.

'Are you willing to risk a scene, *mi perla*?'

'Let me go!' Trapped, Désirée hissed the words at him, but he shook his head, an unholy light of amusement gleaming in his jet-black eyes.

'Not until you agree to my request.'

Request! He was blackmailing her and he knew it!

'Very well,' she said through gritted teeth. 'But you'd better have a good reason for this. . .this piracy!'

He laughed. 'I shall see you at supper,' he said and released her.

Afterwards, Désirée could never remember a word of what she had said to Elena and her friends. She supposed she must have smiled and nodded in all the right places, a legacy of a lifetime's training in behaviour appropriate for a lady, but it was a complete blur.

Recovering her composure at last, thanks in part to a glass of the excellent champagne which Elena had charmed out an *afrancesado* wine merchant, she began to circulate. As promised, there were several French officers and their ladies present among the Spaniards. However, the atmosphere was extremely civilised, with no trace of sour resentment to spoil the party.

To her own surprise, Désirée found she was enjoying herself. . .until she happened to glance across the room and caught sight of Rafael bending his dark head to listen to a voluptuous beauty in a crimson satin dress cut daringly low.

Her breath suddenly shortening in her tight chest, Désirée watched them. The raven-haired woman, who-ever she was, possessed a ripe, enticing allure. . .and a provocatively sensual laugh!

All at once, Désirée experienced the depressing con-viction that her new evening gown of lilac silk-gauze was dowdy. Rosita had dressed her hair in a high knot of curls, elegantly threaded with lilac and silver ribbons, and she was wearing her pearls, but compared to that glowing creature over there bedecked with rubies the size of hen's eggs, she felt washed-out and dull.

'May I offer you another glass of champagne?'

Désirée whirled round to find herself being regarded by an elderly exquisite, clad with formal splendour in maroon velvet.

'*Gracias*.' Désirée thanked him and took the wine he held out to her.

The man, who did not introduce himself, smiled at her with languid amusement.

'I see you are watching Don Rafael flirt with my wife. They make a handsome couple, but you have no need to worry.'

She threw him a startled glance. 'You are very frank, *señor*.'

'A privilege of advanced age, Mademoiselle Fontaine. One of the few worth having, I might add.' A faint smile curved his thin mouth.

Désirée nodded. She could hardly argue with him on that score, but she couldn't let his earlier observation pass unchallenged.

'You have the advantage of knowing who I am, *señor*, but you are mistaken. I assure you I have no interest in whether or not your wife is flirting with our host.'

'Neither have I.'

His calm reply took the wind out of Désirée's sails and she stared at him round-eyed.

'Perhaps I should introduce myself. I am the Marques de Aranda. My wife and Don Rafael are old friends.'

He saw her raised eyebrow and chuckled quietly.

'Inez knows I trust her to behave with discretion. She will not overstep the mark in public, but in private? Ah, now that might be another matter.'

Désirée gulped. 'The Marquesa's behaviour is your business, *señor*, not mine.' Her voice strengthening, she added more firmly, 'Nor, am I pleased to say, is it any concern of mine what Don Rafael does. I don't care who he flirts with.'

His lined face broke into a disbelieving smile.

Nettled, Désirée let her gaze return to the couple they were discussing.

Rafael was smiling, that warm intimate smile which transformed his austere features. He said something and the Marquesa laughed, her great dark eyes flirting with him over the top of her painted fan.

'Very affectionate, I agree,' said the Marques, observing Désirée's disastrously expressive face. 'But, I repeat, do not allow yourself to be deceived by appearances, *mademoiselle*. You have no need to feel threatened. I think you'll find that Don Rafael's romantic interests lie rather closer to home.'

Désirée swivelled round until she was facing him once more. There was a knowing look in his cynical old eyes.

'You listen to gossip, sir,' she retorted, unconsciously adopting the clipped tones employed by her grandfather whenever he was displeased.

He nodded. 'I find it instructive.'

Her lips tightening, Désirée curtsied with exquisite grace.

'Pray excuse me. I have just seen someone I wish to speak to.'

He inclined his silver head and Désirée swept away into the crowd.

As the Fates would have it, she immediately bumped into Armand. His pleased greeting was balm to her soul and she smiled at him with a warmth that made him catch his breath.

'A splendid party, *oui*?' He waved one hand in an expansive gesture. 'Doña Elena is to be congratulated.'

'Indeed.' Désirée strove to calm her ruffled feathers. She managed to murmur correct responses to Armand's enthusiastic praise of the excellent musicians and the lavishness of the refreshments, but her mind remained preoccupied.

That cynical old man was a mischief-maker, she'd lay

odds on it! He had enjoyed seeing her squirm, but all the same, he had unwittingly done her a favour. He had made her realise that the nature of her friendship with Rafael was already the subject of gossip. It was infuriating!

'But your glass is empty!' Armand suddenly interrupted his voluble discourse. 'Let me get you some more champagne.'

'No, thank you. I've had enough.' Désirée was beginning to wonder how much Armand had imbibed. There was a slightly glassy look in his pale eyes and his manner was unusually boisterous.

'No?' Armand eyed her up and down and then quite abruptly said, 'That's a very pretty dress you are wearing. Colour suits you, you know. You are the belle of the evening.'

Désirée didn't believe a word of it, but she acknowledged the compliment gracefully.

'Etienne said his little sister was a beauty.' Armand beamed at her happily. 'And now you are an heiress too.'

Deciding he was foxed, Désirée was willing to overlook his painful lack of tact, but she was relieved when they were interrupted a moment later by Monsieur Dubec.

'Ah, Major, I need a word with Mademoiselle Fontaine. You'll excuse us, won't you?'

For an instant, Armand glared belligerently at the dapper little secretary. Then it seemed to penetrate his hazy wits that it would be a mistake to come to cuffs with one so close to the King.

'I'll see you later,' he muttered gruffly to Désirée and walked off.

'Our gallant Major is displeased with me.' There was an amused twinkle in the secretary's eyes. 'However, I shall not hold his ill manners against him.'

'I fear he is a little the worse for Doña Elena's champagne.'

Dubec chuckled. 'To be honest with you, *mam'selle*, he is inclined to drink too much. Most soldiers do but, unfortunately, Armand does not carry his wine well. He either turns surly or, worse, over-affectionate!'

'So I had noticed,' Désirée remarked drily.

From her tone, Dubec guessed she had not been displeased by his interruption. He had wondered whether he ought to warn her that Evrard was heavily in debt and on the look-out for a rich wife, but if she was not enamoured of the Major's charms it wasn't necessary and he had a more urgent matter to discuss.

'I'm sorry, but I'm afraid I'm going to have to mar this delightful occasion with some bad news.'

Désirée cocked her head enquiringly at him.

'There's no way to wrap it up in clean linen so I'll come straight to the point. The owners of the house in the Calle de Clavel are influential *afrancesados* whom the King wishes to keep happy. They offered your brother the place rent-free for as long as he wished, but now they have changed their minds. They want it back.'

Désirée stared at him, the colour draining from her face. Her heartbeat accelerated, but she managed to hang on to her composure.

'When do they want me to move out?'

'As soon as possible.' Grateful to be spared a fit of hysterics, Dubec attempted to soften the blow. 'However, I'm sure they could be persuaded to to give you time to sort yourself out.'

'I could pay them rent if they let me stay.'

He shook his head. 'I doubt they will accept your suggestion. They don't need the money.'

'The King has agreed to their demand?'

'Not yet, but he will have to if he wishes to retain their goodwill.' Dubec gave her a hard look.

Désirée knew that Joseph couldn't afford to quarrel with his Spanish supporters. It would be unfair to put pressure on him to support her.

'I have no desire to inconvenience His Majesty. You may tell him I won't cause trouble.'

Dubec's smile was approving. 'I believe Colonel Thierry's wife has already offered to accommodate you?'

Désirée admitted it, her tone reluctant. 'I am grateful for their kindness, but I think I would prefer to hire a house.' She gave a little shrug. 'I have been my own mistress for too long. I value my privacy.'

The King's secretary sighed. It was well known that the lovely Mademoiselle Fontaine was unusually independent, but he felt he had to try and make her see sense.

'Take my advice, *mam'selle*. Accept the hospitality you have been offered or go home to France. This is not the place for a a woman without a man to protect her.'

'Have you no faith then in the efficiency of our gallant forces, *monsieur*?' Désirée couldn't keep a note of mischief from her tone.

'I think you know I have been too long a courtier to admit to anything of the sort,' he said wryly.

Désirée's face lost its teasing smile. 'I cannot go home,' she said simply. 'Not yet.'

He understood and thought her brave, if misguided. 'I hope you won't regret it,' he said quietly.

'I won't,' Désirée answered with more confidence than she felt.

It was customary to play cards at a *tertulia* and several small card-tables had been set up in rooms adjacent to the main *sala*. When one of Elena's friends asked Désirée to partner him at whist she agreed, glad not to have to think about what Dubec had just told her.

'Well done, *mademoiselle*. You played an extremely good hand.'

They had just won their second game and Désirée, who had been well taught by her grandfather, smilingly accepted his congratulations.

The others around their table called for another game and Désirée's partner demanded an increase in the stakes.

'We'll make our fortunes, *mademoiselle*!'

Désirée was reluctant. She liked playing cards, but she wasn't addicted to gambling. She had seen it do too much damage.

They protested at her decision to withdraw, but Désirée

held firm, adding, 'Doña Elena has given the signal for supper to be served.'

'*Sí*, you are right.' Désirée's partner drew out a handsome gold watch from his waistcoat pocket. 'It has already gone eleven.'

All around them card games were breaking up and people drifting away towards the dining-room.

'Here comes Don Rafael.'

Désirée looked up and her pulse quickened.

How broad his shoulders were beneath that elegant blue coat. He made every other man in the room seem insignificant!

Rafael greeted the others politely and then turned to Désirée. 'I have come to escort you in to supper, Mademoiselle Fontaine.'

Désirée's chin came up. Was he counting on the fact that she was too well-bred to embarrass him by refusing in front of his guests?

'You did promise to favour me with your company,' he reminded her with a slight smile.

'So I did.'

Excusing herself to her companions, she allowed Rafael to whisk her away.

'Are you hungry?' Rafael asked as they traversed a long corridor.

'Not particularly.'

'Good. Then we can give supper a miss.' Rafael changed course and led her to the book-room.

It was empty, but a branch of candles standing on a large reading-table in the centre had been lit, warding off the gloom. Hundreds of leather-bound volumes lined the walls, lending a dry dusty scent to the air.

Désirée moved to examine the nearest bookcase. Picking out a volume, she recognised a valuable copy of Pliny's *Historia Naturalis*.

'You have an excellent collection,' she murmured, replacing the book in its rightful place.

'It belonged to my father. This used to be his refuge whenever he came to Madrid. He hated city life and consoled himself with buying new books every visit.'

He smiled at her, that slow intimate smile which warmed his patrician features. 'Would you like to see his favourite acquisition?'

Désirée nodded, feeling strangely unsure of herself, and Rafael got down another of the heavy volumes and placed it on the table.

'Come and see. The illustrations are exquisite.'

Désirée joined him and forgot the nervous apprehension twisting in her stomach, becoming caught up in the beauty of the medieval Book of Hours.

'Thank you for showing it to me,' she said as he closed the volume.

'I knew you would appreciate it.'

There was a tiny silence.

Désirée was very aware of the irony of the situation. It felt odd to be standing here next to him, their minds in accord when she had been expecting a quarrel!

She had been so angry with him. He had rejected her twice, once in the forest and yesterday when he had pretended she was a stranger, but tonight in this quiet peaceful room as she looked into his dark face she forgot her hurt pride. All she was conscious of was how much she loved him.

'Désirée.' Rafael took her hand and conveyed it to his lips, pressing a kiss against the soft skin of her inner wrist.

A little shudder ran through her slender frame.

'About last night. . .' Rafael's deep voice was unusually hesitant. 'I give you my word that I had no wish to ignore you. I know it may have seemed that way, but—'

'You were discussing private business and I was *de trop*.' Désirée's tone was dry.

He nodded. 'Are you very offended?'

'I was,' Désirée admitted slowly, realising it was no longer true.

'I'm sorry. I was startled, but I ought to have handled

it better.' He pulled a wry grimace. 'You have a habit
of addling my wits until I forget all sense.'

Knowing he alluded to what had happened the last
time they had been alone together, Désirée experienced
a *frisson* of solidarity.

'Then we are both in the same boat,' she blurted out.
'*Mi perla*?'

'I wasn't going to admit this, but in view of what you
have just said it is only fair to tell you why I was so
offended and angry with you. I thought you were deliberately paying me back for not speaking to you the last
time I came here.'

He stiffened. 'Do you really think I would let my
behaviour be governed by mere spite?'

She coloured and gave a little shake of her head. 'No,
of course not. I was letting my emotions cloud my judgement. Trying, I suppose, to justify my own guilt.'

His black brows shot up as he grasped her meaning.

'*Querida*, you have nothing to reproach yourself with!
I was very flattered by your offer.'

'I resented your refusal! I blamed you for my humiliation, but I had no right to press you. My behaviour was
shameless and you had good reason to reject—'

'We both know I wanted to make love to you,' he said
firmly, bringing her agitated recital to a halt. He took
her into his arms. 'I still do.'

His dark head dipped, his lips finding hers in a kiss
as sweet as it was brief before he released her and
stepped back.

'But I cannot. It would be wrong.'

Désirée stared up into his night-dark eyes, seeing a
reflection of her own sadness there.

'The chains of honour bind us both, Désirée. Break
them and we risk destroying all that that makes us ourselves.'

Silence returned to the room. Désirée shivered, knowing he was right. Conscience could not be easily denied!

He had apologised and she ought to be satisfied,
yet she could not shake off the conviction that there

was something seriously wrong. Something was
troubling him!

Désirée felt cold all over. What secrets was he keeping? She longed to know, longed to help if she could,
but she had no right to ask.

'I saw you talking to Joseph's secretary a little while
ago,' Rafael spoke at last and something in his expression
told Désirée he knew what they had discussed.

'You know about the house?' she exclaimed.

'I heard the news the day you came to visit Elena. I
wanted to warn you then.'

'But I wasn't in the mood to listen.' Désirée sighed.
She had been acting like a prize idiot! 'Is that what you
wanted to talk to me about tonight?'

He nodded. 'I thought you ought to know what was
happening so you could start making alternative plans.'

'Dubec wants me to accept Madame Thierry's offer
of hospitality.'

Watching how she fiddled nervously with the silver
sticks of her fan, Rafael guessed that she had been
advised to go back to France. 'Is that what you want?'

'No! I am thinking of hiring a house.'

'I have another proposal you might like to consider.'
Rafael motioned her towards a chair.

Désirée sat down and looked at him expectantly.

'Unless you return home you will need—'

'I am not prepared to leave Spain!'

'I wasn't going to suggest it,' Rafael replied mildly.
'Only that you leave Madrid.'

She blinked at him. 'I. . .I don't understand.'

'Come back to Casa del Aguila and be our guest. Elena
needs someone to keep her company.'

'She is going to be a nun,' Désirée protested weakly.

'Not immediately. The arrangements have yet to be
made. It will take several weeks.'

Rafael leaned back against the library table, resting
his lean hips against the edge. His pose was outwardly
casual, but tension coiled itself into the pit of his stomach.
It was important he got her out of Madrid, but he dare

not tell her why. It wasn't fair to burden her with the dangerous knowledge that Wellesley was almost ready to march into Spain. If the British were successful. . .if Joseph attempted to defend the capital, she would be caught up in the inevitable bloodshed!

Luckily, his suggestion to Miguel that he would be justified in asking for the return of his house on the Calle del Clavel had fallen on fertile ground. But it wasn't going to work if Désirée proved stubborn.

'People might think it odd if I suddenly leave Madrid. Everyone knows I am seeking vengeance for Etienne.'

'Perhaps, but they also know you have been under a lot of strain. What better way to relax than to visit old family friends?'

Désirée nodded. That made sense, particularly as, thanks to the deception which had begun in Burgos, everyone assumed her family had been acquainted with Rafael's for years. Visiting Casa del Aguila would seem natural.

'Think about it.' Rafael's attractive voice took on a persuasive note. 'Elena likes you and you could be a help to her. Knowing my sister, she will want everything to be in perfect order before she leaves for Frias. I should feel happier if there was someone to stop her from doing too much and straining her health.'

Désirée's thoughts were whirling, but she managed to ask him why he couldn't keep an eye on Elena himself.

'I am often away.'

Désirée's expressive face revealed she was wondering what would happen when he was home.

'It is a big house. We wouldn't be falling over each other and quarrelling every minute if that is what is worrying you,' Rafael said humorously. 'You could have all the privacy you need.'

'Have you mentioned the idea to Elena?'

'Not yet. I wanted to talk to you first, but I know she will approve. She is very devout and spends a good deal of her time at prayer, but she isn't a hermit. She would enjoy your company.'

Désiré needlessly smoothed a fold of her skirts, avoiding his gaze while she grappled with her thoughts.

She was very tempted. His offer would solve her immediate problem and provide a welcome opportunity to see more of the country she found fascinating. But there were several drawbacks.

'It would make it more difficult for me to keep in touch with Major Evrard.'

Rafael's brows lifted. 'The fellow is a calculating upstart who drinks too much.'

Désirée felt obliged to protest. 'He has been very kind to me and he is an efficient officer.'

'You could always write to him.' Rafael dismissed the Major.

'I suppose so.'

'Do you have any other objections for me, *mi perla*?' Rafael gazed down at her, a smile in his eyes.

Désirée bit her lip. How could she admit that the real problem was whether or not she could keep her unruly emotions in check! She had already made a fool of herself once and paid the price in utter humiliation. Much as she still longed for him, she did not want to risk another rejection.

No matter his personal desires, Rafael had been it clear he would not bed her. Was it sensible to take a chance on her own willpower when living with him day after day would strain it to the utmost?

'Would you like more time to think it over?' Rafael asked, hiding his anxiety.

Désirée accepted the suggestion gratefully. 'I promise to give you my answer soon.'

'Good. Now, I think we had better rejoin the other guests before supper is over and we are missed.'

He held out his arm to her and Désirée placed her hand on it with a smile that told him they were friends again.

A week slipped by and Désirée was no nearer a decision whether or not to be Rafael's guest at Casa del Aguila.

Every time she made her mind up, she would think of another reason to change it again.

However, she was well aware that time was running out. A formal letter had arrived, requesting she vacate the house by the end of the month and with only another week of June left to go, she knew she had to act.

Her choice finally crystallised when Madame Thierry, who also attended the fashionable Collegiate Church of San Isidro, drew her aside after Sunday Mass and tried to persuade her to come and live with them.

'I'm sorry, *madame*. It is most kind of you to ask and I am grateful, but I really do have other plans.' Désirée tempered her refusal with polite courtesy, but the colonel's wife was persistent and eventually Désirée was forced to admit she meant to leave Madrid for a time.

'But where do you intend to go, *petite*?'

'Doña Elena de los Dolores de León and her brother have invited me to stay with them,' Désirée answered, ruefully reflecting that the gossip would probably travel faster across the city than her letter of acceptance to Rafael.

The next morning, she called her servants into the *sala*.

'I have asked you here to tell you that I no longer require your services after the end of this week.'

There were startled exclamations and Désirée became aware of a look of reproach on Rosita's face.

She quickly explained she had no complaints about their work, promising them excellent references and extra wages to make up for the short notice.

Rosita lingered behind as the others filed out and asked for permission to speak.

'I have really enjoying working for you, *señorita*. I want to stay on as your maid, if you will have me.'

Désirée shook her head regretfully. 'I will be sorry to lose you, Rosita, but I'm not staying in Madrid. I am going to be the guest of Doña Elena for a few weeks.'

'I don't mind leaving the city,' Rosita said stoutly.

Désirée was touched by her loyalty. 'But don't you have family here?'

'No one close enough to care.' Rosita shrugged.

Désirée sensed the hurt behind the girl's brave front. 'Do they object to you working for a Frenchwoman?'

Rosita nodded in a shamefaced fashion. 'We no longer speak,' she muttered.

'Perhaps you can be reconciled with them when I have gone.'

'It is too late for that, *señorita*.' She blushed, twisting her hands together awkwardly. 'You see, it's not just you. They know the Colonel and I were lovers.'

Désirée sat down suddenly. 'What. . .what did you say?' she asked faintly.

'I was your brother's woman.' Rosita's colour was high, but she held Desiree's startled gaze proudly.

'I didn't even know the two of you had met!'

'One evening just before Christmas, when I was hurrying home from the milliner's shop where I worked, two soldiers stopped me and dragged me into an alley. They were drunk.' Rosita shuddered. 'Etienne happened to be passing. He heard me scream and rescued me.'

A little smile shone on her pretty face.

'He called at the shop the next day to see how I did and. . .well. . .I fell in love with him.' Her voice trailed away and strengthened again. 'I know it wasn't serious for him. He was lonely and needed a woman, that's all, but he didn't care that I was a Spaniard and only a working girl. He treated me like a princess.'

Désirée had recovered her breath. 'My brother was a kind man,' she said quietly.

'You aren't angry, *señorita*?'

'Why should I be? Etienne's private life was his own business.'

'I miss him,' Rosita murmured.

Désirée nodded, her throat closing with sudden sadness. Etienne had possessed qualities which endeared him to many diverse people.

'When I heard that Monsieur Dubec was seeking

servants to work here, I decided to apply.' Rosita sniffed away the tears which threatened and continued with her explanation. 'Etienne often spoke of you and I thought I could repay a little of his kindness by looking after you. Monsieur Dubec could see I was keen and he was having difficulty filling the position, so he hired me even though I didn't have the proper experience.'

Désirée had always wondered why Rosita had been so friendly towards her when most Madrileños made no secret of their detestation of the French. Remembering the younger girl's unflagging cheerfulness and eagerness to help, she was glad that Dubec had given her a chance.

'Why didn't you tell me all this before, Rosita?'

'I didn't want to bother you, *señorita*. You had enough in your dish,' the maid said simply. 'And you needn't fear embarrassment on account of anyone important knowing about me and the Colonel. I asked him to keep our affair a secret. Not that I was ashamed, you understand, but I wanted to try and spare my family's feelings.'

Désirée was silent for a moment, thinking over what she had just heard. Contrary to what Rosita had assumed, she was glad Etienne had found her rather than some haughty married beauty out for amusement. Rosita might not be well-born, but she was a generous and warm-hearted girl who must have eased Etienne's loneliness and given him happiness in the brief time they'd had together.

'Thank you for confiding in me, Rosita. It would probably be better if we didn't speak of this again, but since I already know I can trust you, I would be very happy to take you with me to Casa del Aguila. If you are sure that is what you want?'

Rosita's face broke into a wide grin and she nodded enthusiastically. '*Gracias*.'

'But I cannot make any promises for the future,' Désirée added in a warning voice. 'Remember, I must return to France one day soon.'

'I'm willing to let the future take care of itself, *señorita*.' Rosita replied with her usual cheerful smile. 'It's no use worrying before something happens, is it?'

'No, I suppose not.'

'Shall I start sorting out your clothes for packing?'

Désirée nodded. The die was cast. All she could do now was pray that she didn't make a fool of herself at Casa del Aguila!

Chapter Eight

'Rosita, I want you to lay out my best carriage-dress,' Désirée informed the maid as she came in to open her bedroom curtains. 'We are going to call on Major Evrard at the garrison after breakfast.'

Rosita gulped nervously.

Désirée gave her a sympathetic smile. 'I know, but I must speak to him. I haven't told him yet that I intend to leave Madrid the day after tomorrow.'

Désirée had been putting off the task, although she had paid several other calls of farewell, but she felt she owed it to Armand to explain her decision face to face.

'*Sí, señorita.* Shall I order a carriage after I have brought up your hot water?'

Désirée nodded and Rosita hurried off to carry out this new task.

The French were garrisoned in the Retiro Park, a huge garden over three miles in circumference belonging to the Palacio del Buen Retiro. The beautiful rooms of the palace had been shut up on Napoleon's orders and the garrison established in the old royal porcelain-making factory which stood in the grounds.

Napoleon had also decreed that no Spaniards were to be allowed inside the Retiro, but Désirée felt confident of gaining admittance. Her optimism proved justified and the guard on the main gate waved them through.

Once inside, she marvelled at the freedom from dust and the quiet. There was even a pleasant breeze, probably the result of the palace having been built upon an elevation.

When they reached the Porcelaine, Désirée sent in a message; after a short delay, Armand came hurrying out.

'I'm sorry to disturb you, but if you can spare me a few moments I have something to tell you,' Désirée informed him after they had exchanged greetings.

'Of course. Let's seek a little privacy,' he suggested. 'There are several pleasant walks where we won't be disturbed.'

Désirée allowed him to hand her down.

'Wait for me here, Rosita. You will be quite safe, won't she, Major?'

He gave Rosita a reassuring nod. 'Just stay in the carriage,' he ordered. 'We won't be long.'

Armand led her in the direction of the lake and, as they strolled along a walk shaded by horse-chestnut trees, Désirée admired the views of the Guadarrama mountains.

'There must be a wonderful panorama of the city from the Palace,' she murmured.

Armand agreed. 'We also get very impressive sunsets. But you didn't come here to discuss scenery, did you?'

Désirée shook her head and, halting, turned to face him. 'I came to tell you that I'm leaving Madrid.'

His fair skin paled still further. 'When?'

'On Friday.'

'But why this sudden decision?'

Désirée explained about losing the house and Rafael's invitation.

Armand frowned. 'I had no idea you were so close to Velasco.'

'He is a friend, nothing more.' To her annoyance, Désirée felt herself blush.

'I see.' There was an angry note in his voice which puzzled Désirée.

'I am glad to hear you have no stronger tie,' Armand continued. 'I don't think he is trustworthy.'

'Armand!' Désirée gave a shocked gasp. 'Such criticism does not become you.'

'I am aware that I have been a guest in his home,' he retorted stiffly. 'But my duty as a soldier is greater than any social obligation. Velasco claims to be an *afrancesado*, but I've recently discovered that he has been asking a lot of questions about our forces. Too many questions for an innocent civilian.'

'Do you have any proof of what you are implying?' Désirée demanded.

'Not yet.'

'Then I suggest you stop making unfounded accusations, which might very easily rebound on your own head! Have you forgotten that Don Rafael belongs to an important family?'

'I know that the King is too soft on these Spaniards,' Armand growled in reply. 'He ought to hang a few of them instead of trying to placate them.'

Désirée was tempted to remark that diplomacy was obviously not his strong suit, but she resisted. She didn't want to quarrel.

The two men clearly disliked one another. It wasn't surprising. They held widely different beliefs and views. Armand's distrust could be prompted by his antipathy or even unconscious envy.

Désirée thought it over. Like her brother, Armand had started out with few advantages. He came from a respectable but impoverished family and had achieved his present position through hard work and good fortune. Many would say he had done well, but he was an ambitious man. Exposing a spy would add to his credit.

'It isn't a crime to be interested in politics, surely?' Désirée laid her hand on the Major's sleeve, trying to ignore her suddenly rapid pulse. 'Don Rafael is an intelligent man. It is only natural he wants to know what is going on.'

Armand drew in a deep breath. 'I can see that you aren't going to listen to me.'

Désirée crushed the doubt Armand's words had aroused. Rafael might detest the French, but she couldn't believe he was a spy. He wouldn't stoop to anything underhand.

'I'm sorry, Armand. The last thing I want is to mar our farewell with a quarrel. You have been kind to me and I appreciate your help, but Rafael de Velasco is my friend and I cannot let you blacken his name.'

Armand forced a smile. 'You are a loyal little creature, Désirée, and I admire you for it.' He patted her hand. 'Very well, let us agree to disagree.'

Désirée hastily removed her hand from his arm. 'My visit to Casa del Aguila won't change anything. I am still very anxious to see my brother's murderers caught.'

'I am relieved to hear you say it. I believe I am on the point of making a breakthrough.'

Désirée's eyes widened. 'Has Moreau recovered enough to speak?'

'He woke up in his right senses this morning. The doctor tells me that I may question him later.' Satisfaction filled Armand's light tones.

'You'll let me know if. . .if—'

'Of course.' Armand took her both hands in his own and squeezed them gently. 'I'll send a message straight away.'

'Oh, why couldn't this have happened earlier!'

'There is a solution.'

Startled, Désirée stared at him. His pale eyes were gleaming with excitement. Uneasily, she realised he was now gripping her hands in a tight hold.

'You don't have to leave Madrid at all. Not if you don't want to.

'Armand, what do you mean?' Désirée felt a flicker of panic shoot through her as she tried to pull her hands away and failed.

With surprising strength, he jerked her into his arms.

'I want you to marry me, Désirée.'

'I am astonished at you, Major.' Désirée struggled free from Armand's embrace, evading his attempts to kiss her. 'You know I have recently suffered the loss of

someone very dear to me. How can you think I would
entertain the notion of marriage!'

'I am not proposing a romantic entanglement.' Armand
stood very stiff, his face flushing at the cold fury in her
voice. 'I find you an extremely attractive woman, but my
reason for offering marriage is not based upon physical
desire.'

He paused and tugged at the collar of his uniform in
a nervous gesture. 'I see I have gone about this business
in the entirely the wrong way. Please let me apologise
for offending you and give me leave to explain.'

Curiosity overmastered her anger. 'Pray continue.'

'Thank you.' Adopting an air of brisk logic, Armand
launched into explanation. 'To be frank, Désirée, I need
a rich wife. As you may have heard, I have large debts.
You are a considerable heiress. What's more, your connections would be of great advantage to me in furthering
my military career.'

'And just what advantage would *I* gain from such a
match, *monsieur*?'

'You said you wished to remain in Spain, but it is
neither desirable nor sensible to try to manage on your
own. You need a protector. I come from a respectable
background, am in good health and have excellent
prospects.'

'You are proposing a marriage of convenience?'

'Why not? At your age a girl ought to be wed and I
consider myself a desirable *parti*.'

Désirée suppressed an unseemly urge to giggle. *Dieu*,
she hadn't dreamt he could be so pompous!

'You may be good husband material, Armand. But
marriage is a rather drastic solution to my current problem. It would be simpler to return home to France.'

'That, of course, is your privilege.' Armand inclined
his ruddy head. 'However, I don't think you will. You
want to see Etienne's murderers captured. . .' he paused
significantly '. . .And I am the best person to help you
fulfil that wish.'

Désirée bit her lower lip, all urge to laugh fleeing.

A brief smile of satisfaction flitted across Armand's face as he saw his shaft go home.

'I know I have taken you by surprise, but I beg you to give my proposal the attention it deserves. You will see it has many advantages.'

'Armand, I know you mean well, but I couldn't enter into a marriage of convenience. I think love is necessary—'

'Oh, surely not? Love is a fairy-tale, *chérie*, invented to persuade nervous young girls into accepting the harsher practicalities of marriage.'

The amused scorn in his voice made Désirée frown. 'I am sorry to hear you speak in such a cynical fashion,' she said slowly. 'It merely confirms my belief that you and I are not as well suited as you seem to think.'

'Don't give me your final answer now, not when you are upset. You need time to consider the idea. I can wait until you return to Madrid.' He smiled at her encouragingly. 'You wouldn't regret accepting me. I may not share all your beliefs, but in general we deal together well and I should do my best to make you a tolerable husband.'

'Do you think we would be happy?' she asked bluntly.

'I dare say we have as much chance of happiness as any other married couple.' Armand gave a dismissive little chuckle. 'Now come, let me escort you back to your carriage. It is bad to keep the horses standing and I must return to my duties.'

Désirée was thoughtful on the way home. On arrival, she retired to the *sala*, taking a pot of tea with her. Tea-drinking was a habit she had acquired from her English grandparents and she prided herself on being able to brew it properly.

Sipping her tea, Désirée wished she had been more firm and convinced Armand that she meant her refusal. She could never marry a man like him. He was too calculating, too cynically ambitious!

In fact, she was willing to wager that he would never

have mentioned his debts at all if she had fallen into his
arms and accepted him straight away. Her revulsion at
his attempt to woo her in a romantic fashion had forced
him to change his tactics and adopt a frank approach,
but she had seen through his selfishness.

Désirée shivered. All Armand had achieved by proposing was to spoil their friendship. He had forced her to
acknowledge the cold calculating ambition she had
always secretly suspected to be the well-spring of his
character. It was a flaw she found deeply unattractive
and had tried to ignore. Now it was out in the open and
it overshadowed his good points.

Rising to her feet, she crossed to the little satinwood
writing-desk, but even as she picked up her pen she
paused.

Armand was still in charge of the investigation into
Etienne's death. If she wrote now, rejecting him, would
he allow it to affect his diligence? He claimed to have
been Etienne's friend, but she was no longer sure whether
his zeal for justice was genuine or whether he had made
opportunistic use of his position to try and attach her
affections.

Désirée put the pen down. It was a risk she didn't
want to take. She would let him think she was undecided.

'And if my conscience hurts at deliberately deceiving
you, Armand,' she murmured, 'I shall remind myself that
you did not deal fairly with me, but tried to use my
brother's death for your own advantage!'

Final preparations for their departure occupied most of
Thursday and Désirée was glad when everything was
ready. Rafael was going to come for her at first light
so that they could make a good start before the day
got too hot.

She intended to dine at home and have an early night,
but after her evening bath she ignored the gown Rosita
had put out for her and slipped into a plain black walking-
dress.

When Rosita returned to tidy up, she had already

arranged a black silk *mantilla* over her hair to conceal its brightness and thrown a dark shawl around her shoulders.

'You are going out, *señorita*?' Rosita eyed her in surprise.

'There is one last thing I have to do.'

'I shall get my outdoor shoes—'

'No, Rosita, I don't want you to accompany me. This is something I want to do alone.'

Rosita opened her mouth to protest and then the sombre note in Désirée's voice penetrated her affronted dismay.

'*Si*, I understand,' she said softly and stepped aside to let her mistress pass.

Désirée had never been out without a protective duenna before, but she was certain of her direction and walked along confidently. In her plain attire she knew she was an inconspicuous figure and the streets, busy with people returning home to their supper, held no terror for her.

There was a flower-seller on the corner of the narrow *calle* she sought and she purchased a large bunch of red roses, glad that her Castilian was now good enough not to occasion comment.

The church of San Martin was sturdy and plain, as befitted the patron saint of soldiers. As a child, Désirée had loved to hear Etienne tell the story of how this Roman tribune had taken his sword and slashed his cloak in half to share it with a nearly naked beggar and been rewarded for his charity with a vision of Christ.

Désirée slipped into the church, which was empty save for an old woman praying on her knees before a statue of the the Virgin which adorned the side altar. She didn't stir as Désirée walked past, her flat sandals soundless on the cool marble.

Candles burned on the main altar. Désirée knelt and their flickering flames blurred before her eyes as tears ran unchecked down her pale face.

When she had finished her prayer, she rose and moved to the iron stand holding rows of candles lit by

supplicants, which stood to one side of the altar. A small
tray, holding fresh candles, was fastened beneath together
with a box for money. Désirée dropped a generous handful of coins into the box; taking a new candle, she lit it
from one of those already burning and stuck it firmly
down into a free holder.

It glowed with a fresh bright flame, a promise of life
eternal.

Saint Martin, protector of cavalrymen, had remained
Etienne's favourite saint. He had asked to be buried in
the tiny churchyard here.

Outside, Désirée sought his grave. It was set aside
from the others in a quiet corner, marked by a simple
headstone in the form of a cross, which Désirée had
ordered to be carved.

The stone bore only his name. Désirée had wanted to
have his dates and a proper tribute inscribed, but
Monsieur Dubec, who had escorted her here that first
time, had advised against it. She had been sickened to
think that anyone might be depraved enough to desecrate
a grave, but so many dreadful atrocities had already been
committed in this war that she accepted it was wise not
to flaunt the fact that a Frenchman lay buried in this
piece of Spanish soil.

Stooping, she placed her flowers beneath the cross.

Roses, red as blood. A symbol of her undying love . . .
and a pledge of vengeance.

'Farewell, Etienne,' she whispered and turned away.

Hurrying towards the exit, half-blinded by tears, she
almost failed to recognise the tall man striding
towards her.

'Désirée. Are you all right?'

The cool velvet voice was unmistakable.

'Rafael.' Realising her face was wet, Désirée hastily
wiped her cheeks with the edge of her *mantilla*. 'How
did you know where I was?'

'Rosita told me I would find you here.' He smiled at
her very gently, his heart touched by her sorrow.
'And why.'

Désirée flushed, disconcerted by the sympathy in his eyes. 'You regarded my brother as an enemy,' she muttered.

'True,' he replied quietly. 'But I have no quarrel with the dead. By all accounts your brother was a brave soldier and I can honour him for his courage, even though I loathe the uniform he wore.'

'I hate leaving him here all alone.' Désirée's lower lip trembled.

'He is not alone.' Rafael placed an arm around her shoulders and hugged her tightly. 'He is safe with God. One day you will both meet again.'

He released her. 'Now let me take you home.'

'Thank you.' Désirée pushed back a lock of stray hair from her hot face, feeling oddly comforted by his unexpected compassion.

Relieved to see she had recovered her composure, Rafael moved to offer her his arm and then stopped abruptly. '*Ay de mí*!' he exclaimed, irritated by his own carelessness. 'I almost forgot. I have a letter for you.'

'For me? Is that why you came after me?'

He looked up from delving into his coat pocket. 'My actual purpose in visiting you this evening was to discover if you needed any last-minute help. I arrived on your doorstep at the same time as a messenger from the garrison. He told Rosita that the letter was urgent and since I had already decided to follow you here in order to offer you my escort home, I brought it with me.'

He handed it to her. 'I hope it is not bad news.'

Désirée had already guessed the letter must be from Armand. She ripped it open and scanned the few lines it contained.

'On the contrary, it is excellent news! Major Evrard has discovered the identity of Etienne's murderers.'

'He knows who attacked your brother's patrol?'

Désirée was too excited to notice the sudden hoarseness in Rafael's voice.

'He says the *guerrilla* leader responsible is named El

Verdugo.' Désirée lifted shining eyes to his. 'What does that mean, Rafael?'

Rafael cast a backlong glance towards the lonely grave they were leaving.

The name means The Executioner,' he said heavily.

Accepting the arm he held out to her, Désirée was too excited to wonder why he looked so grim.

Désirée, who had elected to travel on horseback, soon understood why Rafael had chosen a small but sturdy gig instead of a larger, more comfortable carriage as transport for his sister and Rosita.

'Are we really going to climb up there?' she asked in awe.

Rafael, who was slightly ahead of her, reined to a halt and watched how her eyes widened as she gazed at the road, winding its way forever north into the mountains.

He laughed, his teeth very white against his brown skin. '*Sí*. Over the hills and far away, *querida*!'

In his old battered travelling jacket, outlined against the blazing blue sky, Rafael de Velasco sat on his magnificent stallion looking utterly at ease.

'I think you are enjoying this,' Désirée murmured in a faintly disbelieving voice.

'Let's say I prefer it to the city,' Rafael retorted with a dry humour that made Désirée laugh.

Her confidence restored, she patted the neck of her own mount, the well-behaved chestnut gelding she had occasionally hired in Madrid. She had decided to purchase him when she realised she would need a reliable horse for this trip.

'I hope you ate a good breakfast, Madrigal, I think you are going to need it!' she chuckled, urging him forward to catch up with the grey stallion.

Désirée herself had been too excited to eat much. Up and dressed in her riding habit soon after dawn, she had greeted Rafael and his party with eager impatience, anxious to embark upon the journey.

She hadn't realised then how awe-inspiring these mountains were!

'You know, I was pleased when you said that you wanted to follow the most direct route,' she announced with a wry grin. 'I thought it sounded adventurous!'

'Think of the time we are saving. Travelling by way of Valladolid adds days to the trip.' He flashed her a sharp look. 'You aren't really worried, are you? I assure you it is safe enough in summer, although I wouldn't want to chance it in winter.'

'Napoleon did,' Désirée replied and then could have kicked herself for her thoughtless lack of tact as a shadow darkened his face.

'I would never deny your Emperor possesses great daring and courage, but I think even he might have baulked at crossing the Sierra de Guadarrama with women in tow.'

'You think my sex so weak then, *señor*?' Indignation banished Désirée's remorse.

'You yourself just admitted that these mountains frighten you,' he pointed out.

His reasonable tone fanned the flames. 'That's because I'm not used to them,' she retorted with unanswerable logic. 'It has nothing to do with any lack of stamina or courage!'

'Women can possess both those qualities, but you must admit that you cannot match a man's strength or powers of endurance. It is simply a matter of greater muscle.'

Désirée smiled at him sweetly. 'Sometimes, *señor*, brains are to be preferred to mere brawn.'

Rafael threw back his head and laughed. '*Pax*! I give in!'

'You aren't going to argue with me?' Désirée gazed at him uncertainly, feeling a little bit cheated.

A wicked grin split his dark face. 'On *that* subject I wouldn't dare.'

'Now I know you are teasing me!' The innocence in his voice didn't fool Désirée. They both knew that although she was extremely well-read for a woman, his education had been more extensive.

He nodded, admitting it. 'Do you mind?'

'No. I like it.' A slightly sad smile curved her pink mouth. 'Etienne used to tease me sometimes too. He said I needed it when I got on my high horse and started lecturing him about the rights of women.'

'No doubt too much book-learning had turned your brain?'

Désirée opened her eyes wide in mock horror. 'How did you guess?' she murmured, her tone bubbling with suppressed laughter.

'I'm glad your grandfather ignored convention,' he replied rather obliquely.

'Is that a compliment?' she demanded suspiciously.

'I hope so.' His smile was a warm caress. 'You see, *ninfa*, pretty women can be found almost everywhere and clever women are plentiful enough, but a woman who is both beautiful and clever is a much rarer creature.'

Désirée blushed but, rallying, managed to retort, 'Be careful, *señor*, or I shall take you at your word and fancy myself a paragon indeed!'

His smile deepened. She had just proved his point. She always gave as good as she got, defending her views with a wit and spirit he found immensely attractive.

Women who simpered bored him. Most of his friends liked their wives docile and submissive, but he didn't want someone who always agreed with him. He needed challenge, but was honest enough to know that his ideal woman would have to temper independence with integrity. He would have to be able to trust her implicitly for his pride could never endure a wife like Inez who was unfaithful.

'I concede your victory. . .this time, *mi perla*.'

'Were we engaged in battle, *señor*?' Désirée gave him an innocently provocative grin.

'A mere skirmish.'

'"For this relief much thanks,"' Désirée quoted with mock solemnity.

'Shakespeare?' Rafael asked cautiously.

'*Hamlet.*'

Rafael laughed. 'Conversations with you are never boring, *ninfa*, and for that alone your grandfather deserves my thanks.'

The admiration in his dark eyes told her he was serious in spite of his joking tone.

Désirée's pulse quickened with pleasure. It was refreshing to be with a man who wasn't daunted by an educated woman. In his company she could say what she liked. She didn't have to pretend to be empty-headed to avoid being thought a bluestocking.

'Don Rafael!'

A shout from one the outriders who accompanied them shattered their bantering mood and made them wheel their horses round.

When she saw that the gig had become stuck, Désirée forced down her irritation at the interruption and hurried to lend her assistance.

It was the first of several such delays and, as the day drew on, Rafael began to frown.

'We are losing a lot of time,' he said, glancing up at the afternoon sun. 'I had hoped to reach Buitrago by nightfall.'

'Does that mean we will we have to camp in the open overnight?' Désirée asked.

Rafael looked back towards the gig. Rosita was taking a turn at driving while his sister rested, weariness etched on her thin face. 'I hope not. We have enough supplies, but Buitrago would be more comfortable. It is a small place, but there is an inn.'

Désirée was dubious. In her experience, the facilities offered by small remote inns tended to be primitive. All in all, she thought she would prefer a night spent on hard ground to one being eaten alive by bedbugs!

She asked Elena what she thought during a short stop to rest the horses.

'I'll go and tell Rafael I don't mind sleeping in the

open,' Elena announced. 'He is inclined to treat me like an invalid, but I shall manage well enough.'

By the time dusk descended they were still several leagues from Buitrago and, spotting a sheltered gully, Rafael decided against pushing on.

He called a halt. 'We'll spend the night here.'

Relieved to dismount, Désirée stamped up and down for several moments to restore her circulation while around her the outriders who accompanied them began to unload their mounts and make camp.

They lit a couple of small fires and soon the air was filled with the scent of beans, bacon and onions cooking with aromatic spices.

To her surprise, Désirée enjoyed the rough meal.

'That tasted wonderful,' she said, setting down her empty tin plate. She grinned. 'I thought I would find it indigestible.'

'The mountain air has given you an appetite,' Rafael answered.

He was sitting opposite her, across the fire, cradling a cup of red wine in his long fingers and it occurred once again to Désirée that he looked thoroughly at home.

Watching him, she reflected that he was a man of many parts. He always managed to surprise her! He looked like a patrician, dressed like a brigand, had the razor-sharp mind of a scholar but possessed the soul of a true romantic.

'Well, all this fresh air has made me sleepy,' Elena declared, rising to her feet. 'I'm for bed. Are you coming, Désirée?'

Désirée opened her mouth to say she wasn't tired and found herself yawning.

'Go and get some rest.' Rafael cut across her apologies in an amused voice. 'We must make an early start tomorrow.'

Wrapping herself in one of the blankets Rafael had provided, Désirée tried to make herself comfortable. It was growing cold, much colder than she had expected.

Gradually the camp became silent. One of the fires

was put out and the other allowed to die down as everyone except the guard set by Rafael settled themselves for sleep.

Désirée lay on her back, looking up at the stars. Listening to the sound of a night-bird calling, she felt herself drifting off.

She awoke to hear a murmur of voices. Stiff and cold, she struggled to sit up, sleepily wondering what the time was. The remaining fire was still burning and she could just make out someone at the edge of the camp.

The tall figure walked towards the light and she realised the man was Rafael. Coming fully awake, she scrambled out of her bedroll and moved towards the fire.

'Désirée?' Rafael, who was in the act of adding wood to the fire, paused and looked up in surprise. 'Is something wrong?'

'I am very cold. Is there any coffee left? I could do with a cup.'

'Come and get warm while I have a look.' Rafael checked the tin coffee-pot. 'There is a little, but it needs heating.' He set it over the flames. 'Couldn't you sleep?'

'I woke up a few moments ago.' Désirée sat down next to him. 'I thought I heard voices.'

'I was making an inspection of the camp. When I've had my coffee I'll relieve the guard for an hour or two.'

'Have you slept at all?' Désirée was amazed at his stamina.

'I can sleep later.' He smiled at her, the slow lazy smile she loved.

Désirée felt her heart twist with longing. All of a sudden, she was very conscious of the fact that everyone else was asleep, very conscious of his nearness. If she reached out, her hand would encounter his flesh.

Quickly, she clasped her hands together, burying them in her lap.

Her rapid breathing sounded too loud in the silence surrounding them. Désirée fought for control. But the air was very crisp and pure. It went to her head like wine.

'We might almost be the only people left on earth,' she murmured, her eyes glittering in the starlight.

With his usual swift perception, he caught the drift of her thoughts.

Their eyes locked and they both felt the ever-present sexual tension which lay between them tighten its grip.

'Do you ever wish it could be so? That we could be like Adam and Eve?' Désirée couldn't prevent herself from asking the question, her voice soft with longing.

What would he do if there were no barriers between them? Would he take her in his arms and make love to her the way she wanted him to and turn this quiet hillside into Paradise?

'Désirée, don't!' Rafael's voice was hoarse. 'We both know that there can be nothing more than friendship between us.'

'Forgive me.' Désirée let out a little sigh, her head drooping dejectedly on the fragile stem of her neck. 'I didn't mean to tease. I just wish...oh, well, you know what I wish!'

Like a knight of old, he believed honour was paramount and she had promised herself she would never beg for his love again, but at this moment she would have traded her hopes of Heaven for him to forget his scruples.

She lifted her head and met his sombre gaze with a faint rueful smile. 'Forget I ever mentioned the subject.'

'For the sake of my sanity, I must.'

His voice contained a note of dry humour, but in the flickering firelight Désirée saw the wealth of regret in his eyes and felt strangely comforted. Like the mountains he could not be moved, but she was beginning to believe he cared more than he was willing to admit.

'Your coffee is ready.'

The business of pouring out a cup of the strong brew and handing it to her, then pouring another for himself gave Rafael time to bring his emotions under control.

He wanted her so much! But he had no intentions of giving in to desire. He had persuaded her to leave Madrid to keep her safe. Tempting though it was to take advantage of the opportunity offered by this starlit night, nothing else had changed.

Désirée cupped her hands around the coffee, welcoming its heat. 'These mountains would make good cover for an ambush,' she murmured thoughtfully.

'Are you afraid?'

She shook her head vigorously, sending tendrils of hair flying. 'I can't imagine feeling afraid when I am with you.' She smiled at him with utter certainty. 'You know these mountains. What's more, I'd wager my best earrings that you wouldn't panic in a crisis. You don't get upset or lose your temper when things go wrong. You are so. . .steady and brave!'

'*Gracias*. Now who is paying flattering compliments?' Amusement coloured Rafael's deep voice.

'I'm serious! You know how to handle your men to get the best out of them. Etienne always used to say that was a very important skill. He swore a man couldn't be a good officer without it.'

Rafael nodded. 'Your brother was right.' He stared at her, the calm expression on his lean face hiding his bitter disquiet.

She looked so young and innocent tonight! Before going to bed she had loosened her hair from its travelling braid and it fell over her shoulders in a silvery flood that glistened in the firelight. Her riding-habit, which had begun the journey in immaculate condition, was creased and streaked with dust, but her dishevelment didn't matter. She would always appear beautiful to him.

Rafael's heart slammed against his ribs in short thick strokes as the realisation how he truly felt about Désirée Fontaine crashed over him.

Heaviness settled over his spirit. How could he be such a fool!

'I thank you for your good opinion, *mi perla*, but don't place too much faith in me, will you?' he said lightly, his cool languid tones concealing the maelstrom of emotion that raged within his breast. 'I should hate to disappoint you.'

Désirée laughed. 'Don't worry. I know you are no saint, *señor*!'

Frustration boiled in Rafael. She had turned his warning aside! And he didn't know whether to be glad or sorry!

'If you are warm enough now, I think it's time you went back to bed. Otherwise, you'll feel terrible in the morning.'

In spite of his casual manner, Désirée sensed something had gone wrong. However, it was equally clear he did not wish to talk so she nodded and rose obediently to her feet.

She rolled herself into her blanket, her eyes heavy. She was almost too tired to think, but his sudden withdrawal into himself had made her feel uneasy and sleep wouldn't come.

Then, she felt her rumpled blanket being tucked in more securely around her and heard his deep voice say softly, '*Buenas noches, querida*. Sleep well.'

His footsteps receded again and, reassured, she closed her eyes.

They reached their destination on the evening of the third day. Désirée sat up straighter in her saddle, ignoring the ache across her weary shoulders as they rode in through the gates set into the stone wall that surrounded the estate.

The *finca* lay in a small fertile valley a few leagues from the medieval town of Covarrubias. Vineyards and cultivated fields stretched on either side of the dusty road leading up to the house. Situated on a slight rise, she'd been told that it overlooked a large paved courtyard while to the rear were gardens, stables, various outbuildings and the main vineyard.

Désirée had Elena to thank for these facts but nothing had prepared her for her first sight of the Casa. It was a large, lovely building, its upper stories constructed of wood and white-painted plaster which gleamed in the

last of the sunshine. Désirée knew it must be very old,
but everything was well tended and spoke of much care.

'You have a beautiful house,' she exclaimed impul-
sively to Rafael.

She could tell by his smile that the compliment pleased
him, but there was no time left to talk as servants and
dogs spilled from the big wooden doors with loud cries
of welcome and excited barking, turning the courtyard
into a laughing melee as the new arrivals dismounted.

'Come with me, Désirée.' Elena approached her guest,
a happy smile on her face. 'We shall drink something to
cool our throats and then I shall show you to your room.
You must be dying to wash off all this dust and change
into clean clothes.'

They stepped into a massive, high-ceilinged entrance
hall. The stone-flagged floor and bare walls, decorated
only with a selection of highly polished weapons, made
it seem austere, but it was blessedly cool. Removing her
hat and riding-gloves, Désirée handed them to a waiting
servant and followed Elena up a flight of shallow stone
steps into what she assumed was the main *sala*.

It was a big room but the bright rugs scattered over
the wooden floorboards and the colourful embroidered
cushions decorating the heavy solid furniture helped
create an informal atmosphere.

'Sit down. I'll be back in a moment. I want to be sure
that Ramona is preparing lots of lemonade. I could drink
a whole jugful myself!'

Elena whisked out of the room. Désirée could hear her
speaking to someone and then Rafael came in.

'Welcome to Casa del Aguila.' He smiled at her. It
gave him pleasure to see her sitting there by his hearth.
'I hope you will enjoy your visit.'

'I'm sure I shall.' Désirée returned his smile shyly.

He sat down opposite her and stretched out his long
legs. '*Ay de mí*! It feels good to be home!'

'You must be very tired. You didn't get much sleep
on the journey.'

Rafael acknowledged the remark with a slight nod. 'I

am in need of rest,' he admitted frankly. 'But tomorrow
I should like to show you around the estate, if you think
you might feel up to it?'

'I should like that.'

Elena returned, followed by a young, dark-haired maid
carrying a large silver tray.

'Let me help you with that, Ramona.' Rafael rose
swiftly to his feet and took the heavy tray from her.

'*Gracias*, Don Rafael.' Blushing rosily, the girl asked
if she should light the candles.

Rafael set the tray down. 'Leave it for now,' he
instructed, giving her a friendly smile as he spoke.

Watching the exchange, Désirée experienced a sharp
pang of jealousy. It lanced through her unsuspecting body
like a keen blade, making her gasp.

'Are you all right, Désirée?'

Turning the sound into a little cough, Désirée nodded.
'I've just got a dry throat, thank you, Elena.'

Dieu, she must get a hold on herself! Such jealousy
was more than stupid, it was downright irrational!

'I have the remedy for that.' Dismissing Ramona,
Elena poured out the lemonade and handed a fine crystal
goblet to Désirée. 'Drink up, there is plenty more.'

It tasted like nectar after the strong bitter coffee and
rough wine on their journey.

'I've told them to serve supper in an hour. Will that
give you enough time, Désirée? Rosita is already preparing a bath for you.'

Désirée expressed her satisfaction at this arrangement
and accepted a second glass of lemonade. When she
finished it, Elena announced that she would show her to
her room.

Rafael rose politely to his feet and escorted them both
to the door.

'I shall see you at supper,' he said to Désirée. 'Your
luggage has already been taken up. If there is anything
else you need, just let one of the servants know.'

Désirée nodded. 'Thank you.'

'There is no need to thank me, *ninfa*. Remember, *mi casa es su casa*.'

The warmth in his dark eyes made Désirée forget her idiotic jealousy of Ramona. She might have no claim on him, but she was becoming more and more certain that he cared, at least a little, for her.

Mi casa es su casa. My house is yours. Oh, how she wished that could be really true!

Chapter Nine

Désirée couldn't explain it, but for the first time in her life she felt settled. After just over a week at Casa del Aguila she felt as if she belonged here, her restless urges soothed by its slow, ancient rhythms.

'Which, if you consider it logically, my girl, is totally idiotic!' she told her reflection in the dressing-table mirror.

Her reflection nodded obediently.

Désirée let out a strangled laugh. *Dieu*! The situation was impossible. No wonder she had begun talking to herself!

Living here with Rafael was torment, a torment of the sweetest kind. To be so close to him and yet so far! They had ridden out most days and he had shown her over almost every inch of the estate. Hour after hour, they had enjoyed each other's company, talking and laughing, wrapped up in a bubble of happiness that shut out the rest of the world.

Somehow, the very fact that he had behaved impeccably made it harder to bear.

She longed to feel his arms around her, longed to feel his lips on hers. . .

Désirée sighed. She should have stayed in Madrid!

Rising to her feet, she left her bedroom and made her way down to the shaded patio at the rear of the house where breakfast was usually served. Already, although it was not yet eight, it was another hot day and she could see one of the kitchen cats basking lazily in a patch of sunshine beyond the patio.

To her surprise, there was no sign of Elena, who was normally an early riser.

One of the servants brought her coffee and Désirée asked the girl if Elena had already breakfasted.

The maid said she thought that a tray had been taken up to the Doña's room.

Désirée was just finishing her meal when Elena herself appeared, looking rather pale.

When asked, Elena admitted to a headache. 'But I promised I would go down to the village today. I want to deliver those coloured lanterns and help with the last-minute preparations for the *fiesta* tomorrow.'

Désirée nodded. Elena had been spending quite a lot of time lately in the small village of Riofrío, which lay a half a league to the south. It was home to many of the Casa's servants and estate-workers.

Elena sat down, her weariness evident. 'I don't want to disappoint them,' she said, confirming Désirée's guess that the bond of loyalty existed on both sides. 'It will be the last *fiesta* I attend, so I want everything to go off properly.'

'Why don't I go in your place?'

Elena looked doubtful. 'It seems unfair to impose on you—'

'Elena, I should *like* to help,' Désirée interrupted quickly. 'You have been amazingly kind to me. Let me do this small thing for you.'

'It will a long hot ride,' Elena warned.

'All the more reason for me to go,' Désirée said firmly. 'You aren't feeling well and I am as strong as an ox.'

Chuckling softly, for she had never seen anyone less like an ox than her dainty guest, Elena accepted her offer. After thanking her and explaining the necessary arrangements, she declared that she would go back to bed.

Désirée hurried to change into her riding-habit and was just descending to the cavernous entrance hall when she encountered Rafael.

'*Buenos días*. Where are you off to in such a hurry?' he asked.

Désirée explained her mission.

'I'll go with you.'

'But you've just come in.' Désirée eyed his dusty riding-clothes.

'Give me a few minutes to drink a cup of coffee and I'll join you out by the waggon.'

Delighted at the thought of having his company, Désirée agreed with a glowing smile.

She couldn't help torturing herself. Where Rafael de Velasco was concerned, she had no willpower and very little sense!

The village of Riofrío consisted of a well-kept church, a small tavern and a cluster of whitewashed houses grouped around a central square. Backed by fertile fields and pasture, the houses, with their ochre-tiled roofs, were in good repair. Désirée thought it looked a prosperous place; there was even a fountain in the square where the women could do their washing.

She knew that many villages in Spain were not so lucky. Famine and hardship had abounded even before the French had arrived. Riofrío's situation in a sheltered, well-watered valley was favoured, but she suspected that having the Velasco family as its patron was equally important.

Their waggon was soon surrounded by a noisy throng. Every face wore a smile and there was a buzz of excited welcome and conversation.

'This lady is a friend of mine.' To her surprise, Rafael held up Désirée's hand and kissed it in full view of everyone. 'You will treat her as you would Doña Elena.'

Realising that the demonstration was to make sure of her safety and comfort, Désirée forced a smile.

She was horribly aware of the sudden silence and couldn't help wishing that a few of the smiles which had been bestowed so lavishly upon Rafael might flicker in her direction.

The uneasy tension dissolved and loud cheering broke out when Rafael announced he had brought an extra barrel of wine for the *fiesta*.

'Now I see why you are so popular,' Désirée remarked, turning to him with a broad grin.

Rafael shrugged. 'These people work hard. They deserve their fun.'

His cold tone made her realise he had misinterpreted her jest. 'I. . .I didn't mean to criticise.'

Rafael's expression softened. 'No, I know you didn't. Forgive me, I am so used to having to defend my views that I go on the attack without thinking.'

'I understand.'

'Do you, *mi perla*? So many of my countrymen treat their people like dogs. They think me mad to try and alleviate the lot of my villagers. They don't see why I am endeavouring to improve the old ways, why I bother seeking methods to prevent famine and disease.'

His words confirmed her gut feeling that he was a good landlord, but she felt indignant that he should imagine she might side with his old-fashioned, heartless detractors.

'No one should have to go hungry or cold! Even discounting the simple fact that starving people don't make good workers, therefore it makes sense to treat them well, such neglect is morally wrong. The poor are entitled to a chance of comfort and happiness just as much as those born in better circumstances.'

'Spoken like a true daughter of the Revolution.' Rafael's voice was tinged with amusement but beneath his pose of cynicism lay genuine approval and admiration.

He might have known she would share his idealistic views. Her nature was kind and she treated Rosita and other servants with a consideration not often found in well-born ladies.

'I hold no brief for the kind of misplaced fervour which resulted in the death of my adoptive father,' Désirée said awkwardly, her colour rising in embarrassment. 'But I cannot help speaking my mind. I thought you knew that about me by now.'

He nodded. 'I should hate it if you felt you had to mince your words with me.'

His smile reassured her. *Maman* had often scolded her for her outspokenness, but at least this time her lack of tact had not caused offence.

The task of unloading began. Désirée insisted on helping. She noticed one or two of the women giving her speculative looks, but their expressions remained impassive. She was obviously on trial, but at least they hadn't rejected her outright.

Under Rafael's direction everything was quickly sorted out and distributed. When the job was done, jugs of cooling lemonade were brought out. Désirée accepted a beaker with a shy smile and murmur of thanks in her best Castilian.

'*De nada.*' The middle-aged woman, who had handed it to her waved her hand dismissively, but Désirée fancied that she saw a spark of approval in the dark brown eyes.

Then Rafael drew her to his side and put one arm loosely around her waist, while he sipped his drink. Désirée saw the gesture did not go unnoticed. She knew he had done it to impress upon the villagers that she was under his protection, but she couldn't prevent happiness flaring up inside at his touch.

A tiny scandalised voice whispered in her head that they would think she was his woman, but Désirée didn't care.

Gossip be damned! She wished she *was* his woman.

Her whirling thoughts made it hard to concentrate and she kept losing the thread of the rapid conversation. In the end, she was content to rest quietly against Rafael's shoulder, absorbing the lively atmosphere and revelling in his nearness.

'It's time to leave, *mi perla.*' Rafael bent to whisper the words into the delicate curve of her ear.

Désirée nodded, loath to tear herself away.

They said their farewells and mounted up.

'Isn't Domingo coming back with us?' she asked in surprise, noticing the waggon-driver still chatting in a group of men.

'He lives in the village. I have given him leave to spend the *siesta* here. He will drive back later.'

The ride home was very hot. Désirée could feel her riding-habit sticking to her and felt only sympathy when Madrigal began to fidget as they came in sight of the river, a tributary of the Arlanza. The summer drought had caused its level to shrink, but the water that was left glittered invitingly.

'Can we stop for a moment? Madrigal is thirsty.'

Rafael nodded. 'There's some shade over there. We can rest for a while if you wish.'

They watered their horses and tethered them to a branch of one of a pair of wild olive trees which were growing close to the river. Their canopy threw a patch of shade over the bank and Désirée sat down, glad of the respite.

'I don't think I have ever been so hot in my life!' she exclaimed, pulling off her hat and ruffling her hand through her curls in an attempt to cool her scalp. 'I wish I could go for a swim.'

It didn't surprise Rafael that she knew how. 'Why don't you?' he asked with a lazy smile.

Désirée was sorely tempted, but she shook her head. Taking off her clothes in his presence was not a good idea! It would only encourage her wanton imagination!

'Perhaps not.' Rafael struggled to put a tantalising image out of his mind. He could picture only too well how lovely she would look, her delicious curves nude, her pale silken skin glistening with droplets of water. . .

There was a tiny silence and, conscious of the tension between them beginning to spiral Rafael quickly cast about for some innocuous remark.

'Did your grandfather teach you to swim?'

'Actually, it was my father.'

'I didn't realise that you knew him.'

Her face went white and Rafael winced, realising how tactless he must have sounded.

'Please accept that I didn't mean to be offensive. From what you said in Burgos, I'd assumed that your birth was the result of an illicit affair.' A puzzled frown knitted his dark brows together. 'Did your parents go on to marry?'

Désirée sighed. 'No, although Papa wished for it at the end, but it was too late for the vicar to perform the ceremony.'

Glancing across at him, she saw that her answer had only deepened his puzzlement.

'It is a complicated story,' she murmured, fidgeting with a fold of her riding-habit. Summoning her courage, she looked up into his dark eyes. 'Would you like to hear it?'

'Very much,' answered Rafael, who, although he was trying to hide it, was consumed by curiosity. In addition to his deep desire to learn more about her, he had a feeling that her tangled parentage might hold vital clues to her character. The more knowledge he had about the way her mind worked, the more confidently he could predict her reactions.

One day soon he intended to tell her the truth, come what may! And in that dark hour he would need all the help he could get!

Taking a deep breath, Désirée began sensibly at the beginning.

'My mother was the youngest of five daughters. The family was of noble blood but not rich. When she was seventeen, a wealthy widower offered for her. A retired military man, he was more than twice her age, but she was happy to accept. There was very little left in the family coffers for her dowry and she'd feared she might never attract a suitor.'

'Was she as beautiful as you?'

Désirée coloured. 'Far more lovely,' she said with a frown that warned him not to disturb her concentration with frivolous interruptions.

'Etienne was born within a twelvemonth of the wed-

ding, and *Maman* was happy enough living quietly in
the country until Le Chevalier took her on a visit to
Versailles. They left Etienne at home with his nurse—
he was almost seven. It was the first time *Maman* had
been to Court. There was some political tension in the
air, of course, but they hired a house in Paris and she
found the whole experience wonderfully exciting.'

'Would that be about a year before your birth?' Rafael
hazarded a guess.

Désirée nodded. 'Almost. That was April 1787 and
my birthday is at the end of January.' She paused and,
shifting her position, drew her knees up to her chin. 'My
father chose that same April to visit friends in Paris. They
were introduced at a ball. They were exactly matched in
age and were immediately attracted to one another.'

Her shoulders lifted in a tiny shrug. 'You can imagine
what happened.'

Rafael could.

'I think they both got more than they bargained for,'
Désirée continued wryly.

'Yourself?'

She shook her head. 'A baby might be a logical if
unwelcome result of a passionate affair. No, what I meant
was that they fell deeply in love, but there was nothing
they could do about it! Papa was on the brink of offering
for a well-dowered girl his parents approved—he had
come away to make his mind up. He knew that if he
succeeded in persuading *Maman* to run away with him,
they would be furious and say he had ruined his life.'

Rafael nodded. A French Catholic, a married woman
and carrying a bastard child! Not the kind of girl many
parents amongst the English gentry would welcome!

'*Maman* felt very guilty. She had deceived her husband
and he would be publicly shamed if she deserted him.
She also knew that he would never let her take Etienne
away with her and she couldn't bear to abandon him.'
Désirée stared fixedly at her knees. 'So, in the end, they
were forced to part and *Maman* was heartbroken.'

It was an old story, Rafael decided. A bored young

wife seeking excitement she could not find with her elderly husband. The stuff of dozens of witty comedies. . .and yet for Corinne Fontaine and John Cavendish it had been all too real, all too agonising!

'She discovered she was with child soon after her arrival home. By this stage of their marriage, due to his poor health, she rarely shared her husband's bed. They had not done so in all the weeks they had been in Paris.' Désirée's pretty mouth twisted. 'When she confessed, Le Chevalier was extremely angry, but he forgave her and apparently doted on me when I made my arrival.'

Rafael almost made the mistake of saying that she must have been an adorable baby, but then thought better of it.

'I loved him too.' Désirée's bleak expression softened for an instant before tightening again. 'I don't suppose they would have ever told me the truth about my real father if Fate hadn't taken a hand.'

After the mob had attacked the château, Corinne had decided to seek refuge in England. She'd had no contact with her lover since they had reluctantly said goodbye, but she pinned her hopes on the conviction that her John would not see them suffer destitution.

'*Maman* knew my father's elder sister lived in Portsmouth. Aunt Caroline took us in and sent messages to my father. She was very kind.' A ghost of a smile touched Désirée's face. 'But she didn't have the courage to warn *Maman* that Papa's wife was a veritable virago!'

'Your father had married that rich girl?'

Désirée nodded. 'From what I have gathered since, I don't think he ever really cared for her, but his parents were keen on the match, so he'd eventually decided he might as well please them.'

Scarcely aware of her actions, Désirée's fingers plucked restlessly at the surrounding grass. It was dry and brittle, just like her voice.

'When Aunt Caroline wrote to him it had been six years since his visit to Paris. He had put the past behind him. He wasn't even aware of my existence. Le Chevalier had insisted on that.'

Rafael could understand why. It must have galled the old man's pride even if he had managed to forgive his wife's indiscretion.

'I think *Maman* was relieved when Papa answered straight away. He came to see us and she told me later that, after the first awkward hour, it was as if their separation had never existed. But he could not offer *Maman* marriage for now he was no longer free.'

Désirée shrugged. 'So she became his mistress.'

Rafael just managed to prevent a low whistle escaping him. *Dios!*

Interpreting his expression correctly, Désirée nodded. 'You're right. It did set the cat amongst the pigeons. His wife was a jealous woman who had never conceived in the five years that they had been wed. She longed for a child, so it was imperative to keep our existence a secret. For a time all went well. Papa had inherited an estate from his godfather and he arranged for us to be housed in a cottage tucked into its most remote corner. He also gave *Maman* a generous allowance. We saw him nearly every day and *Maman* was happy.'

'Did you like him?'

Désirée wriggled uncomfortably. 'I don't know,' she confessed. 'I remember him as a big, fair-haired man with a loud laugh, but I was a little afraid of him. He was so different from Le Chevalier!'

'It must have been a strange time for you.'

'It was worse for Etienne! At least I was young enough to adapt and Papa was interested in me, but Etienne felt unwanted and in the way.' Désirée shook her head in rueful remembrance and then carried on in a determined voice.

'Some months after we moved into the cottage, Papa's wife found out that he was keeping a mistress. He fobbed her off, continually promising to give *Maman* up. There were dreadful scenes apparently, but she went on swallowing his excuses. I don't know why.'

'Maybe it was easier for her pride to pretend you did not exist.'

'Perhaps. At least, it was until someone teased her spitefully about me at a soirée they were attending one night; then she finally gave Papa an ultimatum. On the way home she told him that, unless he agreed to send us packing, she would sue for a divorce.'

Rafael's brows lifted. Such a move would have caused a dreadful scandal.

A grim frown creased Désirée's delicate features.

'Papa was driving. They began to quarrel violently and he must have lost concentration. The carriage ended up in a deep ditch. His wife was killed outright. Her neck was broken, I believe. Papa was very badly injured. They were closer to the Manor than his own property, so he was taken there and Grandfather immediately summoned a doctor, who told him to send for the vicar.'

Désirée let out a long sigh.

'Papa confessed the whole story to my grandparents and begged them fetch *Maman*. They were shocked and refused at first, but by dawn it was obvious that Papa was dying and they gave in.'

'Did he ask for you?'

Désirée nodded. 'I was taken in to see him for a few minutes, but I cannot remember it well. I was too young, too sleepily confused to realise what was happening. *Maman* was allowed to stay. She always used to tell me that Papa asked her to marry him on that last morning of his life but, sadly, he died before the ceremony could actually take place.'

'And then your grandfather took charge.'

Désirée acknowledged this blunt statement with a slight inclination of her tousled head.

'Papa had begged him to look after us. Grandfather wanted me, but I suspect his original intention was to buy *Maman* off and send her away.' A faint grin touched Désirée's face. 'I screamed and struggled so much that they decided it might be better not to separate us. When I continued to prove unreasonable, *Maman* and Etienne were permitted to move into the Manor too. I suppose my grandparents felt obliged to honour Papa's wishes but, as far as *Maman* was concerned, they never got over their prejudice.'

Rafael regarded her half-averted profile. Her calm voice held no trace of self-pity, but he could imagine how harrowing it must have been for a sensitive child to find herself in such a difficult position.

'My grandparents took over my upbringing and education. They grew fond of me, I believe, but I always remained a pawn in the game they played to thwart my mother.'

Dependent upon their charity, Corinne had been in an impossible situation. Day by day, week by week, she had seen her little girl grow slowly away from her, becoming more and more alien, more and more English.

'However, they disliked Etienne. To be fair, he always behaved in a very insolent and disobedient way towards them, but that was because he hated living in England, hated living on their charity. He ran away back to France in ninety-seven. *Maman* confided in me later that she wished she'd had the courage to follow him, but she was unwilling to deprive me of my inheritance. You see, Aunt Caroline, who was married to a naval officer, had only daughters. There was no direct male heir and I was Grandfather's favourite.'

'What happened during the Peace of Amiens? Did your mother take advantage of the lull in the war to return to France?' Rafael had been doing mental arithmetic. Désirée would have been fourteen, a vulnerable age to endure such upheaval.

'She wanted to, but Grandfather applied pressure on her to stay. He promised her that he would make me his heir if she could persuade me never to return to the country of my birth.'

Désirée shrugged. 'I didn't know. I thought she was content enough in England until one day I found her weeping over a letter of Etienne's. He'd managed to make contact via a smuggler who was willing to carry messages and had written to say that he could now support us.'

A little sigh escaped Désirée.

'*Maman* wanted to go home, of course. She still felt a foreigner in England, just as Etienne had. But she didn't want to go without me.'

'And you, how did you feel, *ninfa*?' Rafael kept his voice level, although he thought he could predict her answer.

'I didn't know what to think!' Désirée exclaimed, confirming his shrewd guess. 'England was my home! I had almost forgotten France. My grandparents were very strict but I knew they cared for me. I kept hoping that the situation would improve.'

She pushed back her tangled curls from her hot forehead.

'It didn't, of course. Public feeling against the French grew as fears of invasion mounted. Even people who had known *Maman* for years became hostile and her health deteriorated under the additional strain. She became very low in spirit, especially when Etienne wrote to say that he was buying back the château. So I was forced to choose.'

She paused for a moment, swallowing the lump in her throat that the memory had induced. She had been sixteen years old and torn between two opposing loyalties. In the end, her mother's illness had tipped the balance.

'I told my grandparents I wanted to leave. They tried to persuade me to change my mind; when they couldn't, Grandfather flew into a rage.'

'He threatened to cut you off?'

Désirée nodded. 'He felt betrayed.'

They had left the Manor that same day and, with the help of Aunt Caroline, she had made contact with Etienne's smuggler who, for a very large fee, was willing to convey them back to France.

It had been a wretched homecoming. In spite of her joy at seeing Etienne again, Désirée had felt a foreigner in her own country.

'It took me months to settle down. I didn't remember the château at all. Everything was strange. Everything!'

She gave a wry laugh, but there was a catch in her voice as she continued. 'For years I'd been taught the French army was my enemy and Napoleon Bonaparte was a monster. Now I had to accept him as Etienne's friend and patron!'

Tactfully, Rafael stared out at the river, giving her a moment to recover her composure.

'It grew easier for me, of course, as time passed. *Maman* never fully recovered her health, but at least she was content in her final years—she had suffered so much unhappiness!'

'Did you think of returning to England after your mother's death?'

Désirée shook her blonde head. 'There was no point. Grandfather never forgave me. He altered his will immediately after we left, excluding me completely. I don't think he would have changed his mind in any event, but seven months after our departure, Aunt Caroline finally managed to produce a son and he had no need to forgive me.'

Rafael wondered if knowledge of her condition had prompted Caroline to speed her niece's departure. From the wry expression in her lovely blue eyes, he knew it was a thought which had also occurred to Désirée.

'He died shortly afterwards. Aunt Caroline wrote to tell me and concluded her letter by saying that my grandmother blamed me for hastening his death. She warned me that I would receive no answer if I tried to get in touch with her. She was right.'

Désirée shrugged her shapely shoulders. 'I continued to write to Aunt Caroline, but her answering letters grew shorter and shorter. At first, I tried to tell myself that she must be too busy, but when I finally realised that our correspondence embarrassed her I stopped writing. That was some three years ago and I haven't heard a word since.'

Sympathy for her plight welled up in Rafael. She had told her story in a straightforward manner with no trace of self-pity, but he sensed that her hurt was deep.

'You did the right thing, *mi perla*,' he said softly.

'I hope so. It is very hard to choose between two loyalties when both have a strong claim.' Désirée's expression was bleak. 'I wanted to please them both and I couldn't!'

'Did you ever think of trying to please yourself?'

Désirée laughed. 'An interesting notion, *señor*! Do *you* believe it is possible to balance personal happiness and honour?'

Rafael was silent for a moment and Désirée saw that he was wrapped in thought.

He lifted his gaze. Delicate white clouds, like the breath of angels, drifted slowly across the intensely blue sky.

'As God is my witness, Désirée, I don't know,' he said at last, returning his dark gaze to hers. 'I pray that it might be so, but I just don't know!'

All trace of Rafael's sombre mood had vanished by the time they sat down to supper that evening. Pleased to see him smiling again, Désirée didn't notice at first how quiet Elena was.

'Are you feeling quite well, *mi hermana*?' Rafael asked. 'You have barely touched a thing.'

'I'm not very hungry.' Elena tried to shrug off his concern, but when Désirée asked her if she still had a headache she finally admitted to feeling ill.

'Perhaps you should go to bed early,' Désirée suggested.

'I think I will.' Elena laid down her knife and fork and pushed back her chair. 'Will you both excuse me? A good night's sleep is probably all I need to restore my energy.' She gave a rueful grin. 'I certainly hope so—I don't want to miss tomorrow's fun!'

Désirée offered to accompany her up to her room.

'There is no need.' Elena smiled her thanks.

'But I've finished, anyway. It's no trouble,' Désirée insisted cheerfully.

Rafael thought his sister looked about to faint. 'If you

fall on the stairs, you certainly won't be up to the *fiesta*. Either accept Désirée's help or mine or I shall call your maid.'

Elena gave in and allowed Désirée to escort her.

Désirée wasn't surprised to find the dining-room empty on her return. Rafael rarely lingered over his wine, but when she entered the *sala* she found it, too, was deserted.

Where could he have got to? They had fallen into the habit of spending the hours after supper in here, sometimes playing cards, sometimes poring over volumes taken from the enormous selection in Rafael's library, and sometimes making music together. Both Rafael and his sister were gifted musically. Elena had a lovely singing voice and Rafael played the guitar with a skill that had surprised and delighted Désirée.

After waiting for some time, Désirée became restless and decided to see if Rafael was busy choosing a book. His private study was situated near the library. She heard voices as she passed. One was Rafael's. The other voice was also male, but she did not recognise it.

About to pass on into the library, she saw the study door opening and curiosity made her linger.

The unknown visitor emerged. He was wearing the rough clothes of a peasant and his face was dirty. Désirée could see him clearly, although she knew that he hadn't spotted her, hidden as she was in the library's shadowy doorway.

Puzzlement rose in Désirée. In the light given off by the candelabrum set on a marble-topped console-table next to where he was standing, his face was familiar, but she didn't know why.

He moved away and Désirée entered the library. She now knew where Rafael was located, but she wanted a moment to herself. She felt strangely shaken and disturbed by the man she had just seen.

He had moved with a confidence which spoke of familiarity with the Casa for all that he was poorly dressed.

And his swaggering walk was at odds with his rough clothes.

A *real* peasant would be nervous in a these grand surroundings.

'Now I remember him!' The exclamation burst from Désirée.

The last time she had seen that fellow he had been dressed very differently. He had worn the garb of a gentleman then, that evening on the banks of the River Manzanares when she had interrupted his private conversation with Rafael!

Barely had this realisation struck home than Rafael himself walked in.

'Ah, here you are! I've been looking for you,' he said. 'Shall I ask them to bring in your tray of tea to the *sala* or do you wish to wait a while?'

Désirée's fondness for tea had become something of a joke with them. In the evenings, when Rafael had drunk *rosole*—a mixture of brandy, cinnamon and sugar Désirée found too heady—and Elena sipped fruit juice, she had always asked for tea.

To Rafael's surprise, she shook her blonde head.

'I don't want any tea tonight, thank you. I've decided to emulate your sister and go to bed early.'

Wondering if she was perhaps regretting her confidences of that afternoon, Rafael concealed his disappointment and bade her a polite goodnight, adding softly, 'I hope you know you can trust me not to repeat what you told me earlier. Your secrets are safe with me.'

Désirée managed a smile. 'Thank you.'

She hurried up to her bedroom. It was a large room decorated with style and comfort. Having expected plain austerity, Désirée had found its elegant modern furnishings a delight. There was even a good-sized hip-bath in the adjoining dressing-room, but the feature Désirée liked best was the wide balcony overlooking the gardens.

Opening the large double windows, she stepped out on to it and sat down in the cane chair placed in one corner. She risked being bitten by insects, but it was cool out here and she found the starlight soothing.

Her pulse was still unsteady. Désirée tried to calm herself by taking several deep breaths, but her brain continued to whirl with agitated speculation.

There could be many reasons to explain Rafael's odd visitor. It was foolish of her to be suspicious!

'You should have stayed and asked him for an explanation,' she said to herself crossly.

But would he have told her the truth?

With a sense of shock, Désirée realised she wasn't sure. Alarm bells were ringing in her head. Was there something going on here at the Casa which was being deliberately kept from her? Rafael sometimes disappeared without warning, but Elena never seemed worried, even if he was gone for many hours.

Until this evening Désirée had assumed he was busy on estate business, but where did that oddly dressed man fit in? Had he followed them from Madrid?

With a sigh, she shook her head. It was a mystery.

Rafael had told her he would keep her secrets safe. Now it seemed that he possessed secrets too. She would have to school herself to patience and wait until he, in his turn, was ready to honour her with his confidences.

Unless she wanted to confront him with her vague uneasy suspicions and risk insulting his fierce pride, it was all she could do!

The *fiesta* was in honour of Saint Veronica, whose feast-day it was. Riofrío's church was dedicated to this compassionate woman who, when Jesus fell beneath His cross on the road to Cavalry, wiped His face with a towel on which a picture of the Holy Face remained imprinted.

The celebrations would begin after the day's work had been done and evening had brought a measure of coolness to temper the fierce July heat.

Désirée decided to wear her white muslin gown with the pretty embroidery and a white *mantilla* to go over her hair.

'Do you think it wrong of me, Elena?' she asked a shade defiantly, encountering the older girl on her way downstairs.

Elena shook her head slowly, her startled expression fading. 'I am just a little surprised. I know how much you mourn your brother.'

'A couple of months after *Maman* died, Etienne asked me to leave off my black gowns, saying that he hated to see me in them and that true mourning took place in the heart and had no need of outward show.' Désirée gave an awkward shrug. 'I know it might shock some people, but I think it is time to begin wearing colours again.'

'I agree.' Elena smiled at her reassuringly. 'You must honour his wish.'

The look in Rafael's eyes as he came out to meet them in the hallway told Désirée that he understood and approved of her decision.

The festivities began with an painted plaster image of the Saint being carried in procession around the village to the sound of much loud singing and clapping of hands. Désirée walked at Rafael's side near the head of the procession. Elena, who was beginning to look rather pale, elected to wait in the church, where it was cooler, for their return.

Désirée wondered if her friend should have stayed at home, but, already, she could understand why Elena hadn't wanted to. The air of happy excitement was palpable!

Bright flags and masses of flowers decorated every house and everyone was wearing their best clothes. As they wended their way along the processional route, Désirée felt again that strange affection for this harshly beautiful land stirring in her heart.

She had wanted to hate Spain because it had deprived Etienne of his life, but she hadn't been able to. She was fascinated by its ever-changing moods. She had never seen landscapes so bleak. . .or so beautiful. High mountains, green valleys, magnificent palaces, a fertile grove of orange trees at sunset, all were mixed up in her memory of the past eleven weeks since she had crossed the border.

To put it plainly, she felt at home here in Castile. Despised as a foreigner by its people, the land itself had reached out to lay claim to her heart.

She could easily surrender and learn to love Spain, just as Rafael had prophesied, if it were not for one thing. Somewhere, hidden in its high hills, lurked the man she hated.

Determined to stay on until she learnt the truth about how Etienne had died, Désirée had discovered that merely knowing the details wasn't enough. She wasn't ready to go home yet.

'An eye for an eye' said the Bible and her brother's blood cried out for vengeance. Until El Verdugo had been captured and punished, she would have no real inner peace.

Darkness was beginning to fall as they returned to the church. The statue of Saint Veronica was lovingly returned to its place of honour and Father Gomez said Mass. Désirée noticed several of the villagers absenting themselves during the service; when everyone else emerged after it was over, the village square had been transformed.

Elena's coloured lanterns had been lit and torches blazed, illuminating a long table set in the centre, which had been covered in white cloths and heaped with an abundant variety of food.

'Your lanterns look very pretty,' Désirée said admiringly.

Elena thanked her for the compliment, but her voice sounded a little weary.

Désirée threw a glance at Rafael. He seemed preoccupied tonight. Had he noticed how tired his sister seemed?

To her relief, Elena brightened up when the little band of musicians began to play and the wine barrels were broached.

'Here, try this.' Rafael handed Désirée a beaker. 'It is from the barrel we brought over yesterday.'

The wine was smooth and aromatic and Désirée sipped it with appreciation.

The food was handed round and when everyone had eaten their fill, the musicians struck up a lively tune. People started getting to their feet; Désirée remembered that Elena had mentioned that there might be dancing.

'Nothing formal, of course. It is very much a spur-of-the-moment thing with the band deciding what to play and people joining in,' she had said.

Désirée loved dancing. She wasn't very good at other ladylike pastimes like sketching or playing the piano-forte, but all her tutors had agreed that she had a natural talent for dancing, with an enviable ability to pick up steps quickly and gracefully.

But perhaps it was too soon for her to dance again? Struck by sudden doubt, she turned to Elena. 'Do you think I ought to take part if I'm asked?' she whispered anxiously. 'I don't want to offend anyone by refusing, but perhaps it would be unseemly.'

'I don't think your brother would object,' Elena replied firmly. 'Remember, tonight is an occasion for joy and I'm sure he would want you to enjoy yourself.'

The music paused with a dramatic flourish and every-one's gaze turned towards Rafael. Their expectant faces made Désirée realise that it must be customary for him to open the dancing.

Slowly he rose to his feet, a tall, commanding figure, and Désirée's pulse quickened in sudden, hopeful antici-pation.

Chapter Ten

Shooting a rueful glance at Désirée, Rafael held out his hand to Elena.

With an iron effort of will, Désirée managed to prevent her disappointment from showing on her face. Of course, Rafael would have to open the dancing with his sister! She was being unpardonably foolish!

Father Gomez, a small, wiry man in his early forties with a pockmarked face, saw what was happening and immediately came up to Désirée.

'Will you allow me to partner you, *señorita*?'

Désirée accepted with a polite smile, but her innards began to quake. *Dieu*, was she about to make a fool of herself? Thank heavens she'd had the sense to ask Rosita to show her some steps from a few of the most common dances!

'You are enjoying the *fiesta*, *señorita*?' Father Gomez asked as they moved to take their places.

Désirée murmured an affirmative. She sensed that he wanted to put her at her ease. He seemed a kind man— look how he had hurried to rescue her from a potentially embarrassing situation—but she was acutely aware of the many curious eyes watching her and it was making her nervous!

Straightening her spine, Désirée forced herself to ignore them and concentrate on the music.

To her infinite relief, she found the *seguidilla* rather similar to an English country dance. The priest, who possessed a quick intelligence and energy for all his quiet manner, unobtrusively helped direct her steps and she managed to acquit herself well enough not to suffer embarrassment.

'Congratulations! You performed very skilfully. . .and made an excellent impression,' Rafael murmured as the dance finished and they all returned to their seats.

'*Sí*,' agreed Elena. 'Father Gomez is a good man. He is not like some of the priests who preach violence against the French.'

The dancing continued and Désirée saw Elena losing her private battle against fatigue.

'Don't you think you should sit down?' she whispered as they passed each other during one especially lively figure.

Elena hesitated, but when it was over and they retired to their seats she announced she would dance no more that evening.

'Are you all right, *hermana*?'

There was an odd urgency in Rafael's tone and Désirée sensed an undercurrent of something she didn't understand in his apparently innocent question. This conviction intensified when Elena replied. Her hasty reassurance was followed by a flood of words too swift for Désirée to comprehend.

Rafael answered in the same low rapid voice, much too fast for Désirée to catch what was being said.

A flicker of unease prickled between Désirée's shoulder-blades. She had a distinct feeling they didn't want her to know what they were saying. Her Castilian was now good enough for everyday purposes, but she still had difficulty with rapid speech and they both knew it.

However, she would have laid odds that they were arguing! In fact, it sounded as if Rafael was planning to do something his sister disapproved of.

'*Lo siento*! You must forgive us, Désirée. A minor family squabble, you understand,' Rafael said at last, breaking off and turning to her with an apologetic smile.

Désirée inclined her head gracefully. 'Of course,' she

said, managing to keep all trace of suspicion from her tone.

Just then, one of the youngest men in the village gruffly asked Désirée to stand up with him.

Désirée had seen Father Gomez talking to the lad and guessed the invitation had been the priest's idea, but she accepted with a smile. During the dance, another *seguidilla*, she did her best to prove that she wasn't some fork-tailed monster, but she had a feeling that her unwilling partner wasn't convinced.

Father Gomez might be willing to discount her origins and judge her by her behaviour, but it was obvious that his parishioners were not ready to abandon their prejudices.

Seeing the slight downcurve of her pretty mouth on her return, Rafael gave vent to a silent curse.

He held out a fresh beaker of wine to her. 'You must be thirsty.'

Désirée took it and thanked him. Had he guessed how out of place and dejected she was feeling? There was a warm sympathy in his voice and a note of encouragement too. Her spirits lifted.

'I don't know how those musicians can keep going,' she murmured lightly, determined not to give way to dejection. 'It's so hot!'

Setting down her empty wine-cup, she unfurled her fan and wielded it vigorously, trying to ignore the way her heart was hammering. When he looked at her like that with such tenderness in his eyes, it was all she could do not to blurt out her true feelings for him!

'Are you too hot to dance me with me?' Rafael asked a moment later as the music changed.

Désirée's mouth went dry and she couldn't answer.

'I promise not to stand on your toes.'

Finding her voice again, Désirée laughed and said, 'I most sincerely trust you will not, *señor*!'

She took the arm he held out to her, placing her fingers lightly upon his sleeve. He was wearing a splendid coat tonight in black velvet, heavily embroidered in silver. Its

style might somewhat old-fashioned, but there was no
denying its formal grandeur accorded well with his lean
proud features. He looked every inch a *hidalgo*, a nobleman of the blood!

The velvet was luxuriously soft, but it could not negate
the strength which lay beneath and a thrill of pleasure
shot through Désirée as she remembered how he had
held her in his arms.

'We have never danced together before,' Rafael said
abruptly.

His expression was impassive, but a muscle by the
corner of his well-cut mouth flickered and Désirée sensed
his tension. Without having to be told, she knew he was
plagued by the same bittersweet memories.

'I'm not sure we should be dancing now,' she replied
with a breathless little catch in her voice.

'Because of Etienne?' Rafael asked quietly. 'Or
because you think it will make it more difficult for me
to keep my word and behave as a gentleman ought?'

Désirée stayed silent. How could she admit that she
didn't want him to treat her honourably? She still longed
for him to make love to her, but such a confession was
dangerous! If she gave way to her true feelings, then her
position here at the Casa would be untenable and she
didn't want to leave!

They took their places and Désirée was surprised to
discover that the new dance was not performed in sets
but by separate couples.

'What is this dance called?' she asked, realising that
it wasn't one of those Rosita had shown her.

'The *fandango*.' Rafael's dark face split into a wicked
grin. 'The Inquisition said it was immoral and forbade
it, but it remains very popular.'

Désirée could understand why. The music had a throbbing beat which held blatant passion!

Borne up by its vibrant rhythm, she found it wonderfully easy to follow Rafael's lead and copy his steps.

'You are a good dancer. You have a natural gracefulness,' Rafael murmured, enjoying the sparkle in her lovely eyes as she grew more confident.

'*Gracias*!' Désirée deliberately chose to treat his compliment as a joke, but the final traces of her earlier dejection vanished, swept away by the sheer exhilaration of dancing under a starlit sky with the man she loved.

It seemed altogether in keeping with the magic of the night that instead of leading her back to Elena, he whisked her away in the opposite direction.

'Where are we going?' Désirée demanded.

'I want to talk to you. In private.'

Désirée had absolutely no objections to this plan, so she saved her breath for keeping up with the rapid pace he set.

'One of the advantages of a misspent youth is a sound knowledge of the village's quietest spots,' he announced with a chuckle as they left the houses behind them.

'Indeed. You must know every single inch of the place or you have the eyes of a cat,' Désirée observed tartly to cover her excitement as he led her quickly down a tiny path.

'Take my hand. I won't let you fall.'

It was very dark. They were far beyond the reach of the lanterns and torches that had rendered the square almost as bright as day. Delighted to have an excuse to cling tightly to his hand, Désirée was sorry when the path they were following stopped.

It opened out into a small grove of lemon trees. Here and there, glossy leaves shone silver as fickle moonlight played over the scented glade, which lay wrapped in peaceful silence.

'How beautiful it is!' Désirée exclaimed, enchanted by this fairytale vision.

Rafael agreed, but his gaze was fixed upon her face, not the moon-silvered trees.

Becoming aware of his regard, Désirée felt her heartbeat quicken. He was still holding her hand, his strong fingers encircling hers in a firm but gentle grip.

'All the same, you, *señor*, are a rogue!' Désirée

declared, trying to hide her perturbation with a pretence of scolding. 'Dragging me off almost before the dance had finished! What will people think!'

The laughter in her voice betrayed her and Rafael grinned as he replied, 'Do you really want to know the answer to that question?'

Désirée shook her head. She could guess all too well. Let the village think they were lovers—she only wished it was true!

Rafael repressed the fierce urge to draw her into his arms.

'I must tell you why I brought you here,' he said, reluctantly releasing her hand and taking a step backwards. He found it hard to think when she was close and he could smell the intoxicating perfume of her hair.

'Is something wrong?' Désirée felt suddenly chilled, her instincts warning that danger threatened.

'I wouldn't describe it that way,' Rafael replied heavily. 'But I am going to have to go away for a while.'

Désirée lifted her gaze to his. 'Can you tell me why?'

'I don't think that would be wise.' Rafael had decided against trying to explain. Duty called him and he could not refuse, but when he told her the truth he wanted to stay and face her anger, not rush away like a coward.

Silence fell between them. Désirée longed to ask if his decision had anything to do with the man she had seen last night, but it might seem as if she'd been spying on him.

The last thing she wanted right now was a quarrel.

'You will be perfectly safe here at the Casa. The villagers hate the French, but you are my guest. They would never seek to harm you.'

Désirée bit back an unladylike exclamation. Damn what the village thought of her! Every sense screamed it was Rafael who was the one at risk, not herself.

'If there is anything you need in my absence, ask Elena. And you'll find that Father Gomez gives good advice. He is an intelligent man and helpful.' A faint smile chased away Rafael's sombre expression for a moment. 'He hands out stiff penances in the confessional, but his heart is as soft as butter.'

A light breeze had sprung up and it blew a stray curl over Désirée's forehead. Her elegant coiffure had suffered from the energetic dancing, but Désirée was too disturbed to be concerned over her appearance and impatiently brushed it aside.

'Does Elena know you are leaving?'

He inclined his dark head in assent. 'She is aware of my plans.'

There was a slight stiffness in his voice and Désirée exclaimed, 'That's why you were quarrelling! She doesn't want you to go, does she?'

Rafael gave a rueful shrug. 'You are too perceptive, *mi perla*.'

Curiosity warred with anxiety in Désirée's breast. Where was he going and why? It must be something outside the usual scope of a gentleman's affairs if Elena disapproved.

'However, much as I love my sister, I don't need her approval.' There was a determined look on Rafael's face. 'I am leaving tonight. Everything is arranged.'

'So soon?' Désirée felt as if someone had punched her in the stomach.

He nodded. 'Immediately after the *fiesta* finishes. That's why I brought you here. So I could say goodbye in private.'

There would be no time later. Once he had seen the two women home, he would change his clothes and leave.

'Why? Did you think I might rail at you in front of the servants?' Désirée said, afraid that she might cry and trying her hardest to inject a note of humour into her voice to conceal it.

The moonlight reflected the sheen of tears brightening her eyes and Rafael's resolve melted.

He stepped close again. 'I told myself I merely wanted to reassure you, but I was only fooling myself.' He reached out and clasped both her hands in his. 'The real reason I brought you here was because I didn't want an audience. You must know why.'

Conscience told him that he was behaving badly, but he wanted to kiss her! It might be the last time he ever had the chance.

Désirée tugged to free her hands. For an instant, he resisted and then let her go.

'I'm sorry,' he said stiffly. *Dios*, did she no longer feel the same?

'So am I,' she answered softly and closing the tiny distance between them, lifted her arms and wound them around his neck. 'More sorry than I can say to see you go.'

His frown vanishing, Rafael tightened his arms around her slim waist and Désirée whispered, 'Say goodbye properly, Rafael, or I'll never forgive you.'

Their lips met with an urgent hunger, igniting the desire that constantly smouldered beneath their mutual pretence of control.

The kiss was long and deep and they were both breathless when at last Rafael raised his head.

'We must go back,' he said hoarsely, but did not release her from his tight embrace.

'Just one more moment,' Désirée begged, abandoning pride and tangling her fingers in the dense black curls which clustered at his nape. 'Please.' She pressed herself against his tall, strong body, unable to get close enough.

'*Querida!*' Rafael succumbed to temptation and kissed her again with a skilful passion that sent Désirée's pulse wild.

Every nerve seemed to tingle, every square inch of flesh aroused and demanding more, but she knew that this was neither the time nor the place to try and force him to change his mind and acknowledge their passion had the right to exist, the right to be consummated.

Reluctantly, she allowed him to break off the kiss.

'Elena will be growing concerned for you,' he said quietly, still holding her.

With a sigh, Désirée rested her head upon his chest.

She could feel his heart beating beneath her cheek. She wanted to lose herself in him and never let him go.

It took every ounce of her willpower not to cry out in protest when, after dropping a last, gentle kiss upon her hair, he released her and stepped away.

'Farewell, *mi perla*.' Rafael managed a crooked smile. 'I promise to do my best to return home as swiftly as possible.'

'*Vaya con Dios,*' Désirée answered and meant it with all her heart.

Désirée wasn't surprised when Elena failed to appear for breakfast the next morning, but as the day wore on she began to feel uneasy.

'Her maid fobbed off my enquiry, but I feel that something may be wrong,' she said thoughtfully to Rosita.

Rosita sniffed expressively. The servants here were a clannish lot. Respect for their master kept them civil, but their lack of friendliness echoed their unspoken disapproval of the strangers.

Désirée grinned. 'I know! All the same, I think I'll try again. There might be something I can do to help if she is feeling ill.'

Juana, Elena's middle-aged maid, answered her knock.

'Come, *señorita*, come!' A look of relief appeared on her sun-weathered face as she dragged Désirée over the threshold of Elena's room.

'What's wrong? Is the Doña ill?'

'*Sí.* She has a fever. It is very bad.' Panic fringed the woman's voice.

Désirée hurried over to the bed. Elena lay flat on her back, her slight form buried beneath heaped covers. Her skin was pale, except for two spots of colour burning in her cheeks and she was moaning and tossing restlessly.

'Elena? Elena?' Gently, Désirée touched the older girl's shoulder, but she gave no sign of being aware of Désirée's presence.

'How long has she been like this?'

'About an hour. She complained of feeling feverish this morning, but told me not to fuss.'

'Have you sent for the doctor?' Désirée was sure that there must be a medical man in Covarrubias.

Juana shook her head and flapped her hands nervously. 'The Dona does not like Doctor Vargas. She told me not to bother him.'

Désirée laid her hand on Elena's forehead. It felt very hot and dry. 'Send for him at once.'

Juana nodded and hurried away, her expression revealing her thankfulness at being able to relinquish responsibility.

Glancing round the room, Désirée located the washstand and, wetting a towel, bathed Elena's face and attempted to make her more comfortable before using the bell-pull to summon a servant.

'The Doña is ill. Bring me a bowl of fresh water and more towels,' she ordered. 'And send Rosita to me.'

When Rosita arrived, Désirée instructed her to fetch the pot of salve from her dressing-table. 'Her lips are already cracked. It might help soothe them.'

'What is wrong with her, *señorita*? Do you know?'

Désirée shook her head. 'Let's hope the doctor gets here soon.'

In the event, it was several hours before Doctor Vargas arrived. Désirée was furious to discover that he had delayed to change his clothes, donning his best suit to visit his illustrious patient.

From the smell of him, he'd wasted time pomading his hair too!

After peering at Elena and prodding at her in a solemn manner, the doctor declared that she had a pernicious fever.

'She needs to be bled. Now, this instant, and regularly each day until she recovers,' he announced. 'And she must be wrapped tightly in red flannel. Also feed her eggs whipped in strong broth every two hours. By force if necessary.'

Désirée stared at him in amazement.

'She is barely conscious, sir,' she snapped. 'Such treatment must do more harm than good.'

He stared at her, his bushy eyebrows meeting in a frown.

'Are you a member of the family, *señorita*?' he demanded.

'I am a friend of Don Rafael's,' Désirée answered impatiently.

'I see.' The doctor pursed his full lips. Dress and manner revealed this lovely looking girl was well-bred, but her accent made it plain she was a foreigner. He had heard rumours that Don Rafael had brought his mistress to the Casa.

'I understand that Don Rafael has been called away?'

Désirée nodded warily.

'He left you in charge?'

'Of course not!'

'In that case, since you dispute my diagnosis, may I enquire whether you have medical qualifications?'

Désirée bit her lip. 'No,' she said shortly. 'But I do know it would be madness to bleed Doña Elena in her present condition.' She glanced across at the bed. Already, Elena seemed much worse. 'She is too weak.'

'Nonsense! I'll not answer for her recovery if my orders are not followed to the letter.'

'Then prescribe a more sensible treatment!'

The doctor began to gobble in outrage, demanding to know by what authority Désirée dared to thwart his orders.

In the middle of his diatribe, Désirée rang the bell and told the servant who answered it to show him out.

'You'll regret this!'

'I doubt it,' Désirée said coolly.

He glared at her angrily but, mindful that she was favoured by the most powerful man in the district, he managed a curt bow. 'I will call again tomorrow.'

'Don't bother. . .unless you can bring some Jesuits' bark with you.'

His thick eyebrows flew up. 'You know of *quina*?'

Désirée nodded. Her Aunt Caroline had managed to get hold of this rare and expensive stuff, which she had called quinine, when her grandfather had contracted a severe fever. The bitter tea it made had cured him.

'I don't have any in stock,' the doctor muttered. 'But I'll see what I can do.'

'*Gracias*.' Now that she had won, Désirée was prepared to be polite.

When he had gone, she summoned Juana to sit with Elena, instructing her to keep on bathing her mistress's hot face and limbs with tepid water.

'And don't pile those blankets back on the bed. She will be more comfortable if she is cool.'

Juana nodded, but her expression was doubtful.

The energetic young doctor Aunt Caroline had found to care for Grandfather had advocated these methods as well as the Peruvian bark, but Désirée had no time to waste reassuring Juana.

'Call me if there is any change,' she said and swept off to find Rosita and the housekeeper. Together, they inspected the Casa's stock of herbs, unguents, and medicines, which were kept in a cool dark storeroom off the kitchens.

Désirée wished she had paid more attention to Aunt Caroline's chatter. Her aunt, who was something of a hypochondriac, had a great interest in herbalism and concocted many medicinal cures and potions which she was forever pressing her relatives to try.

She had attempted to impart some of her lore to her niece whenever Désirée visited. Unfortunately, all Désirée could seem to remember at the moment was that cloves were good for toothache, which wasn't much use!

'Do you recognise any of these?' she asked, passing a glass bottle filled with some cloudy liquid to Rosita. 'I can't make any sense of the label. The handwriting is terrible.'

Rosita uncorked the stopper and sniffed the contents cautiously. 'Mullein, I think.' She tasted it. 'In red wine.'

Désirée frowned. If she remembered aright, mullein was supposed to be a cure for agues and coughs. It might help. But what if Rosita was mistaken?

'It's too dangerous to use anything we are not absolutely certain of,' she said, picking up another bottle.

This time she recognised the contents easily.

'Take this lavender-water up to Juana,' she instructed the housekeeper. 'It will help cool the Doña.'

Dusk had fallen by the time they had finished their inventory, and to Désirée's immense relief she had found a couple of items she was sure were safe.

'Go and get your supper now, Rosita, and try to take a nap. I might need your help later on.'

'What about you, *señorita*? You ought to eat something.'

'Ask them to send some food up on a tray to the Doña's room.'

Taking the medicines with her, Désirée returned to Elena's room. To her dismay, Juana had lit a fire and it was as hot as an oven.

With an impatient exclamation, she flung open the shuttered window.

'*Señorita*!' Horror filled the maid's dark eyes.

'Don't worry, Juana. I haven't run mad.'

'But we must sweat the fever out of her!'

'Perhaps, but she'll suffocate if we don't give her air,' Désirée said firmly.

Juana looked doubtful.

'Besides, a doctor in my father's country told me that too much heat was bad for the body.'

'But. . .but. . .'

'Do you want to boil the Doña's brains in her skull?' Désirée demanded crisply.

Juana goggled at her, her mouth falling open.

'Then trust me. . .and put that fire out.'

Juana scurried to obey and Désirée set out the medicines she had found on the night-table by the bed.

During the long night that followed, she managed to

spoon an infusion of catmint between Elena's parched
lips but, for all that it was supposed to induce perspiration
and soothe restlessness it did little good.

Désirée's confidence began to ebb as Rafael's sister's
condition remained unchanged. Endless day followed
endless night, but no matter what they tried, the fever
remained high.

Doctor Vargas returned and reluctantly Désirée
allowed him to bleed Elena, but even this treatment made
no difference.

It didn't help Désirée's frayed nerves that no one
seemed to know where Rafael had got to.

'Or if they do, they aren't telling! But I must get a
message to him,' she said anxiously to Rosita as the third
day of Elena's illness dawned. 'Vargas says her condition
is critical.'

Rosita shrugged fatalistically. 'Doña Elena is in
God's hands.'

Désirée nodded, a wave of exhaustion suddenly sweeping over her. She had barely slept at all the last two nights.

'Why don't you go and get some rest? You'll make
yourself ill if you carry on like this. Juana and I can
watch her.'

Knowing her maid was right, Désirée agreed.

Stumbling to her own room, she removed her shoes
and fell on to her bed fully clothed, too tired to undress.

She was asleep before her head touched the pillow.

It felt like only moments later that she was awoken
by screaming. Sitting up groggily, her tired brain at first
refused to take in the sunshine streaming in through
her unshuttered window. Several hours must have
passed! Jamming her shoes back on, she ran from the
room, following the anguished wailing, which was
coming from Elena's bedchamber.

Her mouth dry with fear, Désirée experienced a spurt
of relief when she saw the bedcovers stirring slightly.
Elena still breathed!

'For pity's sake, stop that noise, Juana!' She rounded

on the crying maid, her eyes snapping with annoyance. 'You will disturb the Doña with your hysterics!'

The woman took no notice and Désirée was forced to shake her. The screams stopped, but Juana's plump body continued to shudder, an expression of horror in her wide staring eyes.

Alarm filled Désirée. Releasing Juana, she swung round to her maid. 'Rosita? What has happened?'

Rosita, who had lost all her usual colour, gestured nervously towards the bed. 'See for yourself, *señorita*,' she gasped hoarsely.

Her legs feeling suddenly leaden, Désirée moved closer and saw the rash disfiguring Elena's thin face. In the cruel morning light, it was unpleasantly vivid.

'*Mon Dieu!*' Gulping hard, Désirée slowly withdrew the covers.

The same rash covered Elena's palms and the soles of her long elegant feet.

Désirée lifted her appalled gaze and met Rosita's scared eyes.

'*La viruela*,' the maid said as she nodded, confirming her own diagnosis.

Juana's sobbing filled the silence.

Smallpox. A sentence of death more feared than the French!

Rafael approached the tent, conscious of a tightening in his chest. There was a soldier on guard, his red coat bright in the sunlight. Catching sight of Rafael's escort, he came to attention and stepped smartly aside.

It was hot inside the tent and crowded, but Rafael only had eyes for the man sitting behind the paper-strewn campaign desk.

At first sight there was nothing particularly impressive about his spare figure. Unlike most of the other men present, he was not in uniform, but wore a neat blue frockcoat and his dark hair was liberally flecked with grey, although Rafael knew he was barely forty.

He was writing something, his pen moving with

extreme swiftness, but he looked up when Rafael and his escort approached and Rafael saw that he had a long pale face, clear grey-blue eyes and a remarkably large aquiline nose.

'Señor Velasco, sir.'

'Thank you, Grant.' Sir Arthur Wellesley laid down his pen. 'Welcome to our camp, Señor Velasco.'

'I am delighted to make your acquaintance, sir.' Rafael bowed politely. 'I understand from the Major here that you are in need of an interpreter. May I be of some service to you?'

A flicker of pleasure warmed Wellesley's cool, self-contained expression. 'Your English is damned good! Even better than I was led to expect.'

Rafael acknowledged the compliment with a slight inclination of his head.

The British commander gestured him to take one of the folding stools opposite the desk.

'I do stand in need of someone who can reliably convey my intentions to General Cuesta. Your help would be appreciated.' Wellesley's tone was brisk and business-like. 'However, I believe you also have other. . .ah. . . interests here?'

Rafael smiled broadly. 'Your intelligence officers are efficient, sir.'

'Let's hope we can keep Marshal Victor from saying the same.' Wellesley gave a short bark of laughter.

'My *guerrilleros* have combined forces with others in the area to keep your movements blanked out from the French,' Rafael confirmed Sir Arthur's hopes. 'I am certain that no one in Madrid knows yet that you have marched into Spain.'

Wellesley permitted himself a smile. It was the best news he'd had since leaving Portugal.

Led by El Capitan-General Don Gregorio de la Cuesta, a haughty ancient who had never won a battle in the whole of his long life, the Spanish army was disorganised, ill-armed and unreliable. His own troops were on half-rations, supplies and transport, supposedly assured by the Spanish commissariat, having failed.

It was not an auspicious beginning.

But one thing had remained constant: the courageous determination of the *guerrillas*. Like this man before him, they were willing to sacrifice everything. He had already learnt to admire their daring and tenacity. Now he was beginning to think that they might become Spain's last hope, if her generals failed her.

The partisans would continue to fight, he was sure of it. And so long as they fought on and his army remained in the Peninsula, the French would be in a quandary, unable to smother the revolt without fatally exposing themselves to the British.

'It is my belief, sir,' he said to Rafael. 'That if the war lasts here in the Peninsula, then Europe will be saved from Bonaparte. Therefore, whatever happens in the next few weeks, I intend to be patient.'

Rafael nodded. 'I am glad to hear it, Sir Arthur,' he said gravely.

It was good to have assurance that his new ally would not give up easily, for he knew the deficiencies of his own army as well as Sir Arthur did. Cuesta was too old and too set in his ways. It was galling to Rafael's pride to have to admit it, but he knew the British were a much superior force.

Spain needed Wellesley's well-drilled troops, but in turn the British needed him and all the other *guerrilleros*, whether or not Wellesley knew it.

Looking into Sir Arthur's clear eyes, Rafael came to the conclusion that he did and his estimation of the man went up several notches.

'General Cuesta has agreed to join forces with us at Oropesa. From there we intend to advance on Victor together.' Wellesley steepled his fingers together and gave Rafael a direct look. 'Can you furnish me with a set of good maps? The ones we have are poor.'

'I can do better than that, sir,' Rafael replied confidently. 'I shall find you a dozen reliable guides.'

'By God, sir, I think you and I shall deal very well together!'

Rafael left the tent, his ears still ringing with Sir Arthur's thanks.

The meeting had gone better than he had dared let himself imagine. Now all he had to do was make good his promises!

A grin split his dark features. He was a reasonable hand at drawing. The maps would be no problem and he already had in mind the men he would select to act as guides.

When he had first received a message from Sancho, asking him to come to Plasencia, he had assumed his help was required in concealing the British advance. But Sancho had also boasted of his cousin's excellent command of their own tongue to the English leaders.

Luckily, thanks to all the practice he'd had lately, he had more than justified Sancho's claims. It was odd to think how much he owed to his talks with Désirée.

His smile faded. *Dios*, but he missed her! Since they had parted, not an hour had gone by without his thoughts straying in her direction.

Sternly quelling a hope that she might be missing him, Rafael turned his mind to another problem. He had told Elena he would be back within a couple of weeks. Now it looked as if he might be here longer since he could not leave while Wellesley required his services.

Somehow or other, he was going to have to convey that message to Casa del Aguila!

'*La viruela* strikes more fear into people's hearts than the Devil himself.' Father Gomez let out a deep sigh. 'Doctor Vargas has ignored my appeal for help. He will not endanger himself to save peasants.'

Désirée let out an unladylike snort. 'The man dishonours his sworn duty to tend the sick!'

Vargas had also refused to enter Elena's room. As soon as he heard that her rash had developed into pustules, he had hastily gabbled instructions on the best method to treat them before thrusting the package of medicines he had brought, which fortunately included a small quantity of quinine, at Désirée and fleeing the house.

Disgusted at his cowardly behaviour, Désirée had been glad to see the back of him.

'I agree, *señorita*. A doctor should show more courage, but I can understand his fear.' The priest fingered the small, pitted scars on his face. 'Smallpox devastated my own village when I was a child. I was one of only a handful of survivors. Everyone else died.'

Désirée shivered in spite of the warmth of the small room.

They were sitting in the spartan parlour of the priest's house. It was the first time that Désirée had ventured outside of Casa del Aguila since Elena had fallen ill two weeks ago. Father Gomez's housekeeper had brought them wine, but there was no other pretence of social courtesy. Sitting bolt upright in his chair, his face creased with anxiety, the priest told his visitor the extent of the disaster that had struck Riofrío.

Désirée had decided to answer the priest's appeal herself when a message had arrived asking if the Casa had any medicine to spare. Now that Elena, who had pulled through a second bout of fever, was at last starting to mend, she felt it was safe to leave her.

It had been wonderful to feel some fresh air on her face and experience Madrigal cantering beneath her, but Désirée's elation had swiftly vanished when the priest had informed her of the severity of the outbreak which had erupted in the village.

'At least it is good news about the Doña.' Father Gomez firmly dismissed his uncharitable thoughts of Doctor Vargas and poured Désirée another glass of wine. 'But tell me, how are your other patients doing?'

Fourteen of Rafael's servants had fallen victim to the disease. Nine had already died. The housekeeper was rapidly recovering and the others were still fighting for their lives.

'I shall pray for them.' The priest's pockmarked face

creased into a little smile. 'I think God must be delighted
with you, *señorita*.' He handed Désirée the glass. 'Unlike
Vargas, you have shown steadfast loyalty and courage
in dealing with this dreadful affliction.'

Désirée blushed. 'I've only done what was needed,'
she muttered gruffly, taking a hasty sip of her wine.

'You could have left the Casa and returned to Madrid.'

Désirée gave him a startled look. The idea of abandoning Elena had never occurred to her. Even when the
infection had spread to the servants and the task of keeping the Casa going had fallen on to her shoulders, she
had gritted her teeth and carried on.

Désirée had never worked so hard in her life. Every
limb and joint ached with tiredness and her hands were
red and sore from constant immersion in hot water. With
the help of the servants left on their feet, she had taken
care of the sick and in her spare moments boiled sheets,
scrubbed floors, and cooked nourishing soup to feed to
her patients.

It was an endless, exhausting round and yet nothing
she had ever done before had given her the same sense
of achievement!

'Have you had any word from Don Rafael?' Tactfully,
the priest allowed her a moment to recover her composure.

Several days ago a letter had arrived for Elena. After
some hesitation, Désirée had opened it. She recognised
Rafael's handwriting, but could make no sense of his
message. It appeared to be in some kind of code, but
Elena was too ill to be questioned.

Désirée had set the missive aside. She was much too
busy to try and decipher it. 'We received a short letter
from him some time ago. Now that she is getting better,
Doña Elena will soon be up to reading it for herself. I
just hope she won't resent my having opened it first.'

Father Gomez shook his greying head. 'The Doña is
not so foolish. But even if she was annoyed with you,
she would have to forgive you. She owes you a great
debt of gratitude.'

'Not as much as you might imagine, *Padre*.' Désirée gave a small embarrassed shrug. 'It is extremely unlikely that I shall catch the disease.'

'I hope you will not, my child, but—'

'Let me explain,' Désirée interrupted him with an apologetic little flutter of her hand. 'A few years ago I received a new treatment which prevents smallpox, something called an inoculation. A doctor in my father's country had noticed that farmers and dairymaids who'd had cowpox didn't catch smallpox and he devised a medicine to pass on this protection. His experiments showed that giving someone a weak dose of cowpox works to prevent them succumbing to smallpox.'

'Is such a thing truly possible?' The priest's eyes were wide with awe.

Désirée nodded. 'Doctor Jenner published a tract about his discoveries and when my aunt, who has a keen interest in such things, read it, she had herself and her daughters inoculated. After some argument my grandfather agreed to let me be inoculated too. So you see, I don't have to be brave.'

'Perhaps, but you have still worked very hard for those at the Casa.' The priest's glance fell to Désirée's hands. On the night of the *fiesta* they had been the pampered hands of a lady. Now their soft white perfection had vanished, leaving reddened knuckles and broken nails to tell their own tale of unremitting toil.

He hesitated for a moment and then said quickly, 'I have a request to make of you.'

Désirée gave him an enquiring look.

'I know you must be very tired, but are you willing to help me nurse the sick here in the village?' The priest's voice trembled with suppressed eagerness. 'You have the experience and skill we need.'

For an instant, Désirée longed to refuse. She had been looking forward to a chance to rest, but that was before she knew smallpox had surfaced in Riofrío.

'I must return to the Casa and check on my patients there, but I will return as soon as I can.'

'*Muchas gracias.*'

Embarrassed, Désirée waved away his thanks and rose briskly to her feet. 'Before I go, if you'll take me to your housekeeper, I'll show her how to brew a tisane made from holly-leaves to treat the fever. They make quite an effective febrifuge and I noticed that you have a good-sized bush in your garden.'

Father Gomez smiled. 'Of course.'

He had not been mistaken in his estimation of her character. Whatever the state of her morals, and he *had* heard the rumours, Don Rafael's woman had a heart of gold!

Chapter Eleven

'Limonada! Limonada fresca!'

'Over here,' Rafael called out to the lemonade vendor, a big muscular man from Valencia, who trotted over and poured out a measure from the barrel he carried slung on his back.

'*Gracias*.' Rafael handed the cup to his cousin and then paid for a second measure for himself, draining it in one long thirsty swallow.

The vendor moved off again, crying his wares and finding eager customers amongst the troops toiling across the barren plain.

'The most popular man in the army,' Rafael commented wryly to Sancho.

The July heat was intense and clouds of dust marked the lines of columns moving eastwards towards Talavera de la Reina.

When they reached the town they discovered that Marshal Victor had retreated in haste behind the River Alberche a few miles to the north-east.

'The drought has reduced the water to only knee-deep!' Rafael turned to his cousin, his eyes glittering with anticipation. 'We have them!'

His view was shared by Sir Arthur.

'Your *guerrillas* have done their work so well that we've caught Victor's army napping. We outnumber him two to one,' Wellesley said with quiet satisfaction at a hastily summoned staff meeting.

Rafael felt a surge of pride. Early the next morning, however, his elation turned to bitter disappointment.

'Where is he?' Sir Arthur demanded impatiently as dawn broke and still there was no sign of General Cuesta.

Finally, they had to ride over to the Spanish camp to find out what was going on and Rafael undertook the humiliating task of translating one feeble excuse after another as Cuesta refused to fulfil his promise and attack.

'I do not see why he is hesitating!' Sir Arthur fumed. 'Can't you make him understand, Señor Velasco, that if we wait Victor will use the delay to escape?'

Rafael did his best, but the obstinate old man would not be budged.

Sir Arthur's fears were realised. The French flitted eastwards along the Madrid highroad and reports came in from both the British scouts and the *guerrillas*, warning that other enemy forces were concentrating in that direction.

'This is a black hour for Spain,' Sancho said heavily, lighting another of his endless *cigarillos* and trying to draw some comfort from it as he and Rafael breakfasted together.

Rafael scowled. Privately he thought that the old Capitan-General's wits had gone a-begging, but he managed to refrain from saying so. Sancho admired Cuesta, although he did not always agree with him.

Losing his appetite for their frugal rations, Rafael went off to see if he could discover what was happening.

'Ah, just the man I want to see,' Sir Arthur declared. 'Come with me.'

They sought out the Spanish commander and a heated discussion arose.

'Good God, he's as reckless now as he was over-prudent yesterday!' Sir Arthur's famed cool restraint was in danger of disintegrating. 'Tell him that in no circumstances will I accompany him on such a wild goose-chase. There are at least fifty thousand French in the neighbourhood of the capital.'

Rafael translated, using all his tact, but it was to no

avail. Nothing would satisfy the old man but to launch his army after Victor.

'I assume he thinks Victor is fleeing before him. Well, let him continue with this madness if he must, he will pay the consequences of his delusion soon enough. But I will not risk my army on such a fatal venture!'

His high-bred nose quivering with disdain, Sir Arthur withdrew.

The Spanish camp jeered, their mood jubilant.

Rafael bit back a curse.

Frustration boiled in him. They could not afford to quarrel with the British. There was no hope of crushing the French unless they worked together.

'You will fight with us, Don Rafael?' Cuesta gazed at him, his eyes sharp beneath their wrinkled lids. 'You will honour your duty to Spain?'

'*Sí.*' Rafael inclined his head abruptly.

No matter his personal feelings, he could not refuse. To do so would stain his name, bringing shame on his family. The best he could hope for was that there would be something left of Spain's army when this stubborn old man had finished with it.

And pray that Wellesley would not lose patience and withdraw to Portugal while they were gone!

Désirée finished spooning the soup into the little boy's mouth and smiled at him.

'Good boy! You have finished it all.'

She settled him back on the straw mattress and made him comfortable.

'Rest now, Dario,' she murmured. '*Buenas noches.*'

Straightening, she put a hand to her aching back and rubbed it for a moment before tip-toeing out of the barn.

Outside, she took a deep breath of fresh air and for an instant was able to imagine that night had brought a measure of coolness.

July was burning to a close and still *la viruela* held sway in Riofrío.

'*Mon Dieu*, I wish it would rain,' she murmured aloud,

staring up at the cloudless sky. Perhaps she wouldn't feel quite so exhausted if it did!

Father Gomez had persuaded the villagers to accept her suggestion that all the sick be isolated in the biggest barn and kept away from the others.

'It will make it easier to nurse them that way,' Désirée had announced. 'And it might stop the infection spreading.'

A small rota of helpers had been established and Désirée had organised the preparation of food and washing of laundry. She was insistent that their makeshift hospital be kept as clean as possible. Aunt Caroline always claimed that dirt was harmful in some way and Etienne had said wounds seemed to heal better if they were kept clean.

The Spaniards thought she was mad but, although they grumbled about the extra work, they humoured her.

At first Désirée couldn't understand why they accepted her advice. Then she overheard one of the older women berating a girl who ignored her request to sweep the floor.

'Do what *La Inglesa* tells you! She is Don Rafael's woman. In his absence, she speaks for him.'

Désirée had opened her mouth to point out that she was neither an Englishwoman nor Rafael's representative and then shut it again. What Dolores had just said might not be strictly true, but it was useful.

Stretching her tense shoulders, Désirée yawned and forced herself to move. There was still a one last task to be done before she could seek her bed in the small guest-chamber of the priest's house.

Staying in the village saved time and travel, but a sigh escaped her as she strove not to think of how happy she had been at the Casa.

Dieu, but she missed Rafael! It was like a constant ache, ignored only by an effort of will.

'Stop it!' Désirée warned herself sternly. 'You cannot afford to think about Rafael now! You've got work to do.'

Father Gomez was seated at the big pine table when she entered the kitchen.

He rose politely to his feet. 'Come and join me,' he invited, indicating his informal meal. 'I sent Maria off early. She was very tired after washing all those sheets, but she left supper ready. You don't mind eating in here, do you?'

'Actually, I'm not hungry.'

A frown drew his brows together. 'You must eat, my child! If you won't share my rabbit pie, at least have some of this hot chocolate.'

'Maybe a little food might help keep me alert.' Désirée sat down at the table. 'I must attend to those in a minute,' she said, indicating the large bunch of marigolds she had picked that morning and left standing in a pail of water. 'If I don't squeeze their juice tonight, they will wilt and be wasted.'

'Are we running low on marigold-juice again?' Father Gomez asked, filling another cup from the pot in front of him.

Désirée had come across this supposed cure for small-pox in a seventeenth-century herbal in Rafael's library when Elena had first fallen ill. Desperately searching for some advice on what to do, she had struggled to translate the crabbed Latin, hoping it would work.

'Yes, and the *quina* is all finished.' Désirée nibbled glumly on a piece of bread. 'I wish we could obtain more!'

In spite of all their efforts, eighteen people had already died and Désirée had found each death harrowing.

'You mustn't start blaming yourself, child. We must accept God's will.'

Désirée finished her bread and shrugged awkwardly. 'I know, but I do wish there was more we could do to ease their suffering.'

In addition to the shortage of medicine, it was impossible to keep their makeshift hospital cool and the disagreeable smells associated with sick bodies seemed even stronger in the stifling heat.

'You have done all that can be done.' The priest gave her a tired smile. 'No one could have tried harder and I believe that God will reward you for your compassion.'

A blush coloured Désirée's cheeks. 'I want no reward,' she murmured.

A deep and sincere concern for the welfare of these people had grown within her. She cared what happened to them and the knowledge that she had been able to help some of them recover had been enough to compensate her for her efforts.

They sipped their hot chocolate and then Father Gomez said, 'None the less, I shall continue to hope that in return for your kindness to us God will grant you peace of mind.'

Her incredibly blue eyes flew to his in astonishment.

'What. . .what do you mean, *Padre*?'

'You still hunger for the death of those who killed your brother, *si*?'

Désirée's expression tightened. 'I cannot help my feelings!'

'You are very young to be so full of hatred, my child. I shall pray to God asking him to deliver you from this desire for revenge. Such bitterness can only destroy your life.'

Désirée was silent for a moment. In her heart she suspected that the priest was right. She had known no real peace of mind since she had heard how Etienne had died, but she couldn't find any forgiveness in her.

'I do long to see El Verdugo punished,' she admitted slowly. 'I elected to stay in Spain in the hope of seeing him executed.'

A sigh escaped her. How simple things had seemed in Burgos! She had hated Spain, hated all Spaniards! But since then her feelings for Rafael had deepened and everything had grown much more complicated.

Would Etienne blame her for having fallen in love with one of the enemy? Or understand and forgive?

'You do realise that there is little likelihood of El Verdugo being captured unless the French can somehow gain mastery of the hills?'

Father Gomez's quiet remark dragged her from her

confused thoughts and she nodded grimly. In all these weeks, she'd had no word from Armand.

In fact, they'd had no news of any kind for many days. Fear of smallpox had prevented the usual traffic between Riofrio and her neighbours. God alone knew what was happening in the outside world!

'They say that revenge is a dish best eaten cold. I can wait. El Verdugo will have to come down from the mountains sometime.'

'He is a hero to my people. They will not betray him.'

'You need not remind me that many Spaniards have been treated badly by my countrymen,' Désirée retorted, flushing.

She was silent for a moment and then said more quietly, 'I could have accepted Etienne dying in battle, but he died because of a cowardly ambush and I cannot forgive that!'

'But can you not see it is time to bring all this hatred to an end? Both sides have inflicted death and pain. Both have suffered. Seeking revenge only continues the circle. Let your bitterness go and join me in praying for peace!'

'I am willing to pray for peace, *Padre*. I want this war to end. Believe me, I want it more than you can possibly imagine,' Désirée declared passionately.

If the war was over, there might be a chance for Rafael and her. . .

'But ending the war won't bring my brother back,' she continued, her voice trembling. 'And only El Verdugo's death can assuage my grief.'

The priest wore a troubled expression. He opened his mouth and then hesitated. 'I shall pray that you change your mind and give up your hatred,' he said at last.

For an instant Désirée had the strangest feeling that he had intended to say something else, but then she dismissed the thought impatiently.

'Don't waste your time, Father Gomez. Whatever the cost to my own soul, I mean to go on hoping that El Verdugo rots in hell!'

*   *   *

Rafael watched the sun rise over the French lines. As the light grew stronger, the huge dark silhouette sharpened into forty thousand men drawn up in serried columns.

He took a deep breath and was suddenly glad that Sancho had heard his confession last night.

His cousin had been wounded in the clash with Victor's force at Torrijos thirty miles away. Realising he was now vastly outnumbered, Cuesta had promptly given the order to retire back to Talavera. Thankful that the old general had seen sense at last, Rafael had concentrated his attention on helping Sancho, who had a received a nasty sabre-cut on the thigh and could barely walk.

But when they reached the Alberche, Cuesta perversely halted, refusing to cross and rejoin their ally, and urgent messages from the British had no effect.

Rafael couldn't believe it. 'Is the man mad?' he raged. 'How in God's name does he expect us to defend ourselves here!'

'Perhaps the general has a plan of his own,' Sancho argued, trying to ignore the pain in his leg as he allowed one of Rafael's men, who had a reputation for healing, to change the blood-stained dressing.

'Wellesley is waiting for us in the only possible defensive position,' Rafael retorted.

'Sometimes I think you hold the British in too high a regard.' Sancho's expression was offended. 'We Spaniards also know how to put up a good fight!'

Rafael's dark features creased into a sour grin.

'I hope so, because if Cuesta doesn't change his mind, the chances are we'll all be slaughtered, Spaniards and British alike!'

It appeared that Sir Arthur had come to the same conclusion and, at five o'clock on the morning of the twenty-seventh of July, he arrived in person to add his entreaties to the rest.

Summoned to Cuesta's headquarters, Rafael performed the necessary translations. He could feel his temper slipping at the old *hidalgo's* arrogant stubbornness and he marvelled at Wellesley's cool restraint.

'Well, Señor Velasco, it seems there's no other help
for it!' Sir Arthur said, a glint of humour gleaming in
his eyes as he dropped to his knees and humbly begged
for assistance.

The tactic worked. His pride appeased, Cuesta gra-
ciously consented to take up the position allotted to him.

Furiously ashamed, Rafael had stormed off as soon as
the meeting was concluded. Later, when they had reached
Talavera and his temper had mended, he curtly informed
Cuesta that he intended to fight alongside the British.

The old *hidalgo* sniffed disdainfully but, knowing he
had no real authority over Rafael, did not try to stop him.

After their meagre supper, Rafael gave the *guerrilleros*
who had accompanied him the choice of going home to
Casa del Aguila or lending their aid to the regular army.

'The job we came to do is done. I intend to stay and
fight with the British centre. I shall not blame you if you
decide to leave, but Sir Arthur needs good marksmen,'
Rafael told them.

To a man, they took up the challenge and Rafael smiled
at them proudly.

Fearful of an infiltration round his left flank, Wellesley
had positioned Spaniards from Bassecourt's reserve div-
ision among the rocks of the Sierra de Segurilla half a
mile to the north.

'Their officers will give you your orders,' Rafael told
his *guerrilleros*. 'We will meet again after the battle
is won.'

Sancho decided to join the sharpshooters.

'Are you sure your wound won't hamper you too
much?' Rafael asked casually, striving to hide his anxiety
as he watched his cousin struggling to exchange his
dusty, stained soutane for a pair of breeches.

Sancho shook his head. 'I can manage. It is my
duty to go.'

Like many other Spanish priests, Sancho believed that
it was a sacred duty to rid their soil of the invader. While
he did not go so far as to claim, as some did, that it was

no sin to kill a Frenchman, he firmly believed that God would forgive him for it.

'Good luck, *amigo mio*!' Sancho embraced Rafael in a quick fierce hug and disappeared into the darkness with the others.

Comforted by the knowledge that his friends would be in a relatively safe position, Rafael set off to join Major-General Hill, who had been appointed to hold the Cerro de Medellin. French capture of this height would spell doom to Wellesley's army. An attempt had already been made to take it earlier in the night, but had failed.

Rafael hoped it was a good omen.

He managed to snatch an hour or two's sleep, rolled in his cloak, rifle and sword ready at his side, but even in his sleep he was aware of the sounds of artillery being moved into place at the top of the hill.

It was still dark when he woke. Major-General Hill invited him to share an early breakfast with the officers; when the brief, frugal meal was over, Hill called him to one side and spoke to him.

'Wellesley told me you want to serve in the line, Señor Velasco.' There was was a note of faint puzzlement in 'Daddy' Hill's genial voice. 'Is that correct? You wish to stand with the ordinary soldiers?'

Rafael smiled faintly. 'Unlike many of my *guerrilleros*, I am no marksman, sir. My talent lies with the sword. But I have watched your battalions drill and I can take orders. Let me be of some service to you in the line where I can fire with the others until we close with the enemy and I can put my sword to use.'

His smile changed to a wolfish grin. 'And then I shall show you how a Spaniard fights!'

Hill laughed. 'Done! I accept your offer with pleasure, sir. Away with you now. Lieutenant Richards will show you your place.'

The red dawn grew brighter and day broke. The waiting was almost over.

'Any minute now, I reckon,' announced the redcoat on Rafael's left with laconic resignation.

Even as he finished speaking, smoke curled up into the air and they heard the report of a single, French cannon.

The signal for attack.

'*Si*. The battle begins, *amigo*,' Rafael replied. 'And may God have mercy on us all!'

Désirée handed Madrigal's reins to the groom with a smile and walked into the Casa with a happy feeling of coming home.

'Désirée! You are back at last!' Elena came hurrying across the hallway and enveloped her in a hug of welcome.

Désirée returned the embrace. She had grown very fond of the older girl and she was delighted to see her out of bed and on her feet again.

'Elena. I can't tell you how pleased I am to see you. How are you feeling? You look so much better!'

She eyed her friend critically. The unsightly pustules disfiguring Elena's thin cheeks and brow had vanished, leaving behind small scars which were healing nicely. With any luck, her skin wouldn't be too badly marked.

'I am very well,' Elena reassured her. 'Come. I have a bottle of cold wine waiting in the *sala* and Dorotea has baked some of your favourite almond cakes to celebrate your return home.'

Over this refreshment they exchanged their news. Désirée demanded a progress report on the health of all those who had survived the smallpox outbreak at the Casa, then told Elena what had been happening in the village.

Elena's eyes widened as she listened. Désirée was too modest to claim any credit, but it was obvious that her friend had been instrumental in saving many lives.

But all her hard work since *la viruela* had first struck a month ago had taken its toll. When she caught sight of Désirée approaching the house, Elena had been shocked to see how thin and pale the younger girl looked. If anything, Désirée had lost more weight than she had!

'Father Gomez insisted that he could manage on his own now that the worst was over,' Désirée said, coming to the end of her recital. 'There have been no new cases for three days.'

She pulled a wry grimace. 'He told me I needed proper rest or I would become ill myself and, to be honest, I have never felt so exhausted in my life!' She gave a little chuckle. 'I must look a complete fright. I am longing for a proper bath!'

'I thought you might. I told Rosita to get hot water ready when I saw Madrigal ride up.'

'Bless you!' Désirée's smile grew wider. Oh, it felt so good to be back!

After an emotional reunion with Rosita, who had thankfully escaped the ravages of *la viruela*, Désirée surrendered to her ministrations and, feeling clean again at last, lay down on her bed, allowing her tired body to relax.

Only one thing spoilt her bliss. Rafael wasn't home.

Désirée had managed to conceal her disappointment, hoping that Elena would know his whereabouts, but Elena declared that they'd had no further word from him and that his letter had not mentioned when he would return.

Désirée had the feeling Elena was lying.

She suspected that Father Gomez was also in on the secret. He had evaded all her questions, but Désirée had seen him hand a letter to one of the villagers who'd subsequently disappeared. Later, the man's wife had said something which confirmed Désirée's growing suspicion that it was a message for Rafael.

But, surely, if he had received word of his sister's illness, Rafael would have hurried home? In view of the tense situation, she'd expected him to return anyway. Casa del Aguila wasn't near Talavera, but the whole country was like a tinderbox, ready to flare into violence.

A shudder ran through her. Reports of the battle said that a running flame had ignited the parched grass on the Medellin, making a horrible roast of dead horses and engulfing the helpless wounded who didn't manage to scramble clear.

By all accounts, it had been a particularly murderous battle. Rumour had it that Wellesley had lost over 5,000 men and the French even more. Blinding heat, choking dust, clouds of flies swarming amid the cannons' roar and rifles' rattle. . .it must have been dreadful for the men taking part.

Désirée sat up suddenly, her heart pounding.

The Spanish had fought with Wellesley. Was *that* where Rafael had gone? She had been so busy and tired she'd had no time to stop and think, but now she came to consider it, volunteering for a soldier seemed the most likely explanation for his prolonged absence.

What else but war could be keeping him away from home so long?

Rafael paused and wiped the sweat from his brow with the back of his hand.

'We'll halt for an hour,' he announced and heard smothered groans as his men dismounted and tried to find a patch of shade amid the pitiless rocks.

Even his hardened *guerrilleros* were finding it difficult to match the killing pace he'd set. Their stoicism had already been tested to the limit by weeks of short rations and gruelling marches, but Rafael was in a hurry.

'An hour,' he repeated firmly. 'The sooner we are home, the sooner all the girls will be welcoming us as heroes with more kisses than we can handle!'

A burst of ragged laughter greeted his words and Rafael grinned back at his filthy, unshaven tatter-demalions.

He'd never seen a more unlikely bunch of heroes!

His smile faded. They had fought and won, but it had all been for nothing.

For the space of a single day after the battle of Talavera it had looked as if things might be different. Everyone's mood had been optimistic. They had actually beaten

Napoleon's invincible army and the road to Madrid lay open.

Then reports had come in that Marshal Soult was advancing south and threatening to cut Wellesley's lifeline to Portugal.

A conference was immediately called between the British and Spanish commanders. Required to translate, Rafael could practically touch the tension vibrating in the air. Cuesta wanted Wellesley to split his army and, with the help of the Spanish forces, hold off both King Joseph and Soult. Sir Arthur refused. He would deal with Soult and leave the Spanish to handle Joseph.

'How are your hands, Señor Velasco? Are your burns healing?' Sir Arthur asked when the meeting was over.

Rafael had come through the battle unscathed, save for several burns to his hands and arms when he had helped rescue some of the wounded who were trapped by flames.

'They are improving, thank you, sir.'

Sir Arthur nodded and after a slight hesitation added, 'I should be very glad of your services for a while longer.'

Rafael bowed. 'I promised you my help, sir, for as long as you needed it,' he said, concealing his reluctance.

Sancho was forced to remain in Talavera. His wound needed resting and Rafael asked him to get word to Elena.

'I've no time to write, but I don't want her worrying,' Rafael said, fervently hoping that his sister would reassure Désirée. *Dios*, but he longed for the sight of her moon-gold hair!

'In a few days, as soon as my leg heals, I'll go to the Casa myself, *amigo mio*.'

His cousin's promise comforting him, Rafael set off for Oropesa accompanied by his *guerrilleros*, who refused to leave him.

It was the beginning of the end. Forced ever westwards, they had marched across the rugged and waterless hills. The tracks were steep and the big guns had to be hauled up by hand, inch by painful inch. Lack of food continued to be a problem. Wellesley was furious at being let down by his allies, refusing to believe that the Spanish had nothing left to give, and everyone was plagued by flies and insects.

Rafael felt sorriest for those who had fair skin or blond hair. They made him think of Désirée and he shuddered to think of her lovely skin blistering and peeling under this fierce sun. Much as he missed her, he could not wish her with him here.

His own burns were healed by the time they reached Jaraicejo, where they camped beside cork and oak forests. The rolling terrain held a picturesque beauty, but scorpions and snakes haunted their bivouacs, causing more than one man to scream aloud in panic.

Personally, Rafael disliked the leeches more. They lurked in the pools where the men obtained their water and clung to the nostrils and mouths of any unwary horse or man who drank there.

'Damn things! They're worse than the bloody mosquitos!' swore Lieutenant Richards, using the end of a glowing *cigarillo*, which Rafael handed to him, to burn off a leech clinging to his chin.

The leech dropped off.

'Thanks.' Tom Richards handed the *cigarillo* back. 'You're a handy fellow to have around, Rafael. Don't know what we would have done without you.'

'You would have managed.' Rafael grinned back at him. 'Somehow.'

They had struck up a friendship at Talavera, an easy comradeship which Rafael knew he would miss.

In his heart he knew that the parting of the ways must come soon. It was obvious that Wellesley could not hold this position much longer. His army was discouraged and hungry and outbreaks of dysentery and fever had already begun.

Too late, a message came from the Supreme Junta, Spain's ruling body, rewarding the victor of Talavera with the captain-generalship of their forces. Wellesley replied with an elegant letter of thanks and a dignified refusal to become a burden on the country's finances.

'I hear old Cuesta has suffered a paralytic fit,' Lieutenant Richards said, coming to join Rafael at his campfire one night. 'They say he has lost the use of his left leg.'

Rafael nodded. 'Perhaps they will appoint La Romana or Castanos in his place. They are better generals.'

Tom diplomatically kept the thought that they couldn't be worse to himself and turned the talk to other matters.

A few days later Tom heard an even more important rumour and went dashing off to find Rafael.

He found his friend sitting slumped with his head in his hands and all the *guerrilleros* around him cursing violently.

'It's true, then? Venegas has been routed at Almonacid?'

Rafael nodded heavily. 'I was there when Wellesley received the message,' he confirmed, his voice bleak.

It was another disaster for Spain. General Venegas had commanded the only remaining sizable force in the north. Now the French were undisputed masters of Madrid once more.

Tom sighed. 'Well, that's it. There's no point us remaining in Spain any longer. Your armies are scattered and we're just about done in.'

Wellesley plainly agreed with this judgement.

On hearing him announce his intention of leaving Spain, Rafael experienced a strange mixture of anger, disappointment and relief.

It was over. There was nothing more he could do here. He was free to return home at last. Home to where Désirée waited for him.

A fierce impatience to be gone sent him seeking Wellesley, who broke off his busy preparations for the withdrawal to see him.

'I wish to tender the resignation of my services, sir,' Rafael announced with a formal gravity. 'My place is here in Spain with my *guerrilleros*. We must continue the struggle.'

'Indeed you must, Señor Velasco.' Wellesley rose from behind his campaign desk. 'I have kept you from your home for too long.' A smile warmed his usual cool expression and he held out his hand. 'My thanks to you, sir. Your help has been invaluable.'

They shook hands and Rafael choked back the emotion rising in his breast, knowing that the older man would not welcome any display of sentiment.

'You know your Junta have sent messages asking me to stay?' Wellesley remarked suddenly.

Rafael nodded, wondering at the unexpected question.

'I cannot oblige them. I have already lost a third of my army. Unless I remove to Portugal where I can be properly supplied, I shall lose the rest.'

The grey-blue eyes met his and to his surprise Rafael saw a genuine regret underlying the commander's steely determination.

'I think many of your countrymen will say I am betraying Spain,' Wellesley continued slowly. 'Yet it was never my wish to abandon her. Necessity forces me to do so.'

'I understand, Sir Arthur.'

The last vestige of Rafael's anger fled. Wellesley was right. Nothing could be gained by remaining here. Others might blame him, but Rafael could not.

'Good.' The sombre note vanished from Wellesley's voice. 'Now let me offer you my very best wishes for a safe journey.'

Rafael bowed. 'And mine to you, sir.'

Sir Arthur smiled. 'God willing, we shall meet again, Señor Velasco, for I swear to you that I intend to return to Spain one day, driving the French before me!'

An answering grin broke out on Rafael's dark features. 'I shall look forward to rejoining you!'

That mood of optimism was still with him now even after three days hard riding.

'Come on, you lazy good-for-nothings,' he shouted cheerfully, urging his men to their feet. 'We've got a long way to go!'

They might have failed to throw the French out of

Spain this time, but Wellesley and the British wouldn't give up.

And neither would he.

But right now he was going home and nothing, nothing in this world, was going to stop him from making Désirée his own!

'I'm going for a walk, Elena. I will see you later.' Désirée stuck her head around the door of the *sala*.

'Very well.' Elena looked up from her embroidery. 'But don't be late for supper. We must put some more flesh back on your bones!'

Désirée laughed. 'I have done nothing but eat and sleep for almost a week,' she protested.

'*Sí*. You have recovered your health and looks,' Elena agreed with an air of satisfaction. 'But you must not tire yourself out.'

Between them, Elena and Rosita had bullied her unmercifully and, if the truth were known, Désirée had been glad to obey their strictures and do nothing. But today she had woken up, feeling full of energy again.

'I promise I won't go too far,' Désirée announced in her meekest tones. 'All I want is a little fresh air.'

Leaving Elena chuckling at this strange English passion for exercise, Désirée waved farewell.

She took the road that led towards Riofrío. It was cooler now that the sun was sinking, but she didn't plan to walk to the village, only down to the river. That pair of wild olive trees which offered shade to the bank would be far enough.

As she nearer her destination, she noticed a horse tethered to a branch of the one of the trees. Curiosity quickened her step.

A man was kneeling by one of the remaining pools in the riverbed. He had his back to her and was busy laving double-handfuls of water over his head and bare torso.

Désirée watched the water turning his thick black hair into a sleek gleaming seal's pelt before streaming down over his broad shoulders. It glittered in fat droplets on his olive skin, highlighting the hard muscle beneath.

Finishing his ablutions, the man rose to his feet. He shook off the surplus moisture and stood still, his tall lean body glowing like a golden statue in the rays of the sinking sun.

The breath caught in Désirée's throat as if a giant hand had squeezed all the air from her lungs.

The man turned and Désirée knew her sudden hope was real.

It *was* Rafael!

She began to run towards him and saw his startled expression change to one of sheer joy.

'Désirée!' Rafael ran back towards the bank and, giving a wild leap, landed right in front of her.

Without stopping to think, Désirée flung her arms around his neck and hugged him. 'Rafael!'

'Careful, *mi perla*. You'll get wet.'

'I don't care! Oh, Rafael, I've missed you so!'

'Have you?' he asked unsteadily. His arms tightened around around her waist. 'I missed you too,' he said, bending his dark head swiftly to hers.

All thought of caution fled. He had meant to keep his emotions in strict check but, caught off guard by Désirée's unexpected appearance he couldn't control the hunger that flared through him.

She felt so good, so soft and warm! He could smell the perfume of her hair and the clean fresh scent of her skin. As her lips parted, her little tongue eagerly seeking his, Rafael could taste the honey sweetness of her mouth, feel her fingers clutching frantically at his shoulders as she pressed herself against him.

Desire roared in him, deafening the voice of conscience.

'*Querida*!' He rained kisses upon her upturned face, from soft lips to cheek and eyelids and on up to smooth brow before seeking her lips again.

With a sigh of pleasure, Désirée took his hand from her waist and guided it to her breast. 'Hold me,' she murmured against his mouth.

Casting his scruples to the wind, Rafael tugged at the low-cut neckline of her gown, pulling the flimsy muslin aside. Cupping her naked breast with the same eager hand, his long fingers caressed its soft, full warmth, teasing the pink nipple until it stood proud and hard.

She shivered in his embrace and kissed him even more passionately.

Rafael's pulse was hammering and he thought he might explode with longing by the time the long kiss finally ended.

Désirée smiled up at him, her eyes misty. 'I can hardly believe you are here at last,' she whispered, reaching up to stroke his cheek.

'Good job I shaved, eh?' Rafael joked in an unsteady voice, trying desperately to regain control of himself. 'Or my beard would have cut your lovely skin to ribbons.'

Glancing down, Désirée noticed a razor alongside the dirty shirt he had discarded. 'You were tidying yourself before coming up to the house,' she murmured.

'I may not be presentable now, but you should have seen me before.' Rafael chuckled ruefully. 'You wouldn't have let me indoors!'

'Actually, I think you look rather attractive,' Désirée said naughtily, ruffling her fingers through the dark hair that covered his chest.

Encountering a hard copper nipple, she began to caress it.

Rafael bit back a groan and caught her hand. 'Don't,' he pleaded hoarsely.

'Why not?' Désirée met his gaze boldly. 'Don't you like it?'

'Little temptress! You know I do!' Rafael conveyed the hand he held to his lips and kissed it. 'But if we carry on like this I am never going to be able to resist you. I will end up making love to you right here and now!'

'Oh, do, please!' Désirée's grin was wicked as she pressed herself even closer against his aroused body. 'I know you want to.'

Abruptly, Rafael let her hand drop, an unaccustomed glow of colour heating his cheeks.

Désirée giggled at his embarrassment. 'I know, I'm a shameless hussy but. . .' she twined both arms around his neck, looking up at him with a provocative smile '. . .it does seem a pity to waste such a perfect opportunity.'

Employing every ounce of willpower, Rafael shook his head. 'Oh, no, *mi perla*,' he said gruffly. 'We are going to do things properly. The first time I enjoy your lovely body it will be in our marriage-bed.'

Désirée went very still 'What. . .what did you say?'

'I love you, Désirée Fontaine.' Rafael's voice was firm, almost defiant. 'And I am going to make you my wife as soon as the ceremony can be arranged.'

'You want to *marry* me?' Désirée gasped, her arms falling limply back to her sides.

'I shall be the proudest man alive if you consent to be my bride.'

He loved her! He had said that he loved her. Joy filled Désirée as the realisation sank in.

Rafael swallowed hard. She looked so beautiful with that smile illuminating her face. *Dios*! His heart sank at the thought of telling her the truth.

'It won't be easy for us, *Guerida*. We will face opposition from both sides from people who cannot understand that love is more powerful than hate. We. . . we have much to discuss.'

Rafael paused, awkwardly. It was unthinkable that he leave her in ignorance. She *had* to know everything, but how in God's name was he to begin?

Taking advantage of his silence, Désirée reached to touch his cheek lovingly. 'Can't all this talking wait?' she murmured, smiling up at him. 'It is perfectly proper, you know, for betrothed couples to exchange a kiss!'

Rafael struggled with his conscience for an instant. He ought to confess now! But surely they deserved this moment of perfect happiness after their long separation?

His need for her too strong, Rafael swiftly bent his head once more and captured Désirée's willing lips.

Chapter Twelve

Rafael's return generated a storm of excitement. The entire household flocked to welcome him home and it was suppertime before peace was restored.

Over the meal Elena spoke of the smallpox outbreak, lavishly praising Désirée's nursing skills. Embarrassed, Désirée tried to make light of her exploits.

'No, no, I cannot let you refuse the credit,' Elena insisted. 'I owe you my life and so do many of the villagers.'

Feeling Rafael's eyes on her, Désirée coloured. 'I did what anyone would,' she muttered.

To her relief, Elena let the subject drop, but later, when his sister left the *sala* for a few moments, Rafael thanked her for her efforts with a heartfelt sincerity.

'You helped me when I was in need,' Désirée replied simply.

'You have more than amply repaid the debt, *querida*.'

The three of them sat up late, talking and laughing. Désirée noticed Rafael carefully avoided any mention of his absence, but she was too happy to have him back to question him.

He spent most of the next morning engaged in dealing with estate business. Désirée hoped they might have the afternoon together, but after the *siesta* Father Gomez arrived and Rafael took him off to his study.

When they emerged, Rafael announced that the priest had accepted an invitation to supper. Désirée went off

to change her gown, a feeling of puzzled irritation beginning to take hold of her. If she didn't know better, she
might almost imagine Rafael was avoiding being alone
with her!

Supper was a lively affair. The cook had produced a
veritable banquet to celebrate Rafael's return home and
several bottles of excellent wine were broached.

It was very late when Désirée finally fell into bed.

She wasn't surprised to discover that she had overslept
the next morning.

Only Elena remained at the breakfast table.

'Rafael has gone into Covarrubias,' Elena announced,
answering Désirée's question. 'He said something about
being back around noon.'

Désirée bit her lip. After a moment she said, 'I think
I might go for a ride.'

'Alone?' Elena looked slightly disapproving when
Désirée declined the offer of a groom.

'I need a little time by myself to think,' Désirée replied
lightly and, finishing her simple repast, went to change
into her riding-habit.

Two hours later she reined in her horse, her expression
baffled.

'Whoa, Madrigal! I think we are lost!'

Désirée didn't recognise these hills at all. Had she
been so wrapped up in distracted thoughts of the future
that she had strayed beyond the boundaries of the Casa?

A quick glance showed her that the sun had travelled
much closer to its noon-day position. She had been riding
for a lot longer than she had realised.

'Damn and blast it!' she muttered. Rafael would be
home soon and she wanted to be there to greet him.

If only she could manage an uninterrupted talk in private with Rafael, all the stupid nervous doubts which
had been slowly growing in her mind over the last two
days could be put to rest.

'I will feel more settled once we have announced our
plans,' she murmured, patting Madrigal's glossy neck.

She knew she needed to get used to the idea of

marriage, but last night when he had escorted her upstairs at the end of the evening she had sensed that Rafael was troubled too.

'There is something we must speak of, *mi perla*,' he had said abruptly as they neared her door. 'Something I should have told you a long time ago. Something I cannot keep putting off.'

His sombre expression had alarmed Désirée. With a start of surprise, she noticed that his hands were shaking.

'Rafael? Is something wrong?' She had never seen him look this way before. He seemed almost nervous.

'Did you never wonder why I was away so long?' Rafael began awkwardly. 'Or what I was doing while I was gone?'

Désirée let out a sigh of relief. 'Oh, Rafael, it's all right! I know what you are trying to tell me, but it doesn't matter.'

He stared at her, plainly dumbfounded. 'You know? But, in that case, why aren't you angry with me? I was sure you—'

'I'm not saying I approve,' Désirée interrupted hastily. 'But I can understand your need to fight. It is only natural that you should wish to join your country's army.' She gave him a faint smile. 'You fought at Talavera, didn't you?'

'*Sí*, but the situation is not as you imagine.' Rafael turned pale beneath his tan.

'Are you are trying to confess that you are only on leave and have to rejoin your regiment?' Désirée asked helpfully.

'The Spanish forces were shattered at Almonacid! There is nothing to rejoin, even if I wished to do so!'

She had recoiled from the violence in his voice and Rafael had immediately apologised and changed the subject.

Dismissing the unsettling memory, Désirée re-focussed her concentration on which route to take.

'I think it's this way.' She encouraged her horse into a trot. 'Let's get back.'

'*Quién esta ahí?*'

The man suddenly appeared at the side of the track and, startled, Désirée reined to a halt.

'I am Désirée Fontaine,' she answered his question. 'Surely you remember me? I was in the village only a few...' Her voice trailed off in dismay as she realised her mistake. This man wasn't from Riofrío.

Nor were the other two men who now rose from their cover behind boulders to confront her.

The first man spat on the ground. 'You have a French name, woman.'

He raised the barrel of his rifle and stared at Désirée with unconcealed venom.

'What do you want? I have no money on me.' Désirée forced herself to speak calmly.

'El Verdugo might value you as a hostage.'

'You...you are El Verdugo's men?' Désirée's voice faltered as she spoke the hated name. Suddenly she felt very afraid.

The man smiled as if her fear pleased him. 'I see you have heard of The Executioner. Good. Then you know it is best to do as we say. *Vamonos pronto.*'

Désirée obediently kicked Madrigal into motion. 'Where are you taking me?'

'To our camp. El Verdugo can decide whether we kill you or use you as a hostage.'

Horrified, Désirée fell silent. For one mad moment she considered trying to escape, but decided not to risk it. Any hasty move would undoubtedly bring violent retribution!

The track they took climbed upwards, becoming very rough. After a while they made her stop and she was blindfolded with a dirty neck-scarf. The reins were taken from her and her wrists bound with a thin piece of rawhide.

Désirée remained silent. There was no use protesting.

It was impossible to judge how long she was led. It felt like hours! At last she became aware of other noises, other voices. Abruptly, Madrigal was halted and she was

hauled unceremoniously from the saddle. The blindfold
was removed and she saw a crowd of men and a few
women. They were mostly dirty and roughly dressed,
their faces hostile as they gazed at her.

'This way.' The man who had captured her prodded
her with the butt of his rifle towards a group of small
tents that had been set up under a couple of pine trees.

He jerked open the tent-flap of one and shoved her
roughly inside. Désirée stumbled. Unable to save herself
because of her bound hands, she fell awkwardly to
the floor.

Cruel laughter was followed by the sound of the flap
being secured once more and then the tramp of booted
feet moving away.

Struggling into a sitting position, Désirée blinked away
the tears which threatened.

'Damn and blast it!' she whispered, fighting the urge
to scream.

No one knew where she was! How would anyone from
the Casa be able to find her here? She might never see
Rafael again!

'Stop it!' Désirée's sharp little teeth bit savagely into
her lower lip. If she didn't try and think more positively,
she would lapse into panic.

At least they hadn't hurt her. She had been very afraid
that they might. Rape was the common fate of women
taken in war.

Désirée swallowed the bile that rose in her throat at
the thought of one of those men touching her.

Desperately she glanced around the tent, but it was
empty save for a couple of grubby blankets. There was
nothing she could use to cut her bonds.

She tried wriggling her fingers. Her wrists were
already sore. The rawhide strip was very tight and she
couldn't loosen it with her teeth.

After a while she gave up and sat in apprehensive
silence waiting for something to happen. The minutes
ticked by, but no one came.

It occurred to her that El Verdugo might be away from

the camp. Or perhaps he was too busy to deal with her. Either way, it looked as if she could be in for a long wait.

It was very hot and airless in the tent and she was horribly thirsty. After an hour or so, when her eyelids began to droop, she decided not to fight to stay awake and allowed herself to slide flat. She doubted she would be able to sleep properly, but her discomfort and thirst wouldn't seem so bad if she could doze.

The sound of shouting jerked her awake. The sun was no longer beating on the canvas walls of her prison, but it was still light outside so she didn't think she had slept long. She wriggled back into a sitting position, longing for a drink, and moistened her dry lips with her tongue.

The tent-flap was suddenly wrenched open and she had to conquer the desire to scrabble away into a corner.

Two men were standing at the entrance. Dazzled by a shaft of low sunlight which came lancing in, she blinked at them, her vision blurring.

'Désirée.'

For a moment she thought she was hallucinating, until he came closer and she felt herself lifted gently to her feet.

'Rafael!' His name escaped her lips in a frightened gasp. 'Oh, what are you doing here? Did they capture you too?'

'Let me untie you, *querida*.' His strong fingers were busy with the rawhide.

The tears she had held back for so long began to trickle down Désirée's face. Somehow he must have discovered she was in this awful place and tried to rescue her.

Without turning his head, Rafael threw the strip of rawhide to the ground and snapped a curt remark to the guard who was still standing in the entrance. Désirée wanted to tell him not to antagonise their captors, but she couldn't force the words out past her sobs.

'Don't cry, *mi ninfa*.' Rafael gently smoothed back her dishevelled hair and pulled her into his arms so that she could rest against his shoulder.

Désirée gulped hard, struggling to regain her composure. When she looked up again she saw that the guard had gone.

Rafael examined her wrists and swore beneath his breath at the angry red marks which the bonds had left. 'Did they hurt you in any other way?' he demanded hoarsely.

She shook her head. 'No. I'm all right.'

'Thank God!'

The expression in his eyes told her how worried he had been and she tried to smile reassuringly at him.

'Oh, my brave little love!' His self-control cracking, Rafael kissed her, his mouth urgent.

Désirée answered his passion with the same fire. For hours she had thought they might never see each other again!

But they weren't out of danger yet.

'You shouldn't have come after me, Rafael,' she exclaimed, pulling away from him. 'These men belong to El Verdugo. They are very dangerous.'

'I know.'

Désirée scarcely registered the irony in his tone. 'What do you think they will do with us?'

'Don't be afraid. I won't let them hurt you.'

The sound of footsteps approaching made Désirée jump. Rafael swung round, his expression turning hard.

One of the *guerrillas* who had taken Désirée prisoner ducked in through the flap. To her surprise, he carried a tray filled with food and wine.

'Leave that and get out.' Rafael's voice was cold.

Anxiously, Désirée touched his arm. 'Don't anger them,' she said softly in English.

'*Señorita*, if we had only known who you were—'

'Go. We are not to be disturbed again. Is that clear?'

The young man's face turned red and he hurriedly backed out.

Confused, Désirée watched Rafael pour out the wine. He handed her a beaker and she took it automatically, her thoughts whirling.

Rafael drank deeply. Watching him, Désirée became aware that he was extremely tense.

'Rafael, what is going on?' Désirée took a nervous gulp of her wine. It had sounded as if he was giving that man orders, but that was absurd!

He took a step towards her and then halted, a very uncharacteristic expression of indecision appearing on his face and she gazed at him in sudden alarm. 'Have you. . .have you come to some sort of arrangement with them?'

The first *guerrilla* had spoken of hostages. Was it possible that Rafael had offered to take her place and they had agreed?

'I will not allow you to sacrifice yourself for me,' she declared fiercely. 'Whatever is to happen, we will face it together.'

Rafael stifled a groan. *Por Dios*, why did it have to be here of all places that he must finally explain!

'Désirée, listen to me. We aren't in any danger. These men won't hurt us.'

Désirée stared at him in utter bewilderment. 'How can you be so sure?'

Rafael's dark eyes clouded with pain. 'I know it— because *I* am El Verdugo.'

Was she going mad? Had fear turned her brain? This was *Rafael*, the man she loved. How could he and that vile murderer be one and the same?

'I. . .I don't understand!' Désirée felt panic rising in her. Why did he stand there in silence, making no attempt to end her torment? 'That means *you* killed Etienne!'

'No!' Her horrified exclamation released Rafael's frozen tongue. 'I wasn't even there that day. The ambush was mounted in my absence. It wasn't planned. My men took a chance when they saw the patrol.'

He took a step towards her, his hand stretched out in entreaty. 'Désirée, we hadn't even met when it happened. How was I to know that colonel was your brother?'

Désirée backed away from him. 'But you would have

done the same? You would have attacked his patrol?'

She waited with bated breath for his answer, her eyes huge and violet in her pale face.

Rejecting the temptation to lie, Rafael jerked his head in assent and watched her features twist into a mask of bitter hatred.

'Then you are just as guilty as they are!'

'Désirée, for the love of God—'.

'Don't touch me!' Désirée struck his hand away as he reached for her.

Rafael took a deep breath. 'Please, listen to me. I wanted to tell you the truth, but at first I didn't know if I could trust you—'

'I trusted you!' Désirée screamed. 'Did it amuse you to flirt with me, knowing that you were responsible for my brother's death? How you must have secretly laughed when I offered myself to you!'

He paled at the accusation. 'Is that what you truly think of me?'

'I think you are a liar and a cheat, only interested in your own self-preservation. What better way to make sure that I never achieved the revenge you knew I sought than to make me fall in love with you!'

Désirée shuddered. What a fool she had been! With the benefit of hindsight, she could see that both Armand and Father Gomez had tried in their different ways to warn her. Well, now she was paying the price for her blind folly!

'I know I have hurt you. Believe me, it is the last thing I wanted and I am desperately sorry for it.' Rafael raked one hand wildly through his thick hair. 'I've been trying to find the right moment to explain ever since my return.'

'Really?' Sarcasm flooded Désirée's voice. 'And just when did you plan to finally pluck up the courage to tell me? At the altar?'

Rafael winced. 'You have every right to be angry. It was cowardly of me not to tell you sooner, but I knew you would be. . .upset,' he muttered, floundering for words.

'*Upset*!'

Dios, but this was even worse than he had imagined! She was looking at him as if she wanted to knife him.

'I realise that this has come as a terrible shock to you,' he ploughed on, his usual possession in shreds. 'But try to remember that, until I knew you could be trusted, I had to put my duty to Spain before my own wishes.'

'Is that what you call your killing and spying?' Désirée's voice was filled with loathing. 'Oh, don't look so surprised. I may be gullible, but I'm not a complete fool. You came to Madrid to gather information, didn't you? That's why you invited French officers to your house and pretended to be an *afrancesado*.'

No wonder he'd been annoyed when she saw him with that man who had later re-appeared at the Casa. It was obvious now that he'd been bringing Rafael news about the British advance.

'How could you stoop so *low*?'

Her scornful tone brought a flush of colour to stain Rafael's cheeks, but his dark eyes held hers steadily. 'I told you war is a dirty business.'

Désirée glared at him, hating him. How could he stand there so coolly when he had destroyed her dreams, wrecked every hope she'd had for the future?

'I'm not proud of some of the things I have done.' Rafael strove desperately to breach the barrier she had erected and make her realise that his role as a *guerrilla* leader had nothing to do with his feelings for her. 'I did what I had to. Your brother was a soldier. He would have understood.'

'Don't you dare speak of Etienne to me! You are not fit to wipe his boots!'

She was trembling, her face whiter than bleached linen. Realising that she was too overwrought to listen to logic, Rafael abandoned his attempt to explain his motives. In this mood, he doubted she would even accept that he'd wanted her out of Madrid to ensure her safety lest the British capture the city.

'Désirée, what's past is past. Don't let it stand in the way of our future. I love you.'

She stared at him wildly. 'I don't think you even understand the meaning of the word! If you loved me, you wouldn't have deceived me. All you feel, all you can ever have felt for me, is lust!'

Rafael caught her by the arm, pulling her towards him. '*Querida*, don't! Don't let your grief drive a wedge between us. Give me another chance. Let me prove how much I care. I swear on my word of honour that I will never keep the truth from you again.'

The touch of his hand ignited the same flame of desire in her as it always had and Désirée hated herself for her weakness. If he kissed her, she might give way to the tears that were stinging behind her lids and surrender to her crazy longing to trust in his words of love.

'Let me go, you hypocrite!' With all her strength she struck out with her free hand, hitting him so hard that the imprint of her fingers stood out clearly on his brown cheek. 'I wouldn't accept your word now, not even if you swore it on a stack of bibles!'

He released her, a stunned look of disbelief in his eyes.

'You must be mad if you think I would marry you!' she hissed at him, taking a bitter pleasure in seeing him flinch. She wanted to hurt him as much as he had hurt her and harsh words were the only weapon at her disposal. 'I loathe the very sight of you! You disgust me!'

He stepped away from her, his expression a proud mask.

'So be it. I will ask for your understanding no more. Let everything we have meant to each other end here.'

The anguish in her heart was as if a knife was being twisted into it, but Désirée ignored the pain and said coldly, 'I never want to have to speak to you again.'

He bowed with exquisite grace. 'I shall arrange for your immediate return to Madrid.' A faint mocking smile touched his lips. '*Vaya con Dios*, Mademoiselle Fontaine. We shall not meet again.'

'My dear *mam'selle*. I did not know you had returned to Madrid. Welcome back.'

'Thank you, Marques.' Désirée swept him an elegant curtsy. She rose with a polite smile pinned to her lips. The King's drawing-room was no place to show her dislike of this cynical old man.

'You missed all the excitement, my dear. Only imagine, we almost found ourselves evicted by the British.' The Marques de Aranda's hooded eyes took on mocking gleam. 'I hear they have given Wellesley a title for his efforts. Viscount Wellington of Talavera. Such generous creatures, those countrymen of yours.'

Désirée struggled to conceal her surprise. How had he found out that she had English blood? It was not commonly known.

'Are you enjoying the concert, *señor*?' she asked, determined not to let him see that he had startled her.

'Not particularly. However, this interval affords the opportunity of some amusing conversation. Everyone seems to have been invited to the Palace tonight.' He fluttered the bejewelled fan he carried in a languid gesture, indicating the crowded room. 'Speaking of friends, my dear, surely you did not come on your own?'

'Major Evrard escorted me.' Armand had gone to fetch her a cooling drink. She hoped he would hurry back.

'Ah, the gallant Major.' The Marques permitted his lips to crease in a thin smile. 'I understand his search for El Verdugo continues. How disappointing for you that he has had no success.'

Désirée stiffened. 'I must accept God's will,' she murmured, taking refuge in a platitude he dare not dispute.

She had only arrived back in Madrid a few days ago and had not yet decided what her next move should be. Although logic dictated that she denounce Rafael, she shrank from revealing him to be El Verdugo. She kept telling herself this hesitation was merely because she did not wish the world to know what a gullible fool she had been, but in her heart she knew she was lying.

Even now, her love for him was not entirely dead and she could not face repaying his betrayal with the deliberate denunciation he so richly deserved.

'I thought you would decide to stay on at Casa del Aguila.'

'Why?' Désirée hastily reined in her wandering attention.

Lifting pained brows at her bluntness, the Marques murmured, 'Isn't it obvious? Rafael de Velasco is your *novio*.'

'You are labouring under a misapprehension, *señor*. He is most certainly not my sweetheart.'

'What a pity.' He gave a malicious chuckle. 'Your marriage would be a perfect way to cement the new relationship between our two countries! It would disappoint my wife, of course, but don't let that weigh with you.'

'Do not be absurd!' Désirée's cheeks flushed with sudden rage. 'I have no wish to marry or even see that man again. In fact, your whore of a wife can have him with my blessing!'

His mouth gaped open in speechless affront and Désirée seized her chance to escape back to Armand.

Noticing her high colour, Armand asked if the Marques had been up to his usual tricks. 'You mustn't let him upset you. He enjoys baiting us.'

'I swear he only supports King Joseph out of expediency.' Désirée threw back the contents of her wine-glass in one angry swallow.

'Probably. However, he does possess influence.' Armand cast a cautious glance around and, dropping his voice, added softly, 'They say he employs an army of spies.'

So that explained how the Marques knew of her real ancestry!

Désirée already regretted her outburst and not only because Aranda might seek revenge. The Marquesa's reputation was dubious, but she had never given Désirée cause to insult her and Désirée was ashamed of her spiteful remark.

'I'm not really in the mood for the rest of the concert,' she said abruptly. 'Will you please take me home?'

Armand inclined his fiery head in assent and offered her his arm.

Désirée was lodging with Colonel Thierry and his wife. She hadn't had the heart to look for a house of her own. In truth, she no longer had the heart for anything.

The shock of discovering that Rafael was a *guerrilla* had robbed her of both appetite and energy and she was so white-faced and silent during the journey back to Madrid that Rosita had been seriously worried.

Outwardly, Désirée had now recovered, but within her soul the nightmare continued. Every night she cried herself to sleep, but tears could not ease her distress. Rafael's betrayal had polluted everything, cutting her off from all happiness and joy. Even the simple pleasures of life had no meaning, her very food seemed tasteless. She felt like a ghost cut off from the world, nothing was real.

When Armand had appeared on the Thierrys' doorstep, it had been too much trouble to send him away. He was eager to resume his courtship and had beseeched her to accompany him to the concert tonight.

Listlessly, Désirée had agreed. His calculating ambition had lost its power to affect her. It didn't matter. Nothing mattered.

Now, as they left the Royal Palace, she realised with a jerk of surprise that her encounter with the Marques of Aranda had shattered the apathy which had engulfed her since leaving Casa del Aguila.

'I think it is better if you don't come in, Armand,' she said as he escorted her to the Thierrys' door.

Startled, Armand asked if he had done anything to annoy her.

Désirée shook her head. 'I just need to be by myself.'

'Is something wrong?'

'I want to think. I must make plans for my future.'

'Are you considering leaving?' Armand stared at her in dismay and Désirée cursed her expressive face.

'Is it the Marques? Don't worry, I shall deal with—'

'I don't give a damn what Aranda or anyone else says about me,' Désirée interrupted fiercely. 'I don't need his approval or yours! From now on I intend to live my life as I see fit!'

To please *Maman* and Etienne she had concealed her English blood and striven to be a good Frenchwoman, but now they were gone, as was Grandfather. She was free to live her life in whatever manner she chose and, right now, all she wanted was to retire quietly somewhere far away and lick her wounds in private!

With a stab of bitter amusement, she realised that Aranda couldn't hurt her. Society already disapproved of her desire for independence—they might as well have something else to gossip about. Let them all know that Fate had moulded her into a hybrid who didn't belong to either France or England! After the way Rafael had broken her heart, it scarcely seemed to matter.

A rush of sadness swept aside her amusement. She had already found the home she really wanted. Everything had gone wrong and she could not stay, but she belonged here in Spain where she had more in common with Father Gomez and the people of Riofrío than Madame Thierry or Armand Evrard.

'I thought you were going to accept my offer.'

Hearing the note of offended puzzlement in Armand's voice, Désirée struggled to collect her thoughts and find an answer.

'I am grateful for the friendship you have shown me, but I don't want to marry you, Armand,' she said carefully.

'Why not?' he demanded. 'I swear I'd be a good husband.'

'I don't love you.'

'Forget your romantic ideas, I beg of you, *chérie*! We can be happy without such nonsense.'

Désirée shook her head. 'Marriage between us wouldn't work, Armand. Our values are too different.'

'You can't leave Spain! Think of your quest for vengeance!'

'I have not forgotten it.'

Désirée had sworn on Etienne's grave that she would

see his killer punished. Pain twisted within her as she
realised that she would never have the strength to carry
out that vow.

'I don't understand you,' Armand muttered sulkily.

A bleak smile touched Désirée's lips. 'I don't want to
marry anyone, Armand. I just want to try to forget I ever
came to Spain.'

It was the only way to free herself from the past.

'I can't say I blame you, I hate this accursed country!'
Armand let out a gusty sigh of sympathy. 'It's only fit
for savages! But as my wife you wouldn't be stuck here
forever, you know,' he added persuasively. 'My advance-
ment is certain. As soon as we throw the English back
into the sea, I'll be able to ask for a transfer to Paris.
You'd be able to enjoy a civilised life, mixing in the best
society.'

'Armand, please!' Désirée was rapidly losing patience.
'I'm not even sure if I wish to go on living in France,
but I do know I don't want to be your wife.'

Armand's eyes narrowed. 'Is there someone else?' he
demanded.

Désirée denied it quickly.

'I don't believe you! We were getting along famously
until you went to Casa del Aguila. There is no reason
for you to have decided against me unless...' His pale
eyes bored into Désirée's face and to her annoyance she
couldn't help flushing.

'*Merde!* It's Velasco, isn't it?' An ugly note of jealousy harshened Armand's light tones.

'No! You're wrong! I hate that man!'

Armand gave a short bark of laughter. 'Here's a pretty
change of tune! When I told you that I suspected he
might be a spy, you nearly jumped down my throat.'

Désirée shrugged, feigning calm, but her knees were
shaking. 'My reason for changing my opinion concerning
Rafael is personal. I have no desire to discuss it.'

Armand eyed her speculatively. Something didn't add
up here. 'Velasco is a powerful man,' he said slowly.
'But I don't trust him. In fact, I'm thinking of starting

up an investigation into his activities. You see, I heard a rumour the other day that he was amassing guns.'

Désirée strove to keep her expression blank, but her mouth dried in sudden alarm.

'As you know, I have special authority from the King to root out *guerrillas*.' His gaze hardened. 'If you know anything, it is your duty to inform me of it.'

'There's nothing to tell.' Désirée could feel her heart-beat pounding dizzily in her ears.

'Are you sure?' Armand glared at her. 'I think you are hiding something.'

'Armand, will you please stop this!'

'You are in love with him, aren't you? That's why you went to the Casa, why you are shielding him.' His expression was contemptuous. 'You are a fool, Désirée! Did you really think he would return your sentiments? Can't you see that a man like that would only want to use you?'

Hysterical laughter bubbled up into Désirée's throat.

'And what about you, *monsieur*? Would you have offered for me if I had been poor?'

'Don't be absurd! My feelings have nothing to do with it.' Armand shrugged off her question with a look of affronted outrage and returned to the attack. 'Just what is it that you are concealing?'

'Nothing! Désirée turned away with an impatient gesture, intending to bid him goodnight, but Armand forestalled her.

'Wait!' He grabbed her by the arm. 'If you won't consider helping me, think of your brother! You owe it to Etienne to tell the truth!'

Désirée paled and, sensing her hesitation, Armand increased his pressure. 'Is Velasco one of the *guerrillas*?' He noted the flare of alarmed anguish in her wide blue eyes and sucked in his breath. '*Mon Dieu*! He is, isn't he?'

'No! You're wrong!' Désirée pulled away frantically, her voice trembling.

An unholy glee lit up Armand's pale gaze. 'I knew it!

I always knew that bastard was up to no good! It wouldn't surprise me if he turned out to be someone important—' He cut himself off sharply, watching how her alarmed expression changed to one of horror.

He let her go. 'El Verdugo himself,' he breathed.

Désirée hesitated just a fraction too long and Armand let out a crow of triumphant satisfaction.

'Armand, you are mistaken—'

'Oh I don't think so, *chérie*.' He chuckled lightly. 'I don't think so at all!'

'*Senorita*! Thank God, you are awake.' Rosita cried as she answered Désirée's bell the next morning.

Désirée, who was seated before the dressing-table of her borrowed bedchamber, turned with a start.

'They are saying that Don Rafael is a *guerrillero*,' Rosita exclaimed before she could ask what was wrong.

'Where did you hear this?' Désirée demanded, her hairbrush falling from suddenly nerveless fingers.

'At Doña Mercedes's. You were sleeping so I thought I'd go and try to match that torn lace.'

Désirée took a deep breath. 'It's true. Don Rafael is El Verdugo.'

Rosita paled and Désirée waved her into to a chair before continuing, her expression hard. 'Major Evrard asked me for the truth last night and I. . .I laid information against Don Rafael.'

'*Madre de Dios!* But you love him!'

'Not any more.' Désirée's mouth began to tremble. She wasn't surprised that Rosita had guessed her true feelings. Servants often were the first to know what was going on. 'He killed my love for him, just as he killed my brother.'

After Armand had guessed the truth, there seemed little else to do but admit that Rafael was responsible for Etienne's death. She owed her brother that much at least.

'I think you are being unjust, *señorita*,' Rosita announced slowly. 'I too loved Etienne, but I don't hold

Don Rafael personally to blame for his death. We are fighting a war and, in a war, soldiers often die.'

'You are a Spaniard. You are bound to see things differently.' Désirée could feel the thin thread of her self-control stretching almost to breaking point.

'I see the truth. Do you want Don Rafael's blood on your hands?'

Désirée began to shake uncontrollably. 'He deserves to hang! I won't let you try and make me feel guilty. It was my duty to confess!'

'*I* did not speak of guilt, *señorita*. It is your own conscience that is telling you that you have done a wicked thing.'

'You have no right to criticise me, Rosita!'

Désirée told herself she had nothing to reproach herself for. She hadn't set out to denounce Rafael. Armand had guessed his identity.

'All I did was confirm the truth. He *is* a traitor! And he betrayed my trust! He ought to be punished!'

But why did she feel no satisfaction?

Rosita saw the fury fade from Désirée's pale face, leaving behind an expression of bewilderment. 'Go to Major Evrard, *señorita*,' she urged. 'Tell him that you were mistaken.'

'I can't,' Désirée gasped, her voice cracking and her eyes filling with tears. 'It's too late. Armand would never believe me!'

Rosita jumped up and, hurrying to kneel at Désirée's side, put an arm around her, murmuring words of comfort that Désirée scarcely heard.

'Why didn't I go on denying it?' she sobbed. 'Dear God, I don't know what possessed me! I don't want Rafael to die!'

'What will the Major do?'

Struggling to master her emotion, Désirée answered, 'He told me that he will seek permission to lead an attack on Casa del Aguila. He had no doubt it would be granted.'

'He will have to move fast if he hopes to surprise

Don Rafael,' Rosita said thoughtfully. 'And he will need many men.'

'The King will give them to him. The capture of El Verdugo will demonstrate French power and show everyone that the *guerrillas* need not be feared.'

'Can't you plead with the Major? He likes you. He might let Don Rafael go if you begged him to.'

Désirée let out a wild laugh. 'You mistake the extent of my influence, Rosita! Even if he was willing to give up his chance of winning glory, Armand wants promotion. He has many debts.'

'You could offer him money.'

'I can't match a colonelcy.' Désirée dismissed this suggestion.

She rubbed her temples. Her head was throbbing and a sense of hopeless frustration filled her. There seemed no way to prevent the attack.

'What about sending a message to warn Don Rafael?'

'How? Who can we trust to take it?'

Désirée had gathered from Armand that he expected to be able to leave tomorrow morning at the latest. Their messenger would have at least one company of *chasseurs à Cheval* hard on his heels.

'I cannot ask anyone to undertake such a dangerous mission—' Her voice suddenly stilled for an instant. 'But I will deliver the warning myself.'

'*Senorita*! You cannot!'

'Why not? I'm a capable rider and I wouldn't get lost.'

'But. . .but. . .you are a woman!' Rosita's expression was scandalised. 'What will people say!'

'They won't know. I shall dress as a man.'

'Even so, it would be dangerous to travel alone.'

'I'm not taking one of Madame Thierry's grooms,' Désirée retorted, her mouth setting into a stubborn line. 'I don't know them well enough to trust them.'

'Then I shall come with you.'

Désirée shook her head.

'I can ride,' Rosita said stoutly. 'Not as well as you, but I promise I will keep up.' When Désirée continued to hesitate, she added softly, 'Please, *señorita*, don't shut me out. I would feel that I was letting Etienne down if I allowed you to go alone.'

'Very well,' Désirée whispered, her heart too full to say more as she clasped Rosita's hands in gratitude.

Rosita returned the pressure for an instant and then sprang to her feet. 'I know a place to buy suitable clothes.'

Recovering her composure, Désirée handed over her purse.

'Buy an outfit for each of us and hire a horse for yourself from Señor Gonzales. I'll pack a few necessities and think of some excuse for the Thierrys while you are out.' Her brow creased in thought. 'I can say I have a fancy to visit that shrine Madame was talking about yesterday. I'll also mention that we might stay on for a short while at the convent there.'

Rosita nodded and hurried to the door.

'Be as quick as you can, Rosita. We must leave before the *siesta* begins or it will look odd.'

They couldn't afford to arouse any suspicions. There was too much at stake!

Chapter Thirteen

'**W**ho are you? Where is Don Rafael?'

Désirée stared in consternation at the big, heavily built man who came awkwardly to his feet at her whirlwind entry into the *sala*. He wore the black soutane of a priest, but he was a stranger.

Disappointment washed over her. It had been a gruelling journey, fraught with hardship and the danger of discovery, and she was close to exhaustion.

She was also extremely nervous. It had taken all of her courage to enter Casa del Aguila. The idea of actually facing Rafael again after all the terrible things she had said made her feel dizzily breathless.

'I am Sancho Ortego y Castuero,' the priest said curtly. 'My cousin Rafael is not at home.'

His brown gaze swept appraisingly over her. Glad that she had stopped a few leagues back to change out of her masculine attire, Désirée dipped a brief curtsy.

'Delighted to make your acquaintance, *Padre*,' she murmured politely, subconsciously attributing his lack of warmth to surprise. 'My name is—'

'Don't bother. I can guess.' His tone filled with contempt. 'You are the French bitch who has broken my cousin's heart!'

Désirée flinched from him in shock. 'You. . .you don't know what you are talking about,' she stammered, too taken aback to defend herself.

'Ah, but I do!' A wealth of hostile dislike glittered in

his eyes. 'Rafael is a changed man since you deserted him, Mademoiselle Fontaine. I haven't seen him smile once since the day I arrived.'

'I don't know what he has told you—'

'He hasn't said a word,' Sancho interrupted her roughly. 'Others told me what happened.' He glared at her. 'I suppose you've come back to apologise, but it's too late. He's better off without you. We don't need any accursed French spawn here.'

Désirée lifted her chin proudly, ignoring her weariness. 'What passed between us is none of your business,' she said in a tone as cold as his own. 'I do not have to justify myself to you. All I will say is that I am here on urgent business and must see Rafael at once.'

He shook his dark head. 'If you think I will let you near him again, you are sadly mistaken. His work is too important to Spain to have his mind troubled by the likes of you. You had your chance and threw it away. Now get out.'

Désirée drew in a deep breath. 'Your manners ill befit your calling, *Padre*,' she snapped, her eyes flashing with rage. 'How dare you try to browbeat me! I have come all the way from Madrid and I *will* speak to Rafael.'

She crossed determinedly to a chair and sat down with every appearance of composure. 'Now, unless you mean to pick me up and throw me out bodily, have the goodness to ring that bell and desire Ramona to bring me some lemonade. I am parched.'

His heavy brows drew together in a thunderous frown, but after a short tense silence he gave a begrudging nod and did as she bade him.

Désirée saw that he walked with a bad limp. Elena had once revealed that her favourite cousin was serving as an army chaplain. She hadn't mentioned his handicap, but it seemed almost certain that this must be the same man.

'I can understand your dislike of me,' she said in a quieter tone as he turned to face her again. 'But the sooner you tell me where I may find Rafael, then the sooner I shall be able leave.'

'You don't intend to stay?'

'Not one moment longer than it takes to deliver my message.'

'And what is this oh-so-important message?'

Désirée hesitated. She was reluctant to explain her actions to this hostile man. He might not even believe she deeply regretted her folly.

'I should prefer not to disclose that information, except to Don Rafael or his sister,' she said stiffly.

'Elena is down at the village.' Sancho eyed her suspiciously. 'Why won't you tell me?'

'I assure you I mean Rafael no harm.' She clasped her hands tightly together to stop them trembling. 'Believe me, it is vital he hears my news.'

He shook his head. 'I don't trust you. I think you are planning mischief.'

Désirée let out an impatient sigh at his stubbornness. 'Very well. My purpose in coming here was to bring warning that the authorities know Rafael's secret identity and plan to capture him.'

He let out a bellow of rage and to Désirée's alarm grabbed her by the arm and yanked her up out of her chair.

'And who betrayed him, eh?' he demanded, thrusting his face close to hers. 'Was it you?'

Désirée refused to show the fear she could feel welling up in her tight chest. 'It was a mistake. I want to make amends.'

'Liar!' Sancho shook her arm roughly. 'You have come here to trap him, but—'

'*Let her go.*' The deep voice cut across Sancho's angry yelling, bringing instant obedience.

Freed, Désirée whipped round to see Rafael standing in the open doorway.

Greedily, her starved senses drank in his appearance. Clad in riding-boots, black cord breeches and a billowing-sleeved white shirt open at the neck, his tall figure radiated vitality, but to her dismay there was no glimmer of welcome in his dark eyes as she took an impulsive step towards him.

She came to a halt, her courage failing.

'Stand away from her, cousin. I don't need you to fight my battles for me.' Rafael walked into the room, his manner casual as he tossed the riding-whip he carried onto a side-table, but Désirée's heightened senses picked up the tension coiled within his lean frame.

With a mutter of protest, Sancho reluctantly obeyed.

'Why have you come back, Désirée?' Rafael's voice was coolly controlled.

'I came to warn you that Major Evrard is on his way here.' Désirée forced herself to speak calmly and ignore her thudding heart. 'He knows who you are.'

'I suppose you told him?'

The mocking scorn in his voice sent a chill down Désirée's spine, but she held his eyes bravely. 'Yes, I did.'

'I wondered if you might.' For an instant Rafael let his bitterness show.

Swallowing hard against the dryness in her throat, Désirée continued doggedly. 'Your capture is his first priority, but he also means to raze this house as a warning to others not to rebel.'

'How many men does he have?'

'I don't know exactly. Enough.'

'Don't believe her, Rafael. She has betrayed you to the French once already. This is a scheme to hand you over to them.'

Désirée threw Sancho a furious look. 'And just how am I supposed to achieve such an aim? Am I going to tie him up, toss him over the back of my horse and ride off with him?'

Sancho had the grace to look discomfited.

Désirée turned back to Rafael, a militant expression in her eyes. 'I don't care what you think of me,' she lied. 'But I don't want harm to come to Elena or any of the servants.'

She would not tell him that she couldn't bear the pain of knowing she was responsible for his death.

'Please.' Her angry voice dropped. 'Don't let mistrust of me allow you to risk their lives. Armand is only a few hours behind me. They will be here soon.'

She saw from his expression that he believed her.

'Sancho, call all the servants together and tell them we are evacuating the Casa.'

'I say we should fight!'

'*Dios*!' Rafael ran one hand through his wind-blown hair in a gesture of exasperation that was painfully familiar to Désirée. 'We haven't enough men here to defend the house and I won't waste lives in a futile attempt! We take refuge in the hills, understood?'

Sancho glowered, but gave a reluctant nod of assent.

'I want you to organise the transport we'll need. Avoid the heavier carts. We can't take them with us.' Rafael delivered the order crisply.

He flicked a mocking glance at Désirée. 'I'll get Elena and warn the village to take precautions. If we elude him, Evrard may vent his spite there.'

'Rafael, are you sure you can trust her? Maybe this is some kind of—'

'Go, *amigo*! We are wasting valuable time in arguing.'

With a final angry look at Désirée, Sancho limped out.

Left alone with Rafael, Désirée felt the nervous dryness in her throat increase. He was staring at her, his expression a mask she could not read, and, ridiculously, she found herself wishing she was wearing the one pretty gown she'd managed to pack instead of her dusty riding-habit.

'Why did you change your mind?'

His abrupt question made her jump, but she did not pretend to misunderstand him.

'It was dishonourable to make use of information I had obtained as your guest to betray you,' she said stiffly. She had meant to explain that she hadn't deliberately set out to reveal his identity, that grief and hurt pride had led her to foolishly confirm Armand's guess, but his manner did not invite confession. 'I owed you the warning.'

He was looking at her so coldly! She ached to touch him, to tell him how much she had missed him, how much she loved him, but too much bitterness lay between them.

He nodded, his face shuttered and grim. 'I suppose I ought to thank you for coming, but somehow I can't quite bring myself to do it.'

The icy scorn in his voice made Désirée flinch and something inside her snapped, releasing the torrent of anguish she had bottled up ever since their last meeting.

'I know it is too much to expect you to forgive me, but at least I'm trying to make amends for the trouble I've caused,' she declared in a shaking voice. 'I behaved badly, but I never wanted to hurt you. Can't you understand that?'

'Not so long ago I asked you that the same question.' Rafael flung the words at her with cold fury. 'I told you I loved you and you answered me with insults and disdain.'

Désirée shuddered at the memory of that dreadful day and despair coursed through her as she finally realised how deeply she had offended his pride.

She had thrown his love back in his face and he would never forgive her for it!

'Perhaps I should have tried harder to accept your explanations, but you are also to blame, Rafael de Velasco! You say you loved me, but you didn't trust me—'

Her voice broke and unable to go on she turned to flee before her last reserves of pride failed. . .unaware that he had seen the tears glittering in her eyes.

'Wait!' His command stopped her at the door. 'Do you really mean it about wanting to make amends for bringing Evrard down on us?'

She nodded silently, unable to force a single word out past the unshed tears choking her throat.

'I'm going to try to save some of the Casa's valuables.'

Rafael's tone was off hand, almost uninterested. 'You could help the servants pack.'

Désirée's heartbeat accelerated. Was it her imagination or was there a slight unbending in his stiff form? A slight hint of warmth in his dark gaze?

Sancho was right, she had hurt him badly. He wouldn't ask outright for her love again, but she sensed there might still be a chance to heal the breach. Only this time *she* would have to make the first move.

'Where do you want me to start?' she asked breathlessly.

The mid-afternoon sun was beating down on the rear courtyard as Désirée helped Luis and one of the grooms load the last of the carts.

Elena came hurrying out of the house with Rosita a few steps behind her. 'We're ready to leave,' she announced. 'All the stores and food we can't take with us have been spoilt as Rafael ordered. Those troopers won't be able to use them.'

'The gig is waiting for you.' Désirée continued to hand up items to Luis as she spoke.

'Aren't you coming with us, *señorita*?' Rosita asked.

Désirée shook her head.

'Everyone has been ordered to leave.' Elena wore a worried frown.

'I know.' Désirée's busy hands didn't stop. 'I'm nearly finished' She gave them a quick smile. 'Go on. I'll catch you up.'

They hurried off towards the stables and Désirée forced her attention back to her task. There were blisters coming up on her hands and sweat was trickling down her back, but she had no time to think of discomfort or weariness.

'What are you doing, woman!' Sancho came limping round the corner. 'It's time to go.'

'In a minute.' Ignoring him, Désirée handed up the last item.

'Do you *want* the French to find you here?'

A sudden iciness shivered down Désirée's spine. Could she talk her way out or would she be branded a traitor?

'Rafael won't risk his neck waiting for you.' Sancho's heavy face wore a sardonic expression as if he understood her uneasy thoughts. 'He'll be at the stables by now. He'd just finished poisoning the well when I left him.'

Désirée couldn't prevent a quick frown.

'You object?'

She met his gaze steadily. 'No. This is war and I have learnt the hard way that war is a dirty business. But that doesn't mean I have to approve. I still can pity the suffering such a brutal trick will inflict.'

He nodded and for the first time she noted a spark of approval in his eyes. 'Your compassion does you credit, *señorita*,' he said gruffly. 'I too regret the harsh measures we are forced to use, but make no mistake, they are necessary.'

'Everything is secured,' Luis called, unceremoniously interrupting their conversation.

'Hitch up the horses, Eneco,' Désirée ordered and the groom sprang down from the cart to obey.

'Leave us.' Sancho's tone was autocratic. 'I can manage. Luis, move over. I shall drive.'

Belatedly realising he meant to travel on the already heavily laden cart, Désirée opened her mouth to protest, but Sancho forestalled her.

'My leg was slashed in battle,' he said stiffly. 'It makes riding difficult.'

Désirée had seen how badly he limped. No wonder he hated the French!

To his annoyance, she insisted on helping him to climb up to the driver's seat. 'You can't do it on your own so stop wasting time,' she told him briskly.

The minute he was settled, she ran to assist Eneco to finish his task.

'You know the rendezvous point?'

Eneco nodded and she sent him on his way.

Sancho flicked the reins and the cart rumbled forward.

'Don't just stand there daydreaming, woman!' he shouted over his shoulder. 'Move!'

'I'll tell Rafael that you have left. Take care,' Désirée yelled back and, picking up her skirts, ran like a hare for the stables.

'Where the devil have you been?' Rafael greeted her, his voice rough.

Désirée saw that Madrigal was already saddled and he was just fastening the girth of his own horse.

She started to explain, but Rafael made an impatient gesture.

'Never mind! It doesn't matter.' His fingers flew. 'We are ready now.'

He cast a final glance around to make sure they had not left anything which might assist the French before picking up the brace of pistols which he had set down earlier on the bench nearby.

'Will you let me have one of those? I know how to shoot.'

'I suppose your grandfather taught you?' Rafael handed a pistol over, stifling a sudden urge to laugh as he watched her expertly check its balance.

'But of course.' Désirée grinned back at him, a tiny flicker of hope springing into life as she caught his spurt of amusement.

At least they still shared the same sense of humour!

The pistol was already loaded so she tucked it into the wide sash she wore at her waist to disguise the looseness of her riding-skirt. It felt cold, heavy and wonderfully reassuring!

'Come, we must hurry. We are the last to leave.'

Before she had time to steel herself against his touch, he seized her by the waist, ready to throw her up into her saddle.

Their eyes met and she saw that he had felt the same jolt of desire.

'*Por Dios!*' Rafael bit off the oath.

They stared at each other, caught in thrall for an instant

longer, before Rafael managed to shrug off his paralysis.

'Up with you,' he muttered.

Désirée could feel herself shaking as she watched him spring up into his own saddle.

They clattered out of the stable-yard and were soon out amongst the vineyards which lay to the rear of the estate. Beyond the boundary of Casa del Aguila a narrow twisting track led away up into the hills. Galloping down it too fast for safety, Désirée was aware of a wild exhilaration.

She had done it. She had saved Rafael from capture.

Barely had this thought sung joyfully in her brain, than she heard the sound of gunfire and yelling coming from ahead.

'French scouts,' Rafael said tersely as she glanced at him in alarm. He kicked his mount into greater speed. 'They must have spotted one of us.'

Désirée copied him. Armand would probably concentrate his efforts on the main gates, but he wouldn't neglect other avenues of escape. His scouts would be out pinpointing information to assist the attack.

As they galloped round the next bend they saw the cart Sancho had been driving. It lay on its side, goods scattered. One of the horses was clearly dead, the other screaming in shrill pain.

Désirée couldn't see Luis, but Sancho was crouched behind the rear of the cart. A blue-uniformed soldier lay spreadeagled and unmoving a few yards away.

A volley of shots warned them that there were others.

'Get down,' Rafael yelled.

Désirée obeyed the command without hesitation. As soon as her feet hit the ground, she swiftly slapped Madrigal on the rump. The horse, already frightened, veered off with a neigh of alarm and she dropped flat on to her belly, crawling after Rafael into the shelter of some boulders at the side of the track.

'Good girl.' Rafael gave her a quick grin of approval. 'Where are they?'

'Over there.' Rafael jerked his head to the left. 'Behind those thorn bushes.'

Just then there was another crash of fire and this time Désirée spotted the betraying puff of smoke. 'I see them.'

The injured horse had stopped screaming and there was nothing but silence.

'I'm going to try and take them from behind. Stay here.'

'No!' Désirée hissed back at him. 'I'm coming with you.'

He shook his head. 'It's too risky.'

'You need someone to give you cover.'

'Sancho will help.'

'You don't know how many bullets he has left,' Désirée pointed out with a calmness she was far from feeling.

'Shooting a man isn't like culping wafers or going after rabbits.' Rafael's face was grim. 'And these are *French* soldiers. Your compatriots.'

Désirée swallowed hard. 'I know I haven't any experience of fighting, but I promise you I am on your side. I won't hold back,' she asserted, knowing that even the slightest hesitation on her part could prove lethal.

Rafael's frown deepened. What had happened to make her change her mind? She had always vowed she despised the *guerrilleros*. Why was she willing to abandon her hatred and throw her lot in with his?

A flicker of hope danced in his heart, but he suppressed it ruthlessly. Their situation was too dangerous to let himself be swayed by foolish sentiment.

'Please. I swear you can trust me.'

Sincerity shone in her lovely eyes. 'Very well, I accept your offer,' he said, recklessly throwing caution to the winds and electing to trust his instincts.

Relief washed over Désirée. She couldn't have borne it if he had rejected her help! She desperately wanted to prove to him that she had finally realised that he had been right that day in the *guerrilla* camp. The love they shared was much too special to waste. It was more important than anything else.

'We must act quickly.' Rafael's rapid voice broke into
her euphoric haze. 'It will be a bloody business, I'm
afraid.'

Désirée forced herself to concentrate as he swiftly outlined his plan. 'I understand,' she nodded, determinedly
quelling the fear rising in her breast.

She was very pale. 'Are you sure you want to go
through with it?'

'I won't faint,' she promised stoutly.

Rafael permitted himself a slight smile. 'Remember,
wait for my signal, *mi perla*.'

Désirée nodded, a surge of lovely warmth at his use
of the familiar endearment easing the knotted cramping
in her stomach.

Rafael went first, moving like an eel. Désirée was too
wound up to notice the sharp stones which dug into her
flesh as they crawled forward over the rough ground
using the scrub and outcrops of broken rock to hide their
progress. Her mouth was dry and her heart was banging
like a drum, but her mind was strangely clear.

She had no idea how long it took them to achieve their
object. Time seemed distorted into a slow dream, but her
senses remained crystal-bright, each volley shocking in
its loudness as Sancho and the soldiers exchanged fire.

At last Rafael jerked his hand in a signal to halt.

Désirée watched him crane his neck carefully forward
round the patch of cover they were employing.

'As I thought. Three of them,' he whispered.

'Do you think they are an advance party?' she
mouthed.

Rafael was sure of it. The sound of gunfire would have
drawn any other troops by now. But they couldn't count
on their luck holding. The main body of Evrard's force
couldn't be far behind. He had to deal with this obstruction to their escape and fast!

Rolling carefully over, he silently scooped up a large
pebble and skimmed it low and hard back in the direction

they had come. It hit the edge of the boulder where they had been sheltering, making a loud noise.

Immediately, an answering flurry of French shots struck chips off the rock.

'They think we are still down there,' Rafael whispered, his eyes glittering. 'But Sancho knows we are not. He'll hold his fire now and give us our chance.'

Désirée indicated her comprehension. The element of surprise would be on their side.

She checked her pistol, swallowing hard to try and moisten her dry mouth.

'Ready?' He gave her a swift smile and her quivering nerves steadied.

'As I'll ever be,' she whispered back.

They leapt to their feet in the same instant, firing with a smooth co-ordination.

'*Santiago!*'

Under the cover of her fire, Rafael hurled himself at the Frenchmen, screaming the name of Spain's beloved guardian saint and, to Désirée's utter astonishment, the same savage yell erupted from her own throat as she raced after him.

One soldier went down instantly, blood pumping from his chest. The second managed to let off a shot that whistled past Désirée's ear before Rafael reached him. She saw a flash of light reflecting off the knife in Rafael's hand before they closed.

Even as the Frenchman slumped to the ground, the third soldier raised his empty rifle and swung it at Rafael's head.

'Behind you!' Désirée shrieked a warning.

Rafael whirled, flinging up his arm to parry the blow, and the rifle-butt thudded into the muscle of his shoulder.

He stumbled back from the force of the blow and Désirée saw his knife fall from benumbed fingers, leaving him weaponless. With a shriek of fury, she dropped her own empty pistol and threw herself on to the Frenchman's back.

He let out a roar of startled surprise, trying to dislodge

her clinging form. Several of his wild blows landed, but Désirée hung on, her nails clawing into the exposed flesh of his neck.

They writhed together in a macabre dance and she could feel her grip loosening. Just as she was sure she was about to be thrown off and trampled, Rafael recovered and dived in under the man's flailing arms.

The Spanish blade found its target and Désirée rolled free as the wounded scout crashed to the earth.

She scrambled to her feet. 'Are you all right?' she gasped anxiously.

Rafael gave her a crooked grin. 'I think I should be asking you that question.'

'I'm just bruised,' she muttered, trying to ignore the trembling in her knees.

She glanced back as they left. A slight movement caught her attention and she halted, realising that the last soldier to fall was still alive. His eyes opened, a spark of recognition flaring into them as he got his first good look at her.

Her gasp of dismay made Rafael swing round.

'No! Let him live.' Compassion overcoming fear, Désirée clutched Rafael's arm to prevent him turning back. 'He's no threat to us now.'

Rafael frowned, but consented. 'Very well, I'll spare him, but we must hurry.' His long stride lengthened. 'We've got to get out of here before his companions come and find him.'

And when they did, Désirée thought to herself, he would undoubtedly reveal to Major Evrard that she was a traitor!

Désirée watched the plume of dark smoke rising to merge with the dusk. Too far away to be certain, she thought she could see a red glint competing with the final rays of the sun as it sank below the western horizon and in her imagination she heard the roaring crackle of flame.

'Oh, Rafael! Your lovely house!'

She stretched out an impulsive hand to the tall stiff

figure standing at her side on the mountain's slope.

Rafael de Velasco slowly turned from witnessing the destruction of his home. His expression was so bleak Désirée's heart ached for him, but to her surprise when he spoke his words lacked bitterness.

'Casa del Aguila will rise again. I shall rebuild when this war is over and we have peace once more.'

'I thought you would be utterly furious at its loss,' Désirée murmured, burdened by shame and regret.

'People are more important than possessions. Thanks to your warning, my sister is safe and I still have my freedom. I owe you a debt of gratitude.'

'But it's all my fault you've lost the Casa!' Désirée could hardly believe her ears. He didn't sound angry with her any more.

Rafael shrugged ruefully. 'You were the catalyst, but I was always at risk of being exposed and I knew what the consequences would be.' His mouth hardened, setting into a grim line. 'However, if he thinks to push me into rash action with this destruction, Evrard is mistaken. For the moment, I am only interested in ensuring the safety of those who depend on me.'

'I'm so glad everyone escaped.' Désirée gave a nervous little laugh. 'I was so scared!'

'No one would have guessed.' A smile suddenly warmed Rafael's austere features. 'You fought like a lioness!'

Désirée blushed. She didn't deserve his praise. 'Poor Luis will have a lump on his head for days to remind him he was knocked unconscious. He is lucky to be alive.'

'So are we. For a while I doubted if any of us would make it to safety,' Rafael answered truthfully.

Désirée shivered at the memory. Both Luis and Sancho had been injured. While she had bandaged their wounds with strips torn from her petticoat, Rafael had sweated to round up their mounts. Without the cart, they'd had to double up, the other two men taking Rafael's big grey while she rode behind him on Madrigal.

In spite of the danger, her senses had thrilled to be

close to him and a certain tension in his broad back told her that he was aware of the same attraction.

To her immense relief they had not encountered any more of Armand's men and they'd reached their destination shortly before sunset, the last of the fugitives to do so. She had felt very strange, re-entering the *guerrilla* stronghold, painful memories of day she had been brought into the camp as a captive crowding in on her, but the *guerrilleros* were anxious to make her welcome.

A bowl of hearty stew and the red wine they had pressed on all the new arrivals had eased some of her weariness and she had slipped away as soon as she could, desperate for some peace in which to think. Rafael had appeared soon afterwards when she had halted on the mountainside.

Turning from the destruction her folly had begun, she lifted her gaze to his dark face.

'Were you following me?' she asked, acutely aware of her thunderous pulse.

'You don't know these hills.' There was an awkward edge to his normally smooth tones. 'It isn't safe to wander alone when night is drawing on.'

'Why should my safety concern you?' Désirée felt suddenly breathless. 'I thought you wanted to be rid of me.'

'So did I.' Rafael saw her flinch. 'But I was wrong.'

'Are you saying that you can forgive my betrayal?'

'I think we must forgive each other, *querida*,' Rafael replied unsteadily. 'For I know that there will no happiness for either of us if we remain apart.'

He held out his arms to her. *'Te quiero, mi perla'*

'And I love you, Rafael.' Désirée melted into his embrace, laying her head upon his shoulder as he hugged her tightly to him.

'You'll never know how much I missed you,' he whispered, pressing his lips to her pale hair. 'I wanted to chase after you the moment you left. Only the belief that you were certain to reject me again stiffened my resolve.'

Désirée lifted her head and met his gaze. 'I might have

sent you away,' she admitted. She swallowed hard. 'I didn't realise then, you see, that I angry with you for my own sake, not Etienne's.'

'I don't understand.'

'Armand guessed you were El Verdugo. I ought to have gone on denying it, but I didn't. I betrayed you.' Désirée sighed. 'Justice for my brother had little to do with it. I thought you'd been playing with me and I wanted to hurt you in return. I knew in my heart that Etienne was a casualty of war, but my pride was smarting. I wanted revenge!'

'Revenge is a dish we Spaniards understand,' he said softly, stroking a comforting finger down her cheek.

'But it only breeds further hate. Father Gomez told me I might regret wishing to see El Verdugo dead and he was right! I was too unhappy and angry to stop and think of the consequences, but if I could turn back the clock I would!'

Her lovely eyes were brilliant with unshed tears and Rafael's arms tightened protectively.

'Do not distress yourself, *querida*. The past is over, it is finished with. Now we must think of the future.'

He released her and drew out a tiny silk pouch from within his coat. 'I bought this that last morning when I went into Covarrubias. It has lain next to my heart ever since. Will you wear it for me?'

Désirée took the pouch and undid it to reveal a heavy gold wedding-band. It gleamed in the faint light and, speechless with emotion, she could only nod in consent.

'Are you sure, *querida*? There's still time for you to go back to Madrid. We can make up some story to explain today but, if you stay, your mother's people will surely brand you a traitor.'

'I know.' Disappointed in his ambitions, Armand would not be kind. 'But I can live without their approval.' A wry smile touched her mouth. 'You told me once that, faced with having to decide between my mother's needs and my grandfather's, I ought to have considered what

was best for me. I never really understood I had that
choice before.'

She paused. 'I have learnt many other things about
myself too since I came to Spain. I realise now that I
only supported Napoleon for Etienne's sake.'

The Emperor's vaulting ambition had always disturbed
her, but she had tried to suppress her doubts out of loyalty
to her brother.

'Napoleon seems willing to sacrifice everything in
order to conquer. Truth, honour, justice—he disregards
everything that matters!' Désirée sighed. 'Already, too
many men have died to satisfy his ambition. It is time he
was stopped or he will bring total ruin down on France.'

'So you will support our fight for freedom?' Rafael
asked eagerly.

Désirée nodded. 'I don't approve of the methods your
guerrilleros use, but I accept that they are necessary.
You needn't fear that I will try to interfere.'

'Then you have decided? You truly wish to stay?'
Rafael's dark features lit up in a joyful smile.

Désirée answered him with confident nod. 'I want to
be with you, Rafael. I know the price. I shall be a *persona
non grata*, exiled from France, but you needn't worry
that I shall feel sorry for myself. Your people shall be
my people, your cause mine, I swear it.'

Rafael let out a shout of triumph and drew her back
into his embrace.

Revelling in the feel of his strong arms enfolding her,
Désirée asked if he could arrange to send several letters
for her. 'I must write to my friends and to my lawyers.
Proper provision must be made for my cousin Hortense.'
A tiny sigh escaped her. 'I just hope she will try to
understand.'

'One day, when this war is over, we will visit your
château,' Rafael promised.

Désirée thanked him and then asked where would they
be living. 'I should be quite happy in one of those tents,'
she added hastily in case he misunderstood her curiosity.

Rafael laughed. 'The situation isn't quite that bad! I

have some money safely hidden and there is still my hunting-lodge near Frias.' He ran a caressing hand over the enticing curve of her hip. 'We can spend our honeymoon there.'

Désirée hugged him in delight.

Rafael's face sobered. 'Yet afterwards. . .? All I know is that, even to be with you, my conscience will not allow me to give up the fight to free Spain. We shall have to endure long separations, I'm afraid.'

'No!' Désirée's voice rose in protest. 'I shall go wherever you go. My place is with you.'

'Désirée, it is too dangerous. I cannot allow it. You must remain behind. I shall be hunted, but the French dare not attack in the high mountains.'

She smiled a little. 'I wondered how long it would be before you began to order me about again,' she said, her tone affectionately teasing.

Rafael gave her a crooked grin. 'You know me too well, *querida*. But, in truth, the life of a camp-follower is hard and you are a well-born lady.'

'Aren't you forgetting how I was reared, Rafael de Velasco? I won't faint at the sight of blood or turn squeamish if I'm asked to get my hands dirty!'

Désirée's flash of indignation faded. 'Oh, Rafael, I know it will be difficult, but being apart from you would be worse.'

She smiled mistily at him.

'All my life I have felt rootless and unsettled. Now, for the first time, I know where I want to be. I am your woman. I belong at your side.'

'I swear I shall make you happy and be worthy of your love.' Rafael's tone was husky as he looked down into her radiant face.

Désirée wound her arms around his neck. 'I can't promise to be a very obedient wife,' she murmured mischievously. 'But I intend to be a loving one.'

Her lips parted in sweet invitation and Rafael stopped resisting his need to kiss her.

The touch of his mouth on hers, so sweetly gentle and

tender, blotted out all the pain and terror, obliterating the recent past. The nightmare was over.

Rafael deepened the kiss and urgent with passion they clung together, touching, exploring and delighting in each other until at last they broke breathlessly apart.

'How long do you mean to make me wait, *mi perla*?' Rafael demanded hoarsely, thinking that Frias seemed as distant as the moon!

'Weddings take a good deal of arranging,' Désirée retorted wickedly, for the sheer pleasure of seeing his eyes flash with brilliant fire. 'I shall need a new gown, a lace veil, new shoes, bridesmaids. . .'

Désirée solemnly ticked the items off on her fingers, but couldn't maintain her pose. She began to giggle and Rafael let out a growl of mock fury, realising she was teasing him.

'Come here and I'll teach you how a proper Spanish wife should behave!' he laughed, sweeping her back into his arms to kiss her again.

The sound of voices calling in the distance gradually penetrated their rapt absorption.

'Our absence is causing alarm,' Rafael observed dryly. 'I think we had better head back to camp.'

He slipped an arm around her waist and, entwined, they began to walk slowly in the direction of the shouts.

Rafael cocked his head, listening carefully. 'That sounds like Sancho.'

'He should be resting,' Désirée exclaimed with a frown.

'True, but I suspect he is feeling on edge. He told me earlier tonight that he had misjudged you. He wants to apologise.'

'He had cause to doubt me,' Désirée replied generously.

Rafael smiled. Her kind heart was one of the many things he loved about her.

'I'm glad you bear him no grudge, *querida*. He has a hot temper, but we are good friends and I know he is already feeling guilty because wound-fever prevented him from delivering the message explaining my delay in coming home.'

'So that is why we didn't hear from you!'

'*Sí*,' Rafael nodded. 'And Father Gomez's messenger missed me. We had already left Talavera by the time he arrived so I didn't know about the smallpox outbreak until I got home.' He shuddered, thinking how close he had come to losing his sister.

They walked on in silence, each momentarily preoccupied with their own thoughts, and then Désirée revealed what she had been thinking.

'Perhaps if we asked him to marry us, Sancho would know I am willing to become his friend?'

Rafael let out a whoop of approval. 'You are as clever as you are beautiful, *mi perla*!'

'Flatterer!' Désirée coloured happily.

Bobbing torches ahead warned that their solitude was about to come to an end.

Abruptly Rafael halted. 'Do you really want an elaborate wedding, Désirée?'

She stared at him puzzled for a second and then a joyful smile lit up her face. 'There's no need for us to wait, is there?' she exclaimed excitedly, the last trace of her weariness vanishing. 'Sancho can marry us tonight.'

'I know I am being selfish in depriving you of the usual—'

She laid a finger quickly against his lips, silencing him. 'I don't need a special gown or veil. I've got you and that is all that matters.'

He pressed a kiss into the palm of her hand and enfolded it in his. 'Then let's go and tell everyone.'

An hour later, the ceremony began under the starlit sky. Désirée wore her white embroidered dress, glad she had remembered to pack the matching shoes in her saddlebag. A sapphire-studded gold cross, loaned with delighted congratulations by Elena, shone around her slim neck and her pale hair streamed loose beneath a

circlet of wild flowers lovingly fashioned by
Rosita's hands.

She carried a posy of the same flowers and Rafael
thought he had never seen a more beautiful bride as Luis
proudly escorted her towards the main campfire where
he and his cousin stood waiting.

Sancho began to recite the words of the service and a
hush fell over the crowd gathered to watch them
exchange their vows.

'With this ring I thee wed. . .'

Désirée heart was so full she thought she might cry
as she felt Rafael slip the heavy band onto her finger
and a moment later Sancho pronounced them *marido y
mujer*—man and wife.

'You may kiss the bride, *amigo mio*,' he concluded
with a broad grin.

Loud cheering broke out as Rafael took her in his
arms, but Désirée was only aware of the warm tenderness
of his lips on hers.

'I love you, *mi mujer*,' he said, raising his dark head.

Désirée smiled up at him, her eyes brighter than the
stars above.

Her new life had begun.

Historical Romance™

Coming next month

MISS HARCOURT'S DILEMMA
by Anne Ashley

A Regency delight!

Verity's life was not simple. Somehow she'd
become involved in unmasking a spy and
fallen in love with two men—Brinley Carter
and the mysterious Coachman. How would she
ever choose?

TRUE COLOURS
by Nicola Cornick

A Regency delight!

James wanted to know why Alicia had ended
their engagement and why she'd rather risk
another infamous scandal than marry him,
especially when he was *sure* she still loved him.

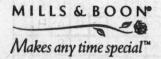

DANCE FEVER

How would you like to win a year's supply of Mills & Boon® books? Well you can and they're FREE! Simply complete the competition below and send it to us by 31st October 1998. The first five correct entries picked after the closing date will each win a year's subscription to the Mills & Boon series of their choice. What could be easier?

OBLARMOL
AMBUR
RTOXTFO   *FOXTROT*
RASQUE
GANCO   *CONGA*

KOPLA
OOOOMTLCIN
MALOENCF
SITWT
LASSA

EVJI
TAZLW   *waltz*
ACHACH   *chacha*
SCDIO   *DISCO*
MAABS   *SAMBA*

G	R	I	H	C	H	A	R	J	T	O	N
O	P	A	R	L	H	U	B	P	I	B	W
M	O	O	R	L	L	A	B	M	C	V	H
B	L	D	I	O	O	K	C	L	U	P	E
R	K	U	B	N	C	R	Q	H	V	R	Z
S	A	N	I	O	O	N	G	W	A	S	V
T	S	I	N	R	M	G	E	U	B	G	H
W	L	G	H	S	O	R	Q	M	M	B	L
I	A	P	N	O	T	S	L	R	A	H	C
S	S	L	U	K	I	A	S	F	S	L	S
T	O	R	T	X	O	F	O	X	T	R	F
G	U	I	P	Z	N	D	I	S	C	O	Q

D8C

Please turn over for details of how to enter ⇨

HOW TO ENTER

There is a list of fifteen mixed up words overleaf, all of which when unscrambled spell popular dances. When you have unscrambled each word, you will find them hidden in the grid. They may appear forwards, backwards or diagonally. As you find each one, draw a line through it. Find all fifteen and fill in the coupon below then pop this page into an envelope and post it today. Don't forget you could win a year's supply of Mills & Boon® books—you don't even need to pay for a stamp!

**Mills & Boon Dance Fever Competition
FREEPOST CN81, Croydon, Surrey, CR9 3WZ**
EIRE readers send competition to PO Box 4546, Dublin 24.

Please tick the series you would like to receive if you are one of the lucky winners

Presents™ ❏   Enchanted™ ❏   Medical Romance™ ❏
Historical Romance™ ❏   Temptation® ❏

Are you a Reader Service™ subscriber?   Yes ❏   No ❏

Ms/Mrs/Miss/Mr ....Intials ....(BLOCK CAPITALS PLEASE)

Surname..

Address ....

....

....Postcode...........................

(I am over 18 years of age)   D8C